Ready, Okay!

Ready, Okay!

A novel

Adam Cadre

HarperCollins*Publishers*

HarperCollins books may be purchased for educational, business, or sales promotional use. For information please write: Special Markets Department, HarperCollins Publishers Inc., 10 East 53rd Street, New York, NY 10022.

FIRST EDITION

Designed by Joy O'Meara

Printed on acid-free paper

Cadre, Adam, 1974–
    Ready, okay! : a novel / Adam Cadre—1st ed.
        p. cm.
    ISBN 0-06-019558-4
    1. Teenage boys—California—Fiction. 2. Suburban life—California—Fiction. 3. Alienation (Social psychology)—Fiction. 4. California—Fiction.
I. Title.

PS3553.A3145 R42 2000
813'.54—dc21   99-058863

00 01 02 03 04 ❖/RRD10 9 8 7 6 5 4 3 2 1

For my sister

Ready, Okay!

One

The day I turned sixteen years old I had no idea that in four months nearly everyone I cared about would be dead. Unburdened by this foreknowledge, it was with a free and unclouded spirit that I went down to the DMV and failed my driving test.

"That's too bad," Peggy said when I told her. Peggy had been my very best friend in the whole wide world for almost ten years now, yet somehow the extent of the tragedy that had befallen me seemed to elude her. "You can take it again in two weeks, right?"

"I guess," I said, watching as she flipped through the channels with the remote control encased in its little plastic bag. The reason it was in the bag was so it wouldn't get dirty. The couches we were sitting on were similarly covered with plastic. At one point Peggy had also insisted on covering the TV with plastic, but after a few minutes of that the rest of the family had decided that being able to see the picture was more important than keeping fingerprints off the screen.

"So there you go," Peggy said. "Two weeks. *I* have to wait a *year*."

Of course, Peggy already had her license; what she had to wait a year for was the breast-reduction surgery she'd been after since middle school. At least, she'd been *talking* about it since then, though she'd usually conclude, "Of course, I could never really go through with it—this is the way God made me and that's all there is to it." But recently she'd become genuinely intent on getting the things lopped off. She'd even gone to see her doctor about it when she'd turned seventeen the week before, only to be told that it wasn't a serious enough problem to warrant such drastic measures and that she'd have to wait till she was eighteen. She immediately went home and circled her eighteenth birthday on the calendar.

A picture worth 423 words or so

Now they say a picture's worth a thousand words, but you could read a thousand *pages* describing someone and not be able to recognize that person as well as someone who'd seen a picture for half a second. But since the only surviving picture of Peggy is thousands of miles away in Illinois, and since I'd really prefer that her admittedly striking bustline *not* be the only physical feature you associate with her, I think I'd better describe her before I get too much older.

Peggy's eyes were, officially, blue. That's what it said on her driver's license, anyway—which, incidentally, she'd gotten on her first try, unlike, say, me. But you only had to look at them for a second to realize that while they were blue around the outside edge, around the pupils they were quite unmistakably brown. In between, the two colors merged into each other in a golden starburst pattern. But I suppose you can't fit all that onto a driver's license.

When Peggy was seven her hair was actually quite reddish. As often happens, a couple years later it darkened to an unremarkable brown. As seldom happens, a couple of years after that she started going gray. By the time she was thirteen or so there was enough gray hair mixed in with the brown that her classmates had started to notice, but she refused to color it: "this is the way God made me and that's all there is to it."

For some reason that policy didn't seem to apply to her freckles. Peggy had freckles liberally sprinkled across her cheeks, which was actually rather becoming, but she hated them. When she was eight she tried to get rid of them by rubbing her cheeks with lemon juice. When that didn't work she tried Tabasco sauce. Luckily we were able to stop her before she could find any hydrochloric acid.

Peggy's teeth were perfectly normal but there was no convincing her of that. She'd had braces put on when she was in the second grade and they didn't come off till she was in tenth. These were hardly the metal monsters of decades past, when you wound up looking like you had a mouthful of barbed wire: they were transparent and virtually invisible. Nevertheless, Peggy got into the habit of hiding her teeth at all times. Even after the braces came off, when she cracked a smile her lips stayed shut tight.

But I'm getting hung up on details here—was she pretty, you ask? That's hard to say. I'm probably the least qualified person to judge that kind of thing. Having known her for nearly ten years, I'd gotten so used to her face—even though it'd changed somewhat between seven and seventeen—that before I even really *saw* it my brain would register, "Hey, it's Peggy!" and since she was a beautiful person, I couldn't help but see her as beautiful. How would she look to me if I knew nothing about her as a person? I can't even imagine.

Back to my humiliating failure, already in progress

"So what did you do wrong?" Peggy finally asked.

"Nothing!" I said. "I obeyed all posted speed limits, I changed lanes safely, I executed a perfect three-point turn, the works. When we got back to the DMV I thought I'd racked up a perfect score. But the guy said I'd almost hit a pedestrian as I was pulling into the parking lot so he flunked me."

"How close did you come to hitting the pedestrian?" she asked.

"That's just it," I said. "There was no pedestrian! The sidewalk was deserted! The whole thing is ridiculous. Who ever heard of a pedestrian in Orange County anyway?"

Right then Mrs. Kaylin came in from the kitchen. In each hand she held a saucer and on each saucer was a cupcake. I assumed mine was the one with the birthday candle in it. "Wow, thanks," I said.

"Mom, you know I can't eat this," Peggy said. "I'll get fat."

"And of course that would be a fate worse than death," said Mrs. K. Peggy's parents were both fairly, uh, plump people, plump and jolly with snowy white hair—at one point there was a rumor going around that they had eight flying reindeer stashed in the backyard—

so Peggy's insistence on staying under four and a half pounds met with little sympathy from the parental front.

"I'm still not eating it," Peggy said.

"Peggy, you could eat a cupcake *factory* and not come anywhere near 'fat,'" I said. The candle was starting to drip wax on my cupcake so I blew it out.

"Did you make a wish?" Mrs. K. asked.

"Nah," I said. "I don't believe in that sort of thing. You know what they say. If wishes were knishes the world would be a deli case, or something like that."

"Okay, I'll eat it," Peggy said. "But get me a knife so I can scrape off the frosting. Please."

"Well, since you asked so nicely," Mrs. K. said. She got Peggy a knife. "So, Allen, did your sister pass? Her driving test, I mean?"

"Mff?" I said. I swallowed. "Echo? No, she doesn't take it till tomorrow morning."

"Snagged the last appointment, did you?" she asked.

"Hmm?" I said. "Oh, no. See, I was born at 11:56 P.M. on February fourth, and she was born at 12:02 A.M. on the fifth, so technically she doesn't turn sixteen till tomorrow."

"Really?" Peggy said. I had finished my cupcake by this point but Peggy hadn't even finished scraping the frosting off hers. "So how come when you had those birthday parties all those years ago you both had them together? And always on the fourth, right? That doesn't sound too fair."

"Beats the alternative," I said. "Better than having one party where five hundred people show up and another where the only person who shows up is a kid from eight blocks down looking to use the bathroom. Having them both together we each got to think, 'Hey, everyone's here to see me!' And better the fourth than the fifth because—"

The clock in the living room struck six. "Six already?" Peggy said. "Oh, no! I've got a date in half an hour!" She put her saucer with its untouched cupcake and pile of discarded frosting down on the coffee table. "I've got to go get ready," she said. "I'll see you later." She dashed upstairs.

"Guess I should've known better than to have my birthday on a Friday night, huh?" I said.

Won't you be my neighbor?

As I walked back home, I couldn't help but reflect on how much the neighborhood had changed since Peggy had first moved in almost ten years before. I didn't reflect on it very long, though, because she only lived two doors down from my house.

We both lived on a eucalyptus-lined cul-de-sac called Hyacinth Avenue in Fullerton, California, birthplace of the electric guitar and, less impressively, of me. Hyacinth was part of a housing development nestled in between Cal State Fullerton on the east, Ilium High School on the south, and Fullerton Creek to the north and west; it was a stumpy little street with only six houses, which made it the choice place for all the kids in the development to hang out since there were practically never any cars coming. On those rare occasions that they didn't get around to setting up the hockey nets, they'd be playing baseball with tennis equipment, or skateboarding, or racing their bikes from the end of the cul-de-sac to the stop sign (a trip that generally took somewhere between 1.3 and 1.5 seconds). My house was at the corner, where Hyacinth met the cross street. I'd never lived anywhere else.

No one in any of the other houses on my street could say the same: even the Kaylins hadn't moved in until I was six. The only people who'd been in the neighborhood as long as I had were the Monihans, and they were an old retired couple who I assume had lived other places in the hundred and thirty years or so they'd been kicking around. They lived on the corner across from us. The other families on our street all had boys about the same age as Echo and me, but they had all moved out by the time we were in middle school. A cranky old man moved into the house at the end of the cul-de-sac—all the kids around would cut across his lawn on the way to school, and he'd yell at us for scaring his cat—and into the house between Peggy's and mine moved a thirtyish stockbroker who for reasons lost in the mists of time we all called "Dooj." He had a pretty wife and a clinically insane dog, a beautiful Siberian husky who did laps around the backyard, around and around and around, running day and night, never eating, never sleeping, and never stopping until the day my brother shot it. Dooj could never figure out why anyone would want to shoot his dog. He also couldn't figure out why every kid in the neighborhood called him Dooj when presumably at least *one* of us had to be bright enough to know how to pronounce "Doug."

The last of the original kids in our neighborhood to move out was a pale, sickly kid named Carver Fringie. He was a year older than me and lived in the house next to the Monihans'. He never played in the street with the other kids—he was never healthy enough—but he always watched: every time the other kids were out playing he'd be sitting out on his front steps, usually with a blanket and always with a book. And we're not talking *The* Perro *in the Sombrero* here—we're talking big, impressive, scary books: literature, history, science, philosophy, you name it. He kept the Fullerton Public Library in business more or less singlehandedly. But then his mom died—apparently, robust health didn't exactly run in the family—and he'd had to go live with his dad in Chino. The house stayed empty for well over a year, until this girl named Cat Nicholls and her mom moved in. Cat was a couple years older than me and every evening she and a couple guys she knew would hang out on the front steps, just like Carver Fringie had. And though every morning as I passed by on my way to school I couldn't help but notice the empty bottles and cigarette butts piled up on the front steps, they never did any of that stuff when any of us younger kids were around. I guess they didn't want to be a bad influence or something.

Not that there were really that many of us left to influence—by this point, Hyacinth had become a fairly placid place. The street was generally deserted. Even when Peggy's brother Grant went to go ride his bike he did it somewhere else. And me, I was never into the sports thing to begin with. I spent most of my time at Peggy's house.

Childhood logic at work

For as long as I can remember, all my friends have been girls. Even before I started school I'd had a lurking suspicion that the female sex was inherently superior, but my first day of kindergarten proved it conclusively. All I had to do was survey the playground at recess. Girls: drawing on the blacktop with chalk, jumping rope, conversing with one another. Boys: throwing dirt clods at trees. QED.

Of course, the problem was that the girls that I thought I might like to be friends with were not without analytical powers of their own, and they had reached essentially the same conclusion I had. Which meant that once I opened my mouth and they found out I was a boy, they would assume me incapable of civilized behavior and not talk to me. This was where having a twin sister came in handy. Not because she could act as a liaison into the female community—far from it. She was actually trying to cross over in the opposite direction: she and a bunch of boys spent every recess playing soccer (which at that age consisted of an awful lot of kicking and not an awful lot of aiming) and had no use for her fellow girls or anything they did. So I passed for her. It wasn't all that hard. All you had to do was find a group of girls looking shifty-eyed and solemn. Chances were they'd be having a mass initiation into a secret club. Every girl in my class other than Echo was a member of at least eighteen or nineteen secret clubs. So I'd stand inconspicuously in the background, and they'd see me and think, "Hmm, one of those Mockery kids," and they'd see Echo out in the field and think, "Okay, there's the boy one, so this one must be okay." And so I'd get initiated into the club, which usually involved learning a password—"alligator" was a popular one—and that was all there was to it. After that, I was in the club, and if I said "alligator" they had no choice but to hang out with me. Which, I might humbly add, they usually didn't find so bad.

So you can imagine my reaction when I went outside one fine summer afternoon and spotted a girl on previously boy-dominated Hyacinth Avenue. She'd dragged a little round table and some chairs out onto the front lawn and was having some sort of imaginary picnic with three stuffed penguins and her sister Kelly, who was five years old at the time and looked bored out of her mind. I took it upon myself to welcome them to the neighborhood.

"Furniture is supposed to go *inside* the house," I said. "Not *outside*."

"This furniture is supposed to go outside," Peggy said. "It's made special just for that."

"What're you doing here, anyway?" I asked. "This isn't your house."

"It is now," she said.

Having gotten the welcoming part out of the way, the time had come to get in on whatever she was doing. "What're the penguins for?" I asked.

"We're having an iced tea party," she said.

"But there's no iced tea!" Kelly complained. "Iced tea is brown. The cups just have *air* in them. Air is blue. Iced tea's brown."

"It's the *sky* that's blue, not air. Air's brown," Peggy said. "Look." She pointed at the horizon, where the air was quite clearly a shade of brown not at all unlike iced tea. "Kelly doesn't know much," Peggy confided. "She's just five and a quarter."

"Actually," I said, "air's clear. It looks brown near the ground because of smog, you know, like the black stuff that comes out of trucks. And the rest of it looks blue because the air molecules scatter the blue light around and let the other colors through."

"Really?" Peggy said. "Is that true?"

"Sure," I said. "You can look it up."

"Is it in the Bible?" she asked.

"It's in science books," I said. "Ask her." I pointed at Echo, who was playing goalie in front of the net the hockey-playing kids had set up at the end of the cul-de-sac. "Or him." I pointed at Carver Fringie, who was sitting on his front porch watching the hockey game.

Peggy looked up. "That's neat," she said.

"There's still no iced tea," Kelly said. She got up and wandered into the house. Peggy looked crestfallen.

"Um, I can do whatever she was doing if you want," I said.

"Well . . . okay," she said. "Sit in her chair." I did as instructed and Peggy handed me a penguin. "Do you want some iced tea?" she asked it.

"Sure, I guess," I said in my best penguin voice.

"No, that's wrong," she said. "Penguins don't like iced tea. They only like fish." She turned to the dolls on her side of the table. "Adelie, do you want some iced tea? No? How about you, Gentoo? No? See, they only like fish."

"Okay, then mine wants some fish," I said.

"Of course," she said. "They always want fish." She turned to confront my penguin. "You can't have any fish," she said. "You'll get fat."

As the imaginary picnic progressed I somehow failed to notice that the hockey game had broken up and Carver Fringie had gone back inside and the sun had drifted lower in the sky. I also failed to notice that I had no idea what my fellow penguineer's name was. I noticed these things only when Kelly came back out. In her right hand she held a slice of American cheese. "Peggy, dinner's ready," she said.

"'Peggy'?" I said. "Is that you?"

"Yeah," she said, but then corrected herself. "I am Margaret Hannah Kaylin, daughter of Robert and Josephine Kaylin of 151 Hyacinth Avenue, Fullerton, California," she rattled off.

Kelly took a bite of the slice of cheese she was holding. "Where's cheese?" she asked.

"In your hand?" I suggested. Kelly looked wonderingly at her left hand. "Other hand," I said.

"She means Keith," Peggy said. "My brother. She knows how to pronounce it but just says it wrong to act like a baby."

"I'm not a baby," Kelly said.

"Then don't act like one," Peggy said. "Keith went to the park."

"Mom says I'm not supposed to go to the park by myself," Kelly said.

"Well, I can't get him," Peggy said. "I have to take the penguins back to my room. Get Mom."

Kelly went tearing back into the house as fast as a five-year-old carrying a slice of cheese can go. "*MOM!* Cheese went to the park!"

A minute later Mrs. Kaylin came out. She looked much the same then as she did ten years later, only her hair was gray instead of white. "Oh, hello," she said. "Have you two been playing out here all this time?"

"We're not playing," Peggy said. "We're having an iced tea party. But it's over now."

"And who are you?" Mrs. K. asked.

"I'm Allen," I said, but then decided to elaborate. ". . . Mockery, son of Andrew and Susan Mockery of 147 Hyacinth Avenue, Fullerton, California."

"Don't tell me she's got you doing that too," Mrs. K. said. "Look, Peggy, if you get lost, just find a pay phone and use your calling card to page me. Don't go bothering strangers."

"But it was in a filmstrip," Peggy said. "They showed it at *school*."

"That filmstrip was from forty years ago," Mrs. K. said. "I saw the same one when I was your age. Now go wash up, kiddo."

"Okay," Peggy said. She gave me a very serious look. "Come back tomorrow," she said. "We'll make cookies."

So the next day I went over to her house and we made cookies. Or, rather, she made cookies and I ate them. I tried to help make them but when she gave me a bowl and said, "Mix this," my mixing technique apparently proved so subpar that after about five seconds or so she took the bowl back and mixed it herself. As for the eating part, I was more than willing to share but Peggy wouldn't eat any because "I don't want to get fat."

The day after that I got invited over for dinner. Wackiness ensued when Mrs. K. cheerfully dropped an enormous hunk-o-beef onto my plate and I had to inform her that I'd never eaten a piece of meat in my life and had no plans to start. Mr. and Mrs. K. were somewhat taken aback and Cheese looked positively incredulous but Peggy seemed very impressed.

A few days later I went to the park with Peggy and Kelly and Cheese. There were actually two parks within a couple minutes' walk of our street, but Greenbelt Park was little more than a hedge around the creek. Acacia Park, on the other hand, was a substantial plot of grass with trees and a baseball diamond and a sandlot with swing sets and monkey bars and stuff. It was usually pretty empty. We got the swings all to ourselves.

I pushed Peggy; Cheese pushed Kelly. Cheese was my age and had really curly hair like me, but otherwise looked nothing like me: he was sort of thick and burly, or at least as burly as six-year-olds get. His head was just a little too small for his body, too, a trait that people kept telling him would straighten itself out as he got older but never did. He hadn't even wanted to come with us, but Kelly had insisted on coming ("I'm not a baby") and so we needed a fourth person to come along or Peggy and I would end up spending the whole time looking after her and there'd be no point in going.

"So where are you from?" I asked Peggy between pushes.

"151 Hyacinth Avenue," she said. "You've been to our house."

"I mean before," I said. "Where did you move here from? What state?"

"State?" she said. "We just lived on the other side of the creek. We only moved because my mom had a baby and we needed a bigger house."

"Oh," I said. "My mom's having a baby in a couple months too. Maybe we'll have to move. I hope not." Then it hit me. "Hey, wait, if you've lived around here all this time then how come I haven't seen you at school?"

"I go to Catholic school," Peggy said. "Are you Catholic?"

"Nope," I said.

"So that's why we haven't seen each other at church either," she said.

"Hey," Cheese said, "do you think that if you pushed hard enough you could get the swing to go all the way around?"

I thought about it for a minute. "Well," I said, "if you take a bucket of water and spin it around really fast the water'll stay in the bucket even when it's upside down. 'Cause the water's going up faster than gravity's pulling it down. So if you could get the swing going that fast you could do it. But I doubt you could push that hard. Especially with a person in it."

"I can too push that hard," Cheese said. He gave Kelly a mighty shove and while the swing didn't go anywhere in particular, Kelly tumbled off it at a surprising speed and landed in a heap on the sand. She seemed to consider the situation for a moment and then burst into tears.

Peggy hopped off the swing. "Keith, go home," she said.

Cheese was so pale it was hard to believe he'd ever had a drop of blood in his entire body. "I—I didn't mean to—I thought—"

"Go home," Peggy said. Cheese ran across the bridge leading away from the park and took off down the street. Kelly rubbed her eyes, which wasn't really the brightest idea since her hands were covered with sand. That got her shrieking *and* bawling for a minute or two till the tears washed the sand out. "Shhh," Peggy said softly. "Shhh. It's okay." She looked at Kelly's hands and knees. "She's not bleeding," she said. "She isn't really scraped up even. She just hit the ground hard."

"So what do we do?" I asked.

"Nothing," Peggy said. She took Kelly into her arms and let her cry on her shoulder for a while. I felt pretty bad since I was the one who'd come up with the stuff about the bucket. "Come on," Peggy said gently. "You think you can walk home?"

"I don't know," Kelly sobbed.

"Of course you can," Peggy said. "You're not a baby. You're big. Right?"

Kelly sniffed. "I guess," she said. "Cheese hates me."

"Keith wasn't trying to hurt you," Peggy said. "He just wanted to see if the thing with the swing would work. He loves you. And I love you, and Mom loves you, and Dad loves you, and Grant loves you."

"Who's that?" Kelly asked.

"The baby, silly," Peggy said. "And I bet Allen loves you too. Right?"

"Uh, sure," I said.

"So there," Peggy said. "Nobody hates you. Come on, let's go home."

"Okay," Kelly said.

She was actually pretty much back to normal by the time we got back to the house, but her face was still stained with tears and other less picturesque fluids. "What happened here?" Mrs. K. asked.

"She fell off the swing," Peggy said. "Didn't Keith tell you?"

"He just went up to his room," Mrs. K. said.

That reminded me of something I'd been meaning to ask. "Hey, Peggy, can I see your room?" I asked.

She looked like I'd asked her to stick her face in a garbage disposal. "Of course not," she said. "That's private."

Also private for some reason was her uniform. I'd caught a glimpse of her in it a couple of times, clambering into her parents' station wagon as I passed her house on the way to school. The uniform was fairly standard—white shirt, red tie, optional white sweater, blue blazer, pleated plaid skirt, white knee socks, and shiny black shoes with shiny silver buckles. But Peggy refused to let me see her in it whenever she could help it. I came over to her house almost every day after school and invariably she'd already changed into regular clothes, even when she'd only been home for a minute or two. It was kind of frustrating. Now don't get me wrong—while it's true that I was a good eight or nine years ahead of my peers in figuring out that girls were sort of soft and pretty and interesting and stuff, not even I had enough discernment at that age to comprehend exactly how much of a turn-on a Catholic-schoolgirl uniform is. What got to me was the way she used it to deliberately exclude me from that part of her life. "My uniform is for school," she said. "You don't go to my school. So you can't see it."

It was strange, because in other ways we were really close. Like sneaking out together in the dead of night—or at least seven-thirty, which in the winter counts as the dead of night. I'd seen a documentary about the KGB and was convinced I had to do something about it. Peggy was waiting on her front porch with a flashlight and a legal pad. Like me, she was dressed entirely in black.

"Do your parents know what you're doing?" I asked.

"I told them I was playing with you," she said.

"Okay, that sounds pretty believable," I said. "Now here's the plan. The KGB is from Russia, so if we find any cars with Russian license plates we'll know there're KGB agents living around here." Peggy nodded solemnly. The first suspect was a station wagon parked across the street. I shined my flashlight on the license plate.

"California," I said. "Write that down."

Peggy wrote it down. She also wrote down the plate numbers of a couple dozen other cars we found on neighboring streets, all of which bore California plates. I was beginning to get discouraged when Peggy grabbed my sleeve. "Look," she said, pointing. A car in a nearby driveway clearly did not have California license plates. We turned off our flashlights for full invisibility as we crept up the driveway.

"Oregon," we whispered together.

"That's between here and Russia," I whispered.

"Maybe it's not a KGB agent but, you know, an assistant maybe," she whispered back.

"A sympathizer," I murmured.

We scouted out almost the entire development and it was past nine when we finally got caught. To my surprise it wasn't Mr. or Mrs. K. who found us, but my dad. "What are you two up to?" he asked.

I tried to come up with a plausible pretext but decided that what we were doing was too obvious to fool anyone. "Looking for communists," I admitted. "Do I have to come in?"

"Oh, not right away," he said. "You can have a few more minutes. I was looking for your counterpart, actually. Have you seen her?"

"You mean Echo?" I said. "She went to the high school parking lot to ride bikes."

"Ah," he said. "Well, enjoy your McCarthyism." He strolled off down the street.

"Who was that?" Peggy whispered.

"My dad," I said.

"Really? How come he doesn't look like you?" she asked. "His skin's different . . ."

"I look more like my mom," I said.

I decided it'd probably be best to head back. Peggy had filled up almost the whole front page of the legal pad with license plate numbers. "Keep that list," I said. "Then next time if we see any of the same cars we won't have to write it down."

"Okay," she said. "I can put them in order, too. On index cards, even."

"Sounds good," I said. I walked her up to her front porch. "Well, see you tomorrow."

"Wait," she said. She looked at me for a second without saying anything. Then she kissed me on the cheek.

Now I'd been kissed before—it was one of the perks of the secret clubs—and it was only common courtesy that when someone kissed you, you kissed her back. And what I felt for Peggy was more than courtesy—she'd been my best friend for months now. So I leaned forward to kiss her. "Don't," she said. She slipped inside and closed the door.

Jumpers

When you're six years old, it's not all that uncommon for your best friend to be the kid next door—or two doors down, as the case may be. After all, little kids don't have much in the way of interests or personality to get in the way of getting along. Chances are that a kid who lives on the other side of the continent isn't going to be radically different from the one who lives across the street, so you might as well stick with whoever's closest.

But once you've been in school for a couple years, your social world widens considerably. You discover that you distinctly dislike the company of certain people. You discover that the person three seats behind you says much funnier things than anyone who lives in your neighborhood. You discover that you no longer feel an instant emotional bond with anyone who happens to be standing in front of your house. You discover that the kids on your street may be your neighbors, but they're not necessarily your friends.

At least, you discover these things if you're not me. But if you *are* me, and I know I am, you discover that no one you meet quite measures up to the girl two doors down. Not because there's anything wrong with the kids in your class or anything. It's more a history thing than anything else. You can hit it off with all kinds of people, but once you've shared a counterespionage run with someone, well, that's the kind of bond that goes deeper than sharing your math notes.

So even as we continued to go to different schools, Peggy Kaylin remained my very best friend in the whole wide world. I'd go to her house almost every day after school, sometimes for twenty minutes, sometimes for the entire afternoon and well into the evening. Since we did go to different schools and hadn't seen each other all day, we always had plenty to talk about. Then, one day, things changed. It was my first day at Vista de la Vista Middle School. When my little schedule card said it was time for PE, I changed into my gym clothes and lined up on the blacktop with forty other kids, all in dark blue shorts and white T-shirts with their last names written across them in black indelible marker. I stood there looking around, seeing if I recognized any of the names and enjoying the way some of the letters could get distorted in the most fascinating ways when attached to the right shirt on the right girl, letting the names the teacher was barking out just sort of wash over me since I knew he wasn't anywhere near the M's, when one name came barreling out of the teacher's mouth, flew into my ear, and crashed into my brain. "KAYLIN!"

After I picked my jaw up off the asphalt and snapped it back in place, I craned my neck around wildly looking for who the teacher could possibly have been talking to. Sure enough, standing a couple rows over was none other than Cheese. "What're *you* doing here?" I asked.

"No talking during roll call!" shouted the teacher. "Five laps after class!"

So five seconds after school ended—well, maybe more than that,

since doing all those laps left me too tired to walk home all that fast—
I was at Peggy's door stabbing at the doorbell like a deranged subma-
rine captain firing off torpedoes. Peggy answered.

"What's going on?" I asked. "Why is Cheese at Vista de la Vista?
Why isn't he at Catholic school? Why are you still in Catholic school
if he's not?"

"How many times did you ring the bell?" she asked.

"I dunno," I said. "Maybe fifty."

"Then we get to listen to fifty back-to-back renditions of the Westminster chimes," she said. "We put the system in yesterday."

"Oops," I said.

"Well, come in," she said. "I have something for you. It's in the
kitchen."

She waited for me to come in so she could walk behind me. She
hated people to see her walk. Actually, she hated people to see her at
all. But especially walking. "I feel about as graceful as a cross between
a cow and a minivan," she said. The reason was obvious: she'd
bought the shirt she was wearing just a few months before, thinking
that her prodigious breast development had finally stalled out, but it
turned out that her body had just been resting for a bit and now the
poor shirt was in visible pain straining to keep a handle on her new
physique. Yet somehow she hadn't made the connection between said
physique and the fact that at age thirteen and a half her ex-boyfriends
numbered in the twenties.

In the kitchen were two baskets. The smaller one had three chocolate chip cookies wrapped in cellophane along with half a dozen
strawberries and a miniature round of Gouda cheese in it. The larger
one had the same stuff, only more of it.

"The big one's for your family," she said. "The little one's all
yours."

"Wow," I said. "You went to all this trouble just for me?"

"Not really," she said. "Today was the first day of school so I
made baskets for all my friends and teachers. Except the teachers got
apples instead of strawberries. And since I was already making them I
thought I might as well make a couple for you."

"That's so cool," I said. But her mention of the first day of school
(along with the nonstop Westminster chimes) reminded me of why I'd

come in the first place. "So why's Cheese going to Vista de la Vista?" I asked.

"Well," Peggy said, "it's like this." She looked up for a second as if the best way to explain might be written on the ceiling. "See, at the end of seventh grade we had a picnic for all the kids in my class and their parents, and I overheard a bunch of parents talking about how lucky we all were to be going to 'the good school' with 'the good kids.' And later I was thinking about it and I thought, Hey, if we're the 'good' kids, what does that make public school kids? 'Bad'? And that bugged me. 'Cause I know public school kids that are good—like you—and I know lots of Catholic school kids that . . . aren't." Yeah, I thought, like Boyfriend #1, #2, #3, #4 . . .

"Anyway," she said, "Keith was changing schools anyway, and he wanted to go to public school just 'cause he didn't like the uniforms and the discipline and stuff, so once I talked to Mom and Dad they put him in Vista de la Vista instead of St. Joseph's, and if he likes it, I might end up going to Ilium instead of Rosary next year."

So, one day shy of a year later, Peggy started at Ilium High School. I went over to her house the day before; she'd just gotten back from shopping for school supplies. "Look!" she said, spreading her new possessions out on the coffee table. She opened up a burgundy plastic case. "See, it's a kit! You get two pens in case one runs out of ink, and two pencils in case one breaks, and on the other side you get a highlighter, and a mechanical pencil, and a click eraser, and a white-out pen! You just write over what you just wrote and white-out comes out instead of ink! And built into the case—see? It's a pencil sharpener!"

She put the kit down. "Now look at this!" she said. "You get six notebooks, one for each subject, and they're all recycled paper, and when you're not using them you hook them into this binder so they don't get separated!"

"I can see you feel very strongly about stationery," I said.

"And I got clothes, too!" she said. "Ones that actually fit!" She dug through the bags next to the couch. "Here's a sweater . . . here's another sweater . . . here are some skirts . . ."

I couldn't help noticing that all the sweaters were white and all the skirts were plaid. "Uh, you know, Peggy . . . it's public school," I said. "You can wear anything you want."

"Oh, I know," she said. "But still, it's good to be respectful. Hey, let's see what the weather's going to be like tomorrow."

"This is Southern California," I said. "It's going to be eighty degrees and sunny."

Nevertheless, Peggy picked up the remote in its little plastic bag and turned on the TV. But instead of being in front of a map talking about warm fronts and Santa Ana winds, the weather guy was up on a rooftop holding police at bay with a semiautomatic.

"Oh, no," Peggy said.

"I guess the barometric pressure must've gotten to him," I said.

"Don't come up here!" the weather guy was shouting. "I'll jump, I mean it! I'll shoot you all and then I'll jump!"

"Mel, it's Herb!" came a voice over a megaphone. "Don't do this, man! We love you!"

"I've heard of ratings gimmicks before, but this is ridiculous," I said.

"I can't watch this," Peggy said. She turned off the TV and shivered. "That's just horrible. I'm sure that if he does jump they'll show him going all the way down. Down, down, down, and—" There was a cymbal crash.

Now, I knew Peggy pretty well, but I was reasonably sure I couldn't actually hear her thoughts. "What was that?" I asked.

"Oh, Keith got a drum set," she said. As if to confirm this, Cheese launched into a drum solo. "I just don't get it," Peggy said. "If you're going to kill yourself, you should just do it. Making a big production out of it and hurting other people . . . that makes no sense at all."

"Oh, I dunno," I said. "One could make the argument that if you're going to kill yourself, you should blow away everyone who ever ticked you off first. What are they going to do, execute you?"

"But you're lucky if you don't end up in hell just for killing yourself," she said. "Why kill other people and go for sure?"

"What if you don't believe in hell?" I asked.

"Well . . . I guess you could say that if you're going to be dead, and you don't believe in the afterlife, then it doesn't make any difference to you if you let the other people live or not because . . . because you'll be dead!" she said. "So if it doesn't make any difference to you, why not be nice? This is a stupid conversation."

"This is an inaudible conversation," I said. "I don't suppose there's any way to turn down a drum kit, is there?"

Right then Kelly came in. Actually, Kelly never just "came in"—she threw herself into rooms like she'd been shot out of a catapult. She was wearing a Vista de la Vista PE outfit with the name "KELLY" written across it. "Isn't that supposed to have your *last* name on it?" I asked.

"Yeah, yeah, I know that *now,*" she said, skidding to a stop. "I had to go get another one. Hey, Peggy, are you, like, busy? 'Cause you said you were going to help me, like, practice? And stuff?"

Peggy looked at her watch. "Sure, okay," she said. "But let's make it quick. I've got a date."

Kelly scampered upstairs. "Practice?" I said. "Practice what? And you've got a date? The day before school starts? Who's this, number forty-four?"

"His name's Colin," Peggy said. "And don't worry. He's not like the other ones. I think this time it could really be special."

"Yeah, that's what you said about the last forty-two," I said.

Kelly came crashing down the stairs and into the TV room with a pom-pom in each hand. "Ready, okay!" she declared. "Be aggressive! B-E aggressive! B-E! A-G-G! R-E-S-S— Uh, oops."

She stopped herself before she bounced off the far wall and picked up the chair she'd knocked over. "Kelly, what's the most important thing in cheerleading?" Peggy asked.

"Energy!" Kelly shouted triumphantly.

"Wrong," Peggy said. "It's precision. All it takes is a couple of cups of coffee to get people to jump around. The thing that makes you a good cheerleader is the ability to jump around in the exact same way as a bunch of other girls. And that means you've got to coordinate your timing, which you can't do if no one else is here, and get your routine down, which you can. Let's see it again and this time, precise."

"Okay," Kelly said. She picked her left pom-pom out of the house-plant and stood in the middle of the room. "Ready, okay! Be aggress—"

"Stop," Peggy said. "Your arm. Where's it supposed to be? Up? Down? Out to the side? Out in front?"

"Up," Kelly said. "And it *is* up."

"It has to be straight up," Peggy said. "Don't let it sag. Keep your elbows locked until the routine calls for you to bend them."

From upstairs came the distinct sound of Cheese knocking one of his cymbal stands over. Kelly threw her pom-poms to the ground. "Like, how am I supposed to concentrate with all this *noise*?"

"You mean like at a football game?" Peggy said. "You're not going to be cheering in a library. You have to deal with the noise. Now let's see it again."

"Whatever," Kelly said. She picked up her pom-poms and went through the routine once more; it almost looked like Echo going through her kata back when she was taking martial arts classes. Toward the end Cheese finally gave up on his drum practice. I guess he was even beginning to annoy himself. *"Go! Fight! WIN!"* Kelly concluded. "How was that?"

"That's more like it," Peggy said. "See, that was pretty good."

"Just pretty good?" Kelly said.

"To be honest, yeah," Peggy said. "But 'pretty good' is way better than anything the girls you'll be competing against can come up with. You'll blow them away, easy."

"Really? You mean it?" Kelly lunged over the coffee table and threw her arms around Peggy. "You're the greatest!" She let go and bopped her in the face with a pom-pom. "Uh, sorry I knocked over all your pencils and stuff . . ."

"It's okay," Peggy said. She snapped her writing implements back into their case. "Show Allen out, okay? I've got to get ready for my date!"

The big one–seven

Yet, somehow, when Peggy's seventeenth birthday came around, I was still in the picture while Colin had become just another number in the ranks of Peggy exes. Well, sort of. I was in the picture enough to get invited over for dinner on her birthday, but afterward, when she went on her date, it wasn't with me. I suppose you could say I was in the picture but out of focus.

A few months earlier we'd been hanging out in the TV room talking while Cheese flipped through the channels. One of the shows he flipped past was a calligraphy show; I made a mental note of the way Peggy's eyes lit up as it flashed by, and so when I'd saved up enough money I bought her a calligraphy set. It took me about a week or so to figure out how to wrap the calligraphy set without ending up taping it to my face, but eventually I got it right and so that's what was in the box I was holding as I rang the doorbell (only once—I'd learned my lesson after spending a month with Westminster chimes ringing through my head).

Kelly answered the door. Immediately my heart leaped out of my chest and embedded itself in my rib cage. See, by age fourteen, Kelly Kaylin had metamorphosed into the ninety-nine most desirable pounds of female on the planet. Part of it was because her face was . . . well, I can't say perfect, because that'd be selling her short. She was much more devastatingly attractive than that. If Peggy's face had an unglazed quality to it, Kelly's was glazed, polished, treated with a coat of sealant and unspeakably stunning. Like Peggy, she'd discovered that she was going gray a couple years before, but unlike Peggy she'd immediately dyed her hair black, aggressively black, grab-you-by-the-collar-and-slap-you-silly black. So that was part of it. Another part of it was that she'd developed, not to uncomfortable levels like Peggy, but just to the point that her figure could only be called, in the words of the local *fútbol* announcer describing a Mexican goal, *"perfecto y ESPECTACULAR!"* I'm not just talking about her chest, *perfecto y espectacular* as it was—I'm talking about every delectable square inch of her body. So that was part of it too. But there was more. See, Kelly didn't photograph especially well. When you took a picture of her, she looked fine, but nothing you'd write your congressman about. I therefore theorized that Kelly Kaylin was surrounded at all times by a thick cloud of pheromones that made her seem a good 40 to 50 percent more beautiful than she actually was. My theory was borne out by the fact that when I had a head cold for a week she no longer looked quite so preternaturally amazing as she usually did, but once my sinuses cleared, it immediately became apparent that this girl was freakishly gorgeous, a living breathing wet dream with braces. To spend any length of time around her without feeling the urge to jump her you'd have to down your body weight in saltpeter every morning.

It didn't help that Kelly was something of a minimalist where clothing was concerned. On this particular evening, for instance, she was wearing a flimsy white T-shirt with nothing on underneath, a pair of striped boxer shorts, and one pink sock. "Oh, hey," she said. "Come in."

Once I heard her voice, my torment multiplied. Here I could see her, I could smell her, and now I could hear her, but I wasn't allowed to touch her or taste her. It didn't seem fair. I would gladly have traded the hearing part for either of the other two. "Hey, you," I said. I waved the present at her. "Any particular place I should put this?"

She shrugged, and I swear, the things that went on under that shirt—epic poems have been written about sights less glorious. "Like, you can put it on the table in the living room with the others if you want," she said. "She says she'll open them when she gets back but that'll be, like, the middle of the night. If you want her to open it while you're here, you'll have to, like, you know, give it to her." She flounced off into the TV room. I followed her at a somewhat more measured pace. The forty minutes of preparation I'd put in before coming over hadn't done a bit of good.

As I passed the little dining room I noticed that the table was already set except for a couple of places that didn't have any silver-ware. From under the tablecloth I heard an odd crunching sound. Peggy apparently noticed it too, as she arranged the knives and forks on the table. She lifted up the tablecloth to find Grant underneath munching on a bag of cookies. "What are you doing under there?" she asked. "Give me those!"

"They're mine," Grant said. "I bought them."

"It doesn't matter who bought them," Peggy said. "Get out from under there." Grant crawled out from under the table. "How many did you eat, anyway?" she asked.

"I dunno," he said.

"How can you not know?" she asked. "What, weren't you there?"

"I only had two," he said.

"What does Mom say about eating junk food before dinner?" she asked.

"Not to," he said.

"So you *don't do it*," she said. "Now put those away."

Mrs. K. came in to see what was going on. "You know, Peggy," she said, "there's a reason they have different words for 'sister' and 'mother.'"

"Well, *someone* has to do something about this kind of thing," Peggy said. "You can't just go around breaking the rules. Besides, he'll get fat."

Kelly came careening back from the TV room. "What's all the arguing about?" she asked.

"Nothing," Peggy said. "Can't you put some clothes on? We have *company*."

"Right, like Allen's company," Kelly said. "You need to, like, free your mind or something."

"Do you want this now?" I asked, offering Peggy my present.

"Just put it on the table," she said. She shook her head. "I don't understand. Aren't people supposed to pay attention to you on your birthday?"

"Sure, to *you*," I said. "Whether they listen to anything you *say* is something else entirely."

Before long dinner was served and I had an important tactical decision to make. See, the Kaylins had a tradition—it had started out as just a now-and-then thing but then Peggy started insisting on it—of saying grace before dinner while holding hands around the table. Which meant that if I sat next to Kelly I'd have the opportunity to touch her, at least for a minute or so. But if I sat across from her, I could look at her for the entire meal. Being a long-term thinker I selected the latter course and sat between Peggy and Grant.

So we all held hands. "Lord," Mr. K. said, "we thank you for the meal we are about to receive. And on this special day we hope that in her eighteenth year you will see fit to grant—"

"What?" Grant said. "I wasn't doing anything."

Mr. K. laughed. "Sorry," he said. "We hope that in her eighteenth year you will see fit to *give* our daughter as much joy as she has given us the last seventeen. Amen."

Cheese dabbed at his eyes with his napkin. "That was beautiful, man," he said. "I think I'm gonna cry."

Dinner was salad and a pair of lasagnas: a little one without meat for Peggy and me, and a big one with meat for everyone else. I was the child of two vegetarians so it had never even occurred to me that a hunk of dead cow or a chicken corpse was something that you'd actually want to put in your mouth. Peggy, on the other hand, had converted at age nine after watching a documentary about the meat-packing industry, complete with footage of the killing floor of a slaughterhouse, and after spending the entire night throwing up she'd vowed never to eat a piece of meat again. Shortly thereafter she saw a documentary about the 1982 Tylenol scare and refused to eat *anything* for fear of being poisoned. She lost over twenty pounds and had to be hospitalized for a while. From then on she wasn't allowed to watch any more documentaries.

"Be careful," Mrs. K. said. "The pans are hot. Use the pot holders."

"You always say that," Kelly said. She grabbed the big pan and ladled some lasagna onto her plate. Then she handed the pan to Cheese, who yelped and threw it halfway across the table. Miracle of miracles, the pan neither smashed anything on the table nor spilled its contents into anyone's lap.

"Shit!" Cheese said. "That's hot!" He ran into the kitchen and stuck his hands under the faucet.

"Like, it's not that hot," Kelly said. "You can barely even *feel* it. Wimp."

"Kelly, please don't start a fight," Peggy said. "And, Keith, watch your language. And Grant—"

"What did *I* do?" Grant said.

"—pass the dressing, please," Peggy said.

So we had dinner. Then we had dessert. Mrs. K. brought out a cake with seventeen candles, which Peggy proceeded to blow out somewhat less than enthusiastically. "Did you make a wish?" Mrs. K. asked.

"No," Peggy said. "I made a wish a while ago, and today it didn't come true."

"I dunno why you want that surgery anyway," Cheese said. "Do you know how many chicks would kill for—"

"Only the ones that didn't know what it was like," Peggy said.

"Cut the cake already," Kelly said.

The cake was cut and passed around. It was around this point that my tactical decision paid off, as I got to enjoy the spectacle of Kelly licking frosting off her fingers. It wasn't quite as good as the time I'd seen her devouring a Popsicle, but it was close. Peggy, on the other hand, was just pushing her cake around with her fork, and it wasn't just because she didn't want to get fat. "What's up?" I asked softly.

"Is that your therapist voice?" she said.

"I'm not a therapist," I said. "I'm a peer counselor."

"Right," she said. "And I'm a beverage facilitator."

"So are you okay?" I asked.

"I guess," she said. "I don't know. It's just—this place. Nobody does what they're supposed to, everyone's mean to everyone else, it's totally chaotic. *Totally* chaotic."

"Totally chaotic." I hadn't been over for dinner in the week since then, so that evening and especially that conversation were fresh in my mind as I walked up my driveway. The rest of it—the childhood games, all the afternoons I'd spent at her house between six and sixteen—I can't say I was really actively thinking about. But I didn't have to. It was always there, lurking in the background. Every time I looked at Peggy Kaylin I was seeing her through ten years of history.

Where the heart is, or at least the spleen

Sitting in the driveway was the car that I'd have been free to hop into and drive anywhere I wanted if I hadn't almost hit someone who wasn't there. Echo and I had bought it together: it was fairly tiny, which was fine with me, and it was black, which didn't thrill me but which Echo had insisted on. And it was unlocked, which was a good thing because someone had left the garage door closed and our front walk was so overgrown you couldn't make it to the door without a machete and several canisters of Agent Orange. I got the garage door opener out of the car, clicked open the sliding door, and went inside.

I was greeted by the sight of my brother Krieg standing in the kitchen hunched over a Carnage Pizza—sauce, cheese, pepperoni, ham, sausage, Canadian bacon, regular bacon, ground beef, chicken, turkey, mutton, venison, ostrich, squirrel, and raccoon—that he'd ordered from Pizza Hovel. "Mmmgfmn," he said. He wiped his mouth with the back of his hand, leaving a bloody smear across his face and crumbs of pizza crust suspended in his scuzzy mustache. "Mine," he elaborated.

"Wouldn't have it any other way," I said. Krieg grunted and went back to cramming pizza down his throat.

Echo stood in the corner with her arms crossed. She wore black jeans and a shapeless black sweatshirt, which would normally be a wholly inappropriate outfit for Southern California but which made more sense inside, where every room in the house but one had the air conditioner blasting at least twenty-four hours a day and sometimes more. "So did you get your license?" she asked.

"No," I said. "They said I almost hit someone. *I* didn't see anyone."

"Makes sense," she said. "People are always hurting other people without realizing it."

"Right," I said. "Well, I'd gladly flagellate myself but I left my whip in the cab. So do *we* get anything to eat?"

"We ordered from the Delhi-Catessen," she said. "They should be here any minute. We didn't get anything for you but I guess you can share mine." Outside a car door slammed. "That must be them," Echo said.

She was wrong. The garage door flew open and in came my half-uncle Bobbo with trollop in tow. "Hey, everybody!" he said. "This here's Trina." Trina was exactly Bobbo's type: makeup you'd need an archeological team to dig through, perfume that could kill a cow at thirty paces, hair that didn't looked bleached so much as spray-painted yellow. "Say hi to Trina, everyone," Bobbo said.

"Hi," I said.

"Mgmff," Krieg said.

"So how much do you charge?" Echo asked. "Fifty bucks a night? Sixty?"

"That wasn't very nice," Bobbo said. He turned to Trina. "You want a drink?" he asked. "I've got a minibar in my room." They went upstairs. Thus ends Trina's role in the story of my life.

Moments later the delivery guy arrived. Echo paid him and unloaded the bags onto the counter: garlic naan, samosas, dal makhani, vegetable korma, all kinds of stuff. There was a thumping on the staircase and my sister Molly came skidding into the kitchen. She was thirteen years old and completely naked. "Hey, you're back!" she said. "Did you get your license?"

"No," I said. "I lost control of the car and plowed directly into the DMV office, killing hundreds."

"Figures," she said. She got a paper plate out of the cupboard and started loading it up. "So can I see it?" she asked.

"I actually didn't pass the test," I said. "The fact that I had to drive a taxi instead of my own car didn't help. But I guess Bobbo was too busy cruising for chicks to take me to the DMV."

"Well, you'll get it next time," Molly said. She picked up the phone and punched the buttons. "Jerem?" she said. "It's Molly. Dinner's here." A pause. "I'm not going in there," she said. "It'll ruin my appetite. Yeah, he's here. No, he flunked the test. Okay. 'Bye." She hung up the phone. "Jerem wants you to bring him some food," she said.

"Whatever," I said. "I still don't see why a nine-year-old needs a cell phone." Echo had already made a plate for herself and one for me so I put everything that was left back in the bag and took it upstairs.

Jerem shared a room with Krieg, sort of. They both lived behind the same door, but Jerem had surrounded his bed with an enormous curtain that stretched from the floor to the ceiling. I opened the door and the stench knocked me to the carpet. "Food's here," I said.

Behind the curtain I could hear Jerem's fingers tapping away on his computer. "Place the food on the ground and close the door," he said. "Do not open the curtain. Do not attempt further conversation."

"I'll be sure not to pass go or collect two hundred dollars either," I said. I put the bag on the ground and closed the door.

"It's totally chaotic," Peggy had said. "*Totally* chaotic."

"Yup," I'd said. "Your family's a mess."

What else is on?

Before I went to bed that night I decided to cap off the evening with some guitar playing. In the two years I'd been playing I'd progressed from astoundingly incompetent to merely remarkably unskilled. Despite my lack of talent, I really enjoyed playing—I'd spend several hours every week up in my room pretending to be a rock star. Of course, I only knew about four chords so I had to pretend I was a rock star recuperating from a freak spinal injury that'd left me with grossly impaired motor skills. So anyway, I was merrily rocking out when suddenly I found myself with some unexpected percussive accompaniment: someone was knocking on the garage door. I put down my guitar and was about to go see who it was when the phone rang. The phone was closer so I picked it up. "Hello?" I said.

"Beep!" said the phone. "This is a recorded message from the Ilium High School attendance office. Our records indicate that Craig Robert Mockery missed one or more periods of class today. Unexcused absences can lead to disciplinary action. Beep!"

I hung up and went downstairs to see who was at the door but Bobbo had beaten me to it. It was Peggy. "Yes?" Bobbo said. Then his gaze wandered to about the third button on her shirt. "Whoa, *hel*-lo!" he said. "Come on in! I was expecting a pizza but this is *much* better!"

Peggy's face lit up like the coil on an electric stove. "Real sensitive, Bobbo," I said. "Hey, why don't you go down to that center for the disabled? I'm sure they've got lots of people in wheelchairs you can point at . . ."

"Give me a break," he said. "Have you *seen* this chick?"

"Only every day for the past ten years," I said. I went out into the garage and shut the door in Bobbo's face. "Sorry about that," I said. "I would've answered the door but I had to listen to the Ilium computer tell me that Krieg cut class. Gee, there's a shocker."

"Do you always leave your garage door open?" Peggy asked, looking around. "Anyone could just walk in and steal all kinds of stuff."

"Yeah, I know," I said. "I'd like to say we're demonstrating faith in human nature but really we're just kind of lazy. So how was your date?"

"Not so great," she said. "He tried to . . . I mean . . . he tried stuff."

"Yikes," I said.

"What do you mean, 'yikes'?" she said. "It's exactly what you said was going to happen. It's what you said was going to happen the other ninety-one times, too, and you've always been right. I don't get it. Is it me? Does going out with me short-circuit something in decent guys' brains to turn them . . . not decent? Or am I just the worst judge of character in the world?"

"I wouldn't say that," I said. "It's just that you don't really have a lot of time to judge. Don't most of these guys ask you out at work? Or ask for your number when you're at work and then ask you out after a ten-minute phone call?"

"Not always," she said. "I meet guys in my church, and at school . . . and besides, I've known Mike for weeks! Months, even! He was always hanging out with Dave and Chris when I was seeing *them* and he was always really nice."

"But even over those months that you knew who he *was,* how much time did you spend *with* him?" I asked. "A couple afternoons? Maybe a five-minute conversation every now and then?"

"But that's what I go out with them for!" she said. "To get to know them better! You're a peer counselor—what should I do?"

"Actually, as a peer counselor I'm not allowed to give advice," I said.

"Then as a friend," she said.

"Well," I said, "the thing about dating is, it sort of implies that you're more than friends, or going to be . . . it's like, instead of going naturally from someone being a stranger to an acquaintance to a friend and *then* letting your guard down and opening yourself up to getting closer, you're skipping all the middle steps."

"But I don't want to 'just be friends,'" she said. "I *like*—you know, going out and doing fun things, and kissing and stuff like that."

"That's fine," I said. "I'm not saying you shouldn't see *anyone*— not that there's anything wrong with taking it easy and just staying single for a while. But—I mean, I wouldn't feel comfortable going out with someone that I didn't feel like I already knew inside and out, you know?"

She smirked. "I don't know," she said. "It sounds like you're saying I should go out with . . . my *brother,* or somebody. Or you."

"No," I cut in. "I mean, not *necessarily—*"

"Well, I'll think about it," she said. "Anyway, here." She opened up our outdoor freezer and took out a package. It was gift-wrapped.

"What's this?" I asked. "Will it melt?"

"It's a present, silly," she said. "And that was just the only place I could see to hide it."

I opened it up. It was a little hardbound book, like a diary. I flipped through the pages and found what looked like TV listings pasted inside.

"I know you're always making fun of TV shows," she explained. "So I've been saving up all the dopey listings I've found in the newspaper . . ."

I turned to a page at random:

14 TEEN-VEE
Ashley: The Early Years
Ashley discovers that when her beloved art teacher leans over her shoulder to "help her with her brushwork," he's sneaking peeks down her shirt. Starring Holly Madera as Ashley.

53 THE FORMULAIC TRIPE CHANNEL
Straight Flush
Corey does some bad acid, tries to kill Zeke, but learns her lesson; Annie can't find her favorite hat. Starring Anastasia, Bathsheba, Coriander, Delilah, and Ezekiel Oldenberg as Anastasia, Bathsheba, Coriander, Delilah, and Ezekiel Smith. Guest-starring Mohan Tadikonda, Master of the Martial Arts.

78 THE 1978 CHANNEL
The Love Boat
Guest star finds love on boat. Guest star: TBA.

"This is amazing," I said. "It must've taken you forever."
"Just a few minutes here and there," she said. "It was fun."
"Look, do you want to come in?" I asked. "I can make sure Bobbo doesn't bother you . . . "
"No, it's getting late," she said. "I should go."
"Okay," I said. "Thanks again. And, hey, you know . . . I love you, Peggy."
She smiled. "That's sweet," she said. "Good night."
I watched her self-consciously walk down the driveway and disappear down the street. I shut the garage door and went upstairs.

When I got back to my room I found Echo switching off my amp. "Whoops," I said. "Forgot I'd left that on. Sorry about that." I yawned and put my guitar back on its stand. "I think I'm going to sleep," I said.
"Okay," Echo said, heading for the door. "Want me to turn out the light?"
"Go for it," I said. She turned out the light. In the darkness I heard her close the door and slide into her bed on the other side of the room.

TWO

Echo got up at one-thirty the next morning, spent the next several hours doing whatever it was she did every day before the sun came up, and then at nine A.M. took her driving test and racked up a perfect score driving the same cab with which I'd scored my big zero. She then drove home, got on her bike, rode off somewhere and didn't get back until late that night. The car continued to collect dust in the driveway.

As for me, I had a lot of explaining to do once I got back to school on Monday. Especially once September Young spotted me. "Hey!" she said. "Did you drive your car to school? Can I see it?"

"Why would I drive to school?" I asked. "You can see my house from the parking lot."

"Oh, yeah," she said. "So can I see your license? Did they get a good picture of you? My brother's license picture makes him look like some kind of radioactive mutant."

"I didn't pass the test," I said. "We've got at least another two weeks of Taxi Ocho ahead of us. Sorry."

"Oh," she said. Her face fell for half a second. "Well, that's okay. What's another two weeks, you know? See you after school."

We shall overcome

A couple weeks before my first day at Ilium, I got a manila envelope in the mail full of flyers advertising the various extracurricular activities offered there, things like: "Incapable of constructing a grammatically correct sentence? Not sure what those comma thingies are for? Then Yearbook is for you!" I was about to throw the whole batch of them out when one of them caught my eye. It said:

Peer Counseling

Ilium High School offers peer counseling sessions in lieu of detention time for minor infractions of the student conduct code. If you have been issued a citation for such an infraction and wish to exercise this option, please consult Mrs. Handey in the front office. If you are interested in becoming a peer counselor please see Assistant Principal Todd at 3:30 P.M. on September 10th.

September tenth was a Wednesday, meaning that I'd had a grand total of two days of high school experience under my belt when I went to the office that afternoon. I figured that was more than enough to give me a comprehensive understanding of the whole adolescence thing. A quick glance at my map of the school revealed where Assistant Principal Todd's office was; sitting on a chair right outside the door was a nice-looking girl with long straight honey-colored hair and a well-scrubbed, freshly varnished look. I recognized her from a couple of my classes, not so much for what she looked like as for the faded denim jacket she'd worn the last two days and would go on to wear pretty much every time I saw her thereafter.

I sat down on the ground. "Are you here for the peer counseling meeting?" the girl asked.

"No, I'm here for the sit-in," I said. "Which desk do you think I should cuff myself to?"

"I've been waiting here for fifteen minutes but you're the only other person who's shown up," she said. "I'm September, by the way."

"I'm Allen," I said. "Maybe a lot of people came by but then left once they saw you're the only one who gets a chair."

"So do you know anything about this Doctor Todd?" September asked.

I'd asked Peggy the same question the day before and she'd told me a little bit about him. Apparently, Doctor Dennis Todd was quite the legendary figure around Ilium. When the school had first opened he'd been the football coach—his doctorate was in physical education—but he'd worked his way into the administration as assistant principal in charge of discipline. He was something of a recluse, as only those summoned to his office ever saw him; he patrolled the campus through his proxy, a shriveled German crone named Uta Himmler who had worked for the school since opening day. She spent her days looking for people violating the student conduct code and reporting back to Doctor Todd on her walkie-talkie. Anyone caught breaking the rules received the same punishment, be it for littering or for attempting to kill someone with a forklift: a red ticket. These red tickets had to be redeemed at the front office; sometimes you just had to bring it back with a parent's signature, but you could also get assigned detention or, if it was really serious, you might be sent to see Doctor Todd in his office.

The red tickets quickly became the object of both dread and derision, and Uta was universally loathed. The school had only been open for a couple of weeks when she had a song written about her, one that was passed down from generation to generation; it went a little something like this:

> (sing to the tune of "Theme From *The Monkees*")
> *Here she comes . . .*
> *Walking down the hall . . .*
> *She's old and ugly . . .*
> *And only three feet taaaaalllllll . . .*
> *Hey hey, it's Uta!*
> *Fled from Deutschland after the war!*
> *And now she's come to stop you*
> *From eating in your caaaaarrrrrrrr . . .*

I was halfway through the chorus when September gave me a look like she'd just discovered that the calls were coming from inside the house. "What?" I said, turning around. Right behind me was Uta Himmler herself, all fifty-one chain-smoking inches of her. "Who are you?" she spat. "No vun may see Doktor Tod vitout appointment. He is busy man."

"We have an appointment," September said meekly. "Sort of."

"Ve shall see about dat," Uta said. She put down her cigarette and took her walkie-talkie out of its holster. A couple bursts of static later she raised an eyebrow in surprise. "Very vell," she said. "You may enter." She picked up her cigarette and marched off to the faculty restroom.

Doctor Todd's office was lit only by the light coming in through the open door and had the feeling of a bunker in the closing stages of a war. "Come in," said a gruff yet plaintive voice in the darkness. "Sit."

September flipped the light switch. Bathed in white fluorescent light the office looked much less eerie and much more like a converted storage closet. Sitting at the desk at the far end of the room was, I assumed, Doctor Todd. If Richard Nixon and Adolf Hitler had ever gotten together and had a child, the result would probably look a lot like the man September and I saw before us: he was intensely jowly, with a ski-slope nose and a toothbrush mustache, and his half-hearted comb-over did nothing to cover up his enormous forehead. "Sit," he repeated.

We sat down. September brushed some nonexistent crumbs off her skirt. Doctor Todd produced a stack of red tickets and handed one to each of us. "Citations," he said. "Note list of violations. Items in bold-face fall under my purview. Others possibly referred to you. Brief definitions. Dress code violation. Chief area of concern, bare skin on torso area. Apparel containing indecent slogans. Images also. Specifics unnecessary. Elastic clause: distraction equals violation. Enough said regarding that. Show of affection. Holding hands permitted. Beyond that, increasing penalty concomitant with increasing level of display. Eating in car, very important. No eating in car, ever. Cannot stress enough. Littering, truancy, vandalism . . ."

Doctor Todd continued in a similar vein for about twenty minutes. September seemed to be making a concentrated effort to follow what he was saying, but after a couple minutes I gave up and instead tried counting the words he said like Echo did when we were little. Eventually he stopped talking and handed both of us a set of thick three-ring binders. "Study," he said. "Learn information. Both medical information and counseling tips. Additional training sessions after school with Mrs. Handey before counseling commences. Make appointment before leaving. That is all."

This "additional training" consisted mainly of quizzes on the material in the big binders—"I never thought I'd have to become such an authority on K-Y jelly," September remarked one afternoon—but we also had a few practice runs with various teachers playing the parts of troubled students. (You haven't lived till you've heard an elderly man in a brown suit tell you he's about to be a teenage mother.) Once September and I had proved to everyone's satisfaction that we weren't liable to do anything in a peer counseling session that'd mean a round of costly lawsuits for the school district, there was only one hurdle left to overcome. Mrs. Handey called us into the office at lunchtime one day and announced, "We're ready to begin! In fact, Doctor Todd already has students lined up for you this afternoon. We'll have September take the girls and Allen, you take the boys."

"Come again?" I said.

"You mean we're not working together?" September asked. "But we trained together, we did all those practice runs together! You never had us do it separately!"

"It's a matter of imbalances," Mrs. Handey said. "We didn't think a boy would listen to a girl, or that a girl would open up to a boy."

"Say what?" I said. "What, is this a Daylight Savings Time thing? Like instead of setting our clocks back an hour we set them back to 1958?"

"If we split you up we can cover twice as many students," Mrs. Handey said.

"No you can't," September said. "'Cause I'll quit."

I had to raise my eyebrows at that one. September looked really indignant. "Uh, yeah," I said. "Me too."

Fortunately it was Mrs. Handey and not Doctor Todd we were dealing with, so instead of calling in Uta to drag us away she just threw her hands up in the air. "Fine," she said. "Your first case is at three-thirty."

Deeg patrol

The peer counseling sessions were scheduled to be held in the front office's conference room, which was a long skinny room with two long skinny tables arranged end to end to make a *really* long skinny table. At each end of the far wall was a window stretching from floor to ceiling and about six inches across; these were both shuttered, though, so there were no visual cues to suggest that we weren't miles underground. September was already there when I arrived, looking at a manila folder marked SHARALAYEK, SHARON. "So what's the story?" I asked. "Please tell me it doesn't have anything to do with any kind of explosive."

"Nope, just talking on the phone in class," September said. "I guess they decided to start us off easy."

September was sitting in the seat recommended by our big three-ring binder, ninety degrees removed from the far end of the table with her back to the window; it wasn't immediately obvious where I should sit, though. "Maybe across from me?" she said. "But no, then it's like we were pulling a squeeze play on her . . . maybe two seats down on my side . . . ?"

"I think I'll just roam around," I said. As it turned out, I didn't have much choice—I was already in mid-roam when Sharon Sharalayek came in.

Sharon was quite short and could have been fairly pretty if not for the black lipstick; it was astonishing just how many of the people sent to September and me over the years seemed to think they were striking a blow against society through cosmetics. She was also wearing hammer-and-sickle earrings, a featured item at Nordstrom that month. "Hi!" September said. "I'm September. That's Allen."

Sharon rolled her eyes. "How nice for you," she said. She opened her purse and after some digging around produced a red ticket. "So what do I have to do to get you to sign this thing?"

"Have a seat," September said. She indicated the seat at the far end of the table. "We just need to talk for a few minutes."

Sharon sat down. "So," I said, "how's the five-year plan coming along? Think you'll meet the tractor quota?"

"Huh?" she said.

"Your earrings," I said. "There was a time when if I'd seen you wearing a Bolshevik insignia I'd have followed you home and written down your license plate number."

"Are you like a noid or what?" she asked.

"No, I'm just kidding around," I said. "Why, do I look annoyed?"

"Not 'annoyed,'" she said. "A noid. I can never figure out what the hell you noids are saying."

"So why do you think you're here?" September asked.

"And you're a pod, aren't you?" Sharon asked, turning to September. "'Why am I here?' You mean like God must've put me here for some purpose and you're gonna tell me that if I don't straighten up and accept Jesus that I'm gonna burn in hell, right?"

September looked like she'd just fallen through a trap door. "Um . . . actually all I wanted to know was whether you knew what your ticket was for . . . "

"Yeah, right," Sharon said. "They said it was for talking on the phone in class, but that's just an excuse. *Everyone* was talking except for the drool sergeants in the back row still taking the test. I just got singled out because I'm the only one around here who's, you know, individualistic."

I opened the shutters to the window next to me. Even though it was only six inches wide you could see a good half dozen people with black makeup and Soviet jewelry. They waved.

"Yeah, you're quite the nonconformist," I said.

"Okay, sidebar," September said. She got up and came over to the window. "Look, I think we're sort of stumbling out of the gate here," she whispered. "What should we do?"

"You don't have to whisper," Sharon called out. "You can just spell the words. That's what my mom always did when I was four and didn't want me to know what she was saying. Except she always spelled the wrong ones. 'I caught Joe boffing that fucking tramp A-G-A-I-N.'"

"I have no idea," I whispered back. "It's not like she's a menace to society. I think we just talk to her and try not to be combative."

September went back to her seat. "So, did you decide who's gonna be the good cop and who's gonna be the bad cop?" Sharon asked.

"We're not cops," I said. "If we were cops do you think we'd be *here*? We'd be down at the 24-Seven in that back room or wherever the hell it is the cops go when they disappear into the convenience store and don't come out for six hours."

Sharon's phone rang. She pulled it out of her purse, pulled up the antenna, and switched it on. "Hello?" she said. "No, he's not. No, she's not either. This isn't their number anymore, okay? How many times do I have to tell you? They've moved on with their lives! Why can't you?" She jammed the antenna back down into the phone and threw it back in her purse. "They probably changed their number just to get away from this guy," she fumed. "I bet he's been using the same phone book since 1983."

"Why do you bring a phone to school?" September asked timidly.

Sharon rolled her eyes. "Well, dur-hey. *I'm* at school. If I leave it at home, how'm I supposed to answer it?"

"Couldn't you just let it ring?" September asked.

"I've tried that," Sharon said. "The teachers always complain."

September rubbed her temples. "No, wait," she said. "Couldn't you leave it at home, *and* let it ring? At home?"

"Are you Amish?" Sharon asked.

Suddenly an angle occurred to me. "Yeah, Sep," I said. "You're living in the past, buddy. 'Let it ring.' Sheesh. Now me, if I had a cell phone with all these calls coming in, I'd get one of those automated voice-mail systems. Everyone trying to bother you winds up on a tape in some office in El Paso and there isn't even an annoying blinking light to bug you when you get home."

"It's not 'bothering,'" Sharon said.

"Sure it is," I said. "I mean, you look like you've got better things to do than field phone calls all day. Right?"

"Of course," she snapped. "But, you know, it can't be nonstop excitement all the time. It's better than watching the second hand on the clock go around and around or sitting alone in an empty house—"

"Are you lonely?" September interrupted. She apparently had her own angle in mind—I'd been trying some reverse psychology, but she'd left out the "reverse" part.

"No," Sharon said automatically. "I mean—well, *you* know what it's like when there's no one home and no one'll *be* home for hours . . . "

"Um, not really," September said. "I have eleven brothers and sisters. I've shared a room with two of my sisters for as long as I can remember. I've *never* been alone in my house."

"Oh," Sharon said. "How about you?" she added, turning to me accusingly.

"Four sibs, share a room," I said.

"I take it you're an only child?" September asked.

"Yeah," Sharon said. "So? Maybe my parents didn't feel like contributing to global overpopulation."

"Or maybe they split up before they could have any more," I said.

"Whatever," she said. "So are you gonna sign this thing or not?"

"In a minute," September said. "If you want to be around people after school, have you thought about trying to get a job? You'd have plenty of company and make money besides."

"I'm fourteen," Sharon said. "Who's gonna hire me?"

"So you could volunteer," September said. "Do some work after school for your church or synagogue. Or some other kind of non-profit organization. You wouldn't get paid, but you'd be around people, and you'd be helping out and, you know, doing good."

Sharon looked at September like she'd just gotten off the bus from Neptune. "Volunteering isn't necessarily all that great," I said. "I was working at this place over the summer, a couple afternoons a week, and it was less than fabulous. I thought I'd be answering phones, writing memos, all kinds of stuff. All they'd let me do was make coffee. 'We need coffee! Get over here, Coffee Boy!' I don't even *drink* coffee."

"Where?" September asked.

"This child abuse prevention center downtown," I said. "That's another thing. It was too far to walk so I had to take OCTA buses. I was shelling out ten bucks a week in bus fare."

"You people!" Sharon said. "I was wrong. You're not a noid, and *you're* not a pod. You're deegs! You're both deegs!"

"Um, could someone translate that for me?" I asked. "I haven't taken AP Slang yet."

"You," she said. "You came on like you'd swallowed an encyclopedia. And her," she said, jabbing a thumb at September, "I picked up a real Jesus-likes-me-best vibe coming off her. But you're not trying to show off how smart you are, or how morally superior you are— you're trying to show off how good and kind and wonderful you are. You're goodeegoods. Deegs. Now are you going to sign this ticket for me or what?"

September signed the ticket and Sharon stormed out. A year and a half later she would be dead, her body riddled with gunshot wounds.

Guess who's coming to dinner?

Not too long after our first peer counseling session I found myself in a big house in Yorba Linda surrounded by a hundred thousand blond children—September had invited me over for dinner. "These are some of my brothers and sisters," September said by way of introduction. "I hope you like kids."

"Sure," I said. "Especially simmered in a light cream sauce."

"Allen!" she said. "Seriously, though . . . *do* you like kids?"

"I dunno," I said. "I mean, that's a lot like asking if I like people. In my experience any given kid has exactly the same capacity to be cool or to be a jerk as any given adult."

September's mom poked her head out of the kitchen. She looked like a fairly generic Orange County Republican Woman: some combination of the shade of her lipstick, her slightly vacant expression, and the way you could just tell that never in her life had she sat on the floor. She did a double-take when she saw me but quickly shook it off. "September, I could use your help in the kitchen," she said.

"Didn't she know I was coming?" I asked.

"Yeah, she knew," September said. "Make yourself at home—I'll be back in a few minutes."

I had a look around and noticed that affixed to the wall underneath the landing of the staircase were a couple of embroidered signs that read FAMILIES ARE FOREVER and JESUS IS LORD. I wondered if I hadn't underestimated Sharon Sharalayek's powers of insight. Half a second later September came back into the room, having changed clothes; she'd also apparently decided that her last year and a half of aging hadn't quite worked out, and reverted back to about twelve and a half. "I get to eat in the *kit*-chen! I get to eat in the *kit*-chen!" she chanted, merrily skipping around the room. "I get to eat in the *kit*-chen and *yooo*-ou *do*-on't!" She stopped short. "Well!" she said. "I'm betting September didn't meet *you* at church, hmm?"

It finally dawned on me that this wasn't September at all but some sort of sister. "And who might you be?" I asked.

"Why, I'm April, of course," she said. She flashed me this mischievous smile like she'd been sneaking out her bedroom window every night for the last three months to see me. "You'll quickly find I'm the black sheep around here," she confided, batting her eyelashes at me. "The bad girl. The troublemaker."

"Yeah," September said, emerging from the kitchen. "Like last week, Mom wouldn't let her wear eyeliner to school, so she waited till she was on the bus and put it on anyway. What a rebel!"

"Oh yeah?" April retorted. "Well *your* idea of being a rebel is putting up a poster of Paul McCartney in our room!"

"Why do you keep expecting that I'll die of embarrassment every time you bring that up?" September said.

I decided I'd better cut in before things degenerated into fisticuffs. "So I take it there's some advantage to eating in the kitchen?" I asked.

"*Yeah,*" April said. "You get to talk, and you can eat cereal instead of vegetables, and you can listen to the TV, and you can put your elbows on the table, and you can just grab stuff instead of asking people to pass it, and a million other things." Her eyes lit up at the prospect. "They make you wait so long till you're allowed to eat at the big table and then once you get there you find out that it's all a big rip and you were better off where you were. Now I'm not even *allowed* to eat in the kitchen unless there's company and I get bumped."

April pranced back into the kitchen and August shuffled in. He was September's older brother—I'd seen him around school a couple times but we'd never really talked. "I never get to eat in the kitchen," he moped.

September's parents and older sister followed him in with the last of the food, half of an enormous pot roast; the other half had been parceled out to the kids in the kitchen already. The redheaded older sister closed the partition and the six of us sat down.

We said grace, though we didn't hold hands like over at Peggy's house. Also different was the way that instead of passing things around and taking what you wanted, you had to wait for Mrs. Young to make up a whole plate and pass it to you. I saw a plate covered in gravy heading in my general direction so I thought I'd better speak up. "No meat for me, please," I said. "I'm a vegetarian."

Mrs. Young gave me a look like I'd just declared I was wanted in six states for armed robbery. "I read an article about vegetarianism just a few weeks ago," she said. "Did you know that it says right in 1 Timothy 4:3 that the meats of the earth are to be received with thanksgiving, and not abstained from?"

August burst out laughing. September looked like she wanted to crawl under the tablecloth. "I didn't know that," I said, "but still, salad's plenty for me." In the end I wound up with salad and a roll and some mashed potatoes, which I had to stop Mrs. Young from pouring gravy on. Upon closer inspection the potatoes turned out to be not so much mashed as smushed. From the kitchen I heard the sound of cereal being poured into someone's bowl, and I understood April's glee.

"So," Mr. Young asked after a few minutes, "how are you enjoying the peer counseling?"

"Um, it's fine," I said. "We had a rocky start but I think we're getting the hang of it."

Mr. Young nodded. It was a reasonably painless exchange and September seemed marginally less tense. I was beginning to wonder why she'd wanted me to come over for dinner at all, since from the moment we'd sat down she'd been acting like we were in a room full of angry bees. In fact, everyone seemed a little edgy. Then Mrs. Young asked, "So, Allen, are there *many* black kids at your school?"

August practically choked on his tongue; September actually slapped her forehead. "*Mom!*" she protested.

"What?" Mrs. Young said. "Am I wrong? What nationality are you?"

"Mom, cut it out," September hissed.

"Don't be rude," Mrs. Young said.

At this point everyone had stopped eating but May. (I'd inferred that the older sister's name was May from the way that when people said, "Please pass the salt, May," she passed the salt.) "Oh, I'm a citizen," I said.

"Yes, but where are you from *originally*?" Mrs. Young asked.

"Oh, *originally*," I said. "*Originally*, I'm from Fullerton. Born there, raised there, lived in the same house my whole life."

"What I'm getting at is, where are your *ancestors* from?" Mrs. Young asked.

"Well," I said, "I've only met two of them, actually. Namely, my parents. My dad's from Pennsylvania, and my mom's from New Mexico."

Mrs. Young nodded as if this neatly answered every question she'd ever had in her entire life. "So you're Mexican," she said.

"Actually," I said, "the last time I checked, they'd gone ahead and had New Mexico admitted to the Union. And the last time I checked was 1912."

"I can't say I care for your tone," Mr. Young said. "You're a guest in our house and we expect you to show some courtesy. Now, all she wants to know is what your ethnic makeup is."

"Fine," I said. "If you absolutely positively *have* to know, on my mom's side I'm part African, part Dineh, which is an American Indigen tribe, and part peninsular Spanish. On my dad's side I'm part Lebanese, part Italian, part Scandinavian, and part no one knows what."

"Irish?" Mr. Young suggested. "Your last name's Mockery, right? That sounds like an Irish name."

"Yeah, but that name comes from my dad's stepfather," I said. "My dad's biological father was a Marine on shore leave who decided that nothing quite tops off a night on the town like raping your date. He may well have been Irish but that'd just be coincidence."

Mrs. Young was aghast. September looked like she really wouldn't have minded if the earth were to explode in a nuclear holocaust right that second. May actually got up and left. August, on the other hand, was grinning like he'd just thrown a pie in someone's face.

"Can we *please* change the subject?" September asked.

"I think that's a very good idea," Mr. Young said. He took a sip of water. "So, what does your father do?" he asked.

"Well," I said, "up till a couple of years ago he was a history professor at Cal State Fullerton. But then he got splattered across the interstate by a carload of drunken fratboys while changing a tire one night and since then he doesn't really do a whole heck of a lot."

"Oh, my goodness," Mrs. Young said. "Your poor mother—she must've been devastated—"

"Not really," I said. "She wasn't upset at all."

"What?" Mrs. Young said. "How cold and unfeeling do you have to be to—"

"Pretty cold and unfeeling," I agreed. "But then she had a pretty good excuse, having been dead for a good five years at that point herself."

Mrs. Young blanched. "You'll . . . have to excuse me," she said. She got up and left. I looked over at September. The way she was rubbing her temples you'd think she thought she could massage the last few minutes out of her brain.

"Was it something I said?" I asked.

Pay lay ale, baby

When I got back home that evening Echo looked up from her topology homework and gave me a suspicious look. "Where've you been?" she asked.

"I went to September's house," I said. "You know, September Young? She's in our history class."

Echo smirked. "Oh, *her,*" she said. "So, did she teach you the tokens of the Melchizedek priesthood?"

"Say what?" I said.

"Guess not, huh?" Echo said. "Good thing for her. No sense in getting disemboweled, right? Besides, there's the language barrier. You haven't taken the Berlitz course in Reformed Egyptian yet. And nary a Urim or Thummim in sight to help you out. Poor Allen."

"Um, Eck?" I said. "Don't take this the wrong way, but . . . what the hell are you talking about?"

Echo's face went stony. "Look," she said, "just keep one thing in mind. If you expect to keep any of my respect, you'll stay away from the pods."

"Don't worry," I said. "I managed to alienate everybody. You would've been proud."

Not surprisingly, I didn't get invited over again after that. Not because September herself was upset with me, but because, as she told me the next day, "My mom and dad say you're a bad influence and that they want me to stay away from you. They're not going to make me quit counseling, but we can't hang out after school or go anywhere together or anything like that."

"I didn't know we did," I said.

"Yeah, but—look, couldn't you have just humored them?" she asked. "So maybe my parents don't like hearing about unpleasant stuff. What's wrong with that? Couldn't you have given a couple noncommittal answers and changed the subject?"

"I tried!" I said. "*They're* the ones who asked the questions! I tried to get out of answering them as best I could. And if you're not allowed to associate with anyone whose background is a little 'unpleasant' then chances are you're going to find yourself out of friends before too long."

But September abided by her parents' wishes, and so for the rest of the school year we never talked for more than a minute or two once the peer counseling was over for the day. Nor did I hear from her at all over the summer. So I was more than a little surprised when, the day before school started back up for sophomore year, I received what would turn out to be a fateful phone call.

Ahoy-hoy?

It was about eleven at night and I was playing a little guitar before bed when the phone rang. Living in my house and having the phone ring was much like being a fighter pilot and having a missile fired at you. You had to act fast lest tragedy strike. See, Bobbo had his own line, and Jerem had somehow managed to get hold of a cell phone, but the other four of us had to share the main phone line. Which was fine if Molly or Echo or I answered it, but if Krieg happened to pick it up and it wasn't for him, the best the caller could expect was a grunted "fuck off" followed shortly thereafter by a click. This tended to discourage people from calling back. This was especially problematic when the person on the other end of the line was calling to say something like, "Hi, I'm calling to confirm an appointment to pick up some insulin?"

So the second I heard the phone ring I threw my guitar aside—which was a mistake, since I had the strap on and so all I did was throw my neck out of alignment—and lunged for the phone. I got it on the first quarter of a ring. "Hello?" I said.

"Uh, hi," said the voice on the other end. "Is, uh, Allen there?"

"September?" I said. "This is Allen. What's up? I haven't heard from you all summer."

"Uh, yeah," she said. "Sorry. I wish I could chat but I don't have much time. I'm in kind of a fix. Is there any way you could give me a ride home?"

"Huh?" I said. "Where are you?"

"I'm at Greg Garner's house," she said. "He's having a party . . ."

My jaw hit the floor about the same time the receiver did. I picked up the receiver first. "*YOU?*" I gasped. "*You* went to one of Greg Garner's *SEX PARTIES??*"

"It's not a sex party," September said. "It's a regular one. For the day before school starts. I only went to make sure August didn't get drunk and make a fool of himself, but he did anyway. Now we need a ride home and you're the only one I can think of who won't spread it back to my parents."

"Can't you take a cab?" I asked.

"That'd get *us* home, but then tomorrow morning I'd have to explain to my mom and dad why the station wagon was missing," she said. "It's parked out front. August got his license a couple weeks ago. Um, hey, can you come back in a couple minutes?"

"What?" I said.

"Not you," she said. "I'm up in one of the bedrooms and a couple people just came in. Can you help me?"

"I dunno," I said. "All I have is a permit. Can't you take a cab and then have the station wagon towed home?"

"Isn't that about a hundred dollars a mile?" she asked. "I—I don't have any money."

She sounded like she was either holding back tears or about to have a panic attack or both. "Okay, okay," I said. "What's the address?"

The big house

According to California law, my learner's permit allowed me to operate a motor vehicle provided someone over twenty-five years old was in the car. That meant Bobbo.

I went downstairs to find Bobbo watching TV. Now came the part that would require some delicacy. I knew that if I told him straight out that I needed to pick up my friend and her doofy brother from a party way out in Sunny Hills and then drive them all the way to Yorba Linda, and that I needed to drag him along for the entire trip, that there was no way he'd agree to go. I'd need all the subtlety I could muster.

"Hey, wanna go to a party?" I asked.

"I'm there," he said. He picked up the remote and clicked off the TV. "Let's roll."

I'd never been to Greg Garner's house before, but I knew him—he'd been the business manager at the school paper the previous year, back when Echo and I were staff writers. He'd graduated since then but apparently he still lived in the area. Still in the same house, in fact—he and his older brother had inherited it when their dad had been sent to prison for insider trading about five years back. He had the place all to himself, not to mention a couple million dollars to dispose of as he saw fit. His favorite expenditure was a series of increasingly legendary parties, the most celebrated of which were the ones that doubled as orgies. Each one had a different set of rules. The one I'd heard about went like this: first, you had to bring a member of the opposite sex, be it a friend, sibling, significant other, complete stranger, or what have you; once everyone had arrived, you all drew numbers out of a pink or blue hat, depending on your sex; then you found the other person with your number, retired to one of the bedrooms or cars or closets or whatever, and you can figure out the rest. Refusal was allowed, whether you got cold feet or just didn't like who you got paired with, but those who refused seldom got invited back.

I followed September's directions and soon Bobbo and I found ourselves parked in front of Greg Garner's place. There was an imposing iron gate blocking the horseshoe driveway, but it swung open to let a car out and we slipped in as it was reclosing. The front door was wide open and the walls were shaking with the sound of really loud elevator music, also known as rap. We went inside.

The foyer was roughly the size of my entire neighborhood. The floors were blond hardwood and the center of the parlor—it'd be criminal understatement to call it a room—was sunken and seemed to be lushly carpeted, from what I could see under half a million pairs of feet. I spotted September right away, sitting in the corner closest to the door, scuffing her feet on the step below and looking absolutely miserable. She had the forlorn look of someone waiting at an unsheltered bus stop in the pouring rain with only a discarded scrap of last week's classifieds as protection. "Ready to go?" I asked.

She jumped. "You're here!" she said. "I swear, another few minutes and I was ready to call my parents. Even if it meant being grounded till I was in grad school. Let me grab August and we'll go."

I elbowed my way through the crowd and grabbed Bobbo's arm just as he was heading into the kitchen. "C'mon, let's go," I said.

"Say what?" he said. "We just got here!"

"Look around," I said. "It's all high school kids. You're thirty-six years old. Don't you feel a little out of place?"

"So they'll think I'm a college guy," he said.

"What, a fifteenth-year senior?" I said.

"Whatever," he said. "Look, I'm gonna have a couple drinks, get a few phone numbers, you know, *party*! It wouldn't kill you if you did the same thing. That's what Krieg would do."

"Okay, for one, the only way Krieg could get a girl's number is if he slugged her in the face, grabbed her purse, and copied it out of her address book," I said. "Second, you're not going to win any hearts pointing to him as a role model. The guy's a psychopath."

"He's the only normal one out of all you kids," Bobbo said.

"Besides," I said, "like I said, you're thirty-six. The girls here are fifteen, sixteen, *maybe* eighteen, tops. Isn't that a little creepy? Not to mention illegal?"

"Don't argue legal stuff with *me*," he said. "I didn't go to law school for nothing."

"The school you went to isn't even accredited!" I said.

"It was when I went there," he said. "Go on, beat it. We'll go in an hour or so."

September was waiting by the door with August in tow. He had a flushed look like he'd just wrapped up a full day on the slopes. "Bad news," I said. "Looks like we've got another wait ahead of us. Bobbo's got a hankering for some underage action."

"Huh?" September said.

"My half-uncle," I said. "I only have a permit. I need him in the car before I can drive it."

September groaned. August, on the other hand, seemed not at all perturbed. He had a glazed smile on his face that said, "I have absolutely no idea what's going on, so it must be amusing."

September sat back down on the step and put her hands over her ears. "This is a nightmare," she said.

"Look, why don't you just go wait in the car or something?" I said. "You'll probably be happier out there than in here."

"I would, but I have to keep an eye on *him*," September said, jerking a thumb at August. "An hour ago I went to the bathroom for five lousy minutes and he spent the whole time following girls around saying, 'Yore real purdy.' If I leave now he'll just get into a fight or something."

I looked down at August, sitting on the step and beaming pinkly at the carpet. "Hey," I said. "You'll go wait in the car with September, right?"

August nodded with the amiability that comes with complete disorientation. "I call shotgun," he giggled.

I felt a hand grab my arm. It occurred to me for the first time that I hadn't been invited. It was beginning to look an awful lot like I was about to gain an intimate knowledge of Greg Garner's taste in bouncers. But it turned out to be none other than Greg Garner himself.

The few times I'd spent any time in the same room with Greg Garner he'd always struck me as someone who'd make a good Hollywood brat actor: add one part money, one part cocaine, two parts arrogance, stir well. He was wearing a skinny tie and his face was bright with perspiration. "Hey, I know you," he said. "From the paper. Alex, right?"

"Allen," I said.

"Right," he said. "Hunh. I hadn't been planning for the day-care population to be so well represented, but I guess it's too late to worry about that now. There's still some beer left in the kitchen if you want."

"Um, I think I'll pass," I said. "I'm mainly here to give these two a ride home. I'm just waiting for my, uh, other friend to get ready to go. It might be a while."

"Really?" he said. "Hey, will you hold on a second? I've got a favor to ask you." He disappeared into the next room and came back with a salad bowl. "Can you take care of these?" Greg asked.

I looked in the bowl. It was full of keys. Some were attached to alarm remotes, some were on big gaudy key chains, some were just keys. "What do you mean, take care?" I asked.

"You know, give them back to people when they're ready to go," he said. "Or not, if it looks like they'll plow into a tree. You're into that peer counseling shit, right? This is basically the same thing. Thanks. I appreciate it." He went off to go talk to someone else.

"Wotta revoltin' development this is," I said. "Umm . . . here." I handed the bowl to September.

"Where are you going?" September asked.

"I just want to have a look around this house," I said.

Every room was packed with people. I estimated that somewhere between 60 and 70 percent of the population of California had shown up. Most of the people I didn't recognize; some I exchanged "Hey, I've seen your face around school but have no idea who the hell you are" glances with; a scattered few I knew from classes or peer counseling, but they weren't really friends. Oh, and in the big TV room I saw Bobbo chatting up someone who looked younger than Molly. It wasn't until I got to the game room that I saw someone I knew fairly well.

Second coming

Carver Fringie, as you'll recall, had moved to Chino with his dad, but after middle school and a year of high school, he'd moved back. Not back into his old house—Cat Nicholls lived there now—but back into the school district, so he went to Ilium. To an extent he was still the same: he always carried a book around with him, for instance. (At Greg Garner's party it was *The Sexual Enlightenment of Children* by Sigmund Freud.) But the similarity only went so far. Carver Fringie had changed.

Fringie had always been a sickly kid—he'd had to cover himself with a blanket just to sit on his front porch and watch the kids play hockey out on the street, even in the summer—but apparently during the three years he was away he'd gotten over it. He was an athlete now. Not big and bulky like a football player, but lithe and lean like a swimmer: in fact, heading into his junior year he'd been named captain of the water polo team. And at Ilium, water polo was the premier sport. Not in terms of performance—they won fewer than half their games—but in terms of prestige. Everywhere he went he was followed by his droogs on the water polo team, would-be Fringies with knock-off nicknames like Skippie and Grungie and Buddie (along with some slightly more original ones like Sluggo and Lemming, and the one guy on the team without a nickname, Kevin Love). And, of course, he was followed around by girls. Lots and lots of girls.

Fringie hadn't been back in town for more than a few days before he began to pick up a certain reputation, spread partly by the other water polo players but mainly by his own inability to suppress the evidence. It was a reputation he tried to defuse as best he could. "Look," he'd say, "I'm *not* a 'virgin surgeon.' That's crass. I consider myself more of a 'deflorist.'"

His success in the field of deflorestation was easy to understand. September and I had done counseling sessions with quite a few of Fringie's, er, patients the year before, all up on unrelated charges, and they had plenty of reasons for Fringie's appeal:

Amber Flores: "He's so sensitive. I mean, he's got sensitive eyes. And his lips. You can tell he's deep from the way his mouth is shaped."

Linda Garcia: "He's buff, but not gross. *You* know. It's like, he's got a guy's body, but it's the kind a girl would have if she were a guy. But a girl trying to be a guy, not being a guy trying to be a girl again. You know?"

Erika Christensen: "He's not one of these guys where you go places and make out but don't really know each other—he actually talks to you! All the time! I mean, I didn't usually know what he was saying and stuff, but that's just 'cause he's way smarter than everyone else!" (When I asked how she could tell that what he was saying was intelligent if it was incomprehensible, she said, "Carver says that's exactly what an insecure bourgeois poseur would say!")

No one, however, could convincingly explain Fringie's haircut. He'd always had curly blond hair, but now he'd buzzed the sides and the back really short so that all that was left was the dark roots, and then left a big blond pouf on top like a popcorn beret. It made his head look like an enormous mushroom. I wasn't enough of an expert on fungus to tell if it was the poisonous kind or not.

So here, playing pool with some water polo players, was Carver Fringie. I hadn't really had anything approaching a conversation with him since he'd left Hyacinth Avenue, though I could hardly avoid seeing him around school. Still, we went way back. And now, at long last, we were face to face.

"Hey, Fringie," I said.

He looked up. "Hey, Al," he said.

That taken care of, I headed out to see what the rest of the house had in store. "The penis knows what it wants," Fringie declared as I left.

I looked over my shoulder to see if he was talking to me. I really,

really hoped he wasn't. Luckily, he was talking to a couple water polo players—Sluggo, the one who looked like a third-grader who'd had an accident with a bicycle pump and been blown up to five feet ten, and Lemming, who got his nickname not because he looked like a rodent (though he did) but because on his fifteenth birthday he'd gotten really trashed and done a swan dive into the deep end of an empty swimming pool. Every time Fringie started in on one of his pronouncements the water polo players all got this look on their faces like dogs that've just heard the plaintive call of a can opener. These two were no different.

"The penis is singular in purpose," Fringie said. "It can be side-tracked, diverted, but never dissuaded. The mind can delude itself into thinking it is above what the penis knows it wants and has always wanted, but the penis is purer and thus must prevail. The penis will not be denied that which it has so long sought."

All was still. "Umm . . . what?" Sluggo finally asked.

"Two-ball, corner pocket," Fringie said. He sank the two but the cue ball spun away and careened into the pocket on the other side of the table.

Burn baby burn

I'd pretty much had my fill of Fringie for the time being, so I figured I'd better get back to September. She was still sitting on the steps next to the door. The rap record had been replaced by a bunch of re-remixed remixes of something, and August had taken to the floor like a one-man disco inferno, or at least a disco grease fire. Not surpris-ingly, the crowd had begun to thin out.

I sat down next to September. "Hi," I said.

"Are we leaving anytime soon?" September asked. "I don't believe I have *school* tomorrow. If Mom and Dad get up and see the car's missing, I'm dead. This was the dumbest idea I've ever had."

"Why are you here, anyway?" I asked.

"Well, August was going to go no matter what," she said. "And I wanted to make sure he didn't try to drive back. And I thought if I was here he'd be too embarrassed to, you know, drink too much . . ."

"I thought you all weren't supposed to drink," I said. "I mean, even putting aside the underage part."

"Right," September said. "But August's inactive."

I looked at August frantically swaying his hips and pointing at stuff. "He looks pretty active to me," I said.

"I mean he's not involved with the Church anymore," September said. "He and Dad have been fighting a lot. It's not much fun."

Right then some girl I'd never seen before came up to us. She smelled like she'd been doing laps in a swimming pool full of nail polish remover. She pointed at the salad bowl. "Are those the keys?" she asked.

I looked down at the bowl. "Hey, you're right!" I said. "I was wondering what the hell these were. We figured they must be some kind of casserole."

"So can I have my keys?" the girl asked.

"Which ones are yours?" September asked.

"The ones with my *name* on the keychain," the girl said. "Duh."

"And your name is . . . ?" I said.

"Ingrid," she said. "Ingrid Escajeda." She looked over at another girl woozily leaning against one of the marble columns. "Don't pass out on me, Jill," she said. "If you pass out, I swear, I will *laugh*. I will laugh *so hard* . . ."

I found Ingrid's keys, but I decided to hang on to them—she was looking pretty fermented herself. "Um, just out of curiosity, how many drinks've you had tonight?" I asked.

"Huh?" she said. "I dunno. I didn't *count*."

"You didn't count, or you lost count?" I said.

"Uh . . . what?" she said.

"Why don't you stick around for a while longer?" I said. "I don't mean to be a jerk about this but I'm not all that comfortable with the idea of you getting behind the wheel right this second."

"Are you serious?" she said. "Look, just give me the keys, okay? Jill's got to be back by twelve-thirty."

I thought for a second. "Okay, then, we'll get her a Dial-a-Ride," I said. "We can get you one, too, if you want. You can come back and get your car tomorrow."

"This is stupid," she said. "Come on, they're *my* keys."

I turned to September. "Why don't you find that phone you called me with and go order a Dial-a-Ride or a cab or something?" I said.

She did. Twenty minutes later the stumpy little OCTA bus arrived and whisked Ingrid and Jill and some other people away. I was pleased: I felt like it was entirely possible that I'd just saved a couple of lives. In Jill's case, I may well have been right. In Ingrid's case, all I did was prolong it for nine months, at which point she was felled in a hail of bullets.

A few minutes after the bus left, Bobbo came downstairs and declared that it was time to go. He was visibly toasted. "Marijuana's good for you, Allen," he confided.

"Swell," I said. I found Greg Garner, gave him back the bowl of keys, told September and August we were leaving, and met up with Bobbo outside. "So now what?" I asked.

"You'll have to drive us home," September said. She said something to August and he dug a set of keys out of his pocket. The station wagon was parked across the street. "Okay," September said, "you need to make a right at the light, and—"

"I've been to your house before," I said.

"Yeah, but that was a while ago," she said.

"I remember the way," I said. "Trust me."

Bobbo sat up front, September and August in the back. I started up the car and cautiously steered away from the curb. I navigated the maze of residential streets pretty well but I wasn't used to driving such an enormous car so when I made the turn at the intersection I misjudged the corner and we briefly wound up on the sidewalk. "Maybe we should let the drunk guy drive," Bobbo said. "Safer."

"Quiet," I said. "Just because I don't treat curbs like these metaphysically insuperable barriers doesn't mean—"

"Hey!" Bobbo interrupted, pointing. "Pull in here. It'll just be a second."

We pulled into the parking lot of a 24-Seven. Bobbo hopped out. I kept the car running. There were about a hundred and fifty police cars parked out front. Not because there'd been a robbery or anything—there were always a hundred and fifty police cars out in front of convenience stores. A couple minutes later Bobbo came back with two bags of cookies. He ripped open one of the bags and crammed four cookies in his mouth. "Let's roll," he said.

The rest of the trip was fairly uneventful. We cruised down Bastanchury Road into Yorba Linda and soon we'd reached the entrance to September's development; the dashboard clock said it was a quarter to one. I parked in the Youngs' driveway and we all clambered out. All was silent except for a couple of crickets and the sound of someone's sprinkler system down the street. "See?" I said. "Safe and sound. I *told* you I'm a good driver."

September came over and put her hand on my arm. "Thanks for all your help," she said. "You saved my life. I mean it. I'd invite you in, but, you know . . . if Mom and Dad found out you were here . . . "

"Sure," I said. I gave her back the keys to the station wagon. "Can you do me a favor, though?"

"Name it," she said.

"When you get inside, is there any chance you can call another one of those cabs?" I said. "It's kind of a long walk back to Greg Garner's house."

September looked confused for a second. Then she remembered that *my* car was still there. "Oh!" she said. "Of course." There was an awkward moment where she was standing just a little too close and then she gave me an equally awkward hug. She smelled like peppermint candy. "I guess I'll see you tomorrow," she said.

Bobbo sat down on the curb and continued to devour his cookies. I watched September lead August up the walk. As they went inside I heard him say, "Y'know, if you wurn my sister I'd find you really attractive."

"Glad to hear it," September said. The door clicked shut.

Boy meets girl, which sucks

A week later September and I had an appointment with Doctor Todd to meet the new peer counselors. The recruitment notice had gone out in the information packet just like the previous summer; the first meeting had been Wednesday, and starting the following week September and I were to begin training them. I was really looking forward to it: it was strictly forbidden to try to strike up a relationship with the people who came in for counseling, but there was no rule against fraternizing with your fellow counselors and with any luck we'd get someone cute.

So Monday afternoon we went over to Doctor Todd's dingy little office. "So when are all the new folks going to show up?" I asked.

"Applicants unacceptable," Doctor Todd said. "Two of you will have to handle all cases again."

"Wait," I said. "You mean every single person who showed up bombed out of the program on the first day?"

"No," Doctor Todd said. "Only two applicants, one male, one female. Male applicant said had only been interested as way to meet girls, now had, thus was no longer interested. Female applicant similar, said had been interested in relationship with 'deeg' type of boy, other remaining candidate close enough, thus also no longer interested. Unfortunate. Female applicant showed promise. Also, beauty."

"Hmm," I said. I made a mental note to make sure to spend several minutes beating my head against a wall once the meeting was over.

"Yes, disappointing," Doctor Todd said. "But no great loss. Probably canceling program after this year anyway. Mandate from district: zero tolerance. Still, much work this year for only two people." Suddenly his eyes lit up and he pointed at me. "Excellent applicant would be sister," he declared.

"Uh . . . I'm not so sure about that," I said. "Echo isn't really a people person. Sorry."

"Um, I have a question," September interrupted. "I was thinking . . . last week Allen and I wound up getting stuck taking care of the keys at a party, making sure everyone got home okay, and it was a big mess . . . but it's something that ought to be done, you know? I mean, who knows how many parties there are every weekend where no one takes care of the keys and people try to drive home when they shouldn't?"

"School not responsible for off-campus incidents," Doctor Todd said.

"Yeah, but . . . we can still do *something*," September said. "Like give people rides. We could buy some cars, hire some drivers . . ."

"And a pony!" I said. "I want a pony!"

"Budget too small," Doctor Todd said. "For cars. Also for pony."

"Oh," September said.

"Now wait," I said. "We can't afford a printing press, right? That's why we send the school paper out to be printed, so it can still look like a newspaper and not something that came out of a photocopier. What I'm getting at is, can't we get a contract with an existing cab company? That way we don't pay any overhead for salaries or for cars. We could even probably work out an arrangement where we get a big discount since they know we'll be giving them a ton of business."

Doctor Todd stroked his chin. "Will make a few calls," he said.

Later that week Doctor Todd called us to his office. "Search for a cab company successful. Only one outfit in price range: Taxi Ocho in Santa Ana. Number is 853-OCHO. Fifty percent off with Ilium ID card. Free for you two. Only use for appropriate reasons. Also, one other thing."

"Yes?" September asked.

"Drivers only speak Spanish," Dr. Todd said. "Little call for English-speaking drivers in Santa Ana. Have to make do best you can."

"They only speak Spanish?" September asked. "But I take French!"

"*Quel dommage,*" I said.

Sometimes a clock tower is just a clock tower

So now you understand why September had been so eager for me to get my license. I had a hard enough time communicating with the taxistas; for September, who had only a smattering of the ol' español, it was a nightmare. Somewhere along the line she'd picked up the impression that once I didn't have to drag Bobbo along, I'd be more than happy to whisk her and August to and from any party they cared to go to. My personal take on the matter was that while I'd be glad to give her the occasional lift, if she expected me to act as her personal taxi service it wouldn't be too long before I conveniently forgot how to speak English myself.

I was called to Doctor Todd's office once more a few days later, this time without September. As I headed over there I found myself swarmed as always by a crush of admirers. Well, okay, not admirers exactly. See, unlike September, I was willing to clear red tickets for people who'd received them for silly offenses like eating in their car or breaking the dress code, which made me very popular among people who didn't feel like spending an hour in detention or stuck in the office chatting with September and me. It'd been just an occasional thing my freshman year, but word had spread over the summer and now I always had a couple dozen people waiting to ambush me after class. So I usually wound up spending twenty minutes every day after school signing tickets for half-naked girls who would then go traipsing off in search of Carver Fringie. That afternoon was no exception.

So once I'd finished that, I headed over to the office. I suppose I probably ought to say a few words here about the layout of the school so you have an idea of the geography involved. Ilium High School, viewed from above, was doughnut-shaped. It'd been built back when high-concept designs had been all the rage, and some enterprising young architect had apparently been under the impression that the public was crying out for doughnut-shaped buildings. The office was part of the doughnut, though walled off from the rest: to get there from any of the classrooms you had to leave the building and go in through one of the office doors. The courtyard encircled by the doughnut was called "the wheel," since, being round, you could hardly call it a "quad"; it was paved with hexagonal tiles of volcanic rock, with weeds growing in the cracks and old discarded gum forming a thick crust on the surface. The doughnut itself was a beige stucco affair with a Spanish tile roof, the kind that kids chuck tennis balls at and try to guess which little trough they'll come rolling out of. They'd been trying for a Mediterranean-villa feel to the place, which would have been slightly more successful without the ugly metal lockers lining the wheel. Also, I'm under the impression that few if any actual Mediterranean villas are, in fact, doughnut-shaped.

At the center of the Ilium campus, smack in the middle of the wheel, was an imposing tower, four stories tall with a clock on every face. As I walked to the office I looked up at the clock, which read 9:07. It always read 9:07. The tower had been hit by lightning a couple days after the school opened and the clock hadn't budged since. The official name of this structure was Pergamum Tower, though most everyone called it the Gig thanks to an observation made by Carver Fringie the year before: "Let's think about this for a minute.

Ilium: isn't that part of the pelvis? So we've got a school named after someone's cargo with an enormous erect gig in the middle. Hello? Paging Dr. Freud? Could we *be* any more phallic?" Cue the laugh track, roll the credits. That Fringie was such a card. No wonder all the girls went to find him after I'd signed their tickets.

I arrived at Doctor Todd's office to find him brandishing some sort of worksheet. "Personality profile form," he said. "Given to incoming freshmen at beginning of every year. You know this already. Look at this one." He handed me the sheet of paper. It took me a couple minutes to decipher the scrawl in the answer blanks, but I eventually figured it out:

1. What do you value most in life?

Deth.

2. What do you like best about yourself?

I ruel.

3. What would you most like to change about yourself?

Fuck you. Im perfect the way I am.

4. Where do you see yourself in twenty years?

Ded. Im going to die yung and take as many pepel as I can with me.

5. Who are the people you most admire?

Adolf Hitler becase he rueld the most superier cuntry in the world, and Wilhelm Krieger the leed singer for Crucified Vomit becase he kiks ass and gets all the biches to suck his dik.

"Ah ha," I said. "Well, this is clearly the handiwork of nature's greatest mistake: my brother."

"Troubling," Doctor Todd said. "Shows potential for dangerous behavior. Disruption. Violence. Eating in car. Must be proactive. Prevent unfortunate incidents prior to occurrence. Purpose of diagnostic forms. You agree? Form is not result of simply sick sense of humor?"

"Oh, no way," I said. "Krieg has no sense of humor. This is actually what he's like."

"Very well," Doctor Todd said. He put the form in a manila folder and pulled a different one out. "Send in next case, please."

"You mean there were others like this?" I asked.

"All were like this," he sighed.

"And it was true!" I told Echo that night as we were getting ready for bed. "He had a stack of, like, a hundred forms in that folder. 'What do you value most in life?' 'Death.' 'Killing people.' 'Nothing.' I mean, I like black comedy as much as anyone, but the thing is, you really do have to put the comedy part in along with the black. Otherwise it's not clever, it's just—just—"

"Foreshadowing," Echo said.

Three

Before I started this project, I went down to the library and read every creative writing handbook I could find, everything from Pompus and Jargonlace's *Elements of Rhetorical Stylistics in Extended Narrative Texts* to Elroy T. Funbun's *How to Write Books Real Good*. And the one thing they all cautioned against was introducing a whole bunch of characters at once. Nevertheless, this next bit features a bunch of people I haven't told you about yet, and if that means I have to introduce eight hundred characters at once, well, I guess I'll just have to figure out a way to scrape through life without the approval of Elroy T. Funbun.

More fun than a bunker of führers

Since our school was called Ilium, it was pretty much inevitable that when they got around to naming the school paper, they wound up calling it the *Iliad*. Then someone pointed out that the big doughnut-shaped building they'd just finished putting up didn't have any space for a journalism room. After a brief moment of panic, they remedied the situation by partitioning off a section of one of the teachers' lounges. Of course, the lounge had been asymmetrical, so there were some inequities in the division. We got two more electrical outlets than the teachers did; they got the window. It wasn't until the extra wall had been put up that the designers discovered that the new room had no source of light. This was remedied by installing a flickering fluorescent tube in the ceiling. Which meant that you'd walk into the *Iliad* room full of youthful exuberance and vigor, perhaps humming a little tune about the flowers in the meadow and the birdies in the trees or some such, and then after about five minutes you'd find yourself wondering why it had taken you so long to realize that you ought to hang yourself. I really wouldn't have been surprised to walk in one afternoon and find Eva Braun sitting at the layout table glumly swallowing a cyanide capsule.

The faculty member who was technically in charge of the whole operation was one of the sophomore English teachers, Benito Mussolini. Her real first name was Isabella, but given her last name, the nickname was inevitable. Besides, there was no getting around the fact that she was a dead ringer for Il Duce. Sure, her mustache was a little thicker—more Stalin than Mussolini, really—and as far as I know the actual Benito Mussolini didn't share our Benito's predilection for lime green pants, but still, there was definitely something there. Suffice it to say that she was, in Cat Nicholls's words, "a big ol' slab of wacky androgynous fun!"

Cat—who, as you'll remember, lived on my street—was our editor-in-chief, and we were lucky to have her. Everyone else Benito had ever appointed to that position had tried to play Reichsmarshall, keeping track of every detail and trying to micromanage everything; Cat, on the other hand, had been blessed with a sort of sublime obliviousness that in some cultures would have marked her as a sage. When her PE class played softball, for instance, the ball had once dropped to the ground and rolled up to her feet, and instead of throwing it to first base she'd just picked it up and started counting the stitches. She even looked sort of scattered—she was always bumping into things, and couldn't seem to keep her hair out of her eyes. Speaking of which, she was the only person I'd ever met with naturally occurring burgundy hair: it was a distinctly purple shade of brown and she swore she didn't dye it. She was also the only person I'd ever met under the age of fifty who wore stockings. Burgundy ones, natch.

The editor-in-chief's direct subordinate was the "executive editor," a junior whose task over the course of the year was to learn the ropes:

how all the layout programs worked, how to deal with the printers in Anaheim, how to ensure that people did what they were supposed to and didn't goof off, how to resolve tensions between editors and writers, all that stuff. This post was filled with none other than that enterprising young go-getter, the one and only Miss Peggy Kaylin.

What all the buzz is about

Peggy was a figure of both veneration and derision around the *Iliad*. She was venerated for the way she'd regularly do ridiculous things like bring everybody meticulously prepared baskets of homemade cookies and other treats, or attempt to brighten up the *Iliad* room with strategically placed vases of flowers. She was derided for the exact same reason.

But the main reason most of the senior editors didn't seem to like her very much was that she was ambitious. It wasn't that she was angling to be editor-in-chief next year—the fact that she was executive editor guaranteed that she would be, so there was no jockeying for power involved. Rather, it was that she already had all kinds of grand plans for what she was going to do once she was editor-in-chief, which she kept in a notebook, which she left in the *Iliad* room for a few minutes one day assuming that no one would read it, and certainly assuming that no one would read it aloud. She assumed incorrectly.

Here's what it said:

Problem: The *Iliad* room is ugly and depressing.
Plan: Talk to Dr. Todd in June. See if we can get funds allocated to either: a) knock out the partition and install a translucent glass wall, b) add a skylight, or c) at least put in a window. I can do the painting and/or wallpapering myself. I can also provide new furniture (offer to show the shelves I made over the summer).

Problem: Truancies. Too many people are leaving just because it's the last class of the day and they can get away with it.

Plan: Take attendance at both the beginning and the end of class.
Alternate plan: Give quizzes where students have to analyze passages from the day's newspaper or something. They don't have to be given every day, just often enough to get people to show up every day.

Problem: Attitude. Too many people are taking journalism not because they're interested in it but just to hang out with their friends and because they need the extra class. They don't care about the quality of the paper.
Plan: Talk to Ms. Mussolini about giving bad grades to people who put in a bad effort. If a story turns out badly, make sure there are consequences not just for the writer, but for editors if they don't fix it. This will lead to more effort and thus more quality.

And so on, for several pages. Peggy was naturally upset that people had read her notebook ("That's private!" she'd exclaimed, shocked) but was bewildered by the fact that everyone in the room was upset with her for writing it. "I don't get it," she told me later, as I watched her make brownies and crispy rice squares to bring to school the next day as atonement. "If they don't think my plans are any good, that's fine, but why would they get *mad* at me? If they have better ideas I'd be happy to hear them . . ."

"I don't think that's really the point, though," I said. "I think they're mad for a couple different reasons. One is that it sounds like you're out to give everyone more work. It's like you're the kid in the front row who reminds the teacher right before the bell rings that she forgot to give out the homework assignment."

"What's wrong with that?" she asked, her ears turning bright pink. "I mean, if she *forgot*—"

"But more than that," I continued, "you have to realize that tone is a funny thing and doesn't always transfer to print. You may have just been scribbling down some ideas, but if you just take the words and strip away the earnest-yet-chipper tone you'd normally use to make it clear you don't mean to criticize anybody, it sounds like you're saying the *Iliad* sucks and that the reason it sucks is that the people on it are slackers."

"But don't you think that's pretty accurate?" she said, putting the brownies in the oven.

"Excuse me?" I said.

"I don't think that's mean or unfair," she protested. "I mean, if you tell someone that they're ugly then that's cruel, because that's just the way God made them and there's nothing they can do about it. But if all you're doing is saying that they're not doing their work, and they aren't, then that's fair because they can do something about it. If they feel guilty it's their own fault. If they'd just do what they're supposed to, they wouldn't get their feelings hurt." She poured a bag of marsh-mallows into a big metal pot.

"Um, I don't think 'guilty' is really the right word," I said. "I think it's more like 'ticked off that if you get your way you'll ruin the cool thing about the *Iliad*, which is that ninety-nine percent of the time you just sort of hang out and talk and stuff, if you bother to show up at all.' Though now that I think about it that's more like forty-two or forty-three words. But I'm pretty sure it's not guilt because everyone seems pretty darn happy with the situation as it stands."

"Well, I'm not," Peggy said. "Besides, just because you don't feel guilty about something doesn't mean it's okay. I'm sure there are plenty of murderers out there who don't feel guilty about it."

"Don't you think there's more than a little bit of difference between murdering someone and cutting class?" I asked.

Peggy defiantly poured the bowl of cereal into the metal pot. "Most murderers," she said, "probably started out by cutting class."

I scratched my head and tried to figure out if that made any sense.

In any event, that should give you an idea of why Peggy wasn't the most popular person on the staff. But it doesn't really explain the sort of virulent hatred she generated in people like, say, Elizabeth Clarke. Zab was the editor of the opinion page, and she was from Britain. Sort of. Her family had moved to the States when Zab was five, so Zab's thick British accent was largely fake. Not that you needed to know her personal history to figure that out: it was not only fake but a terrible fake, which shifted uncontrollably from BBC anchor to Cockney cabdriver to fifth Beatle and then sometimes she'd throw in some Canadian for good measure. The one authentic link she maintained to the UK was her periodontal care: she must have brushed her teeth with molasses or something because they were stained a rich brown and were half-rotted out of her head. She was also one of the people who tended to go home ten seconds after attendance was taken, and thus would have suffered the most from the plans outlined in Peggy's notebook. So maybe that was her motivation, or maybe it was just a personality clash, but whatever it was, the day after Peggy brought in her peace offering of brownies and marshmallow bars, Zab decided to give Peggy a gift of her own. It was a wicker basket full of flowers.

"That's so nice!" Peggy exclaimed. "Wow, Zab, that was really sweet of you." She picked a carnation out of the basket and sniffed it.

Everyone else looked rather skeptical. "What's this all about?" I asked.

"What?" Zab said. "I just thought it'd be a nice gesture. There's more stuff under the flowers, luv." This was back when Zab was calling everybody "luv." It was annoying, but a million times better than a couple weeks earlier when she'd been calling everybody "guv'nor."

"Really?" Peggy said. "You really didn't have to go to all this trouble. Wow, look! There's some soap, and brownies, and clear balloons, and some kind of jelly, and . . . hmm. What's this?"

Zab had already started giggling at the words "clear balloons," but seeing Peggy looking quizzically at the oblong white plastic object was enough to send her into gales of laughter. "What do you think it is?" she sniggered.

"I don't know," Peggy said, turning it over. "Is it some kind of power tool? It's got a switch on it."

"Why don't you turn it on?" Zab suggested.

"Peggy, don't," I said. "Zab, this is the most dis—"

"Oh, piss off, Sambo," she said. "Go on, turn it on."

Peggy flipped the switch. It made a quiet buzzing noise like an electric toothbrush. "I still don't get it," she said.

All the other *Iliad* staffers had long since stopped what they'd been doing to watch this little piece of theater, but it was only the buzzing that got Cat to put down her copy of *The Dave Clark Five Report*. "Hey, what's going on?" she asked. She looked at Peggy and a puzzled look crossed her face. "Hey, Peggy," she said, "why'd you bring a vibrator to school?"

Peggy dropped it like it was an angry weasel. Luckily the impact broke it so it didn't go on buzzing. "I—I didn't know," she said helplessly.

"C'mon, there's more," Zab said. "See the—aw, don't go away, luv! What, don't you like sex toys? They're the gift that keeps on giving!"

Before the door closed I had a terrible thought and chased after Peggy. I caught up with her just as she was about to lock herself in the faculty bathroom. "Peggy, wait!" I said.

"Leave me alone!" she said, covering her face.

"Okay, just one thing," I said. "Whatever you do, *don't* eat the brownies, okay?"

She gaped at me, her face crimson and distorted with fury. "Why, 'cause I'll get *fat*?" she hissed.

"No, because they're probably full of hash," I said. "And don't use the jelly either, unless you want really well-lubricated toast."

She slammed the door. There wasn't much point in trying to console her—when Peggy said she wanted to be left alone, she meant it. Nor, I was willing to bet, would she be willing to talk about it later. Or ever. And as it turned out, I didn't need to worry. By the time I got back Zab had already eaten half the brownies herself.

Stunt casting

She was also busy receiving one of Hayley Kerensky's low-key tongue-lashings. Hayley was my boss on the *Iliad* and she had figured out that if you really want someone to feel idiotic, yelling doesn't do any good: you have to speak calmly and reasonably like you were talking to a small child. "What exactly was that little production supposed to prove?" she asked quietly. "What do you stand to gain by being pointlessly cruel?"

"A lot more than I gain by listening to you bitch at me," Zab said. She picked up the basket and left. Hayley sighed.

Hayley was a relative newcomer to Orange County; she'd lived in Seattle until a couple years before, when her parents had split up and moved to Alaska and Florida respectively—I guess they really wanted to get away from each other. Hayley had decided to split the difference and live with her sister in Fullerton. Hayley was the youngest of five kids: her brothers were thirty-eight and thirty-six, her sisters were thirty-two and thirty, and Hayley herself was seventeen. It doesn't take a heck of a lot of math to figure out that she was an accident. "But then, so was my oldest brother," Hayley once pointed out. "He's why my parents got together in the first place. Sure, I probably would've preferred it if they'd waited till I was in college before getting divorced, but you have to admit, thirty-seven years is a long time to stay together 'for the sake of the kids.'"

Hayley was quite pretty, especially if you like that sort of hippie-intellectual look. She always wore sandals, even on rainy days, and had round John Lennon glasses with gold wire rims. She had a predilection for T-shirts with the names of film festivals or obscure bands on them, over which she'd wear unbuttoned button-down sweaters in the winter. She also had a thing for long crepe skirts, mainly because they gave her an excuse to wear a slip, which is an intrinsically cool thing to wear. But by far the most memorable thing about the way Hayley looked was her hair. It was very wavy, had a sort of cascading effect to it, and came down to the small of her back. It was a rather dull medium-brown color, indoors; outside, though, when the sun was out, it would blaze with a fiery copper color like it had been spun out of a drawerful of brand-new pennies.

Hayley had managed to find a social niche for herself soon after moving here: she and Cat hit it off right away and soon she was spending several evenings a week hanging out on Cat's front porch along with Cat and Hank and Holdn, who were also on the *Iliad* and who I'll talk about right now.

Hank Andreas, whose real first name was Paul but who called himself Hank because, as he put it, "If your name were Paul, wouldn't you call yourself Hank?," was the *Iliad* photographer and the bane of Benito's existence. It wasn't because he dunked his head in a bottle of hairspray every morning, making his hair do things that would've left Isaac Newton rubbing his eyes and muttering something about finding a new line of work; nor was it the fact that all his shirts had the name "Hank" embroidered on the pocket and that he insisted on buttoning them all the way up; it wasn't even because he shaved his eyebrows. Benito could handle these little eccentricities just fine. It was the photos that Hank turned in that gave her cerebral hemorrhages on a regular basis.

She'd quickly come to expect this particular headache every three weeks, but the first batch of photos in September had really caught her off guard. Hank had handed her a diskette full of pictures and was sauntering out the door when Benito barked, "Wait."

"Is there a problem?" Hank asked casually.

"Is there a *problem?*" Benito repeated. "I'd say there's a problem. Look at this!"

Hank looked at the picture that Benito had loaded up onto the screen. "Yeah, I'm particularly pleased with that one," he said.

"Pleased?" Benito said. She dug a copy of his assignment sheet out of her notebook. "This was supposed to be a picture of the football game."

"It is," Hank said. "The assignment didn't specify which element of the game to emphasize . . ."

"It shouldn't have to," Benito said. "It should be obvious. Someone catching a pass, making an exciting run, celebrating a victory . . . even people cheering in the crowd if the action on the field is too boring. But under no circumstances should your only picture be of the backup quarterback picking his *nose.*"

"But this subject has greater symbolic weight," Hank said. "It's emblematic of not only the game in question but of American sport culture in general. I call it 'Digging In on Third Down.' Besides," he added, "the picture of him hockin' a loogie came out all blurry."

"Look," Benito said, "let me make this perfectly clear. You're not here to make statements about 'symbolic weight,' okay? You're just here to take the pictures. Got it?"

"You're alienating me from the fruits of my labor," Hank said.

"And you're just going to have to deal with that," Benito said.

"Fuckin' bourgeoisie," Hank muttered.

Fortunately, Hank had other outlets for his creative urge. An idea occurred to him one day as he was standing in the wheel, surrounded by lockers in every direction; a few hours of stencil work and several cans of spray paint later, each locker door bore its very own portrait of Andy Warhol. Hank probably would've even been able to avoid getting suspended for vandalism if only he'd been able to resist standing in the wheel and crying, "Ah, the irony! The layers upon layers of meta-commentary!"

Then there was the thing with the tree, but that was more memorable for Holdn's reaction to it than the stunt itself. Holdn Holdnowski was Hank's constant companion, and like Sluggo the water polo player, he looked like a little kid; the difference was that while Sluggo looked like the doofy third-grade bully, Holdn looked like the adorable four-year-old grandson that every nursing home inmate insists on showing you pictures of. He even had permanently pink cheeks like he'd always just come in from playing in the snow. This alone was apparently enough to secure him a steady stream of girlfriends, none of whom lasted for more than a couple of weeks.

Holdn was the ad manager for the *Iliad,* which was a pretty important position: we got almost no funding from the school district, so any expenses we might incur, from printing costs to computer repairs, had to come out of our ad revenue. Greg Garner had managed the books the previous year, and left Holdn with a dozen solid accounts; Holdn, however, tended to think of school as voluntary, and since school included the *Iliad,* those accounts had dwindled down to a microscopic ad for Fred's Quality Footwear on the sports page and the occasional sheet of Taco Junta coupons. Benito was understandably pissed about the fact that we were now bleeding cash like a piggy bank perforated with machine-gun fire, but no one else wanted the job so Holdn was allowed to stick around.

Holdn was reasonably convinced that he was the coolest human being this side of the international date line, but even he had to admit that he couldn't top Hank's stunts. He tried to be gracious about it, but grace wasn't really part of Holdn's emotional vocabulary. So after Hank pulled off the Warhol caper, Holdn pulled him aside in the *Iliad* room and offered his congratulations. "Not bad," he said airily. "I've got a bunch of ideas of my own I've been working on but I can't ever find the time to really do them. We ought to work together, you know? Between my brainpower and your dedication we could really accomplish something."

"Isn't this how capitalism started?" Hank asked.

So a couple of months later Echo and I were walking to school when we noticed that the little tree out in front of the office was drooping. Every branch looked like it weighed a couple metric tons and the whole thing was dripping wet, like it couldn't stop crying. Quite frankly, it looked very depressed. You know society's going to hell when even the trees are overcome with angst.

"What the hell?" I said. "That's one selective rainstorm."

"It's not rain," Echo said. She brushed a fingertip against the trunk of the tree and tested it with her tongue. "It's maple syrup," she said.

It wasn't exactly a big mystery who the culprit was. When Hank showed up for journalism class he received a hero's welcome; we were all congratulating him on a stunt well done when the *Iliad* room door flew open and Holdn stormed in. "Okay," he demanded, "where the hell's Andreas?"

It was kind of a weird question to ask since Hank was standing right in front of him. "I haven't seen him," Hank said.

"Where've *you* been?" Hayley asked.

"I overslept," Holdn said. "Wh—"

"You overslept for seven and a half hours?" Hayley said.

"Yeah," Holdn said. "That's not important. What the hell is with the tree, Andreas? I thought you said we were going to work together on these things!"

"No, that's what *you* said," Hank said. "You need to brush up on your pronouns."

"Well *fuck* you!" Holdn shouted. He kicked one of the trash cans. We had these two big metal trash cans in the *Iliad* room that made a cool *KRONG!* sound when you kicked them. He turned to the rest of us. "You were all in this together, weren't you?" he sneered. "I'll bet you all got together and said, 'Hey, let's pull this *really* cool stunt—but let's not tell Holdn! Let's all just *exclude* Holdn!' That's how it went, didn't it? *Didn't it?*" He kicked the trash can again and put a pretty big dent in it.

"That's not true, Holdn," Peggy protested. "None of us knew any more about it than y—"

"Oh, what the hell do you know about it?" Holdn snapped. "You don't know what they're like! You all just spend your days trying to come up with ways to make me look like an idiot, don't you? *Don't you?*" He picked up the trash can without the dent in it and shook it. I guess it was supposed to be threatening but in reality all it did was make him look like an idiot. "You're all against me! Plotting against me! Admit it!"

"No one's against you," Peggy said, in a voice like buttermilk. "We care about you!"

"We do?" Cat said, scratching her head. "Did I miss a memo?"

"C'mon, this isn't funny," Peggy said. She got up and went over to Holdn. "Holdn, put the trash can down," she said. "No one's plotting against you."

"I am," Zab said.

"*See?*" Holdn screeched, waving Peggy away. "I *told* you!"

"Don't you think you may be making too much of a few bucketfuls of syrup?" Hayley asked.

"*Fuck* you!" Holdn spat. "Fuck all of you!" He took the trash can he was holding and chucked it out the door. It bounced a couple of times and went rolling down the hall.

"What a catharsis," Hank said.

"I think that's supposed to go in the Dumpster, actually," Cat said.

"*Fuck* you!" Holdn shouted.

"Yeah, well, you already said that," Hank said.

The door opened and Uta Himmler came in. "Who trew dis trash can?" she asked. "Whoever trew it vill pick it up right now, *ja?*"

Holdn pushed Uta out of the way and stomped off. "Man, he sure showed *me*," Hank said.

"Isn't anyone going to go after him?" Peggy asked.

"What for?" Cat asked.

"Well, *I* am," Peggy said. She followed Holdn out of the building.

"No vun is picking up de trash can," Uta said. She pointed at me. "You. Pick it up."

"Me?" I said. "I didn't—"

"Do it," Uta said.

"But I just work here," I muttered.

The weird thing is that later that afternoon Holdn was hanging out with Cat and Hank and Hayley on the front steps of Cat's house just like nothing had happened. I asked Peggy what she had said to achieve such stunning results and she just shrugged. "I didn't say anything, really," she said. "Before I could say anything he started going on and on about his dad's girlfriend and then about his sister and then he started talking about baseball and then he got on his scooter and left."

"Uh, okay," I said. "So then why—"

"I asked Cat about it after school," Peggy said. "I was kind of upset but she said he just does this sort of thing every so often." She looked at her watch. "But I can't really talk now. I've got to get ready for my date!"

0°C

That just about covers everyone you need to know on the *Iliad*. Which isn't to suggest that half a dozen people comprised the whole operation—far from it. There were other editors, and loads of staff writers and whatnot. Still, the other people on the paper were sort of ephemeral presences, unknown faces that would occasionally wander timidly into the *Iliad* room to hand in a story and quickly scamper away. Sure, there were a few you could recognize—the assistant editor on the sports page was Sluggo the water polo player, for instance—but for the most part not many of them were especially memorable. Hank referred to the staff writers collectively as "the vague people," which seemed pretty accurate. They probably thought of us in much the same way.

And then there was Echo.

Echo was the *Iliad*'s copy editor. It was a position Benito had invented specifically for Echo, not because the *Iliad* needed a copy editor so much as because Echo needed a place to go. See, every October, Benito would talk to Mrs. Wennikee, the freshman English teacher, and ask her to pick her top one or two students; whoever she picked would, if they agreed, be signed up for journalism and groomed to take over the top spot three years down the line. Three years ago it had been Cat; the year after that, Peggy (not so much because she was the greatest writer as because Mrs. Wennikee liked her spunk); then last year it'd been Echo and me, Echo because she had, in Mrs. Wennikee's words, "the most elegant prose I've seen in twenty-four years of teaching," and me because I'd gotten my hands on some incriminating photos. (No, not really.) Our first year I wrote mainly for the entertainment page, and Echo for opinion; thus, when I got the job as Hayley's assistant, Benito slotted in Echo as assistant opinion editor—under Zab.

"No way," Echo said when she found out. "I'm not working under Zab, or for Zab, or with Zab, or anywhere near Zab. She's a human cesspool. You could catch gonorrhea just from standing next to her."

"But all the other assistantships have already been filled," Benito said.

"Then I'll just take a different class," Echo said. "You seem to have forgotten this is an elective. And I'd elect to slash my wrists before I'd work for Zab. End of discussion."

So Benito quickly whipped up the idea of having a copy editor and Echo agreed to stay on. She could hardly have asked for a more perfect position: she didn't have to go into the *Iliad* room or deal with people at all. She'd just sit in Benito's room and do her homework, and then after school once everyone else had left she'd look at the stories people had turned in and fix all the typos.

Zab was just as pleased as Echo at the way things had turned out. Every time she went into Benito's room to talk to one of her staff writers or something and saw Echo sitting there in her bulky black sweatshirt on a ninety-degree day, she'd come back with a fresh string of unfunny invective: "Call Guinness, it's a world record! Who'd've thought you could get a stick that far up a person's ass?" I'd tried defending her once or twice, but that just made it worse; Zab would just snort and say, "Ooooh, the pickaninny's mad. Whatcha gonna do, rustle up your homies and do a drive-by on me?" So it was really kind of pointless.

Of course, Benito's room wasn't a much friendlier environment where Echo was concerned. Echo tended to strike fear and loathing into the hearts of the vague people—when she walked into Benito's room it was like chucking a bar of soap into a pot full of grease. No one dared to come too close. Part of it was the way they would hand in an article and within a matter of minutes she'd return it with so many corrections you'd think it'd been written in crayon by a trained monkey; part of it was her frankly ridiculous academic overachievement and the wild popularity that sort of thing inevitably brings; some of it was even a vestige of her third-grade days when she would hand out after-school beatings on a regular basis to anyone who'd been hassling me. Most of it was probably because you couldn't really talk to her without getting the verbal equivalent of a beaker of acid splashed in your face: at the beginning of the school year I overheard many a conversation between Echo and one of the fresh-faced new staff writers that went something like, "Are you Echo Mockery?" "Yes." "Is it true that you got a sixteen hundred on your SATs when you were ten?" "Yes." "So you're, like, really smart, huh?" "Not anymore. Talking to you has been so stultifying that now I'll be lucky if I can still feed myself."

And part of it was undoubtedly because of the way she looked. Echo's face was exquisite, perfect in every detail, with a flawless complexion and cheekbones that 99 percent of the world's models would kill for—but you couldn't really call her beautiful, because her beauty was cruel. Her silvery-gray eyes could bore a hole in you the size of a chicken pot pie and her lower lip was just a little fuller than it really had to be, so it seemed like she was always pouting; it made her look haughty and arrogant, which was unfortunate because she actually *was* kind of haughty and arrogant and didn't need her face to advertise it. Then there was her posture: Echo was the only adolescent in the history of the world who didn't slouch. And she always dressed entirely in black, which is pretty lame but certainly impresses the hell out of most fifteen-year-olds. Molly and I were once watching a movie on TV and there was a scene with this ice sculpture of a muse playing a lyre and Molly said, "Hey, doesn't that look like Echo?" I didn't see the resemblance, myself: the muse's hair was long and flowing, not chopped at her shoulders; she was dressed in some sort of tunic, not in a black sweatshirt and jeans; and I couldn't picture Echo in the same room as a lyre, let alone playing one. I said as much to Molly. She frowned and said, "You're right. *She* doesn't look like *Echo*—Echo looks like her. She's like a living, breathing ice sculpture."

Holdn sees something shiny

So you should now have a pretty good idea of what April Young and Kelly Kaylin were getting into when they walked into the *Iliad* room

Tuesday afternoon. They just kind of stood in the doorway for a couple of minutes until Cat put down her newspaper and said, "Yes? May I take your order please?"

No one else had noticed them standing there, and we all looked up. They were both wearing their black-and-silver cheerleading outfits. I waved to Kelly, but April thought I meant her and waved back. "Um, weren't you all supposed to send a photographer today?" she asked. "'Cause we thought you were sending a photographer and no one showed up. The whole squad's waiting."

Peggy grabbed the photo assignment list and looked up the entries for February 8th. "Two-thirty, cheerleading practice," she said. "Where's Hank?" She looked around. "He was here a minute ago."

I beckoned Kelly inside. "What's this all about?" I asked.

"Huh?" she said. "Oh, like, we're getting ready for the big soccer game and stuff." Every year the guys' and girls' soccer teams played each other as a fund-raiser; it was the one game of the season that charged admission, and more people showed up for that one game than for the rest of the season combined. It was usually pretty brutal: last year the girls had won 22–0.

Peggy went to Benito's room to look for Hank. "So how's it going?" I asked. "Practice, I mean."

"Uh, okay," Kelly said. "We've got a new routine for this year. It's, like, 'Girls are keen! Girls are great! Girls are mean and filled with hate! *KILL! KILL! KILL!*'"

"Yikes," I said, awed and more than a little turned on at her sudden display of rapacity. "How's the one for the guys go?"

"There is none," Kelly said. "If they want a cheer they can, like, cheer for themselves."

April came up and slapped Kelly across the side of her head. "That cheer was supposed to be a secret," she said.

"Hey, no need for violence," I said.

"Sure there is," April said. "B-E aggressive, right? Besides, she can't feel it. Watch." She slapped Kelly across the face with a resounding crack. A bright red handprint appeared on Kelly's cheek but she just blinked. "See?" April said.

"Like, you didn't hit me very hard," Kelly said. "It just *sounded* bad."

Peggy came back in. "I can't find Hank anywhere," she said. "We'll have to reschedule or something."

"Isn't that him under the table?" April asked, pointing.

Peggy ducked down to take a look. "Hank, what are you doing under the table?" she asked.

"Gluing potato chips to it," he said.

"Why?" she asked.

"Because if I glued them to the top no one could get any work done," Hank said.

"Get out here," Peggy said. Hank reluctantly clambered out from under the table. "Now hurry up and get your camera."

"Um, we usually practice in the gym but we can move outside if you need better light," April said. "Want us to?"

"I dunno," Hank said.

"What do you mean, you don't know?" April said.

"I dunno nothin' 'bout no light," Hank said. "I'm jus' heah t' take th' pickchuhs."

"But won't the contrast come out bad if the light's bad?" April asked.

"I dunno nothin' 'bout no contrast," Hank said. "I'm jus' heah t' take th' pickchuhs."

"Um, you better get going," Peggy said. "School's almost over."

"Yeah, yeah," Hank said. He and April and Kelly headed back out to the gym. As they walked down the hall I heard him explain, "I don' know much, but I know pickchuhs."

Hayley coughed. "Don't you think you ought to go with them?" she asked me.

"Me?" I said. "Why?"

"Siren Delaney's a cheerleader, right?" she said. "She was supposed to have her story in on Friday. Then it was Monday. Now it's Tuesday and there's still no story. It's your responsibility to make sure the writers get their assignments in on time. Where is it?"

"I dunno nothin' 'bout no story," I muttered. Still, I went to go follow them.

"Wait, wait, wait," Holdn said as I opened the door. "Mockery. Who . . . who *was* that?"

"Who was who?" I asked.

"That . . . *girl,*" Holdn said. He ran his hand through his hair, which was now dyed half purple and half green. "She was—I mean—"

It was a feeling I knew all too well. "Kelly Kaylin," I said. "You know, Peggy's sister." I looked around. "Hey, where'd Peggy g—"

"Not *her,*" Holdn said. "The other one. The shiny one. *You* know. She looked like she was fucking *laminated.*"

"You mean April?" I said. "April Young?"

Holdn grabbed a piece of scrap paper and scribbled down the name. "That's 'Young' as in 'not old,' not as in 'Freud and,' right?" he asked. I nodded. "Do you know her Social Security number?" he added.

"No," I said. "Why?"

"Well, I'm planning to spend the remainder of the fiscal year running my tongue over her naked body and I figured I'd better report it on my taxes," he said. "It's more fun than itemizing deductions and it gets the IRS guys all jealous."

"You don't pay taxes," Hayley said.

"I could start," Holdn said.

Pretty soon after that it was time for peer counseling and since it was fresh in my mind I thought I'd better tell September about Holdn's designs. "Hey, you know Holdn Holdnowski?" I asked.

"I think so," she said. "Is he the one with the weird hair?"

"Yes," I said, "but that doesn't really narrow it down."

"Two different colors," she said.

"Yup, that's him," I said. I recounted the afternoon's conversation for her. "So what do you think?"

"Isn't he a senior?" she asked.

"Sure is," I said.

"Doesn't he know she's just a freshman?" she asked. "She's not even fourteen yet."

"I think that's part of the appeal," I said.

"I don't get it," September said. "What could they possibly have in common?"

"Um, I kinda doubt he's interested in her for her conversation on long wintry nights," I said. "Anyway, I just thought you'd want to know. I'd rather not get involved."

Reading is fundamental

The next day at lunch some of us were eating in the *Iliad* room—Hank and Hayley and Holdn and Cat because they just sort of hung out there, and me because people were always trying to find me to get their red tickets signed and it was easier when I stayed in one place. Hayley was reading the newspaper; Cat was reading the latest issue of *Rotate;* Hank was reading a big manual called *Building Your Own Nuclear Fallout Shelter;* and Holdn was reading a little book with a watercolor of a young teenage girl on the cover titled *Cap'n Groovy's Guide to Your Changing Body.*

"Hey, listen to this," Holdn said. "'While every vulva is unique, just like a face, they can still be grouped into five main types. See Figure twenty-five.'" He held up Figure 25. "Hey, Nicholls, which kind do you have?"

Cat didn't even look up. "The best kind," she said.

"Where did you get that?" Hayley asked.

"Cal State Fullerton library," Holdn said. "They've got all kinds of crap like this. There was also one for boys but it was only four pages long and two of those were diagrams." He looked at Figure 25 thoughtfully. "Which type is April Young, you figure? Oh well, I'll find out for myself soon enough."

"What makes you think that?" Hayley asked.

"I've got a plan," Holdn said. "I figure I'll get her number from someone, call her up, we'll talk, we'll go out, and pretty soon it's hardcore penetration."

"You think that'll work?" Hayley said.

"Well, sure," Holdn said. "I'm me." He scratched his face. "Besides, I can always go with Plan B."

"Which is?" Hayley asked.

The door opened and April came in—not in her cheerleading outfit, but in jeans and a T-shirt. "Are you Holdn?" she asked Holdn.

"Yeah," he said.

"Got a car?" she asked.

"I've got a scooter," he said.

"Close enough," she said. "Wanna take me for a ride?"

"Let's go," Holdn said. They went.

"I guess that was Plan B," Cat said.

Thirty seconds later the door flew open again and August stormed in. "All right, which one of you is Holdn Holdnowski?" he demanded. He glanced around the room and zeroed in on Hank. "It's you, isn't it?" he spat, grabbing his collar. "You're the one talking shit about my sister? I *heard* you were weird-looking!"

"But I'm jus' heah t' take th' pickchuhs," Hank protested.

"Actually," I said, "Holdn just left—"

"Oh," August said. He let go of Hank's collar. "Well, that's okay then. Uh, sorry about that."

"—with April," I finished. "He's taking her for a ride on his scooter."

"*WHAT?*" August yelped.

"They left like a minute ago," I said. "He usually parks in the faculty lot. You can probably still catch him."

August took off running. I went over to Benito's room and looked out the window. August burst out into the lot just as Holdn pulled out into traffic with April's arms wound tightly around his waist and her honey-colored hair blowing wildly behind her in the breeze. I heard August shouting something about using protection; whether he meant helmets or contraception I couldn't tell.

Carpet with tahini sauce

When I went to the *Iliad* room for lunch on Friday afternoon, August and September were both hanging out in front. September was carrying a paper bag; August had a super-jumbo soda from the local 24-Seven. "What's going on?" I asked.

"It's an ambush," August said. "We're gonna wait for that Holdn guy to show up and then Temberine there's gonna throw that paper bag over his head and then I'm gonna give him the beating of his life."

"I said no beatings," September said. "We're just going to talk to him."

"Then what's the paper bag for?" I asked. September reached in and pulled out a sandwich. "Oh," I said. "Well, have fun." I went inside.

"Just who I've been looking for," Hayley said as I came in. "Did you get Siren Delaney to turn in her story yet? It's now officially a week late."

"I've really got to find somewhere else to eat," I said.

So I wolfed down my delicious repast of cookies and an apple and went to go look for Siren Delaney. I got back just as Holdn and April showed up, fresh from a trip to Cous-Cous à Go-Go. "All right, buddy, hands off the jailbait," August said. "You should be arrested for even thinking about her."

"April, we need to talk," September said.

"Um, is there any way I could get by . . . ?" I asked.

"You better just leave her alone if you know what's good for you," August said, poking Holdn in the chest. "I mean it."

"So . . . Sheila's your prize poodle, and I'm the one-eyed three-legged mutt down the street?" Holdn said. "Is that pretty much how this works?"

"Who the hell's Sheila?" August said.

"I am," April said. "It's my secret name."

"Don't joke about that," September said.

"If I could just squeeze by real quick here . . ." I said.

"Wait a minute, wait a minute," August said. "Did you just call my sister a dog? That does it. Throw the bag over his head."

"I'm not throwing the bag over his head," September said. "Look, April, we just want to talk. I don't think you know what you're getting into here."

"I know exactly what I'm getting into," April said.

"Though technically," Holdn said, "*I'm* going to be getting into *h*—"

"You bastard," August spat. He took a wild swing at Holdn that landed with the resounding thwap of flesh smashing into pita bread.

"My sandwich!" Holdn cried. "You killed my sandwich!" This was true—August's punch had sent Holdn's kefta kabob flying down the hall. It lay on the ground bleeding a pinkish sauce. "That was expensive!"

"Your *medical* bills are gonna be expensive when I'm through with you," August said. He tossed his super-jumbo soda aside and threw himself on Holdn, which was a mistake since the soda hit September square in the chest and gave her a thorough soaking.

"Halt!" cried Uta, appearing out of nowhere. "No fightink on school grounds!" She and April and September and I pulled the two of them apart.

"Leave me alone!" August said. "I haven't finished beating him to a bloody pulp yet!"

"There vill be no bloody pulps here," Uta barked. "Detention for both uff you! And somevun clean up de sandvich! You," she said, pointing at me. "Clean up dis sandvich."

"Me?" I said. "But I—"

"Do it," Uta said. She took out her walkie-talkie and reported in. August stormed off down the hall; Holdn and April laughed and went inside. That left September and me. September looked down at herself in dismay.

"I've got to get this cleaned up," she said. "Come on."

"What?" I said.

"We need to talk," she said.

So after picking up and disposing of the sandwich I followed her down the hall and out to the wheel and into the girls' bathroom, which was reasonably packed. Among the people I recognized were Fringie's current girlfriend, Shelby Streicht, and Fringie himself, leaning up against the wall reading Heidegger's *Being and Time*. "Hey, Al," he said. "Long time no see."

"Funny," I said.

September took off her denim jacket and assessed the damage in the mirror. Her T-shirt had a big brown cola stain all over it. "So what should I do?" she asked.

"Pretreat it with stain guard before you wash it," I said. "I guess you could try club soda, but—"

"That's not what I mean," she said. "I mean about April. And that Holdn guy. You're a peer counselor, and I'm your peer. Counsel me. What should I do?"

"What *can* you do?" I said. "People pretty much do what they want."

"That's no kind of attitude to take," September said. "C'mon, she's in trouble here. Don't you have any advice?"

"Oh, I suppose so," I said. "My chief piece of advice would be not to drag in casual acquaintances who don't want to get involved."

"Allen!" she said. "First of all, obviously you *do* want to get involved or you wouldn't have warned me about Holdn in the first place. Second of all, are you really saying that after almost two years of working together that all we are is 'casual acquaintances'?"

"Well, it's not like we grew up together or anything," I said. "But I meant me and April, not me and you. I've only talked to April maybe half a dozen times in my life. And the reason I told you about Holdn's aspirations was so you could pass it on to April and she could make an informed decision if Holdn tried to pick her up. If it turned her on instead of making her suspicious, well, that's something you probably would've had to start working on a couple years ago to have any effect by now. At this point you can either try to talk to her and hope she listens or you can grab her and tie her up in the backyard."

September sighed and went back to wringing out her sodden T-shirt. "This is hopeless," she said. "I don't even have PE anymore so I can't go to the locker room and change." She put on her jacket and buttoned it all the way up. "I guess that'll have to do. Now I'm going to be sticky the rest of the day."

"Why don't you just take it off?" I asked. "If you're going to wear your jacket like that no one'll know the difference."

September looked at me like I was insane.

The lights and towns below

When I got back to the *Iliad* room, Speedy Wilkins, the sports editor, was going on and on about his upcoming party. "Hey, everyone's coming over to my place tomorrow night, right?" he said. "It'll be great: chips, dips, Bloods, Crips. Anyone who's anyone'll be there. And even some people who, y'know, aren't anyone."

I already knew about the party since Speedy had come up to the office to get someone for key patrol a few days earlier, and since his house was right on Riverside Drive, within easy walking distance from school and thus from my house, I got the assignment. But April, transacting in different circles altogether, was hearing about it for the first time. "Cool!" she said. She grabbed Holdn's shoulder. "We're going, right?"

"Sure," Holdn said.

"Cool," April said. "They'll have wine coolers, right?" The bell rang. "Tell me later," she said. "I've got to get to class." She scampered off.

"Wine coolers?" Hayley said.

"It's a legitimate question," Holdn said.

"So let me get this straight," Hayley said. "Not only is she a child, not only does she have nothing in common with you, but she's also four years early for sorority rush? Holdn, what happened to your taste?"

"Shut up," Holdn said. "It's not my fault she's shiny. It's just the way things worked out. You don't hear me making fun of your little D&D guy with the head cold up in Washington, do you? What's he calling himself now, Jethro Tull?"

"Jefferson Wolf," Hayley said. "And just because he plays role-playing games doesn't mean he's a D&D guy—"

"He named himself after his character!" Holdn said.

"—and he doesn't have a head cold, he has a sinus condition, and actually, you make fun of him all the time," Hayley finished.

"What's wrong with you two?" Speedy asked. "Can't you see you love each other?"

"Shut up," they said together.

By the time Saturday night rolled around, though, I'd completely forgotten about the whole thing—I had other things on my mind. It wasn't until I got a call from September that I remembered where I was supposed to be.

"Do you know where April is?" she asked. "She sneaked out. She isn't at any of her friends' houses and no one has any idea where she went. I know she probably went with that Holdn guy but I have no idea where they'd go."

"They probably went to Speedy Wilkins's party," I said. I looked at my watch; it was past eleven. "I'm supposed to be there myself. I got . . . sidetracked."

"What's the address?" she asked.

I gave her some quick directions and then put on my shoes and left for Speedy's. It was a warm breezy night and the air was thick with the smell of eucalyptus and the wide crumbling sidewalks gleamed in the warm orange light of porches and front walks. Peggy and I had gone for walks all the time on nights like this when we were kids. I almost stopped at her house to see if she wanted to go to the party with me, but I'd already talked to her earlier in the day and she'd mentioned that she had a date that night. She hadn't wasted much time tracking down Boyfriend #93.

Before too long I arrived at Speedy's house, which was a modest one-story dwelling much more in keeping with Fullerton's essential dead-center middle-class nature than Greg Garner's mansion out in Sunny Hills. Cars stretched along the curb as far as I could see. I went inside.

The house was small enough that the front door opened right into the living room, and the first thing that struck me was how few people there were: I was expecting it to be packed, but there were maybe half a dozen people standing around sipping beer out of little plastic cups that made it look like they were drinking urine samples. A couple guys were actually just sitting on the couch watching TV. The sliding glass door opened and Speedy came in. "Hey," he said. "Most everyone's out back—the yard's bigger than the house, and it's a nice night. Plus that's where the keg is. The keys are on the end table there." He pointed and sure enough there was a heap of keys next to one of the lamps. "Glad you made it," he added. "You're the first person from the paper to show up. 'Cept Sluggo."

"Really?" I said. "Then who—" I looked around. "Aw, crap," I said. "They're all jocks."

I felt a hand on my shoulder. "Hey, I know you!" said someone behind me, a big beefy guy with tiny little eyes. "You're Echo Mockery's brother! Or is it sister? Haw haw haw haw!"

I didn't recognize the face at first, but I knew the laugh. "Uh, hi," I said. "Jay Kyeutter, right? I wish we could talk, but I have to go stand somewhere else now."

The door opened and September and August came in. "Where's April?" September asked.

"Nice to see you too," I said. "She's not here. I don't know if she's coming or not."

"Great," September said. She looked outside just in time to see her cab drive away. "I don't believe it!" she said. "I told him to wait out front!"

"Did you tell him in Spanish?" I asked.

"I thought I did," she said. "I guess not. Maybe it was Portuguese or something. *Now* what am I going to do?"

"I know what *I'm* gonna do," August said. "Par-tay! Whoo!"

"Please don't say 'whoo,'" September said.

That was when Fringie strode through the door. "Hey!" Sluggo said. "I didn't think you were gonna show. What happened?"

"Oh, I had to finish dropping Shelby," Fringie said. "I thought it'd be quick but she made a scene."

"You dropped Shelby?" Sluggo said. "But I thought you said the penis was well-pleased, or something."

"Yeah, for a while," Fringie said. "But the contentment of the penis is short-lived. That which is familiar to the penis quickly grows loathsome. Which is kind of a paradox since we all know that in another sense the penis craves the familiar almost to the exclusion of all else. But that which is familiar to the mind and that which is familiar to the penis itself are interwoven but nonetheless different entities."

"Uh, right," Sluggo said.

Then Kevin Love came in and I suppressed a shudder. Kevin Love was spooky. He was the tallest of the water polo players at six feet six, but that wasn't what made him intimidating; what made him intimidating was the fact that you couldn't see his eyes. He had this big shock of dark hair that always hung over them, but even when he brushed it out of the way his eyes were always somehow shadowed—it was creepy. And, like Fringie, he had a rep, but it wasn't quite so benign as Fringie's: if you asked anyone who knew him about Kevin Love, you'd get the same troubled expression, the same hushed tone, and the same answer: "He . . . likes to hurt people." Pause. "Especially girls."

I had a look around the house for a bit and when I got back to the living room I found September sitting in a chair staring out the window and looking morose. "Did you call another cab?" I asked.

"No," she said. "The only phone is in the kitchen and these scary guys are using it. They're—what's the word?—dreadnoks."

"Really?" I said. "Dreadnoks? With the black leather and scuzzy mustaches and everything? What're they doing here? This is a jock party."

"I don't think they were invited," September said. "I think they just wandered in looking for beer."

Sluggo headed out into the backyard. "Whoa!" he said, nearly slipping in a puddle of fresh vomit. "Looks like Ralph was here. Hey, who wants to see me eat a whole bag of potato chips?"

"I don't believe I'm stuck here all night," I said.

Fringie went outside for a bit but then sauntered back into the living room and then into the kitchen. Or at least he tried. There was xsa pair of saloon-style swinging doors hanging between the living room and the kitchen and when he tried to push through them one of the doors smacked into something. "Hey, watch where you're standing," he said. "People are trying to get through." He shoved his way inside.

"Why don't you watch where the fuck *you're* fucking standing, fuckface?" snarled a much too familiar voice.

"Oh, no," I said. "It's evolution gone tragically awry."

"What?" September said.

"My brother," I said.

"Don't have an aneurysm," Fringie said. "I'm just looking for a cup."

"Well you can *fuck* your fucking cup, you fucking fuck!" Krieg said.

"A couple of things for your shopping list, okay?" Fringie said. "One, a thesaurus, and two, a tub of benzoyl peroxide. Get the jumbo size. And throw in a few of those diet shakes while you're at it. Now move it."

"You don't know who you're fucking with, fuckhead!" Krieg shrieked. "I'm gonna fuck you up!"

Fringie turned around and emerged from the kitchen, shaking his head. "Yeah, that's it!" came Krieg's voice after him. "Run, pussy! You better run! You better fucking run!"

"My parents should've stopped with two," I muttered.

August came in from out back, specimen cup in hand. He wasn't exactly drunk yet, but I doubt I would've given him his keys back if he'd had keys. "There's a guy out there eating a whole bag of potato chips," he giggled.

Speedy came in with a glazed look in his eyes. He stood in the middle of the living room and looked around like he was lost. "Anything wrong?" I asked.

"No," he said. "I just have to . . . get something . . ." He went into his room. When he came out a few minutes later he was carrying a baseball bat. He went into the kitchen.

What happened next was kind of weird. The dreadnoks all bolted for the door—including Krieg, huffing and puffing from the exertion of running across the room—but even after they were gone, that wasn't the end of it. Suddenly from the other side of the swinging doors came a horrendous clanging like someone tossing washing machines off the roof of an office building, and when I ran in to see what was wrong I found Speedy all alone in the kitchen bashing the stove with the baseball bat. Before I could say anything a bunch of other people swarmed in to see what all the noise was about.

"Get out," Speedy growled.

He didn't specify whether he wanted us to get out of the kitchen or out of the house entirely, but with all the clanging that followed our retreat, most everyone assumed the latter. Which meant that suddenly September and I were the most popular people at the party since we had everyone's keys. "Who here has a cell phone?" September asked. "No one gets their keys till someone lends me a phone." So she called a bunch of cabs, Speedy went to his room, and the crowd slowly dissipated. The place was pretty much empty when Holdn and April finally arrived.

"What the hell?" Holdn said. "Where's all the people?"

"All the people's gone," I said. "Except him." I pointed at the guy passed out on the couch.

"You're in *so* much trouble," September said to April. "*First* you're grounded and *second* you're out past your curfew and *third* you didn't tell anyone where you were going and when you get home you're not going to be allowed out of the room for a *month*."

April batted her eyelashes. "Wow," she said. "Guess I better not go home then, huh? Thanks for the tip." She wrapped her arm around Holdn's and cocked her head toward the door. "C'mon, let's go," she said.

"Yeah, okay," Holdn said. "Tell Wilkins he throws a hell of a party, okay? Say good night, Sheila."

April blew us a kiss. The door closed.

"I *hate* it when he calls her that," September said. "Why does he call her that?"

"Holdn calls all his girlfriends Sheila," I said.

"And you," she said, turning to August. "Why didn't you do anything? Yesterday you were going to beat him to a bloody pulp, today you just stand around?"

"I've r'nounced the ways of violence," August murmured into his plastic cup.

"Well, I'm going to stop her," she said. "Come on."

It was too late: Holdn and April were already buzzing down the driveway. Just then a cab from Taxi Ocho pulled up. September threw open the door and shoved August and me inside. "Follow that scooter," she said.

The taxista gave me a perplexed look. *"Seguid el,* uh, scooter, *por favor,"* I said.

We rumbled down the street after Holdn and April. "Sheila," September muttered. "He doesn't even care who she *is.* She could be anyone for all he cares." She gave me a bitter look. "You know, when we were in elementary school, the bus home would always pass by the 24-Seven near our house, and April kept asking Mom and Dad to let her get off there and get a candy bar and walk the rest of the way home, and they finally said yes as long as May and August and I went with her. So we all got off two stops early and April brought a dollar from her allowance and she made us all wait outside since she wanted to prove she could buy stuff all by herself—she was six—and so we all hung around out front and it was taking an awfully long time and finally she came out, not with a candy bar, but with a little tin of cat food. Why? Because she'd looked at all the candy bars on the rack and couldn't decide which one she wanted, and since it never occurred to her to just put the dollar back in her pocket and leave without buying anything, she didn't know what to do, since if she got something for one of us instead we'd all fight over it and she didn't have enough for everybody. So she bought a can of cat food since 'it was under a dollar and only the kitty'll want it!' *That's* why he should be going out with her."

"Because they'll always have plenty of cat food?" I asked.

"Because she's a wonderful person," September said.

"Hunh," I said. "I never got the impression you liked her very much."

"What?" she said. "Of *course* I do! I mean, she drives me *crazy,* but—I mean, we've had the same room ever since she was born!"

"I ate the cat food," August interrupted.

"Yeah, and August ate some of the cat food," September said. "Just to prove her wrong." She craned her neck to see if Holdn and April were still in sight. They were—you couldn't miss April's hair blowing around, even this late at night with just the starlight and street lamps and headlights to see by. "What's she doing riding on that thing without a helmet?" September growled. "She's in *so* much trouble. Cutting all that class already has her grounded for three weeks. Every day, it's been, 'Beep! This is a recorded message from the Ilium High School attendance office. Our records indicate that April Laura Young missed one or more periods of class today. Unexcused absences can lead to disciplinary action. Beep!'"

"Her middle name's Laura?" I asked.

"Which is another thing that creep has no idea of, I'm sure," September said. "If he can't even remember her *first* name. But yeah, her middle name's Laura."

"But it's not her *secret* name," August mumbled.

"Quiet," September said.

The cab lurched and when I looked out the window I found that we were pulling into the parking lot of a 24-Seven. Holdn's scooter was propped up by the door. "They must've stopped for some cat food," I said.

Just as the cab came to a complete stop there was a horrendous crash and Holdn and April came tearing out of the store. By the time the guy on duty could hop over the counter and chase after them they were long gone. "Wouldn't you know it," I said. "The one convenience store in the world without a hundred police cars out front."

"Come *on*!" September said urgently. She pulled August out of the cab and obviously expected me to follow, so I did. "*Seguid el* scooter *encore, por favor,*" she said. The taxista looked dubious so she dug a twenty-dollar bill out of her pocket and threw it at him. He shrugged and took off in pursuit of Holdn and April.

"*Seguid el* scooter *encore*?" I said.

"He knew what I meant," September said. "C'mon, we've got to get this mess cleaned up."

"But what good is it going to do to have *him* follow them around?" I asked. "We'll never find either of them."

"We'll just call another cab," September said.

"What good'll that do?" I asked. "How'll we find the first one?"

"They have radios in their cabs," she said.

"Okay, so you're a genius," I said.

September went inside and I followed her in. Holdn and April had overturned the candy rack and knocked over a pyramid of soda cans as well. "Explain to me why we're cleaning this up again?" I said.

"Because she's my sister," September said. "That makes us responsible."

"Oh, okay," I said. "Does that mean you'll help me clean up the wreckage when Krieg blows up my house?"

August woozily stumbled inside. "I'm gonna go lie down," he said. He wandered back to the beverage case and slumped to the ground.

September sighed and righted the candy rack; I started helping the guy on duty gather up the soda cans that'd rolled over most of the store. "What are you doing?" he snapped. "Either you buy something or get out."

"We're just trying to help," September said.

The guy grunted and stopped to light up a cigarette. "See the cameras?" he said. He jerked his head in the direction of the surveillance cameras mounted in the corners. "You see the cameras?"

"Yeah, I see the cameras," I said.

"No tricks," he said. He wandered back behind the counter and turned on the boom box, which erupted with Kyrgyzstani folk songs.

September hummed to herself as she grabbed handfuls of candy bars and tossed them into their respective boxes; I tried to reconstruct the soda pyramid but couldn't get the numbers to work out right and ended up with more of a soda ziggurat. August was curled up on the ground with a four-pack of toilet paper for a pillow, peacefully snoring away. And no wonder: by the time we finished it was past two in the morning.

"I guess I'll go call another taxi," September said, yawning. She went outside to the pay phone and fumbled around for some change before giving up and just using her phone card. After she hung up she stood there for a minute blinking at the phone before rubbing her eyes and coming back inside. She found an inviting-looking corner and sat down.

"Hey," grunted the guy behind the counter. "You buy something or get out."

"What?" she said. "We just spent an hour cleaning—"

"Buy something or get out," he said. He gave me a suspicious look. "What's that in your pocket?" he asked.

"Say what?" I said.

"Empty your pockets," he said.

I took out my wallet and turned my pockets inside out. "Happy?" I said. "Want to frisk me and make sure I didn't stuff a forty of malt liquor down my pants? Sheesh."

"Buy something or get out," he said.

I went out to the parking lot. September grabbed August and dragged him outside too. They dozed on the curb while I paced around waiting for the cab to show up. It took forty minutes.

"*Llamad uno cuatro, s'il vous plaît,*" September yawned. Somehow the driver figured out that she wanted him to radio cab number 14.

"Can't you drop me off at my place first?" I asked.

"I need you," she said. "In case I have to say something complicated."

The taxi pulled back out onto the road and soon we were careening down twisty meandering roads I didn't recognize. "Where are we, Anaheim Hills?" I asked. The cab shuddered to a stop. "Huh?" I said. I looked out the window: we were parked right next to our original cab. I got out and talked to the driver for a minute. September followed me out but August stayed in the taxi, sound asleep.

"So where are they?" September asked, looking around.

"He says they drove around for a while and then toilet-papered someone's house," I said. "Then they came out here and went—up there."

September and I trudged up the hill to find Holdn and April perched at the top, gazing out at the sea of scattered lights below and flipping it off. "Boy, you sure showed *them*," I said.

Holdn turned around. "Mockery?" he said. "What the hell are you doing here? I figured the sibling mafia'd track me down but don't you have better things to do?"

"Oh, shut up," I said. "Thanks to your hormones I got to spend the night in janitor fantasy camp."

"April, you're coming home," September said. "Now."

"Yeah, yeah," April said, rolling her eyes. She kissed Holdn on the cheek. "Thanks for a great night," she said.

"Don't get mushy," he said. "This isn't a fucking romantic comedy. See ya." He hopped on his scooter and buzzed off into the night.

"Get in the cab," September said. April shoved August out of the way and climbed in. September intercepted me before I could get into the other cab. "I just wanted to say . . . what April said goes double for me," she said.

"Say what?" I said.

"Tonight," she said. "It was kind of fun, wasn't it? It was an adventure, anyway."

"It was unpaid custodial work broken up by sporadic periods of riding around in a taxi," I said.

"I guess," she said, scuffing one of her sneakers up against the curb. "Well, good night. And thanks."

"Sure," I said. I got into the other cab and shut the door. "How about you?" I asked. "Did you have yourself a fun little adventure?"

"*¿Qué?*" asked the driver.

Twenty minutes later we finally arrived at my house. I noticed that the house was completely dark, which was odd: Echo had this freakish DNA sequence that wouldn't let her sleep more than three hours a night—four if she was absolutely exhausted—and I was sure she'd be up by now. The car was in the driveway, so she hadn't driven anywhere; her bike was propped up in the usual place too. Still, when I went inside, the house was just as dark as it was on the outside.

I heard a weird halting feathery sound and I felt around for the light switch so I could see what it was (and also so I could make it to the stairs without breaking my neck). It seemed to be coming from the TV room, where I found someone sitting alone in the dark. "Eck?" I said. "Is that you? What's up?"

A sharp intake of breath. "Nothing," she said. "Go to sleep."

I turned on the light and Echo hid her face with her arm. "Are you up late or just getting up?" I asked. "Why were you sitting in the dark?"

"Leave me alone," she said. "Go away."

I caught a glint of light on her cheek and suddenly I realized what I'd heard. "Hey, are you crying?" I asked. "What's wrong?"

"I said leave me alone," she said. "I'm not crying."

"You were," I said.

"I wasn't," she said.

I walked up to her and touched her face. Sure enough, her cheeks were wet. I licked my finger and it tasted salty. "If you weren't crying how did these tears get here?" I asked.

"They're not tears," she said.

I sat down next to her on the couch. "Echo, what's wrong?" I asked. "Are you okay?"

"*Yes*," she hissed. "That's what I've been *trying* to tell you. Now just *go away*, okay? Leave me alone. Just leave me alone. I just want to be left alone. Why can't you just leave me alone? *Leave me ALONE!*"

"Yeah, you sure sound like you're okay," I said. She gave me a look that practically knocked me off the couch. "Okay, okay, I'm going," I said. "If you change your mind, let me know."

So that was kind of troubling. But not sufficiently troubling to keep me from falling asleep five full seconds before my head hit the pillow.

The happiest place on earth

Over the next few days I'd estimate that I spent roughly zero percent of my time thinking about April Young, but that guess might be a little high. So when I happened to pause for a moment when I passed a bunch of cheerleaders out in front of the school as I walked home, it wasn't April I was looking for. But she came bounding over nonetheless.

"Hi, Allen!" she said. "Here to play guard dog?"

"Say what?" I said.

"Since August and September's bus left already," April said. "You're here to watch me, right?"

"No," I said. "To be perfectly honest, it'd take a remarkable effort on my part for me to care less about what you and Holdn do or don't do."

She flashed one of those smiles that made you feel like you were violating some kind of federal statute. "Me thinkest thou doth protesteth too much," she said.

"And me 'thinkest' thou should learn how to conjugate before you try to quote clichés," I said. "I mean, sure, if you were to come in for peer counseling I'd ask you what you think you're doing hanging around with a guy who's gone on record as saying that he's just using you for sex, but as it stands, it's not my problem. You do realize he's had lots of Sheilas over the years, right?"

"But I'm not just any Sheila," April said. "You know what we did Monday?"

"No, but I assume latex was involved," I said.

"No," she said. "We took off from school at lunchtime and went to Tijuana!"

"Great," I said. "Did he try to trade you for a chicken?"

"Huh?" she said. "No, first we just sort of wandered around all these scuzzy little places that had signs out front that said stuff like 'Cheap Dentistry and Upholstery,' and then we went looking for some kind of show Holdn wanted to see with a donkey, but we couldn't find out where it was—"

"There's a shocker," I said.

"So soon it was getting dark and we went to this club and saw this band, they were Americans but they tried to get into the whole Mexico thing by yelling '*Viva!*' and '*Undele!*' in the middle of all their songs, and when they were done and another band was up me and Holdn hung out with them and did tequila shots—"

"Oh, so all he did was smuggle you over the border and get you drunk?" I said. "That's a relief. For a second there I thought he might have been up to something shady."

"The point is, Holdn's just the funnest person I've ever met," April said. "And he's *not* just using me for sex. We haven't even *had* sex yet."

"Yet?" I said.

"Well, you know—anything could happen!" she said, batting her eyelashes.

"Have you talked to any of the Sheilas that have come before you to find out what's *likely* to happen?" I asked.

Before she could answer the bus chugged up the bus lane and wheezed to a stop. "About time," April said. "If we had to wait much longer we might as well've just stuck around till tomorrow." It was getting kind of dark. "Well, see you Saturday!" she said.

"Saturday?" I said. But April was long gone.

But you'll miss all the squirrels

It wasn't long before I found out what she meant. In fact, I already had a pretty good idea what she meant, since I had definite plans for Saturday; I just had no idea she had the same plans. See, Cat and Hayley had managed to talk their way into getting us a tour of the set of *Ashley: The Early Years* and Hayley and I were going to use it as the centerpiece of the entertainment page for next month. Hank was coming along to take the pictures; Holdn was coming because if Cat and Hayley and Hank went, and he didn't, he wouldn't stop whining about it for weeks. But it wasn't until I talked to April that it occurred to me that he'd bring her along.

Once the arrangements for the trip had been finalized, Hayley had asked me to see if Echo wanted to come along. "Um, I guess I can ask," I'd said. "Why?"

"I just thought it'd be a nice gesture," Hayley said. "We work together, and I know nothing about her. She seems smart enough—I'd just like to get to know her better."

So when I got home from peer counseling I went upstairs to find Echo in our room doing her homework. "Hey," I said, "a bunch of us from the *Iliad* are going on a tour of the *Ashley: The Early Years* set— want to come?"

Echo didn't bother to look up. "I don't recall being invited," she said, "so I don't suppose it matters whether I want to come or not."

"Actually, you are invited," I said. "It's for Hayley's page and she specifically asked me to bring you along."

Echo stopped typing and swiveled her chair around. "Hayley said that?" she said.

"Sure," I said. "So are you in?"

"Well . . . ," she began, then shook her head. "No," she said. "They'll just have to get their entertainment elsewhere." She swiveled her chair back around again and that was that.

• • •

When I got to Cat's house Saturday morning the door was open, so as I walked up I could hear April burbling with anticipation. "This is going to be so cool! *Ashley: The Early Years* is the best show on TV! It's so realistic! It's like they got a camera and filmed my life!"

"You mean all your friends have had thousands of dollars of cosmetic surgery?" Cat asked. I banged on the screen door. "Come in," she said.

I went in. It was the first time I'd ever been inside 150 Hyacinth: neither Fringie nor Cat had ever invited me over before. I must admit that I wasn't prepared for the shag carpeting. It was also quite dark inside: the only source of light was that seeping in through the vertical blinds. The furniture in the living room looked like it'd drifted in from a bunch of other houses during a flood or something—April was sprawled on a purple leather couch while Hayley sat in a tie-dyed beanbag next to a matte-black triangular coffee table. Cat was perched on the floor reading the paper and drinking cold coffee out of a martini glass. "Isn't Echo coming?" Hayley asked.

"She said she didn't want to," I said. "So are we going?"

"Not yet," Cat said. "Hank said he's going to be late. And God knows how long it'll take to wake Holdn up." She waved at the hallway; there was a strange rumbling noise coming from it. "I closed the door but you can still hear him snoring," she said.

"That's Holdn?" I said. "I figured you were doing laundry."

April went to go check on him. "Hey, the mail's here," Hayley said. From the beanbag she could see through the screen door out into the street where, sure enough, a mail truck was pulling away. Cat went out to see if there was anything good and came back in with a thick envelope. "Check it out, everyone!" she said. "I got into Berkeley."

"Cool," I said. "Is that your first choice?"

"You betcha," she said. "It's weird. It's like they stuffed the next five years of my life into an envelope and stuck it in the mail." She examined the envelope. "Wow, and they even refrained from calling me 'Catherine.' Excellent."

"My brother Jerem hates his full name too," I said. "He finds the 'y' demeaning."

"That's not it, though," Cat said. "My name isn't Catherine! It's Catalina."

"Like the island?" I asked.

"Yup," she said. "I was conceived there. Good thing, too—if my parents hadn't been on vacation I could've ended up being named 'Tujunga.'"

The screen door opened and Hank came in. "Sorry I'm late," he said. He took a can of condensed split pea soup out of his camera bag, went into the kitchen, stuck it under the can opener, grabbed a spoon, and started eating it like pudding.

"That's disgusting," Cat said.

"It's an acquired taste," Hank said.

"Why would you want to acquire it?" Cat asked.

Hank finished scarfing down his soup and then pulled a tooth-brush and a tube of toothpaste out of his camera bag. He went over to the kitchen sink and began vigorously brushing his teeth. "Do you carry that stuff around everywhere?" I asked.

"Good periodontal care is the key to a powerful bite and a winning smile," Hank said.

I watched Cat flip through the catalog Berkeley had sent her. "So, how about you?" I asked Hayley. "Have you heard anything yet?"

"I'm going to You-Dub," Hayley said.

"Excuse me?" I said.

"University of Washington," she said. "Full ride. Jefferson and I already signed a lease for an apartment in Seattle."

"What about you?" I asked Hank.

"I have no use for your institutional learning facilities," Hank said.

"But you can get away with that," Hayley said. "I have no doubt that inside of a year you'll have a record at the top of the techno charts or something. Holdn, on the other hand, is going to end up collecting unemployment for a couple of years and then get a job as a stockboy at a grocery store and call me every night to complain about his boss and brag about how he copied the key so he can steal cigarettes."

"Speaking of Holdn, shouldn't we get going?" Cat asked. "Now that we're all here? Where is he?"

"Right here," Holdn said. "So you're going, huh? Any excuse to leave me behind, huh? Well I'm sorry I ruined your little plan, but I'm not that easy to get rid of." He stormed outside and hopped on his scooter; April did the same and wrapped her arms around him. "So are we going or what?" he yelled.

We got into the car. Hayley drove; Holdn wheeled his scooter around to settle nicely into her blind spot as we headed out into traffic and hopped onto the freeway. It was a straight shot down the 91 and before too incredibly long we were in Torrance, where the show was filmed.

"Where now?" Cat asked.

"The woman I talked to yesterday said they'd meet us in the parking lot of the high school," Hayley said. "I guess that's them."

Coming toward us were a girl in an *Ashley: The Early Years* T-shirt and a tall guy with a goofy goatee and a bunch of silver rings in his left eyebrow. "Hi!" the girl said. "I'm Melissa, and I'll be doing the tour thing. I like your socks."

"Thanks," Hank said.

"Not you," Melissa said. She gestured at April's feet—she was wearing those colored wool socks only girls can get away with. One was burgundy, one was mustard yellow, just like Ashley's in the pilot to *Ashley: The Early Years*. Hank's socks were argyle.

"Right," Melissa said. "Okay, I usually do this in episode order, so follow me."

"Do you do this a lot?" Hayley asked as we left the parking lot.

"Every weekend," Melissa said. "You brought my fifty bucks, right?"

Hayley pulled out her wallet and handed over the money as Hank whipped out his camera and snapped a picture. "Beautiful!" he said. "I call it 'Pay-Per-View.'"

The tour proved to be something less than a professional operation. Melissa's commentary was perfunctory at best: "This is the gym where the school dance was held in the pilot episode. This is the locker room where most of the field hockey episode took place. This is the cot where Ashley gave Johnny her virginity after they finished practicing for the school play. This is the art room where the teacher looked down her shirt." This stop was where Hank really perked up:

the walls were covered with students' drawings of, for some reason, squirrels, and Hank shot off an entire roll of film photographing each one. "Come on, let's keep moving," Melissa said.

"Wait, I've got a question," Holdn said. He jerked a thumb at the tall guy with the goatee. "Does this guy do anything or does he just stand around looking pissed?" he asked.

"He's the one who works for the network," Melissa said. "I just go to school here. Now let's—"

"Wait," Hank interrupted. "Are there any more pictures of squirrels around here I could look at?"

"Look, I'm doing this as a favor to you guys," Melissa said. "If you don't want to go on the tour you can go ahead and leave."

"Can we just kind of look around on our own?" April asked.

"Fine, whatever," Melissa said. "But I'm keeping the fifty bucks."

She and the sullen guy left. "Okay, let's split up and meet back here in twenty minutes," Hayley said. "Hank, please try to get at least one picture I can use for the story."

"All you capitalists care about is use value," Hank muttered.

And now, a taxonomy lesson

On Monday morning I got to computer class early in hopes of slipping into the lab and sneaking in a quick game of Bloodgnarl before the bell rang. Instead I found September and August standing out front, looking like someone had just run over their dog with a riding mower. This put me in a tricky spot. On the one hand, I was really looking forward to firing up the ol' chainsaw and trying to mow down the gang of orcs that stood between me and level nineteen. And I knew that whatever had the two of them so mopey undoubtedly had to do with April and I didn't really want to hear about it. But on the other hand, September was my friend. And I probably wouldn't be able to clear more than the first couple levels before class started anyway. So the answer was obvious. "What's up?" I asked.

"We're having a family crisis," September said.

"April's ticket," August said, "has officially been punched."

"Everyone was up all night arguing," September said.

"And you were there," August said.

"Excuse me?" I said. "I seem to recall being banned from your house. What do you mean I was there?"

"Not for the arguing," August said. "When she put out for weasel-boy. You were there."

"What?" I said. "Um, I don't seem to remember anyone copulating in my vicinity and I'm pretty sure that's the kind of thing I'd probably notice."

"She told us all about it," September said. "That Holdn guy took her to Cathy Nicholls's house—"

"It's Cat," I said.

"Whatever," she said. "And you came over half an hour later, and she went in to wake him up—"

"And ended up sucking him off," August said. "Now I can't look at my kid sister without picturing her picking Holdn Holdnowski's pubic hair out of her teeth."

"Don't be disgusting," September said.

"So with the minty-fresh taste of weasel-boy's little protein shake in her mouth, she goes to the set of *Ashley: The Early Years*," August continued. "Where the tour guide leads her straight to the most famous cot in the history of television and April decides to get her cargo popped the same place Ashley got hers. And you all run off so she can do just that."

"Really?" I said. "But we all went back to the car after twenty minutes and they were already waiting for us in the parking lot. Though now that I think about it, her socks *had* switched colors . . . but still, that left them, what, fifteen minutes tops?"

"That's what she said," September said.

"Sounds like a tender, loving encounter," I said.

"And naturally she decided to tell everyone in the car on the way to church," September said.

"She just announced it?" I asked.

"Not quite," September said. "Julie asked her where she'd gone the day before and she said, 'I went to the set of *Ashley: The Early Years*,' and Julie said, 'Did you meet Holly Madera?,' and April said, 'No, but I lost my virginity,' and Julie asked what it was like but by that time Dad had already pulled the van over. We actually missed church for probably the first time ever."

"And they grounded Julie, which is seriously lame," August said.

"And we went home and everyone ended up arguing for the rest of the day," September said. "Finally she asked Mom and Dad, 'What, did you think I was going to wait till I was *married* or something?' and they said 'Yes' and she said, 'You're such hypocrites! Did *you*?' and they said '*Yes*.' And she came back to our room looking all confused and I asked what was up and she said, 'That's not the way it happened on *Ashley: The Early Years*.'"

The bell rang. September sighed and went inside. "You want to know what the worst part is?" August confided.

"What?" I said.

"Well—" His voice dropped. "This'll probably come as a surprise to you," he said, "but I've never been too successful when it comes to, y'know, girls."

"I'm stunned," I said.

"It's true," he said. "I know I've got a reputation as kind of a ladies' man, but the truth is, I haven't really had all that many dates. Or any, actually. And I came up with a theory. My theory was that girls—not regular girls, but the really attractive and popular ones— are a different species. Them and the guys they hang out with, whether it's the popular jock types like Carver Fringie or the fucked-up rebel types like Holdn Holdnowski. And that's why regular people like us have no chance with them. It'd be like trying to cross a dolphin with a monkey."

By now a steady stream of people were trying to get into the computer lab, so August stepped out of the way. "But then April started to, you know, grow up," he went on. "And by the time she got to junior high it was pretty obvious that she was part of the other species. She was cute, she had tons of friends, she got on the cheer squad, she always had dates—she was a babe, basically. But she lived at my house. And I got to see that really her life wasn't any different from mine. Sure, maybe she ate lunch with all the cool kids while I ate lunch with September or with loser guys whose conversation was pretty much limited to bong construction. And maybe when the phone rang it was for her about ninety percent of the time and me about zero percent of the time. But she was still just a regular person, you know? She came home and watched TV and ate dinner and watched more TV and went to bed just like anyone else. And maybe we weren't exactly friends, but if I ever said something to her, she'd answer me like I was a person and not just ignore me like I was beneath her notice or something. So I discovered that my theory was wrong, that people are just people, that some have more friends and do more fun things but that there's no, you know, *qualitative* difference or anything."

I looked at my watch since the second bell was about to ring. "But now—I mean, come on, I'm never going to have quickie sex with a virgin cheerleader on the set of a TV show," August said. "That kind of thing just doesn't happen to human beings. But Holdn Holdnowski, hey, no problem, happens all the time. And April too. See, I was right the first time. They *are* a different species. Life sucks."

I went inside half a second before the bell rang.

Worse than senseless things

As I walked home that afternoon I found April out in front of the school looking like the guy who'd run over the Youngs' dog with a riding mower had come back the next day, dug up the corpse, and run over it again. "Hey, Allen!" she asked. "Can you give me a ride home? The bus doesn't come for like an hour."

"What about Holdn?" I asked.

"He dropped me," she said, in a voice that couldn't decide whether it wanted to be bitter or heartbroken. "He said I stopped being 'shiny.'"

"Yeah, that'll happen," I said. I kept walking.

April, however, wasn't about to let me leave without getting some fresh-squeezed pity. "That's all?" she said, grabbing my arm. "'That'll happen'?"

"Pretty much," I said. "What'd you expect? Love and companionship and years of beautiful soft-focus sex? That's not Holdn's style. You were his flavor-of-the-week. Lots of people tried to tell you that but you went ahead anyway. And enough bad things happen to people who *don't* deserve it that I'm not about to send the sympathy truck around for you."

"*Deserve* it?" she said. "I deserve to get dumped? What, because I'm 'immoral'? Because I'm 'bad'?"

"No," I said, "because you're rock-stupid. What you did isn't like robbing the poor or hitting your kids. It's more like finding one of those little packets that says '*Do Not Eat*' and sprinkling it on your cereal. The guy came right out and said he was just using you for sex! Everyone tried to warn you he was bad news. I did, September did—"

"September," April sneered, "is the *last* person who should be giving advice about sex. What the hell does she know? She's the biggest deeg in the world. It's like they say, you have to *go* there to *know* there."

"That's cute," I said, "but it's a load of crap. I've never been to Hawaii but I know not to bring a parka if I go. One of the first steps to wisdom is figuring out that you don't have to jump into the pool to find out if there's water in it."

"Isn't learning from your mistakes another part of wisdom?" April countered.

"No, not really," I said. "It's just part of not being an imbecile. *Everyone* learns from their mistakes. *Wise* people learn from the mistakes of others. It would've taken you five minutes of asking around to get the specifics on Holdn's track record. And then you could've dropped *him* and spent your time gloating instead of feeling sorry for yourself. And maybe even saved your virginity for someone who you'll actually see again at some point in the future."

"So that's what this is really about, huh?" she said. "Figures. That's all my parents cared about, too. But then, they pretty much wrote me off once they found out I wasn't going to turn out exactly like May. The perfect one. The one who did things just to be 'good' and never thought for herself."

"As opposed to you, who do things in order to be 'bad' and never think for yourself?" I said. "I don't really know May—the one time I met her she seemed like pretty much your standard-issue priss—but you seem to have fooled yourself into thinking you're the opposite of her when you're the exact same thing in a different shade. And that's all I have to say."

"Whatever," she said. She rolled her eyes and pulled a cigarette out of her backpack. "Do you have a light?" she asked.

I thought for a moment. "You know, I really have to apologize," I said.

"What, for bitching at me?" she said.

"No, for misleading you," I said. "Because I do have one other thing to say."

"What's that?" she asked.

"You're an idiot," I said. "Everything I said before—that was just rhetoric. I didn't really think you were rock-stupid—I just put it that way so you'd pay attention and maybe let it sink in. Because, sure, everyone's curious about sex. Everyone would be interested if someone they thought was cute said they were interested in them. And sure, the guy's a complete anus and no one deserves the treatment you got. But if you can live on this planet for fourteen years—"

"Thirteen," she said smugly. "I skipped a grade."

"—if you can live on this planet long enough to find out that those things cause cancer and emphysema and wrinkles and coughing fits and still force yourself to choke your way through the first couple packs specifically in order to get yourself addicted to them in hopes of impressing a guy who was treating you like a chew toy"—and here I paused since I was out of breath—"then calling you rock-stupid is an insult to rocks."

And with that I was finally rid of April Young. I'm sure she had no idea why I was so pissed off.

And come to think of it, neither do you. So let me explain.

Four

I don't usually think of myself as someone who gets pissed off easily, but those two weeks were an exception. The start of the trend came when Benito assigned Hayley and me Siren Delaney as the third writer on our page. So let's backtrack a bit—and please, keep your hands inside the vehicle until we come to a complete stop.

Poetry slam

"Oh, you have *got* to be kidding me," I said. I'd just gotten a look at the assignment sheet Benito had posted in the *Iliad* room. "Siren Delaney? Benito stuck us with Siren Delaney? She couldn't have had the courtesy to stick us with a trained monkey or a real bright border collie? She has to go right to the bottom of the intellectual ladder?"

"What's the big deal?" Hayley asked. "Aren't all the vague people pretty much the same?"

"No way," I said. "You don't understand. Let me give you an example. Last year in our English class Mrs. Wennikee made us all write a poem, and after giving out the assignment, she got up and gave us ideas of where to start, like you could base it around a piece of wordplay, or some pretty imagery, or a spiffy metaphor or simile, or something like that. So Siren's eyes light up at the simile part and she comes in the next day and her poem goes, 'My boyfriend is nice / Even when I am bitchy / He's just like a sweater / Except he is not itchy.' This is the kind of mental powerhouse we're dealing with. She's such an idiot she forgets to open doors before trying to walk though them."

"Well, she can't be that bad or she'd never have been recommended for the *Iliad*," Hayley reasoned.

"If only that were true," I said. "But Mrs. Wennikee pretty much makes up her mind who she likes in the first five minutes of the school year and if she likes you then you get a good grade. That poem Siren wrote? She got an A. Mrs. Wennikee said 'its use of polysyllabic rhyme is very sophisticated.' And you can't say I'm just being bitter, because I got the same treatment. I turned in a poem that went, 'Once upon a time there was a cat / That purred and meowed and stuff like that' just to see what she'd do, and it came back with the comment, 'Very Eastern and refined. Excellent use of the traditional seventeen syllables to capture the subject. A plus.' She would've given me an A plus no matter what I'd turned in. I still can't figure out why she liked *Siren*, though. I mean, in my case it was obviously my raw animal sexuality that did the trick, but you can't say Siren got preferential treatment because she's cute, because she *isn't* cute. She looks like a freak. And she's an *idiot*. They made us all go to the career center and the first question they asked us was what our current career plans were and Siren said she was going to be a Laker Girl. And then we filled out these mile-long Scantrons and fed them into a computer and it spit out the results and the printout said that the career Siren was *actually* best suited for was—Laker Girl."

"Really?" Hayley said.

"Yup," I said. "Of course, it also said *I* was best suited to be a Laker Girl, so the program might've had a few bugs."

"What about Echo?" Hayley asked.

"I don't think she'd make a very good Laker Girl," I said.

"I was thinking more about the first part," Hayley said. "I have to admit I'm curious about what a poem by Echo Mockery would look like."

"Same here," I said. "She refused to show it to me. But I'm pretty sure she got an A. It made Mrs. Wennikee cry."

Fired up

Now when I say Echo's poem made Mrs. Wennikee cry, I don't mean she was dabbing at the corners of her eyes with a tissue. I mean she had so much mascara streaming down her face that it looked like she was doing a vaudeville blackface act. We were all taking one of the five hundred standardized tests required by the state as she was reading our poems, and when she went over to ask Echo if she could read it for the class the next day—Echo said no, of course—Siren looked up from her Scantron and you could see her just seethe.

And Mrs. Wennikee wasn't even the faculty member who liked Echo best. That honor went to the one and only Doctor Dennis Todd. See, around the time September and I were finishing up our training sessions for peer counseling, Doctor Todd had got it in his head that we were all morgue bait if disaster were ever to strike. "Must have drills," he would mutter to himself. "Fire. Earthquake. Nukular attack. Woefully unprepared. Massive casualties. Worse than eating in car. Must be remedied. Yes." So he soon instituted a policy of twice-weekly disaster drills. For the earthquake drills we huddled under our desks; for the "nukular attack" drills we did the same thing, except shielding ourselves with pieces of paper to ward off those deadly alpha rays; and for the fire drills we were expected to calmly march out to the field. "USE EXTERIOR EXITS ONLY!" Doctor Todd would bark over the intercom. "INTERIOR EXITS TO WHEEL LEAD ONLY TO CENTER OF RAGING INFERNO IN ACTUAL FIRE EMERGENCY!"

Once we were all out on the field aimlessly milling about, Doctor Todd and Uta Himmler would storm onto the field with megaphones to restore order. On the day when Echo won Doctor Todd's everlasting love and admiration, his attempt to get everyone to line up was no more successful than usual. "LINE UP ALPHABETICALLY BY CLASS! FOUR LINES!" Dr. Todd insisted. "IT IS FOR YOUR OWN BENEFIT! IN REAL FIRE, YOU WILL BE REPORTED DEAD IF NOT FOUND IN PROPER PLACE IN LINE! SPARE YOUR FAMILIES UNNECESSARY ANGUISH!"

"Yeah, I'm sure Krieg'd be all torn up inside," I said.

Echo said something in reply but it was drowned out by a shrill blast from Uta's megaphone—someone had had the misfortune to bring a sandwich to the fire drill. *"NO EATING!"* Uta shrieked.

"LINE UP ALPHABETICALLY BY CLASS," Doctor Todd repeated. "YOU WILL NOT BE DISMISSED UNTIL YOU LINE UP ALPHABETICALLY BY CLASS. I SPENT FORTY-EIGHT HOURS WAITING OUT A TEAM OF GUERRILLAS IN SOUTH AMERICA AND I CAN OUTWAIT YOU!"

Nevertheless, few seemed inclined to line up alphabetically by class. Everyone just stood around talking to friends and smelling the grass cook in the hot October sun. After all, the lunch bell was coming up and then we were all free to go, dismissal or no dismissal. But we'd forgotten what happened every day five minutes before lunch.

Right on schedule the sprinklers went off. Big, industrial-strength ones, black discs embedded in the ground that shot water eight feet into the air. Nineteen hundred students went screaming for cover in the building. "DO NOT LEAVE!" Doctor Todd bellowed. "FIRE DRILL STILL IN PROGRESS! BUILDING HYPOTHETICALLY ENGULFED IN FLAMES! WATER OFFERS CRUCIAL PROTEC-TION!" That was the last thing I heard, since I was much more willing to take my chances with hypothetical flames than with gallons and gallons of nonhypothetical water. Besides, the building was where the nine hundred and fifty sopping-wet girls were going and obviously I couldn't miss *that*.

The lunch bell rang and it was about then that I realized that in the crush to get away from the big wet I'd lost track of Echo. Which normally wouldn't have concerned me all that much except that I had a pretty good idea of where she was. I retraced my steps and made it back outside just as the sprinklers were dying down, and sure enough, Echo was standing in the middle of the field as if nothing had happened. Her bulky black sweatshirt was soaked through and looked like it weighed about four hundred pounds.

"Excellent. Excellent," said a dripping Doctor Todd. "Exemplary discipline. Will be Student of the Month. Sole survivor of horrible conflagration. Excellent. Who are you?"

"Nobody in particular," Echo said. She wiped the water out of her eyes. "Are we dismissed yet?"

"Certainly," Doctor Todd said. "Commendations. Excellent performance."

"Or at least some kind of performance," I said. The grass had been all squishy as I'd started walking toward them but forty seconds later the ground had soaked up all the water and the field was dry again. "What's up? Why are you still out here?"

"I didn't have anywhere in particular to go," Echo said coldly.

"You know this student?" Doctor Todd asked me.

"You might say that," I said. "She's my sister. She pulls this kind of stunt every so often. I'm not sure what it's supposed to prove, but I guess everyone has to have some annoying quirks."

"Yes," Echo said. "Like talking about people as if they're not standing right there." She stalked off. As it turned out, that was the last fire drill ever held at Ilium High—not because of the sprinklers, but because the guy who got yelled at for bringing the sandwich sued the school for causing irreversible hearing damage.

In any event, it came as no surprise when Doctor Todd named Echo as Student of the Month for October. It was somewhat more of a surprise when she was named as Student of the Month for November as well. The December award was even more of a surprise. The January, February, March, and April awards were progressively less surprising as it became increasingly apparent that when Doctor Todd said Echo was going to be Student of the Month, he meant Student of Every Month.

So as we were finishing up our tests and Mrs. Wennikee was trying to fix her makeup, it was pretty obvious what Doctor Todd was about to announce when he broke in over the intercom system. "ATTENTION ALL STUDENTS," he said. "AM PLEASED TO ANNOUNCE STUDENT OF THE MONTH FOR MAY IS ECHO MOCKERY. ECHO MOCKERY MAY PICK UP AWARD IN FRONT OFFICE AFTER SCHOOL. THAT IS ALL."

"Looks like another certificate for the stack," I whispered to Echo.

"No talking during the test," Mrs. Wennikee said.

"So what's the deal?" Siren Delaney whispered. Her freakishly big eyes were shining with hatred. "Are you sucking him off or what?"

"Excuse me?" Echo said.

"No talking," Mrs. Wennikee said.

"That's what the part about the front office is about, right?" Siren hissed. "You go up there and suck him off and he puts you down for the next month's award, right?"

Echo's face went dark.

"People, this is your last warning," Mrs. Wennikee said. "No talking during the test. If you're exchanging answers you'll be in a world of trouble."

The guy who sat behind me cleared his throat. "Uh, can I go to the bathroom?" he asked.

"That's a detention," Mrs. Wennikee said. "I said no talking."

"So does he at least give you a breath mint when you're done?" Siren asked. "Some mouthwash maybe?"

I looked over at Echo. She was literally holding on to her desk to keep herself from springing for Siren Delaney's throat. "You'll regret this," she said quietly.

"What, you'll make sure I never get voted Student of the Month?" Siren said. "You're breaking my fucking heart."

They glared at each other so intensely I was pretty sure that at least one of their heads was going to explode. Luckily, the bell picked that moment to ring. "Pencils down," Mrs. Wennikee sighed.

It rubs the lotion on its skin

"So basically what I'm saying is, this is seriously lame," I said. "Siren Delaney is exactly who Zab would be if she were a couple years younger and had ever heard of fluoride. Can't we trade her to Zab's page for whoever Zab got assigned and maybe a second-round draft pick?"

"You can ask Benito, but I doubt she'll go for it," Hayley said.

"It's worth a shot," I said. I went to go talk to Benito. She was sitting at her desk grading papers. Unlike Mrs. Wennikee, whose grading method consisted of nothing more than looking at the name at the top of each paper, Benito threw in an interval of scowling at each paper before checking the name and giving the grade. "Hayley and I need to trade writers with somebody," I said. "We can't work with who we got."

"Tough," Benito said.

"But the assignments just went out," I said. "You can still change them and no one'll ever know. It'd make everyone involved a lot happier."

"I don't care," Benito said.

"Why not?" I asked.

"Don't whine," she said.

"You know, you're going to be the first one up against the wall when the revolution comes," I said.

Now the next problem was that Siren was taking journalism as an independent-study class, since it was offered the same period as her main elective: cheerleading. I'd also managed to avoid getting her in any of my classes, so I never really saw her except occasionally in passing. I sent her some e-mail over the campus computer network describing her assignment, with instructions to get it in sometime the following week, but the next week came and went and when I came in on Monday morning there was nary a story to be found either in our box in the *Iliad* room or in our inbox on the computer system. Now like I said, I don't usually think of myself as someone who gets pissed off easily, but this was one more aggravation I didn't need.

I was eating lunch in the *Iliad* room when Hayley came in. "Hey," she said, "did—"

"No," I said. "I didn't get my license. I flunked the test."

"I heard," Hayley said. "That's not what I was going to ask. Did Siren Delaney get her story in?"

"Oh," I said. "Uh, no. Can't you take care of it? I hate her."

"Too bad," Hayley said. "I had to go through all this last year when Benito tried to stick that Sluggo guy on entertainment and I'm not going through it again."

So when Hayley ordered me the next day to call Siren out of practice and find out what was taking so long, I couldn't really weasel out of it. It was near the end of school, though, and as I got to the gym I ran into Hank coming out. "Are they still practicing?" I asked.

"No," he said. "They went to the locker room already. I was just taking a picture of the refuse under the bleachers. I call it 'The Trickle-Down Theory.'"

"Swell," I said. "Okay, thanks."

I took a look inside the gym just to make sure Siren hadn't been left behind, but the place was empty. The girls' locker room was right across the blacktop but there were a bunch of dweeby guys hanging out front trying to peep in the door every time it opened; I didn't really want to be associated with them, so I hung back. It didn't help. As Siren strode out of the locker room, accompanied as always by her entourage—Missy Schaeffer, Shelby Streicht, and usually one other random girl—she walked past the dweeby guys and right toward me. "Looking for a cheap thrill?" she sneered.

"Say what?" I said. "What are you talking about? I wasn't anywhere near the door. Look, I need to talk to you."

"Yeah, *that's* gonna happen," she said. Her groupies giggled and they walked out the gate.

So that probably could've gone better. Luckily, the bell rang and spared me from having to face Hayley's wrath right away. But that meant that the next day I'd still have to track Siren down before Hayley found me. I managed to get a copy of her schedule from Doctor Todd and found that she had chemistry right before morning break; I figured I could sign myself out of English five minutes early on "peer counselor business," hustle over to the chem room, and intercept her on the way out. Still, I wasn't happy about it. There's something about hanging around doorways waiting for someone to come out that just screams "demented stalker." All I needed was a love letter to Jodie Foster and a well-thumbed copy of *The Catcher in the Rye*.

I'd expected to have to head-fake a couple of her friends out of the way but to my surprise Siren was alone when she came out. "Uh, hi," I said. I had to walk at a pretty good clip to keep up with her. "Wait up—I need to talk to you for a second."

"I'll make this easy for you," she said. "No, I won't go out with you. No, I won't marry you. No, I won't be the mother of your children. Okay?"

I heard a couple people sniggering and made a mental note never to clear a red ticket for anyone who had chemistry second period. "I'm not trying to ask you out," I said. "Do you have any idea who I am?"

She looked over her shoulder. "Yeah," she said. "You're one of those losers that follows me around everywhere trying to check out my ass."

More sniggering. We were almost out the door at this point so I gave up on any prospect for a conversation. "Look, you were supposed to turn in a story for the *Iliad* on Friday," I said. "Where is it?"

Siren flipped me off and strolled out to the wheel. At that moment I would've given anything for a gigantic bird of prey to swoop down and carry her off, but it didn't happen.

By Friday the situation was getting ridiculous. I made the mistake of walking into the *Iliad* room just as Hayley was putting the finishing touches on our layout sheet, complete with a big white spot where Siren's article was supposed to go. Hayley gave me about thirty seconds to finish my lunch before sending me out to bring Siren in to explain herself. So I went out to the wheel to go look. She wasn't hard to find: like I said, she looked like a freak. Her hair was about eight times bigger than the rest of her body, her eyes were grotesquely big like in a Japanese cartoon, and her lips looked like she'd heard the bee-stung look was in again and gone off and sucked on a hive. So it wasn't like you could miss her in a crowd. On the bright side, she was only about five-one and weighed maybe ninety-two pounds, so while it was true that she was a waste of space, at least she wasn't wasting much.

I found her sitting on a bench out on the wheel watching the student government guys playing volleyball. (They usually set up the net about an hour before lunch started and played till the end of school— like September and me, they had the power to sign themselves out of classes.) I was pleased to find that she had a big ugly bruise on her wrist—apparently there was at least some justice in this world. She was surrounded by her acolytes, as usual; I couldn't help but notice that she was the only one of them who wasn't blond. "Do you have a couple minutes?" I asked.

"Yeah," she said, "but I think I'm gonna keep them."

"Look, what is your *deal*?" I asked. "All I've been asking for this whole week has been one lousy minute to talk about the work you're supposed to have done for a class you signed up for! A lot of people are counting on you getting your work done and one of them's me and I'm getting really sick of you really fast!"

"Don't have an aneurysm," she said. "Are you one of those people that washes your hands every couple minutes too?"

Right then Fringie sauntered over to pick up Shelby for lunch—you'll remember that he didn't end up dropping her till the following day. "Hey, Shel," he said. "Ready to go?" Noticing that I looked like I was about to kick Siren in the face, he added, "Hey, what's going on?"

"Hey, Carver," Siren said. "This guy keeps bugging me about some story or something. *I* don't know. *You're* smart, you figure it out."

"It's *Iliad* business," I said. "Her story's a week late. All she has to do is throw four or five paragraphs together. I've been trying to ask her about it but she keeps blowing me off."

"Is that true?" Fringie asked. "A week late?"

"*I* don't know," Siren said. "I guess. I can't keep track of all this school stuff. I wouldn't have blown him off if he would've just been nicer."

"Nicer?" I said. "*Nicer?* What the hell are you talking ab—"

"Hey, hey, calm down," Fringie said. "I'm sure we can work this whole thing out. Now, Siren, have you even started the article yet?"

"I've got some notes and stuff," she said.

"Okay, and when do you need the finished article by?" Fringie asked.

"Last week," I said. "'If I would've been *nicer*'? That's not even grammatically corr—"

"You're not being very helpful," Fringie said. "How about this? Siren, you try to turn in something after school, and Al, you ease off a little and cut the kid some slack. Does that sound reasonable?"

"Gee, Dad, I never thought of it that way," I said.

"Excellent," Fringie said. "My work here is done. C'mon, Shel, I'm starved."

i thought i told you never to call me here

When I got back to the *Iliad* room after helping September clean up after the sandwich incident, I explained the situation to Hayley: Siren's continued obnoxious behavior, Fringie's intervention, Siren's sudden IQ drop in his presence, the agreement to turn in at least *something* after school. Yet shockingly enough, when I checked back at the *Iliad* room after peer counseling, Siren still hadn't turned in her story, or her notes, or anything. I wasn't beaten yet, though. There was a list of phone numbers for every member of the *Iliad* staff posted on the wall, and I had an access code for the phone. So I called her house.

The phone rang once before it was picked up. "Carol Cameron," said the voice on the other end. It was the voice of someone with a tracheostomy in her near future.

"Uh, hi," I said. "It looks like I may have the wrong number, but is Siren Delaney there by any chance . . . ?"

A long pause. In South America, regimes rose and fell. "Who is this?" she finally asked.

There was a click. "I've got it, Mom," came Siren's voice. "Hi, Brad."

"I'm waiting for an answer," her mother said.

"Sorry," I said. "I'm—"

"Mom, I said I've *got* it," Siren said. "Hang up the phone."

"Don't you dare use that tone with me," her mother growled.

"Why do you always do this?" Siren hissed. "Hang up the fucking phone. I've been expecting this call all week. Can't you just once let me talk on the phone without—"

There was a rattle and another click. "Uh, hello?" I said.

"I know you're still listening," Siren said. "You're not fooling anyone. For God's sake, just hang up."

There was another pause and then a third click. "Okay, I think she's gone," Siren said. "You're gonna pick me up at seven, right?"

"Uh, no," I said. "This is Allen, you know, from the *Iliad,* and I was just—"

"Oh, you've gotta be shitting me," Siren said.

"Umm—"

"Do you have any idea how much shit I'm going to catch for this?" Siren asked. "Do you? Do you have any idea? And for *you?*"

I decided that it probably wasn't in my best interest to answer that question. "Look, you said you had some notes—"

"They're in my locker, okay?" she said. "I'll get it sometime next week."

"Yeah, but you see, the paper actually comes *out* next—"

"And I could give a fuck," she said. She hung up. It was then that I knew that Hayley was going to kill me.

Of course, that was assuming she got the chance, which didn't seem very likely when, as I was walking up the driveway on my way home, the house blew up. Or at least that's what it sounded like. I figured out that the house hadn't actually exploded when a couple seconds had passed and I hadn't yet been buried in flying bits of plaster, but the sound alone was enough to knock me to the pavement. I brushed myself off and went inside to look around—I figured that maybe it'd just been the oven or the dishwasher that'd blown up. But before I could even get to the kitchen there was another explosion, even louder than the first, and this time I could tell exactly where it was coming from: Krieg's room. That's when I get scared, because Krieg plus loud explosions equals bad news.

I dashed upstairs to see what was going on, but when I opened the door, Krieg was nowhere to be found. Nor did there seem to be any more than the usual damage—the mysterious stains on the walls, the missing closet door, the boarded-up window. After I'd adjusted to the stench, I picked my way over the heaps of beer cans and porn mags and month-old half-eaten pizzas and drew aside the curtain surrounding Jerem's bed. "Are you the one making that noise?" I asked.

Jerem squinted at me in bewilderment. At nine, he was the youngest of us Mockery kids and by far the palest—mainly because it'd been years since he'd been exposed to direct sunlight, but partly because of genetics. Being more or less pan racial, we had the potential for any or all of the major strains of skin pigmentation—brown, gold, or pink: I'd wound up with enough of the brown type that most people assumed that my ancestry was at least half African and probably more; Molly's skin was pure shining gold; Echo had landed somewhere in between us and ended up bronze as a statuette. And Jerem, while he somewhat resembled me facially—just as I still got the twelve-and-under menu when we went to restaurants, Jerem got asked if he needed a booster seat—had a light pink complexion and sandy brown hair. As for Krieg, well, it was hard to tell what he looked like underneath all the acne.

"Oh, sorry," Jerem said. "I just got to the level on Bloodgnarl with the intercontinental ballistic missiles. I'll turn it down." The phone rang. Jerem checked his cell phone. "It's not mine," he said. "You better get that."

He reached under the bed and tossed me a phone belonging to the main house line; I hit the TALK button. "Hello?" I said.

It was, of course, Hayley. "Did you get that story?" she asked.

"Well," I said, "it's funny you should ask that, because—"

"You didn't get it," she said.

"There's nothing to get," I said. "She's got some notes in her locker, that's about it. Can't you or I just write something over the weekend to fill the space? Or put in an ad or something?"

"A few issues ago, maybe," Hayley said. "Ever since Benito put Peggy Kaylin's grading system into place, if one of our assigned writers is missing from our page, *we* get graded down. And we haven't had anything to advertise ever since Holdn lost the Fred's Quality Footwear account."

"Fine, so we write something and attribute it to her," I said.

"Wouldn't work," Hayley said. "If we were found out we'd get booted off the paper with failing marks in journalism for the rest of the year. And we'd probably get suspended from school too. And we *would* get found out because Delaney herself could tell on us. You're just going to have to get those notes and piece them together."

"How?" I said. "She'll never come down and get them for me. And now that they have that whole alarm system set up I can't exactly break into her locker."

"Sure you can," Jerem said.

Forgive us our trespasses

"It's easy," Jerem said. He pressed a few keys and soon we'd broken into the Ilium High School computer system. "Their security is a joke," he said.

"I'm not so sure about this," I said.

"Don't worry," he said. "It's completely untraceable. Not only will they not know who broke in, they won't even know they've been broken into. Nothing's being altered, we're just looking at stuff. Unless you want to change some of her grades or something. Want to?"

"No," I said. "That's not what I meant. This is pretty unethical, don't you think?"

"If they didn't want you to do it, they shouldn't have made it so easy to do," he said. "What's her last name?"

I spelled out her last name. Jerem typed it in. "Locker 317, combination 43-49-25," he said. "Wear gloves."

So later that evening after I was sure the campus would be deserted I decided to give it a try. I couldn't find any gloves in the house (who wears gloves?) so I just put some sandwich bags on my hands on the off chance that leaving fingerprints on Siren's locker would turn out at some point in the future to be a bad idea. It was a cloudy and therefore very bright night, the kind of night that tricks you into thinking you can see just fine until you actually try to look at something. I clambered over the gate into the wheel and set about finding locker 317. It didn't take very long—as it happened, it turned out to be right under one of the sodium lights. I dialed up 43-49-25, pulled on the latch, and opened the little metal door. That was when I received my first surprise.

Her locker was stuffed to capacity with all kinds of junk that had nothing to do with school. There were old books (though I couldn't make out any of the titles in the darkness) and trinkets (bracelets and prize ribbons and even an old pocket watch) and three stuffed animals (a bear, a lamb, and an amorphous orange thing that may or may not have actually qualified as an animal). The walls seemed to be covered with pictures, but I could only see little bits of them because of all the stuff in the way. It was too dark to make out any details inside the locker anyway. Suddenly I sensed that someone was standing directly behind me. I froze. Shortly thereafter I realized that standing still didn't make me any less visible to the cop or whoever it was standing behind me, so I figured I might as well turn around to see who it was. It was only the clock tower. Still, it spooked me enough to get moving; I could always come back and explore the contents of Siren's locker some other time, preferably one less scary.

Siren had about half a dozen spiral notebooks crammed in among her memorabilia; I pulled one out to take a look. I opened it up, held it up to the light, and squinted at the first page. Her handwriting was extremely florid without being at all bubbly: it was way too convoluted to classify as elegant, but there was a certain aesthetic appeal in all the unexpected loops and arcs and serifs. It was also practically illegible, especially in the dim trickle of light leaking out of the sodium lamp. This was hopeless. I grabbed all six notebooks and shut the door. I figured I'd sort them out when I got home and then return them Saturday morning.

I climbed back over the gate and hopped the fence back to Hyacinth Avenue. The porch light at Peggy's house was on; I had a sudden urge to make a visit, but I'd have a hard time explaining the stack of notebooks I was carrying and Peggy wouldn't be home on a Friday night anyway. Dooj's dog was still running around and around and around in the backyard as I passed his house, always a good thing. I walked up my driveway, inside through the garage door, and upstairs to my room.

Muy importante indeed

I hopped up on my bed, picked the first notebook up off the stack, and flipped it open. It was full of math problems. The second one was more promising: it at least had words in it. The problem was, I couldn't read any of them. Siren's handwriting was pretty much indecipherable. That is, until I realized I was trying to decipher it into the wrong language; once I made the switch, it was perfectly obvious that the first line read, *"Un burro es un animal muy importante."* Not that that helped me any.

Notebook number three had the advantage of being in English, but since the intricacies of the Mayan calendar were somewhat low on my list of concerns, it wasn't what I was looking for. And number four was just strange. The first page read:

The Admittedly Sporadic Yet Undeniably Historical Chronicle of
SARAH JASON DELANEY THE INTREPID, Adventurer, and Her
Captivity in the Wilds of Uncharted California

I looked up, half-expecting to find a gigantic question mark hovering over my head. This obviously wasn't the notes to her story for the *Iliad*. Still, I was intrigued. I turned the page.

June 25. A terrible anniversary—another full year in captivity has come and gone. In my darker moments I fear I shall never again return to my native shores, yet while truly this land is barbarous and untamed, and the natives have proven themselves exceptionally hostile, never let it be said that Sarah Jason Delaney the Intrepid let her circumstances break her spirit. With the aid of my trusty secret journal, I am certain I can see through the next year, and beyond if need be. Indeed, my chronicle may well provide the public with instruction and delight upon my eventual return to the warm embrace of my homeland.

June 30. Though this is truly a fearsome and savage land, it is not without its pleasures. I went out to get the mail this afternoon and the driveway was glittering as if it were full of crushed diamonds, and when I stepped out onto it I burned my feet. Luckily for me the lawn had just been sprinkled so I just cut through the grass. But that's not even the good part. I went out for my walk at 9:30 or so and the air had a definite chill in it—it hadn't retained any of the afternoon heat at all. But the street had. It was like walking on a pile of laundry fresh from the dryer. The asphalt was even kind of soft from melting in the sun all day. It felt like you could smoosh your toes into it. At least, you could if you were barefoot, which of course I was because, truly, shoes are an abomination. And there's more. You could feel the heat radiating up out of the ground instead of down from the sky, and when I closed my eyes I felt like I was upside down, walking on the ceiling with Velcro boots. I felt sad when I had to open them again.

July 3. I noticed something today. I was on my usual walk down to the mental health center when I heard a buzzing, crackling sound all around me, and the air itself felt ionized, electric. And though I looked all around I couldn't see where it was coming from—it was a quiet summer evening, no cars were passing, no one was around but me. Then I looked up and found where the crackling was coming from: the phone lines. And that got me thinking about phone lines in general. Not about the conversations burbling back and forth along them, or the way my exposure to them while they were acting up is sure to leave me cancer-ridden and sterile, but about the phone lines themselves. They're everywhere. Look up and the sky is crisscrossed with them. It's hideous, it's sky pollution. And I'd never noticed before. In all my years of captivity I never noticed there were phone lines along Rose Drive—my mind just edited them out. In a way, it's scary—what else am I not noticing?—but in another way, I wish I'd never noticed, because now I'll always be aware of the phone lines, and my world just got that much uglier.

July 7. As with every summer, it isn't long before the disappearances begin. This time around it was fairly significant, as when I went to take a few dollars of my babysitting money from its hiding place, it was gone, all $70 of it. When I asked the Queen about it she said she didn't know anything about it and made some lewd suggestions about what I'd done to get it. I suppose it's my fault, truly, for after nine months with the luxury of a locker in which to hide my worldly possessions, I grew rather careless once I had to go back to hiding them around the house. Life would be so much easier if only there were even a single native I felt I could trust to take care of my things for me, but I haven't been able to become close enough with any of them to be able to ask for such an imposition. Far from it—they scorn me if ever I try to even say hello. It would be going too far to say I face overt hostility from my native coevals, but I seem destined to remain locked out of their circles. Which may well be for the best—at least that way I can maintain the customs of my homeland with no fear that they shall be adulterated by the ways of this savage place.

July 12. Visitation Day! Once again I am summarily escorted to the quarters of the King of the Savages for my monthly visit. This time around he spent most of the day watching some car race on television. I looked around for the painting I gave him last time, but couldn't find it anywhere—I almost asked him where it was but I decided I didn't want to know. Then we got dinner at the Taco Junta and he took me back to the Queen's. It was pretty early and she still had some friends over for another one of their scotch-a-thons, and I had to go through the living room to get to my room, and when I did they stopped talking and stared at me as I walked past. And then when I got to the hallway I heard them snickering. I didn't stop to listen to whatever it was they were saying about me. Now I'm an adventurer and not an anthropologist, but those of an ethnographic bent should note that the natives here apparently stop maturing around middle school. Truly, they are a backward people.

July 13. I love you I love you I love you I love you I love you I love you I love you I love you

July 16. Went into my room to find the Queen going through my desk. Royal prerogative, apparently: privacy is not one of the rights accorded to captives of the tribe. She said that I'd stolen a pair of her earrings and she was looking for them. Kind of an odd thing for me to steal since my ears aren't even pierced, but since we obviously both knew it was a lie it didn't really matter how nonsensical a lie it was.

July 22. Walked up to that café on Imperial for lunch today since I was starving and there was no food in the house except for two bottles of vodka and some pesto. As I was ordering I couldn't help noticing the most beautiful boy in the history of the world sitting by himself at one of the tables and I would've done anything to have him come talk to me . . . I know that he was a little older than me and we probably didn't have anything in common to talk about, but anything would've been fine . . . we could talk about his hair or something . . . but then two seconds later this girl sat down at his table and she was tall and thin and beautiful and they were obviously seeing each other and it didn't matter anyway because I'm me and he never would've talked to me in the first place. Especially not with the ugly swollen lip I collected yesterday for not taking out the trash quick enough. I've been Sarah Jason Delaney the Rueful the whole rest of the day. Which is truly somewhat odd because that's one area where I don't really have much to complain about—during the school year I get asked out at least a couple times a month. Just not by anyone good. Brad Chasintek's not bad-looking and he's asked me out twice but I heard him talking to his friends and the whole reason he's interested in me is because he thinks (to use his words) my ass is cute. Truly, these natives' mating rituals are primitive at best.

July 25. I got caught today. The Queen just opened my bedroom door and walked in on me. No, not that. It's much more embarrassing than that. See, the finest day that I've ever had was when I learned that there was a cold place inside me, right next to my heart, and when I was maybe four years old, I discovered that all I had to do was concentrate on that place and tears would spontaneously stream down my cheeks. And the feeling is delicious. Especially when I watch. That's the whole reason I asked for a mirror to put over my dresser all those years ago—so I could stare into it and watch myself cry. And today I got caught. Naturally, I got slapped around, as if she'd just caught me in bed with a boy or something; for truly it is not without reason that she is Queen of the Savages. Unfortunately, while I am in fact an intrepid adventurer, I am not quite as intrepid a linguist. One of these days I'll have to find out what that quaint native phrase "I'll give you something to cry about" means. It certainly seems to be a popular saying.

July 26. I long to have a songbird that would sing a single song and that would sing a dirge for Sarah for her soul is nearly gone and if it sounds as if I'm whining well I think I have the right because it's your fault I'm so heartsick on a dreamy summer night

July 28. I will not get depressed. I am determined not to get depressed. I will not let myself get depressed. I refuse to let myself get depressed. I refuse. I refuse. Intrepid adventurers can stand up to anything. Intrepid adventurers do not get depressed. I am an intrepid adventurer. Therefore I cannot get depressed. The logic in this is perfect, exquisite, and absolute.

July 31.
> *My rescuer, though you've tracked me*
> *To Hades so diligently*
> *I cannot follow you to where*
> *The sunlight sings through crystal air*
> *—a place that I shall never see.*

In flowered fields a young girl plays
How young, how long? Who counts the days?
But then the earth did Dis rip wide
The world was ripped from side to side
—a force I could not keep at bay.

He grabbed me, dragged me underground
The air was thick, I felt the sound
And squinted through the sickly light
At shades that death could not requite
—'twas this place he did show me round.

He offered then to make me queen
Of his realm dark and serene
But howsoever much I wept
He gave me no choice but accept
—though scarce twelve summers had I seen.

What's that you say? Feel no remorse?
No weight have bargains made by force?
My rescuer, do you not see
The change that has come over me
—from Kore to Persephone?

Dis, I know, you much despise—
His bloody hands! His vacant eyes!—
Those hated eyes! See you not how
Their twins, mine, gaze upon you now?
This gloomy realm is mine as well!
Reality breaks childhood's spell!
The world above may not be heaven;
The underworld is surely hell!
Yet my home is this realm below,
For I have nowhere else to go.
To Lord of Darkness I am bride,
Bound to the kingdom of the dead;

On fruits of Hades having fed,
I reign forever by his side.

I turned the page. The rest of the notebook was blank.

I picked up the fifth notebook. Inside I found a bunch of half-paragraphs and sentence fragments that, rearranged and sewn together, combined to make a passable but wholly unremarkable story for the *Iliad* entertainment page. I was disappointed. I expected better of the girl that I was completely and hopelessly in love with.

i want to decide who lives and who dies

But I'm getting ahead of myself here—I wasn't completely and hopelessly in love with her at this point, not yet. Rather, what I felt was a strong sense of cognitive dissonance. For the girl who had written this journal I felt nothing but lovingkindness: I can't say I was especially impressed with her verse or with the profundity of her observations, but her spirit nonetheless seemed to me very beautiful. On the other hand, when I thought of Siren Delaney, I wanted nothing more than to see her head on a pike.

I toyed with the idea that they were actually different people: even though the handwriting was awfully similar to that in the other notebooks and the journal itself seemed relatively fresh, there was no year indicated anywhere. Maybe it was actually fifteen years old and had just been well preserved, and Sarah was a long-dead sister who Siren had been intended to replace. Or maybe she was a cousin of Siren's who went to another school and Siren had stolen her journal at the last family reunion out of spite. Either way, it was better than having to accept that this glorious girl had grown up to become the poster child for postnatal abortion whom we'd all come to know and loathe.

Then the answer dawned on me. Obviously, the whole "Siren" persona was just an act she'd come up with to deal with her environment. Sarah hadn't gone anywhere: she just didn't show her real self to people anymore for fear of getting hurt. Perfectly understandable. She might even still be keeping a diary somewhere. And that was the best possibility of all, since it meant that all I'd have to do would be to get through to her somehow and Sarah could live again. The only tricky part was figuring out the best way to do that. Thus, my first course of action was to assemble a crack research and development team and set them to the task of finding the answer.

I already had a number of candidates in mind for the team, the first of whom lived a few feet away from me. Not Echo—her plan for dealing with Siren would undoubtedly call for too much bloodshed. No, this was a job for Molly. So Saturday morning right after I woke up I knocked on the wall. "You up?" I asked.

"I'm awake," she said. "'Up' is another question altogether." I heard the remote-control lock on her door click open, so I went next door.

Molly's room was tiny compared to the other bedrooms in the house, but she liked it because, being the corner room, it had big panoramic windows along both the north and east walls. It was a high-gloss white room with white curtains and white carpeting and a white emperor-size bed that took up 95 percent of the floor space. It was also the only room in the house that wasn't air-conditioned twenty-four hours a day; Molly even had her own heater to make sure that the room stayed a toasty eighty-four degrees. This probably would have been uncomfortably hot if not for the fact that when she was at home Molly refused to wear any clothing whatsoever.

Her logic ran something like this: "Look, people only wear clothing for two reasons. One is protection from the elements. Which is a consideration when you're living in a cave in northern Europe, but not so much when you're living in a house in Southern California with central heating. And the other is shame. And I don't have any of that." Of course, she was leaving out the third reason: fear of arrest. Which is why she (extremely reluctantly) wore clothes to go to school. But even then she made sure they were extremely hideous ones.

Most people who've heard about Molly's dress code have assumed that it must've been really weird for the rest of us who lived with her—Peggy was scandalized enough that it was near the top of her list of reasons why she practically never came to my house—but it really wasn't that big a deal. First of all, this wasn't something she'd suddenly come up with one day; she'd had this policy for as long as anyone could remember, certainly before she was old enough to be able to articulate reasons for it. She just refused to wear clothes around the house and was lucky enough to have had parents who didn't force her to. And second, there wasn't really anything provocative about it: even at age thirteen, she was still basically just a kid. Her chest could certainly have passed for a boy's, albeit a boy with a serious endocrine disturbance. So no one really seemed to pay it much mind. Bobbo had been kind of freaked out when he first moved in, but he got over it.

Facially, Molly looked sort of like an Egyptian painting: all her features were long. Her face was long, her eyes were long, her nose was long (not unattractively so, but certainly a departure from the delicate little instrument sported by Echo and Jerem and me), and the corners of her mouth seemed to go on forever. Her coloring was golden, with dark eyelids and lips and areoles, and her eyes, through some sort of genetic quirk, were bright green; her hair was a medium brown, and she'd recently let it grow out a bit—it would've gone past her shoulders, but it flared out at the ends before flaring back in to brush the base of her neck. The result left her looking a little like she was wearing one of those wigs that they slap on twenty-five-year-old TV actresses when they're doing flashback episodes and need to make them look thirteen. Since Molly actually *was* thirteen, it looked just fine. She yawned and sat up as I came in. "What's up?" she asked.

I handed her Siren's diary. "Read this," I said.

She read it. "What do you think?" I asked.

"She stole the last part of the poem from Coleridge," she said.

"Okay, let me tell you the story behind it," I said. I did. "So what should I do?" I asked.

"Depends," Molly said. "What makes you think you should do anything? What're you trying to achieve?"

"I dunno," I said. "I mean, I'm intrigued. I have warm feelings for the girl who wrote these pages. But I honestly don't think that it's just that I want her as a love interest. It's more that the world would be a lot better off with Sarah in it than with Siren in it."

"Have you ever read the *Iliad*?" Molly asked.

"Read it?" I said. "Of course. Every issue. I write articles for it every three weeks. What're you talking about?"

"Not the newspaper," she said. "The poem. A big part of it is Agamemnon trying to replace Chryseis of the lovely cheeks with Briseis of the lovely cheeks."

"Is that a clue?" I asked.

"No, just a coincidence," Molly said. "Here's the clue. Which comes first, being cheerful or smiling?"

"Is this a trick question?" I asked. "Being cheerful, obviously."

"Ever tried it the other way around?" she asked.

"What do you mean?" I asked.

"Smile," she said.

I did. After a couple of seconds I started to feel like the day was turning out to be pretty damn good. "Okay, this is weird," I said. "Did you hypnotize me or something?"

"I didn't do anything," she said. "It's just a quirk of physiology. Smiling and feeling good cause one another. If you smile, you tend to cheer up. It's called facial feedback. Works with other emotions too. Scowl and you get ticked off. Obviously if you've just found out you're dying of cancer then forcing yourself to smile isn't going to make you any less upset. But if you're feeling basically neutral you can sort of kickstart yourself in a certain direction."

"So you're saying I should tell Siren to smile?" I asked.

"Don't be so literal," Molly said. "It's a metaphor." She stretched and yawned. "I think I'm going back to sleep. It's too early."

That was a sentiment I could certainly agree with, but I had to return Siren's notebooks to her locker before people started showing up looking to use the pool and the basketball courts and stuff. As I headed down the street I noticed that the Kaylins' garage door was open so I turned around and took the long way around so as not to have to explain what the notebooks were for if one of them saw me walking past. But I made sure to stop by on the way back.

Why must you turn this garage into a house of lies?

I walked up to the garage to find Peggy standing at a workbench with a pile of wood and a bucket of stain. Her hair was flatter than usual and she was wearing a gauzy white T-shirt that was obviously a laundry veteran; you could even see undernea—but of course, I wasn't looking. "What're you up to?" I asked.

"I have to stain this wood," she said. "You shouldn't see me like this. I'm a mess. I wanted to get this done before I took a shower so if I got some on me I wouldn't have to wash twice in a row."

Of course, there was more at stake for Peggy than simply efficiency—a few years back when she'd accidentally spilled a few drops of grape juice on the carpet she'd spent the rest of the day in confession. But I elected not to point this out. "What are you making?" I asked.

"I'm not making," she said. "I'm just staining."

"Fair enough," I said. "Listen, I was wondering if you could give me some advice."

She thought about it for a minute. "Okay," she said. "What about?"

"Okay, you know Siren Delaney?" I asked.

Peggy's face went as icy as I'd ever seen it. "Yeah . . . I know her . . . ," she said.

"Well, as you probably know, Benito assigned her to entertainment this issue," I said. "And obviously I wasn't happy about that because I thought she was a moron."

"That's not very nice," Peggy said. "Accurate as it may be."

"Uh, right," I said. "So, anyway, after a couple of weeks of trying to get her to turn in her story, I, uh . . ." It suddenly occurred to me that I couldn't exactly tell her that I'd broken into Siren's locker. Molly I could tell, but not Peggy—she'd be appalled. I was going to have to ad-lib something. "So, uh, she turned in this notebook, and when I opened it, it turned out that she'd accidentally turned in the wrong one, because after the first couple lines it was pretty obvious that it was some kind of diary."

"So you still don't have the story?" Peggy asked.

"No, I have it," I said. "It was, uh, in the back."

"So then she didn't turn in the wrong notebook," Peggy said.

"I mean it was folded up and stuck in the back," I said. "She could've just turned in the pages separately. The point is, the diary made it pretty clear that she's not as superficial as she pretends to be. And her home life seems to be pretty rough. And—"

"You mean you *read* it?" Peggy asked. "How *could* you? That's private."

"Well I didn't read the whole thing," I said. "Just some. Anyway—"

"Of course, she probably wanted you to read it," Peggy said. "I bet she made up the whole thing just so you wouldn't get her in trouble for being so late. It probably wasn't an accident at all."

"Oh, I'm pretty sure it was," I said.

"Why?" she asked.

"Just a feeling," I said.

"I wouldn't trust her," Peggy said.

This was getting decidedly weird. I figured I'd better wrap it up before I slipped up and got in trouble. "Anyway," I said, "the question is, how do I get her to be more like she is in the diary than she is in real life?"

Peggy shook her head. "That's not your job," she said. "You can try to talk to her and explain everything and hope she changes, but you should never pressure people. And don't try to manipulate people, either. Just be honest. Honesty is always the best policy."

"I'll keep that in mind," I said.

Threesome

"So you want to penetrate her?" Holdn asked at lunch.

I'd made the mistake of turning in Siren's story to Hayley when she stopped by the *Iliad* room at the beginning of lunch Monday afternoon; I thought she'd finally be satisfied, but she gave me a weird look and said, "How did you get this? I talked to her a minute ago in the hall and she said she wouldn't be finished till the end of the day. I was going to call her out of practice and force her to write it in front of me."

So I told her the whole story. And that was when Holdn asked his question. "No," I said, "I don't want to penetrate her. I just want to talk to her. Maybe convince her to switch back to her original personality."

"Right," Holdn said, "and that's the first step toward penetrating her. It's a hell of a lot easier to penetrate a sensitive poet type than a brat. Brats string you along just to be bratty. Sensitive poets, you just toss 'em a couple lines about 'fate' and 'preordained love' and crap like that and next thing you know it's Moaning in America."

"What a lovely sentiment," Hayley said.

"Well, hey, it's Valentine's Day," Holdn said. "Love is in the air."

"You're thinking of smog," Hayley said.

"Oh yeah," Holdn said. "I knew it was one of those."

April showed up at the door. "Ready?" she asked.

"We're gone," Holdn said. They left. As they walked down the hall I heard April say, "I bet they have really good nachos there, huh?" Then the door swung shut.

"So can you still call her out of class?" I asked.

"I suppose," Hayley said. "I'll have her sent over to the teachers' lounge."

Sixth period started off with a phone call. Hayley picked it up. "Hello?" she said. A second passed and she decided to elaborate. "Oh, *HI*!" she said.

"Must be the guy from Fred's Quality Footwear," Hank said.

Hayley cupped her hand over the receiver. "I'm going to need the room to myself for a while," she said. "It's Jefferson."

"So?" Cat said. "What, are you going to have phone sex with him?"

"It *is* Valentine's Day," Hayley said. "In any case, I don't need people eavesdropping. Get lost."

They got lost. So did I. Siren was due to show up in a minute or two, so I opened the door to the teachers' lounge and stepped inside.

Immediately I was hit by a blast of stale tobacco, like getting smacked in the face with a mentholated beach ball. Luckily, it dissipated fairly quickly. Or so I thought at first. After a minute or two I realized that it hadn't gone anywhere—the reason I could no longer sense it was because it had instantly anesthetized my sense of smell. I tried to open a window to let in some fresh air but the windows had all been painted shut. I could feel the carcinogens gleefully prancing through my body. I was displeased.

It didn't help that the entire lounge was so cramped that I could barely move. The room itself wasn't particularly small, but it was crammed with so many stacks of textbooks and haphazardly placed file cabinets and heaps of obsolete computers that I couldn't see more than a couple feet in any given direction. The one clearing I found was dominated by an enormous water cooler the teachers had stuck there like a sedentary Minotaur; I thought about pouring myself a drink before I noticed all the little dead bugs floating at the surface of the water. I elected to leave my thirst unslaked.

I heard the door open and shut. "Hello?" Siren said. "Anyone here?" And that was when I panicked, because I had absolutely no idea what I was going to say to her. I considered hiding and waiting for her to leave, but realized I'd look pretty stupid if she found me. Besides, I might never get this kind of chance again.

"Uh, hi," I said. "Glad you could—"

"*You?*" she said. "I thought I was supposed to be meeting with that hippie chick. Forget *this*." She turned around and pushed the door handle. It was locked.

"Very funny," she said. "Open the door."

"How?" I asked. "If it's locked from the inside then chances are it's hooked up to the timer in the office. Look, it doesn't matter right now. We need to talk."

"Too bad," Siren said, "because I *don't* need to talk to you."

"What makes you think I was talking about you?" I asked. "When I said 'we' I didn't mean me and you. I meant me and Sarah Jason Delaney the Intrepid."

She gasped. For a moment I expected to be slapped. But she didn't slap me. She just flat-out decked me. I didn't even see it coming. Nor did I really feel the impact. All I knew was that one second I was standing upright in my usual way and the next I was sprawled on the ground with a compound jaw fracture and teeth scattered everywhere. (Okay, maybe not. But it still hurt.)

"How do you know about that?" she demanded. "How the *fuck* do you know about that?"

I desperately tried to come up with an excuse, but two voices in my head persuaded me to just tell the truth. One voice was Peggy's, saying, "Honesty is always the best policy." The other was mine, saying, "My head hurts so much that any excuse I tried to come up with at this point would be really lame. Sorry!"

"Okay," I said, "you know how I called you, and asked how your story was coming along, and you said your notes were in your locker? Well, your story *was* over a week late, so I sort of went and got them."

"You *what?*" she said. "You *asshole!* I ought to fucking *sue* you!"

"Sue me?" I said. I clambered to my feet and found one of those olive-green one-piece molded plastic chairs to sink into. "I assume you mean report me," I said, rubbing my jaw. "In which case chances are I'd be suspended for a couple days, or get remanded for peer counseling. Which wouldn't make much sense because it'd mean I'd be counseling myself and talking to yourself is a sign of impending mental collapse. Actually, what'd probably happen is that I'd get fired from peer counseling, and then September would quit either in protest or from overwork, and we'd be left without a peer counseling program."

"Big fucking deal," Siren said. She jerked the handle up and down but the door didn't seem to notice.

"All I'm saying is, it'd hurt more people than just me," I said. "People who don't deserve it. Not that I deserved it when you decided to treat me like your personal fire hydrant for no reason whatsoev—"

"The reason," Siren interrupted, "is that I can smell a loser a mile away. I just made the mistake of assuming you were just a *pathetic* loser instead of a *criminal* loser."

"Look, I'm not going to pretend I'm totally blameless here," I said. "Obviously, I shouldn't have broken into your locker or looked through your notebooks. I might even feel some remorse if not for the fact that you deserve much worse."

"Fuck you," Siren said.

"I can see where you got your rep for brilliant repartee," I said. "But the fact is, while I might deserve a suspension, you deserve to be hit by a truck. You're a front-runner for the single most loathsome excuse for a human being I've ever met and if not for my brother you'd be a runaway winner. If you were being torn apart by a pack of wild dogs I'd splash you with steak sauce. Because you're a murderer and you deserve the chair."

"What the hell are you talking about?" she spat.

"Sarah," I said. "She's the one person involved in all this who didn't deserve to have anything bad happen to her. And she's the one who's suffered the most. *She's* the one whose privacy was violated, not yours. And if that's a crime—and it probably is—it's still nothing compared to snuffing her out. And *you* did that, not me."

"What the hell are you talking about?" Siren repeated. "You're not making any sense. She's me. I'm her."

"Don't flatter yourself," I said. "You can't honestly believe that, can you?"

Siren glared at me. "Whatever," she said. "Even if I *did* kill her, it was a mercy killing. She was miserable all the time. Besides, it's survival of the fittest. She was too fucking *weak* to live."

"Survival of the fittest?" I said. "You know what you're comparing yourself to? Viruses and insects. Which is a pretty apt comparison if you ask me. And don't even *try* the 'mercy' excuse. Sarah may not have been the happiest person around but I've never seen you exactly chipper. If you were you wouldn't be so bitchy all the time. But the fact is that *you're* just as miserable all the time as she was."

"Bullshit," she said. "You don't know anything."

"But I can figure it out," I said. Suddenly everything clicked into place. My sore jaw was really helping me think—all the white noise in my head about caring for Sarah and phrasing things delicately and minimizing my own mistakes had been replaced with one single sparklingly clear goal: making her Siren persona crumble. "You can't be happy," I said, "because you're not a real person. You're just a defense mechanism. You may be better at fending off your parents and winning friends than Sarah was, but it doesn't make you happy because to be happy you'd have to have a whole different set of priorities and you're not *deep* enough to change Sarah's priorities. And fending off her parents doesn't make *Sarah* happy—she doesn't want her mom off her back, she wants her to love her."

"Shut up," Siren said.

"Making friends on the cheer squad doesn't make Sarah happy, because *she* can see that they're shallow as a crêpe pan and their friendship doesn't mean anything," I said. "I'd even bet that the last call that she wanted to take on Friday was from Brad Chasintek because Sarah is unlikely to find happiness spending an evening getting pawed by some idiot hopped up on horse testosterone no matter how much *you* might try to convince her she'd enjoy it."

"Shut *up*," Siren said.

"You've just made everything really clear to me," I said. "You're not a murderer because murderers are just as human as the people they kill. But you're not. You're a virus. You're a *disease*. If I believed in metaphysical claptrap I'd say that Sarah was possessed and we needed to exorcise you. But you're not a demon. You're a coping mechanism gone awry. When people can't cope they either kill themselves or succumb to some kind of mental virus like mindless hedonism or religious fundamentalism or something. And Sarah succumbed to *you*. And if she's ever, *ever* going to be happy in life she's going to have to cast you off. And she can, because if she actually were dead then you wouldn't need to keep all her stuff safe for her. Right, Sarah? You *are* in there somewhere, aren't you?"

Siren covered her ears with her hands (or at least I assume they were her ears—you couldn't really see them beneath all her hair). "Shut *up*," she hissed. "Shut up shut up shut *up*."

There was a click and the door swung open. Uta gasped and dropped her walkie-talkie. "Get *out* vum dere, bote of you," she snapped. "Shtudents are not allowt in de teachers' lownch! Who knows *vut* you are doink in dere?" She whipped out her pad of red tickets but Siren ran off before she had a chance to fill them out.

Déjà vous

When I passed Siren in the hall at lunch the next day she took a swipe at me. Her nails were so sharp that she actually cut me, right on my left wrist, but I kept moving for fear that if I stopped even for a second she'd bite me or something. I have to admit I was surprised: I obviously wasn't expecting her to be happy to see me, but not even my worst-case scenario had involved any bleeding on my part.

Of course, my wrist didn't bother me half so much as the fact that September had me spending all my free time trying to keep April out of trouble. It'd gotten so bad by this point that even when layout for that issue was finished once and for all on Wednesday afternoon and I stopped on the way home to see if Siren might be less inclined to attack me, April came bounding over assuming I was there to see her. "Hi, Allen!" she said. "Here to play guard dog?"

"Say what?" I said.

"Since August and September's bus left already," April said. "You're here to watch me, right?"

"No," I said. "To be perfectly honest, it'd take a remarkable effort on my part for me to care less about what you and Holdn do or don't do." Nevertheless, she took the opportunity to go on and on about her trip to Tijuana. I looked around while she was talking but Siren didn't seem to be around. Eventually the bus showed up.

"About time," April said. "If we had to wait much longer we might as well've just stuck around till tomorrow. Well, see you Saturday."

"Saturday?" I said. But April had already gotten on the bus, which wheezed to life and started chuffing off into the distance. To my surprise, there were still a few people left over; apparently a lot of them had just been standing around talking with the people waiting for the bus and not actually waiting for it themselves. I managed to grab Missy Schaeffer before she wandered off. "Hey," I said. "Have you seen Siren around by any chance . . . ?"

"Oh, don't call her *that*," Missy said, her voice full of mock horror. Shelby giggled.

"Is this an in-joke?" I asked.

"Something like that," Missy said. She and Shelby laughed and sauntered off down the street. They went everywhere together. In fact, four months later, many of the bullets that ended up killing Missy went right through her body and finished off Shelby as well.

I looked around and realized I was alone. There weren't even any cars going by. I was about to cross the street for home when I heard footsteps behind me. It was Siren. Except not really. She looked the same—she was even wearing her black-and-silver cheerleading uniform—but her body language was all wrong. Siren never shuffled, or looked at her feet as she walked, and she certainly would never have been caught clutching a bunch of schoolbooks to her chest. That combined with Missy's remark added up to a hypothesis that was by no means a sure thing but was worth testing out.

"Sarah?" I said.

She looked up. Her face was flushed. "Aw, no," she said. "Don't tell me I missed the last bus."

"Okay," I said. "Would you believe you're really really early for the first one tomorrow?"

She glared at me and put her books down on the ground. She then patted herself down for pocket change, which proved rather fruitless since she didn't have any pockets.

"Sarah?" I said. "Are you okay? I've got some change if you need to make a phone call."

"Leave me alone," she said.

"I'm just trying to help," I said.

"I don't want your help," she said.

"Taxi Ocho doesn't accept collect calls," I said. "Do you have a calling card number or something?"

She scowled at me and turned to the phones. Ilium had two pay phones out front. One had a receiver encrusted with something that resembled three-week-old mustard; the other had no receiver at all, just a cable that dangled like an umbilical cord without a fetus at the end. She elected to go for the one she could actually talk into. She punched in the number of one of those collect-call services and from there on I only heard her side of the conversation.

"Barbara Wellston." Pause.

"Hi, may I please speak to Carol Cameron? This is Barbara Wellston." Long pause.

"Hi, Mom? It's Sarah. Don't hang up. I need—" Pause.

"I stopped calling myself that. Look, I'm stuck—" Pause.

"But I missed the bus and it's getting pretty dark and I don't have any other way to—" Pause.

"But it's only ten minutes out of your—" Pause.

"It's not my fault! I just—" Pause.

"Then how am I going to— Hello?" Dial tone. She hung up.

"Look, I live right across the street," I said. "You want me to call you a cab? I could even drive you home if my uncle's home. I still only have my permit but—"

"I said leave me alone," she said. She sat down on her stack of books and blinked hard at the ground.

"I'm not going to just leave you here," I said.

"I thought you said I deserve to be hit by a truck," she said. "You should be thrilled."

"I said *Siren* deserved to be hit by a truck. But you're not her, are you?" I asked.

"No," she said.

"Then why are you acting like this?" I said. "She's the one who hates me, not you."

"Siren hates you because you're a loser with no friends," she said. "I hate you because you're the creep that went through my things."

"Then let me make it up to you," I said. "Let me get you a ride."

"Fine," she said. "Get me a ride."

"Cool," I said. I checked to make sure there weren't any cars coming and started across the street, but when I looked behind me she was still sitting next to the phones. "Aren't you coming?" I called.

"What for?" she said. "Just have them pick me up."

"And you're going to sit here alone in the dark?" I asked. "It'll probably be forty minutes before they show up. And it's starting to rain." This was probably an overstatement—it really wasn't much more than mist. Still, it was getting pretty unpleasant out. "Come on. You'll be dry, you'll have light to read by . . . I'll even make you some soup." I didn't know where *that'd* come from—there was just something about her looking all forlorn and fragile in the drizzle that filled me with the overwhelming urge to make her some soup. "What do you say?" I asked. "Sarah? It's got to be better than this, right?"

It occurred to me that it wasn't as if she didn't have any other options: all she would've had to do would be to ring a few random doorbells and she could no doubt have found someone willing to take her in while she waited for a cab. Fortunately for me, this option didn't occur to her. She stood up and collected her books. "Which way?" she sighed.

Soup is good food

Sarah Delaney was in my house. Not Siren—somehow I'd managed to forget that Siren had ever even existed. The girl who'd just followed me inside wasn't the obnoxious brat I'd come to loathe over the last year and a half: she was the girl from the diary, Sarah Jason Delaney the Intrepid. Of course, at the moment she was more like Sarah Jason Delaney the Morose, but melancholy had been just as much a thread running through the Historical Chronicle as pluck; the fact that she seemed totally defeated in no way made her any less appealing. "I can make you that soup now," I said.

"I don't want any soup," she said. "Just a phone and a place to do my homework is fine. Are we the only ones here?"

"Looks like it," I said. I went into the kitchen but the phone was missing from its base. I pushed the recall button but didn't hear the reply from the receiver; apparently Bobbo had taken it into the car with him when he'd gone to work again. "C'mon, there's a phone upstairs you can use," I said.

I led her up the stairs and Sarah seemed quite bewildered by all the doors that confronted her at the top. "That's my uncle's room right in front of us," I said, "and then clockwise from there it's my brothers' room, my sister's, mine, the bathroom, and the closet."

"What about your parents?" she asked. "Do you live with your mom or your dad?"

"Neither," I said. "They're both dead."

"Lucky you," she said.

I opened my door and turned on the halogen lamps—we had two of them, five hundred watts apiece—and the room lit up with so much bright yellow light you could practically swim through it. "This is your room?" Sarah asked. "Who's the other bed for?"

"Hmm?" I said. "Oh, that's Echo's."

"I thought you said she lived in the other room," Sarah said.

"That's my other sister," I said. "Molly. Echo lives here."

"You share a room with your *sister*?" Sarah said. "Without a curtain or anything? Isn't that . . . y'know, weird?"

"Oh, I don't know," I said. "Sure, I guess sometimes we kind of get in each other's way. But we can't afford a house with six bedrooms and it's really no big deal. I mean, we spent nine months sharing quarters a lot closer than these. Anyway, the phone's on the desk."

"What's the number?" she asked. "For the taxi place."

"853-OCHO," I said.

"And where are we?" she asked. "What address?"

"147 Hyacinth," I said.

Sarah placed the taxi order, which by my calculations gave me somewhere between forty and eighty minutes of her company—with any luck we'd get a really unmotivated driver who'd stop for dinner and maybe a quick movie on the way to pick her up. She started in on her algebra homework. I noticed that Sarah hadn't let Siren jeopardize her transcript: she was in the same level math I was. I wondered how she justified that to her friends. I hopped up on my bed to read the chapter for Non-Western Civ class. We didn't say anything but it was nice just listening to her breathe. It was thus a rather unwelcome shock to hear a car door slam thirty to seventy minutes before I was prepared to let her go.

I got up and looked out the window at the driveway: it was just Echo. I went downstairs to see where she'd gone and got there just in time to grab one of the bags she was carrying. "'The Albuquookery'?" I said, reading the logo on the bag. "Did that place finally open?"

"No," Echo said. "I broke in and cooked it myself. What do you *think*?"

"I think that if one of these bags isn't full of sopaipillas I'm sending you back," I said. I opened my bag; it was full of entrées positively stuffed with chiles, but that was meaningless without the other half of the equation. I looked in the other bag—nothing but sopaipillas. "You have done well, young one," I said. "You may stay."

"Young one?" Echo said.

"Hey, I'll always have six minutes' seniority over you," I said. "You might as well get used to it now." I grabbed a couple sopaipillas and a plate and went upstairs.

"Care for a sopaipilla?" I asked Sarah.

"What is it?" she asked.

"It's a kind of pastry," I said. "It's one of the very few things my mom ever cooked for us. I mean, not this particular one. This is a fresh one." I put the plate on the desk. Sarah nibbled at it. I devoured mine in about one and a half bites. Then I went to the bathroom to wash the butter off my hands. When I came out I heard Echo coming up the stairs.

"Uh-oh," I said. "This could be ugly."

"What?" Sarah asked. But by then Echo had reached the landing. There seemed to me to be only two possibilities at this point: either Echo would kill her, or she'd say something nasty that'd bring Siren out quicker than a gamma bomb explosion. I wasn't quite sure which was worse.

To my surprise, neither happened. Echo stayed very calm and her voice was only the tiniest bit strained as she said, "Get out of my room, and get out of my house. Now."

"Downstairs," I said. I managed to drag Echo down a couple of stairs, which I figured was good enough. "Look, I'll explain later," I whispered. "Leave her alone, okay? She's leaving really soon."

"No, she's leaving now," Echo said.

"Can't you put up with her for a few minutes?" I said. "One of these days you're going to have to learn how to be civil to people."

"Siren Delaney," Echo said, "does not count as people."

"That's okay, because she's not Siren Delaney," I said. "I'll explain once she's gone. Can't you ease off a little, just this once? For me?"

Echo hit me with a look that would've decapitated me had I not been prepared. Then without a word she went downstairs, out the door, and drove off. This of course meant that she was going without dinner, but I figured that if she was going to do me a favor the least I could do in return was let her be melodramatic about it.

I went back up to my room. Sarah was just kind of staring into the middle distance. "Sorry about that," I said. "Are you okay? You look upset."

"No, it's just . . ." She sighed. "Anything Siren may have said about you," she said, "you deserve. But Echo didn't. Siren was just trying to get at me by slamming her. I guess she saw a resemblance."

"Get at you?" I said. "I thought she was trying to help you out, in her own twisted way."

Sarah's eyes darkened. "Maybe I was a little jealous," she said quietly.

"Maybe you wouldn't have had any reason to be jealous," I said, "if you had turned in 'Persephone' instead of 'My Boyfriend Is Like a Sweater.'"

It suddenly occurred to me that bringing up her diary was unlikely to win me any points with Sarah, but to my surprise she just smirked. "At least you can pronounce it," she said. "When I showed it to my dad he called it 'Purse-Phone.'"

I had to laugh at that one. "'That's right, it's a handbag and a cell phone all in one!'" I said. "'Now how much would you pay?'"

"Something like that," Sarah said.

I sat back down on my bed. "So where are you from?" I asked.

"Yorba Linda," she said.

"I mean originally," I said. "I seem to recall you writing something about wanting to return to your homeland . . . ?"

She sighed. "Wishful thinking," she said. "I used to think that I'd been adopted and my *real* family that actually *liked* me lived somewhere far away and if I could only get back there everything would be great. Then later I realized that being adopted would mean that the people I was living with had actually *wanted* me, and since that was pretty obviously not the case I gave up on the adoption idea. But I still kept my idea of my homeland. I even had a name for it. Since I clearly didn't belong in *Yor*ba Linda, it made sense that I'd be from *My* Balinda. And in My Balinda things were different. The sun rose in the west and set in the east, and people called it the moon. And the grass was red and every day it shrank, and so every so often people would run lawnmowers over it to make it long again. And every day after school all the teachers would go home and the kids would come up with questions for them to answer the next day. See, when school was done the kids stayed behind, and the *parents* came to school till the kids sent them off the next morning. And there were no families. Families were against the law in My Balinda." She frowned. "I can't believe I just told you all that."

"That," I said, "is one of the coolest things I've heard in a long time."

"It's stupid," she said. "I wrote a big long essay about it in fourth grade that they stuck in my school file. Mrs. Wennikee read it when I first got to Ilium and she flipped. She kept trying to get me to write about it again but I'd given it up when I was ten and didn't want to hear about it anymore. And if *I* thought it was embarrassing you can imagine what *Siren* must've thought." She gave a bitter laugh. "When I was six or so I was convinced that My Balinda was real and told my mom that I wanted her to send me there. She said if she could she'd put me on the next plane there. I thought she was being nice."

"What is her *deal*?" I asked. "If you don't mind me asking."

"It's pretty simple, really," Sarah said. "You know how in some countries they force women to marry their rapists if the rapists ask? I think it's even in the Bible."

"You're a rape kid?" I said. "I mean, I'm a rape grandkid, so I sort of know how that goes. But wait—"

"No, I'm not a rape kid," she said. "The point is, if you ask the people who wrote those laws why they did, they'd say they were trying to do the 'proper' thing. Well, I'm what happens when everyone tries to do the 'proper' thing. Mom gets knocked up by some dumb guy she meets in a bar and her parents threaten to cut her off if she goes to the clinic and gets the D&C because that's killing innocent babies, they say. And then they threaten to cut her off if she doesn't marry the guy because I wouldn't be 'legitimate' if they didn't, of course. And Mom's only finished one year of college and is deathly afraid that she'll end up waiting tables for the rest of her life if she gets cut off, and Dad's driving a tow truck or something for a living and figures he could go for marrying into some money as long as he can keep getting chicks on the side, and long boring story short, next thing you know the Bible-thumping parents are dead and the inheritance is secure so it's off to Fleibag Forbes & Schmeck to draw up the divorce papers and before long I'm ten years old with a black eye and a split lip and scars on my wrists because I've never been wanted for a single second of my entire fucking life. Life. What a beautiful fucking choice, huh?"

I was beginning to suspect that the boundary between Sarah and Siren was more fluid that I had initially supposed. I had no idea how to react. The two options that immediately sprang to mind, empathy ("Yeah, life sucks!") and sympathy ("I wuv oo!"), both seemed equally lame. I decided to go with the first alternate response that popped into my head. "Fleibag Forbes & Schmeck, huh?" I said. "My uncle works there!"

"What?" she said.

"He mainly just gets coffee and runs the fax machine, though," I said. Sarah seemed to have caught on to the fact that I was just babbling by this point—she was still looking in my general direction, but seemed to be focusing on a point a million miles directly behind my head. "You know, you could report her," I said quietly.

She blinked and looked at me with huge dark beautiful eyes that seemed to suck all the light out of the room. "It wouldn't change anything," she said. "She still wouldn't—it wouldn't change anything."

"Sure it would," I said. "You don't even have to be the one who does it. I could do it. I know some people. I've done it before in my peer counseling job. They'll just send some—"

"No," she hissed. "*No*. If you try it I'll deny everything. And I'll *never* talk to you again. *Ever*." She turned and went back to work on her math.

I flipped my history book back open to the page I'd been reading, but it was no use. I couldn't concentrate. All I wanted to do was somehow console Sarah for having had a lousy life and the only way I could think of to do that was cuddle with her for a while, and since half an hour earlier I hadn't been sure she wouldn't attack me, that didn't seem like much of a possibility. It was a shame, too, because she was eminently cuddlable. I couldn't believe I'd let spite blind me to this fact for so long. How could I have missed those gorgeous, soulful eyes? I looked at her over the top of my book and watched her work on her math. I watched and watched. Time seemed to wind down like an antique record player. I'd look at the mirrored clock on the wall next to the door and it'd be 5:57, and then I'd spend the next couple of hours pretending to read and when I looked up it'd be 5:57 and five seconds. All my senses suddenly seemed heightened: I could hear Sarah's pencil moving across the page even over the whir of the air conditioner. I could feel each individual nerve in my body and the blood rushing around in my veins and I knew that if I scratched an itch I'd rip my flesh open and bleed to death. Naturally, a hundred thousand itches sprang to life all over my body: my cheek, my elbow, the back of my knee, the tip of my nose, everywhere. Sarah chewed on the end of her pencil. As I watched her, I felt watched. I felt like the Channel 5 NewsCopter was hovering inches from my face broadcasting my every itch and chill on a live feed to a rapt audience. I looked at the clock. It was 5:57 and seven seconds.

I got up and looked out the window. I was acutely aware of the fact that Sarah was female. That the word "ILIUM" emblazoned across her uniform didn't catch the light that way because of any property of the fabric but because of the soft swell underneath. That she was naked beneath her clothes. There was her cheerleading uniform and then there were her underthings and under that she was completely naked. I watched the twilight dissolve into the dull pink glow of night in Southern California and tried not to obsess about this fact. I heard a couple of dull thuds behind me and I looked away from the window: Sarah had kicked off her shoes. This was a mistake, because it drew my attention to her legs. Her beautiful soft legs that didn't stop when they disappeared beneath her short pleated skirt but kept on going. Right on going all the way up. I longed to follow them there. It dawned on me that the solution to all Sarah's problems and all my problems as well would be for us to sleep together. The logic in this was, in Sarah's words, perfect, exquisite, and absolute.

The phone rang and I picked it up. I couldn't understand what the voice on the other end was saying till the blood had a second to rush back up to my brain. "—looked out the window it'd started to rain," said a voice, which I suddenly realized was Molly's. "Can you bring over my rain stuff?"

"Uh, sure," I said. "Where are you again?"

"I'm at Rachel's," she said. "Weren't you listening?"

"Must be a bad connection," I said. "I'll be over in a minute or two." I hung up the phone. "I have to run across the street," I said. "Make yourself at home. *Mi casa es su casa.* You probably shouldn't go into Krieg's room unless you've had your shots, though. I'll be back in a bit."

Sarah didn't look up from her math. "Okay," she said. I stole one last glance at her legs and noticed, right at her hemline, the end of an ugly scar on her thigh. I couldn't tell how long it was but it looked like it'd been a pretty nasty cut. Maybe she'd fallen off her bike when she was little. But I couldn't think about that now; I had a sister to rescue.

I went downstairs and got Molly's bag of rain gear out of the closet by the garage door. It was still barely misting out; it was the kind of evening where you couldn't actually *feel* the rain, but if you were carrying a sheet of paper it'd get all limp and droopy after a few minutes, and that was enough for Molly. Molly wasn't necessarily an aquaphobe in any kind of absolute sense: she liked the kind of water that came out of the faucet enough that a couple years back her main birthday present had been one of those handheld shower massagers and she'd been ecstatic. But water in an outdoor setting—oceans, rivers, lakes, rain, you name it—was her mortal enemy. As far as she was concerned it might as well have been hydrochloric acid. She was convinced that if a drop of it touched her a house would fall on her or something.

The door to the Monihans' was open. Even before I actually stepped inside I was enveloped by the aroma of dandruff and fiber supplements; you could almost tell that the shag carpeting would turn out to be mint green just by smell. The Monihans had an old electric organ that they let Molly come over and play every now and again, though I have no idea if she was any good. They also had a grand-daughter named Rachel who was staying with them while her mom was doing time on a drug charge. She was exactly Molly's age, but all that proved was exactly how meaningless age can be. Molly was probably about eighty times smarter than Rachel, but still, she was just a kid. Rachel, though, well, just from the way she stood you could tell that Rachel hadn't been a kid in years and years. Sometimes I'd see her waiting out in front of the house in her trademark thread-bare orange sweater until some guys in a big car came and took her off somewhere. There was apparently a whole subculture of these way-precocious pre- or just-barely-pubescent girls springing up; some-times September and I would see them at parties we were working, some of them eleven, even ten years old. I suspected that they could take care of themselves a hell of a lot better than I could.

I heard Molly say her good-byes to the old folks and then she came out to the little foyer where I was standing. She was wearing a green-and-orange plaid dress with little pink hearts all over it. "I thought it wasn't supposed to rain in Southern California," she grumbled. "This is the third time this year and it's only February. I swear, I'm moving to Arizona. Or Mauritania." She opened the bag and put on her gloves, knee-high galoshes, and ankle-length raincoat with hood and clear plastic face shield. She was prepared to survive not only a light drizzle but also a level-four biohazard—which, to her, wouldn't have been as bad.

She snapped open her umbrella as we stepped out into the mist. "You know what the worst part about rain is?" she asked.

"It's wet?" I said.

"It's death," she said.

"At least I got the vowel right," I said.

"It doesn't come from anywhere," she said. "We know where the water vapor is, more or less, but it doesn't become rain until it's falling, and once you can tell it's falling, it's already rain. There's no identifiable point at which the nonrain becomes rain. It's like the opposite of a ray. A ray starts at a particular point but doesn't end anywhere in particular. A raindrop doesn't begin anywhere in particular but does stop somewhere: when it smacks into something. Which makes it like consciousness. There's no identifiable point at which consciousness begins—it's a gradual process. But the point at which it ends is very specific. Death. Rain is death."

"Deep," I said.

We went inside and Molly stripped off her rain gear and stuck it back in the bag and put the bag in the closet. Then she pulled off her dress and put it in the hamper, which was also in the closet. Molly kept all her clothes in the downstairs closet. That way she didn't have to get dressed till the second before she stepped out the door. And of course it goes without saying that she hadn't been wearing anything under the dress. I heard a car pull up outside and checked to see whether it was Echo or the taxi. As it happened, it was neither: it was the Pizza Hovel delivery guy. It seemed unlikely that Sarah had called for a pizza while I was gone and gotten really quick service, since Pizza Hovel wasn't exactly known for speedy delivery: their policy was to give you your pizza free if it didn't get there within thirty days. "Did you order a pizza?" I asked.

"Yeah," Molly said from the kitchen. "I didn't know we'd have good stuff already. Oh, well, we can always reheat it." She went back to the closet and threw on her kimono, which was red with a pair of silver dragons on the back. It looked like fine silk from the Orient but was actually made of polyester and came from a sweatshop in Honduras. She wore it mainly to get the mail and answer the door; the latter was a concession to previous pizza guys who'd run off for fear that looking at her in her usual state would get them thrown in jail. "I guess as long as they stay outside, they're still in the world and get to play by the world's rules," Molly conceded. But the same policy didn't extend to people who dared to come in, despite Bobbo's pleas. "This is my home," Molly said. "The fact that I share it with other people doesn't make it any less mine. And I'm entitled to be one hundred percent comfortable in my own home. I spend enough time stuck in those textile coffins outside and I'm *not* wearing them here. If visitors don't like it, they can leave." And sometimes they left. I hoped Sarah wouldn't. Of course, there was always the chance that Sarah would be so concerned that Molly needed clothes that she'd donate hers. I realized that the probability of this was fairly low but just the fact that it was in the realm of possibility meant I was set for later that night.

I went back upstairs to find Sarah plucking a couple of the strings on my guitar. And this time I noticed a fresh cut on her *other* thigh. I wondered how many more there were that I couldn't see. But before I could ask her about it, she asked, "What are the stars for?"

"Hmm?" I said. "Oh, no reason, really. I just thought that a blue guitar with a red fingerplate was just crying out to be covered with white stars. It's actually proven to be really helpful. People are so dazzled by the pretty stickers they don't realize how much I suck. Do you play?"

"No," she said. "I always wanted to learn, though."

"I could teach you the four chords I know sometime," I said. "Then you could learn everything else and teach me."

"Maybe," she said.

Molly came upstairs. "Who's this?" she asked politely.

I looked up. "Oh, uh, hi," I said. "This is Sarah. Sarah Delaney. Sarah, this is my sister Molly."

Sarah looked up and her eyes went wide. Right then Molly placed the name. "Oh, right," she said. "Briseis. Pleased to meet you." She went in her room.

Sarah gaped at me. "D—doesn't she know she's not wearing anything?" she finally asked.

"Sure," I said. "I mean, in the same sense that she knows she's a Sagittarius. If you asked her the question she'd know the answer, but it's probably the last thing on her mind. I wouldn't ask her about it, though. She's prone to launching into monologues at a moment's notice."

"But—doesn't that freak you out?" she asked.

"The monologues?" I asked.

"No," she said. "The not wearing anything."

"Nah," I said. "You get used to it."

"I don't think I could ever get used to something like *that*," Sarah said.

"Sure you could," I said. "You can get used to anything."

Her eyes darkened. "Not anything," she said. I was about to challenge her on that but then I realized she was talking about stuff that wasn't quite so trivial as showing a little extra skin. She turned away and went back to working on her math.

Time passed. Molly finished testing her blood sugar and went downstairs for dinner. Jerem ventured out of his room for a bathroom break. I couldn't think of a time when any of us had had a visitor over for so long, much less one that just sort of did her own thing while everyone else went about their lives as usual. It was as if she were one of us. And if things went well, maybe she would be.

I looked at the clock. "Hey, the cab'll probably be here soon," I said. "If you want to grab some dinner, now would be the time. We've got all kinds of great stuff. Especially if you like chiles."

"Okay," she said. She closed her book and stashed her paper away in the notebook. I was thrilled that she neither gathered up her books nor put her shoes back on before heading downstairs. I followed her to the kitchen.

I couldn't help but notice that she still seemed a little down, and that meant one thing: "Soup," I said. "Want me to make you some soup? We've got all kinds of soup. Tomato dill, cream of broccoli, lentil . . ."

"That's okay," she said, opening the refrigerator. "This is fine." She pulled out Molly's pizza. "Can I eat this?" she asked.

"Sure," I said. She took a slice out of the box and started chewing on it. "Don't you want to heat it up?" I asked. "The oven might take too long, but we've got a micro—"

"This way is fine," she said.

I took an enchilada with green chiles out of the Albuquookery bag and stuck it in the microwave. "What kind of stuff do you usually eat at home?" I asked.

"I'd rather not talk about home," she said.

We ate in silence. After a couple of slices Sarah either got full or realized that cold pizza is no kind of food for tragical girls. I thought about making some soup just for the sake of getting it out of my system but then her taxi showed up. She sighed and went upstairs to get her books and shoes.

I went to make sure the taxista stuck around while Sarah put her shoes on—they were notorious for driving off if no one immediately got into the cab—and right then Bobbo drove up. "Going somewhere?" he asked.

"No," I said. "It's not for me."

"Then who's it for?" he asked. As if in answer Sarah showed up in the door frame. Bobbo seemed impressed. "Yes!" he said. "Now *that's* what you like to see at the end of a long day. Who'd've figured our little Allen-gator would turn out to be a babe magnet? And a cheerleader no less!"

"Shut up," I said. I flashed my student ID to the taxista and explained that the fare should be charged to the school tab. He seemed pissed but acquiesced. Sarah got into the cab. "See you at school," I said. "Thanks for coming over."

"See you," she said. They were the sweetest words I'd heard in a long time.

Downer

I didn't have long to enjoy them, though—Echo came back home. And she demanded an explanation.

"It's a long story," I said. "And you won't like how it begins." I told her about breaking into Siren's locker and finding the diary.

"That's reprehensible, of course," she said. "But then, Siren Delaney deserves to have her eyes eaten out by rats. So you're forgiven for that. But not for bringing her here. And that's the more serious offense. The former only lowers my opinion of you. The latter means you've violated the sanctity of our home. I refuse to sleep anywhere that still bears the stench of Siren Delaney."

"Oh, come on," I said. "First of all, she doesn't have a 'stench.'"

"She has big hair," Echo countered.

"So?" I said. "It's not hairspray big, she just doesn't cut it. There's nothing wrong with that. It's beautiful. And besides, it's like I've been trying to tell you—she's not Siren Delaney."

"What kind of double-talk is that?" she said.

"It's not double-talk," I said. "Siren's just a persona she put on to deal with the crappy life she'd been dealt. Her real name's Sarah and she's really got a beautiful spirit once you get to know her. If you read the diary you'd understand."

"Where is it?" she asked.

"I put it back in her locker," I said.

"Fine," Echo said. "So quote it back to me."

"Right here? This minute?" I said. "Fine, you asked for it."

Echo sat and listened patiently as I quoted the diary back to her. She seemed less than moved. "Of course, I may have the intonation all wrong," I said. "Especially on the p—"

"I doubt it makes a bit of difference," Echo said.

"What's that supposed to mean?" I said.

"Just what I said," she said. "Am I supposed to be weeping for poor lost Siren Delaney now? Because of some affected diary entries and bad teenage poetry? You do realize that she ripped off that whole last stanza from—"

"Coleridge," I said. "So I've been informed."

"The fact is that character is action," Echo said. "If you act like a vicious trollop then you're a vicious trollop. Even if you come home and write reams of self-pitying tripe to try to convince yourself that you're not. But I'll give you the benefit of the doubt and assume that you were moved by compassion rather than testosterone. In which case I remind you that there are lots of kids out there who get whipped with belts, and burned with cigarettes and irons, and raped and sodomized on a daily basis. Kids living surrounded by their own filth in crackhouses or dying of hunger in a desert in Africa. Invite *them* over. And let Siren Delaney and her conveniently morphing personalities rot."

"But that's false logic," I said. "The fact that Hitler was worse doesn't mean Mussolini was a great guy. And the fact that there are kids worse off than Sarah doesn't mean she should be happy with parents who hate her and slap her around."

"Then let me put it this way," Echo said. "Siren Delaney decided that she could win points for herself by trying to humiliate me. I didn't seek her enmity—that was her idea. But as it stands, it's her or me.

You can't associate with both of us. You'll have to make up your mind."

And with that, she strode out of the room. It would've been a dramatic exit if not for the fact that she had to come back twenty minutes later to go to bed.

The power of negative thinking

Sarah didn't come to school the next day. Or at least I didn't see her. And it's not like I didn't look. Believe me, I was looking for her all day. And she was the kind of person who was hard to miss. For instance, Friday at lunch I had no problem finding her, even though she was sitting on a bench in the wheel trying to look inconspicuous instead of hanging out with her usual group—or, rather, Siren's usual group. Unlike Siren, Sarah didn't have any groupies, except maybe for me.

"Hi," I said.

She looked up from the spot on the ground she'd been staring at. "Oh, hi," she said. She sounded distracted.

"Guess what?" I said. "I got my license this morning."

"Good for you," she said.

"Want to help me celebrate?" I asked. "I was going to go out for lunch. There's a café up in Brea that I've been meaning to try. Now I can. Want to go? It's got to be better than—" I looked at what she was eating. "Saltines?"

"It's all we had in the house," she said. "Usually someone on the squad buys me something."

"Then I'll buy you something," I said. "My treat."

She sighed. "Okay," she said.

She wasn't very talkative as we walked back to my house, where the car was parked. In fact, she didn't say anything; she seemed lost in thought. I hit the UNLOCK button on my keychain. "Doors are open," I said. "Hop in."

"Is this a new car?" she asked.

"Sure is," I said. She looked at me expectantly. "What?" I said.

"Aren't you going to talk about the horsepower and the cylinders and the torque or whatever?" she asked.

"Uh, no," I said.

"Brad does," she said.

"Well, there's a difference between me and Brad Chasintek," I said. "I don't have five periods of auto shop."

We buckled our seat belts and I started up the car. I sort of nicked the mailbox with my side mirror on the way out and then kind of overcompensated and hopped the curb with one of the wheels. We still got out to the street okay. "Are you sure you have your license?" she asked.

"Very funny," I said. "Here, have a look." I hit the brake and pulled it out of my wallet. I neglected to mention that the reason I'd gotten it this time was because the guy scoring the driving test had added wrong. She seemed satisfied so I put it away.

We turned and headed up State College Boulevard. Echo had biked up the hill all the time back when she used to bike everywhere, but I'd had neither a bike nor the willpower to make the trip by foot. Driving was cool. "So," I said, "you and Brad—are you serious at all, or . . . ?"

"No," she said quickly. "I mean, maybe Siren is, but I'm not. And she just likes the attention."

"You know, Peggy Kaylin dated him for a while," I said. "Hey, you should talk to Hank—you know, Hank from the paper? He's got a great picture of Brad that Benito wouldn't let him print. It's called 'Digging In on Third Down.'"

Sarah shrugged. I decided to let it go. I'd learned very early in Peggy's dating career that slamming the current boyfriend afforded one exactly zero headway in taking his place. The café seemed fairly busy when we arrived but there were still a few empty tables out front. I found a parking spot and switched off the engine. Sarah didn't seem to have noticed. "You okay?" I asked.

"I guess," she said. "I have a lot on my mind."

We placed our orders and sat down at an empty table outside. Sarah looked at her watch. "Don't worry," I said. "If we're late I can clear the absence. You won't get a call from the attendance computer."

"Okay," she said.

We looked at the cars in the parking lot in silence for a while. "So tell me," I finally said, "how did you make it back?"

"What?" she said.

"I mean, the whole time I've known you, all the way till just this week, Siren's been here and you haven't," I said. "Now you're here and she's not. How did you manage to fight her off?"

"We didn't fight," she said. "It's not like that. It's just . . ." She sighed. "I get up, things happen, I know what Siren would do, I do it. Then a couple days ago I got up and didn't know what Siren would do. She was gone. I'm what's left."

"How can you say that?" I said. "You make it sound like you just had a lobotomy instead of getting over a disease. You're not 'what's left' when Siren takes a holiday. When you're you you're a wonderful person. You're Sarah Jason Delaney the Intrepid."

She looked at me like I'd just declared that I knew for a fact that she was Batman. "That was just as fake as Siren," she said. "I was just trying to force myself to be upbeat. A couple of my teachers made me go in for counseling because they said I seemed down all the time and the counselor told me about the power of positive thinking. I tried it. It didn't work."

"Did you tell the counselor *why* you were down all the time?" I asked.

"He didn't ask," she said. "Even if he did ask I wouldn't have told. It's none of their business."

"He didn't ask about the bruises?" I asked.

Her eyes narrowed. "No," she said. "You think I don't know how to keep that kind of thing covered up? I even used to walk into doors so that if I ever did show up at school with marks on my face everyone would just assume I'd gotten them from being clumsy."

"But why?" I asked.

"Because it's none of their business," she repeated.

"Not because you'd have to admit that a lot of your injuries are self-inflicted?" I asked.

She glared at me. "You don't know anything about it," she said.

"I know some," I said. "It's common enough that there's a whole section in my peer counseling binder about it. Obviously you can't change your background, but there's a bunch of different kinds of medication that—"

"I'm *not* going to be doped up," she said.

"I wouldn't necessarily call it—"

"I would," she said. "I've read all about these antidepressants. They just force you into 'positive thinking' despite yourself. It was one thing as an experiment but I'm *not* going to be forced. If I'm going to be fake twenty-four hours a day it'll be because I want to be, not because some pill is forcing me to be."

I shook my head. "I can't believe that," I said. "The girl who wrote that diary wasn't fake. She was way too genuine to have been just an experiment."

"And Siren was so genuine that you never suspected for a second that she was a put-on till you read that diary," she said.

"Okay, fine," I said. "That I can accept. So Sarah Jason Delaney the Intrepid is your best self, and Siren Delaney is your worst self. That just means—"

"But you're still wrong," she said. "It has nothing to do with my 'self.' I stole the whole Siren thing from someone else. Ever heard of Jessica Pound?"

"What?" I said. "Uh, sure. I mean, I've heard the name, but I don't know her. She's a freshman, right?"

"She is now," Sarah said. "But when I was in middle school, she was in my grade. And she was incredibly popular. Mainly because she was like a walking popularity detector. If she sensed you were a loser, she'd be the most rude and dismissive person you could imagine. If she sensed you were a winner, she'd suck up to you like you were a god and act as dumb as an inflatable doll. Everyone made jokes about her but no one dared to get on her bad side because that'd be like saying you were the same as the noids in the computer lab and the drool sergeants who stuck around after school sitting out front eating crickets. And that's why she was popular. Or at least that was part of the reason. She also put out a lot."

"Yeah, that'd probably do the trick," I said. "So to speak."

"So anyway, over the summer she got knocked up and so she took a year off from school. And we were all going to be going to a new school in a different town now anyway, and that gave me an idea. *Someone* was going to have to fill the void, and since none of the Fullerton kids would have any idea who I was, I decided to be her. I'd act like her, do everything she did—which is why I tried out for cheerleading—everything except the putting out part. And it worked, kind of. I mean, I got friends."

"You mean you got a clique," I said.

"Same thing," she said. "That's just what people like you with no friends call friends."

"It is not," I said. "And I do so have friends. They're just more dispersed. I mean, Peggy's my friend. And September's my friend. And Hayley's my friend. And Molly's my friend. They don't hang out with each *other*, but that just makes it more rewarding because it means I know different kinds of people. And we're *real* friends, which means we talk about stuff the way you and I are right now. And I know you could never have talked to your clique this way because then your cover would've been blown. So what good are they?"

"They tell you who you are," she said. "When I didn't have any friends I was nobody. When I'm hanging out with Shelby and Missy I may not be having any fun but at least I'm one of them. I'm somebody."

"Yeah, but you're somebody else," I said.

"Somebody else," she said, "is still somebody."

Our food arrived at long last. "So where did you come up with the names?" I asked. "For your . . . personae."

"Hmm?" she said, poking at her salad. "Oh, nowhere special. 'Siren' I picked because it sounded like a more exotic version of Sarah. And more cheerleadery."

"And 'Jason' to strike that tomboyish adventurer note, I suppose?" I said.

"No, that's my actual middle name," she said. "My sonogram got misread and so everyone thought I was going to be a boy. I ended up as Sarah Jason because my parents had already put 'Jason' on all my clothes and toys. My dad had been jazzed. A big part of why he agreed to the whole marriage deal was that he thought he was going to get a son. When I turned out to have the wrong kind of gig he split."

"Your dad is a complete fucking idiot," I said. "Uh, no offense."

She looked at me curiously. "You really mean that, don't you?" she said.

"Well, sure," I said. She didn't say anything. "So what was the painting of?" I asked.

"What?" she said.

"Didn't you write that you'd given him a painting?" I asked.

She blinked. "It was a picture of what I saw out my bedroom window," she said. "Except the sun was black. And it cast blackness, so that it darkened everything it shone upon and shadows were brighter than their surroundings. But it didn't look like a negative because the colors were right—the sky was blue, the grass was green, it was just the light and shade that were reversed. It took me a month to get it right. I gave it to him for Father's Day. I guess he threw it out."

"Sarah," I said, "I want to kill both your parents."

"That's sweet," she said.

I'd lost my appetite and it was time to go anyway so I pushed my plate away. Sarah had finished her salad so we got up to go. As we headed back down the hill something else occurred to me. "Sarah?" I said.

"Hmm?" she said.

"Is it really true you can cry on command?" I asked.

I'd expected that maybe if she concentrated for a minute she might be able to get a tear or two to trickle down her cheek. So when without warning she burst into uncontrolled sobs I kind of lost control of the car and swerved into an adjoining development. I pulled up to the curb and switched off the engine. "Hey, are you okay?" I said. "I didn't mean—"

I pulled her hands away from her face and she sniffed. Her face was pink and puffy and streaked with tears and it took her a minute to get her breathing under control. "You mean something like that?" she asked.

"I wasn't expecting it to be quite so dramatic," I said.

"It doesn't have to be," she said. "Depends on my mood."

I pulled back onto State College and eventually into my development and onto my driveway. "Hey, tomorrow I'm going to see the set of *Ashley: The Early Years* with some of the *Iliad* people," I said. "Want to go?"

"I can't," she said.

"Are you sure?" I said.

She shook her head. "I get in trouble if I'm too late coming home from a *walk*," she said. "I could never get away with it."

"Well, okay," I said. "How about dinner Monday? Just say you missed the bus again. You could either come over or we could go somewhere."

She thought about it. "Okay," she said. "I think I'd like that."

"Great!" I said. "That's . . . great." The school bell sounded. I looked at my watch. "First bell," I said. "We still have five minutes. But I guess we'd better get back."

This was going to be cool. This was going to be *so* cool.

The most unkindest cut of all

It wasn't until the weekend that it finally sank in. Sarah and I were on the carpool lane to couplehood. Peggy had been absolutely right: honesty really *was* the best policy. I'd gone ahead and told Sarah about stealing the diary, and not only had she gotten over being mad at me, but it'd turned out to be a great way to get her to open up to me. It'd only been a few days and I was really getting to *know* her—the *real* her, the one she'd never let anyone see. Sure, maybe she wasn't Sarah Jason Delaney the Intrepid, but she was Sarah Jason Delaney and that was intrepid enough for me. And now we were going out for dinner. It was a date! An actual date! Peggy could come over and I could tell her that she'd have to go home early because I had a date! And maybe in time we could double, me and Sarah and Peggy and Boyfriend #107 or whatever she'd be up to by then. It'd be great.

Naturally, I'd have to be careful. I didn't want to scare Sarah off by moving too fast. We'd take it slow at first. Just have some dinner, see some movies, and talk. I was sure we'd have lots to talk about. Sarah had one of the richest inner lives I'd ever encountered. No one who could come up with Sarah Jason Delaney the Intrepid and My Balinda could ever be boring. And I'd learn about her day-to-day life too. Even the littlest things could be magical when they were part of the life of someone you loved. Going out to the backyard and counting the dandelions. Dunking little Styrofoam balls in paint and sticking them together with straws to make molecules for science class. Going out at night and trying to spot some stars. And after a while with just the talking I was sure we'd move on to the cuddling soon enough.

And then she'd be my girlfriend. I'd be able to talk to people and casually say things like, 'Yeah, my girlfriend and I saw that movie just last week' and 'Chicken pox? Oh, I never got it, but my girlfriend did when she was three.' And there'd be no going over to her house to find out she was out on a date because if she *were* out on a date it'd be with me and I would be there. This was going to be so, so cool.

Of course, things would get tricky after a while. College, for instance—we'd have to find one we'd both be willing to go to. Being in the same grade made it easier, since we wouldn't end up in the same situation as Hayley and Jefferson, a thousand miles apart. We'd also have to figure out when we wanted to get married, whether we should wait till after college or tie the knot while we were still young. Combining our last names might be a problem, since they didn't go together so well. Delockery? Mockaney? Hyphenation was even more unwieldy. Maybe she'd want to distance herself from her parents so much that she'd want to just take mine. Kids would be another concern. September already knew exactly how many she wanted to have; maybe Sarah did too. I'd have to find out. Not right away, but eventually.

Just thinking about Sarah made me feel happy. I spent most of Monday daydreaming about her. In fact, that's what I was doing when Hayley came into the *Iliad* room with the new writer assignment sheet. "Looks like we finally caught a break," she said. "Benito gave us Marie Lasker this time around. She's supposedly pretty good about getting things in before the dead—"

"What?" I said. "We didn't get—" I grabbed the assignment sheet out of her hands. "Siren Delaney" was listed under "Sports." "Sports?" I said. "Benito put her on *sports*?"

"Don't rub it in," Speedy said.

I stormed over to Benito's room and threw the sheet down on her desk. "Okay, let me get this straight," I said. "For a week I ask you to take Siren Delaney off entertainment. You refuse. So I go to all this trouble and once she's finally a viable member of the *Iliad* you assign her to someone else? That's not even close to fair!"

"Nope," Benito agreed.

"So are you going to do anything about it?" I asked.

"Nope," Benito said.

I went over to the gym to call Sarah out of class and break the bad news. The doors were locked. "Closed practice," lamented one of the dweeby guys hanging around outside. "They're staying late, too."

This was a problem. If Sarah tried to go straight from school to my house chances were she'd have another run-in with Echo and that could ruin everything, both between me and my sister and between me and my future girlfriend. The bell rang and I went to go see what the peer counseling load for the day looked like. We had only one case lined up so I figured that was manageable. When the guy came in it turned out to be one of Krieg's scary dreadnok friends. "Mark Warner?" September asked pleasantly.

"*Warder,*" he spat. "My name is Warder." He sat down, whipped out a butterfly knife, and started cutting patterns in his left forearm. "I enjoy this," he explained. September was pretty freaked out and I was in a hurry so we just gave him a copy of the "So You're into Self-Mutilation" pamphlet and sent him on his way.

"I don't know," September said. "I've read the section in the binder, but I still can't believe it. Cutting yourself?"

"It seems to be going around," I said. "See you later."

I rushed back to the gym to see if the practice was over yet. It had been over for a while. I still had a chance of intercepting Sarah if she'd stopped to get her books out of her locker. She was just closing the locker door as I arrived. I'd made it in time. Life was sweet again.

"Sarah!" I said. "Am I ever glad to see you. Are you—"

"Sarah can't come to the phone right now," she said. "And I wouldn't bother leaving a message."

Something was wrong. Way wrong. I'd always been able to tell April and September apart with no problem, because even though they had essentially the same face, they did different things with it; the girl standing at Sarah's locker may have had Sarah's face, but she didn't look a thing like Sarah. "Siren?" I said. "You're . . . back?"

"Aw, whatsa matter, loser guy?" she asked. "You look upset. Sad 'cause now you won't get to suck face with your loser chick?"

I felt like I'd just been tossed a bomb reading "0:07"—one wrong move and everything I'd been working for over the past week would blow up in my face, and I didn't have time to think. "Uh, look," I said. "Sarah. Sarah. I understand. Maybe you had a bad weekend.

Had to bring Siren out of the box. But you can't fool *me*. You already told me the secret. I know where Siren comes from. I know it's just an act. A fake personality. You—"

"All personalities are fake," she said.

"That's not true," I said. "Siren is. Maybe even Sarah Jason Delaney the Intrepid is. But Sarah isn't. Not just plain regular Sarah."

"'Just plain regular Sarah,'" Siren said, "was me pretending to be loser-chick from seventh grade. You said it'd make me happier, so I tried it. It didn't work, of course, 'cause you're talking out your ass and don't know anything. I couldn't even get it right half the time. It wasn't the same. About the only thing you *did* get right was that I shouldn't have been trying to hold on to her. So now she's gone. Gone for good. She left you a present, though." She opened up her locker. It was almost empty, just a couple schoolbooks. "You liked her little 'What I Did on My Summer Vacation' thing?" she asked. She pulled something out of her locker and tossed it to me. "It's yours. Have a party."

It wasn't a notebook she'd given me. It was a plastic bag full of confetti. The confetti was the Historical Chronicle of Sarah Jason Delaney. She'd shredded it.

"Oh, I had a big shredding party over the weekend," she said. "In fact, I've only got one thing of loser-chick's left to shred. But that one I'll need some help with." She snickered. "I'm sure Carver Fringie'd be glad to do the honors." She shut her locker again and headed to the parking lot.

I looked at the bag of confetti. I'd memorized every word of the diary, of course, but the violence of its destruction still made me sick. I was about to put it in my backpack when I realized I didn't have my backpack. I'd left it in the *Iliad* room when I'd gone to complain to Benito. I looked at my watch. If I was lucky the custodians wouldn't have locked up yet. I hurried back to the *Iliad* room and opened the door to find Carver Fringie sucking face with Peggy Kaylin.

"Allen!" Peggy yelped. She wiped her mouth with the back of her hand. "Um, it's not what it—"

I closed the door.

On the way home I ran into April. I was pretty hard on her. She had no idea why I was so pissed.

Five

That evening I found myself sitting at a table outside King of the Juice way out in El Modena. It was quite a trip, but I hadn't come just for the strawberry lemonade. I'd come because Peggy had chased after me on my way home and said we needed to talk, but I was in no condition to talk to anyone right then. By the time I'd calmed down and gone over to her house to see what she wanted she'd already left for work, and since I now had my license and making the trip would no longer be a hassle, I figured I'd pay her a visit and we could talk during her break.

And now, a word from our economics correspondent

Now I realized that by doing this I was defeating Peggy's whole purpose in getting a job twelve miles away from her house. After all, there were plenty of employment opportunities within walking distance of school, but as Peggy explained, "I don't want people I know seeing me at work. Work is for working, not socializing. Besides, it'd just make me really uncomfortable." So this was new territory to me. Peggy, I soon discovered, was a breed apart in the juice-dispensing game: while her coworker greeted customers with a simple "Yeah?," Peggy made a point of giving each one a genuine smile before saying, "Welcome to King of the Juice! My name's Peggy—how can I help you today?"

Consequently Peggy's line turned out to be about three times longer than the other girl's. I suspect that suited both of them just fine.

I couldn't help but get a kick out of watching Peggy deal with the people in the line in front of me. Her demeanor actually motivated a lot of people to treat her like a person instead of an extension of the juice machine: one woman complimented her on her earrings, another asked her to suggest a flavor for her, and one guy asked her out—which I didn't get such a kick out of until she politely but firmly brushed him off. The guy right before me in line ordered a smoothie with protein powder and wheatgrass and paprika and ibuprofen and stuff and then it was my turn. "Hi!" I said.

A familiar twinge of distress flashed across Peggy's face, but she quickly regained her composure. "Welcome to King of the Juice," she said. "My name's Peggy. How can I help you today?"

I laughed. "Hey, you're pretty good at this," I said. "Your interpersonal skills are ideally suited to today's service economy."

"Thank you, sir," she said. "What would you like to drink?"

"Uh, I'll take a medium strawberry lemonade," I said. "Did you like my quickie financial analysis? I think my next report'll be on soybean futures."

She set the juice down in front of me. "Can I get you anything else today?" she asked.

"Uh, that's okay," I said, forking over some cash. "When do you get off? You said you wanted to talk."

"We close at ten, sir," she said. "Here's your change. Thank you for choosing King of the Juice."

I looked at my watch; it wouldn't be ten for another couple of hours. "Do you have a break anytime soon?" I asked.

"Enjoy your beverage," she said.

I decided to take the hint. I wandered around the shopping colony, sipping my lemonade; it was a warm night, but that might just have been the lights beating down on me. I decided to kill some time at the big bookstore on the other side of the parking lot. After reading the magazines, enjoying a scone, sampling some music at one of the listening stations, playing a couple rounds of Bloodgnarl in the software section, and dancing a few numbers in the disco, I looked at my watch: ten o'clock. I returned to the juice shop and looked through the window to find Peggy busy putting up the chairs and reconciling the cash registers in her little box flooded with cold fluorescent light—it was sort of like watching TV. Finally, with a last look around, she stepped outside and locked the door behind her.

"Hi," I said. "Did you still want to talk?"

She looked skeptical. "It's kind of late," she said.

"It's up to you," I said.

"Oh, all right," she said. She sat down at one of the little white tables out front. "But only for a few minutes," she cautioned. "Mom and Dad get worried if I'm not back by eleven on a school night."

"Sure, okay," I said. "You know, if you just wanted me to go away you could've said so. You didn't have to pretend you didn't know me."

"But I don't know you, not from work," she said. "I only know you from home and from school."

"So?" I said.

"So, at work I'm a worker," she said. "I can't go letting my personal life mix in with work."

"Don't you think that's kind of weird?" I asked.

"That's your opinion," she said.

"Whatever," I said. "I don't want to argue. So what did you want to talk about? I assume it has to do with you and Fringie."

"Right," she said. She paused to shift around in her seat and sort of shake herself out. One of the first things you discovered in conversing with Peggy was that her hands stayed constantly in motion, making little adjustments; she couldn't leave herself alone for more than a second. "Well," she said, "I just wanted to make sure you didn't have the wrong idea about us. It wasn't what it looked like."

"Really?" I said. "So you weren't actually making out? You just sort of slipped and your faces smushed into each other? That's a relief."

"No, we were," she said. "But it's more than that. I mean, I suppose I've had a lot of boyfriends—"

"Ninety-three," I said.

"—but this is different," she said. "This is true love. And it probably would never have happened if not for you."

It was a good thing I'd long since finished my lemonade or I would've ended up spraying it all over the table. "Come again?" I said.

"Your advice," she said. "That you gave me a couple weeks ago. I did some thinking, and I decided you were exactly right."

"That's funny," I said. "I don't seem to recall telling you to grab the next guy you could find philosophizing at length about his own penis."

"Allen!" Peggy said, her cheeks reddening. "No, you told me to look for someone who I was already really close to. And that's Carver. I mean, we grew up together. You can't get much closer than the boy two doors down, right?"

"Yeah," I said. "Right."

"It was so obvious when I finally thought about it," Peggy went on. "I mean, Carver and me have been best friends for ages and ages—"

"Excuse me?" I said.

"Well, you wouldn't know about it since you're in a different grade," she explained. "But we have all these classes together and we get along really well. And he's really sweet and really smart and *really* cute and he's the captain of the water polo team and—"

"Look, Peggy," I said, "I'm glad to see you so happy, and I wish I could be happy *for* you, but—I *know* Carver Fringie. The guy's bad news."

"Well I know him better than you, and I think he's good news," Peggy said.

"You don't have to take my word for it," I said. "Have you talked to any of his ex-girlfriends? Heard what he's like at the end of a relationship and not just the beginning?"

"Well, of course," she said. "I'm not exactly new at this. But they all said the same thing. He really is just as smart and cool and funny and sweet as he seems. And that it was their fault they ended up breaking up."

"All that means is that he's good at making them think it was their fault," I said.

Peggy frowned. "Why should I be worrying about *that* anyway?" she asked. "Who says there has to be an ending? If it goes the way it's supposed to, there won't be, right?"

I sighed. "How many relationships have you had before Fringie?" I asked.

"Ninety-three, I guess," she said.

"How many of them ended?" I asked.

"Ninety-three," she said. "But all it takes is one."

"And why did those relationships end?" I asked.

"Because the guys I was with . . . tried stuff," she said.

"You mean they tried to pressure you into sex," I said. "Or realized that there was only a certain distance you were willing to go, and dumped you."

Peggy nodded. "But—"

"What is the one thing above all else that Carver Fringie is known for?" I asked.

"That's just a mean rumor," she said. "You mean that he . . . I mean . . . that a lot of girls' first times were with him, right? That's just a rumor. It's not true. He told me himself that it's not."

"But Peggy," I said, "you can't really believe that—"

"Sure I can," she said. "Because it's happened to me. When I was still in Catholic school, a lot of the girls in my class said I was a 'slut' just because my . . . because I . . . *developed* more than they did. And because I had more dates than they did. That's part of why I wanted to go to public school, to get away from the mean girls that teased me and called me names . . . and if it could happen to me, why not Carver? I *know* Carver, Allen. He's not like that."

"Look, Peggy," I said, "it's not like I'm dogmatically anti-Fringie or anything. I just don't want to see you hurt."

"That's sweet," she said, "but you're not going to. I mean, this is it. I can feel it. This is the person I'm going to marry and have kids with and grow old with. I know I've said that before but that was different. I was naive and innocent back then. Now I know when it's real and when I'm just fooling myself. And this is real. I mean, Carver *cares* about me. And he's *interested* in me, as a person. Those other guys . . . a lot of them were really just interested in my . . . you know."

"Right," I said. "Well, I guess that's one thing we can agree on: it's not your breasts that Fringie's after."

So, live around here much?

On the drive home I found my thoughts drifting back to the summer of 1967. Then I turned off the oldies station and thought about some stuff that had happened during my lifetime.

The summer after Echo and I finished fifth grade, my dad's mother and stepfather died of more or less simultaneous strokes. They'd lived on a small farm in Bucks County, Pennsylvania, and my dad and Bobbo had to fly out there to dispose of the property. They took all us kids with them—the one and only time I've ever been outside the state of California. Their mother's maiden name had been Madsen, and the farm had been in the family so long that its official street address was 1 Madsens Lane. We stayed there for a few weeks while Dad arranged to sell it off, then spent some time wandering around the uniform industrial squalor that is the Northeast. All told, we were gone for nearly six weeks.

A week before we returned home, Peggy had gone with her family to spend a few weeks with her grandparents, all four of whom lived in Evanston, Illinois. This meant that during that whole fateful summer I didn't see Peggy once, not from the last day of school in early June till Labor Day weekend. Now, I should make a couple of things clear at this point. The first is that even in June, Peggy's figure hadn't exactly been linear: it'd been clear for some time that she'd begun that miraculous metamorphosis from a pretty much standard-issue kid into one of those unattainable, unfathomable creatures who could make you ache just from the way they were shaped. But even as I marveled that the girl two doors down was showing unmistakable signs of turning into, well, a chick, her maturation seemed to be proceeding more or less in line with that of her contemporaries. The second thing I should make clear is that even upon her return, her breasts were, while admittedly eye-catching, still nothing to contact the media about. They were well within the realm of possibility. So it wasn't simply their size that rendered me temporarily speechless when she first got back. It was the *change* in size, the jump cut between June and September. If the transition between Peggy the unremarkably proportioned and Peggy the impressively endowed had been broken up into ninety little steps, the way it would've been if we'd been hanging out that summer, I might not even have noticed.

Okay, that's an overstatement. Obviously I would've *noticed*. After all, Peggy knew exactly what it was that made my eyes pop out of their sockets and roll halfway down the hallway when she answered the door her first day back.

"See?" she wailed, stomping back into the kitchen, where her mom was placidly chopping up a bunch of celery. "Allen too. I *told* you. I look totally ridiculous. I'm never leaving this house ever again. Stupid body." She threw herself into a chair and blinked furiously at one of the mugs on the kitchen table. The mug had a picture of a teddy bear on it whom Peggy seemed to hold entirely responsible for this turn of events.

"Don't be silly," Mrs. K. said.

"I'm not," Peggy said. "I'm totally serious. This isn't like a pimple or something. This is something I'm stuck with for the rest of my whole entire *life*. Which is now *ruined*. And I'm not even *thirteen* yet—chances are they'll keep on growing for years and years. I'm a complete *freak*."

"Peggy, I'm getting a little tired of this," Mrs. K. said. "You're not a freak. You're not even especially disadvantaged—you're not blind or deaf or in a wheelchair. You've just got a generous figure. Well, that's the way God made you and that's all there is to it. You'll adjust in time. The fact is that this kind of thing runs on both sides of the family. It happened to all the women on your father's side and it happened to all the women on my side. It happened to me, it happened to my sister, now it's happened to you and in a couple of years I'm sure it'll happen to Kelly."

"What?" Kelly shouted from the TV room.

"We weren't talking to you, just about you," Mrs. K. replied.

"Oh," Kelly said, profoundly uninterested. (As it happened, Mrs. K. was wrong. When Kelly's time came, she developed just to the point of being *perfecto y espectacular* and then stayed there. But you already knew that.)

"My life is still ruined," Peggy sulked. "I can't even *walk* anymore—it feels all sloppy. And none of my clothes fit either. Why couldn't I have just stayed the way I was a few months ago? I was perfectly happy with my body the way it was. Now it's lost in time and I'll never ever get it back. I'm stuck like this for the next eighty *years*."

"I think they look good on you," I volunteered.

She glared at me. "What's that supposed to mean?" she asked.

"I'll shut up now," I said.

Despite her woe, Peggy remained unable to resist the lure of school supplies, and the next day Mrs. K. dropped us off at Brea Mall to do some back-to-school shopping. Peggy'd been kind of sullen the whole trip up the hill, and grew doubly so when she had to make the rounds of the department stores buying a whole new wardrobe that she could actually squeeze herself into, but her eyes lit up the moment we stepped into the stationery store and after a few minutes of plucking multisubject notebooks and fountain pens off the shelves she was back to her usual cheerful self. By then I was starving, so I went to grab something to eat in the food court while Peggy looked around for a table. The girl behind the counter was dishing me up a generous helping of congealed ziti when some random guy with a frilly haircut come up to where Peggy was sitting. As I headed back to the table I heard him ask, "Are you a model?"

"No," Peggy said amiably. "You must have me confused with someone else."

"Are you sure you're not a model?" he asked. "Because if you're not, you should be."

"Really?" Peggy asked.

I slammed my tray down on the table and made a fairly elaborate production of sitting down—it was clear to everyone in the entire food court that Peggy and I were sitting together. This jerk seemed not to notice. "Yes, really," he said. "I'm completely serious. You've got the 'in' look these days." He made quote marks in the air with his fingers when he said this. "What's your name?" he asked.

"I'm P— I'm Margaret Hannah Kaylin," she said. "Meg for short."

There were about a million things I wanted to interrupt with at this point: that Peggy was way too young for this guy; that he was obviously just trying to scam on her, using a cheesy pickup line that had been used five billion times over the past few decades and been successful maybe twice; that in the five years I'd known her I'd heard her called Pegleg and Peglet and Pegpen (Cheese was inventive) but never, ever "Meg"; that my ziti was lukewarm at best. But I didn't dare. I was eleven years old. This guy had to be at least five years older than me. And Peggy—well, Peggy may have been only a year and nine days older than me, but she looked a lot closer to his age than to mine. I felt like I'd taken a wrong turn at the jungle gym and ended up at the local JC.

"Well, Meg, my name's Chazz," the jerk said. "Look, uh, I happen to have some contacts in the modeling business—why don't you give me your number, and I'll give you a call if something opens up?"

Peggy blushed. "Oh, I don't think I could—"

"Couldn't hurt, right?" Chazz said. "What's the worst that could happen?"

I could come up with some pretty disturbing scenarios, but before I could propose any of them—as if I would've had the nerve to propose any of them—Peggy went ahead and gave Chazz her number. That troubled me, but at least it got him to go away. "What a nice person!" Peggy said.

"Oh, please!" I said. "'Are you a model?' Who's he trying to kid?"

"Is that so unbelievable?" Peggy said, crestfallen. "Am I that hideous?"

"No, I didn't say—Peggy, that's one of the oldest lines in the book," I said. "Or should I say, 'Meg'?"

"I like the name Meg," Peggy shot back. "Peggy's a little kid's name."

"Fine, whatever," I said. "Look, the point is, that guy was a creep."

"No he wasn't," she said. "You say that about everyone."

"But—" I paused. "Okay," I said, "did you notice that the whole time that guy was talking to you he didn't look you in the eye once?"

"You mean he's not honest?" she asked.

"I mean he was staring at your—" I cut myself off. It suddenly occurred to me that Peggy had finally stopped freaking out about her body and the last thing I wanted was to get her all miserable about it again. I decided to change the subject. "My ziti's cold," I said.

Roll call

Now you're probably patting yourself on the back and perhaps treating yourself to a sandwich for having been perceptive enough to figure out from the moment of his entrance that Chazz would turn out to be Boyfriend #1. The thing is, he wasn't. Sure, he called Peggy up later that night, and they even arranged to go out to dinner, but as soon as Peggy made it clear that he was going to have to meet her parents before they went anywhere, Chazz was history. He didn't even hang up, just ripped the phone out of the wall or something. "It was weird," Peggy told me later. "There was no click—just a weird sound and then a message saying that the line had been disconnected or was no longer in service and I should check the number and dial again. I guess his phone broke."

No, Boyfriend #1 was this guy named Joel Degen, and as he and I were never invited over to Peggy's house at the same time, I never actually got around to meeting the guy. In fact, I didn't know that Peggy even had a boyfriend at all until Cheese blurted it out one evening when I'd been invited to stay for dinner; Peggy brushed it off, though—"He's just someone who goes to my school, let's talk about something else"—and I assumed it wasn't serious. So it was rather disconcerting when one afternoon I came over to help her with her science homework—dipping little Styrofoam balls in paint and sticking them together with straws to make molecules—and when she gave me her notes so I could see which molecules they were supposed to make, I found that she'd written "Meg Degen" over and over and over again on the back of every page. "What's this all about?" I asked.

"Oh," she said, her face lighting up like a stoplight. "It's nothing. I was just practicing."

"Practicing?" I said.

"Yeah," she said. "For when Joel and I get married."

"But that's ridiculous," I said. "You and Joel aren't going to get married. I've never even met him."

Peggy somehow failed to see the logic in this. "So?" she asked.

"So, how long have you known him?" I asked.

"A couple weeks," she said.

"Well, how can you marry someone you've only known for a couple weeks?" I asked. Clearly Peggy was unaware of the statute limiting one's potential spouse to those who were long-standing acquaintances at age twelve. A horrifying thought occurred to me. "Have you kissed him?"

"Well, sure," she said.

I supposed this was marginally acceptable. "Has *he* kissed *you*?" I asked.

"Of course," she said, blushing again. "Look, I don't—"

This, on the other hand, was intolerable. Without question, it would have to be stopped. "Who asked who out first?" I asked.

"He asked me," she said. "Wh—"

"And he could only have known you for a day or two, right?" I said.

"Right, but—"

"So why did he ask?" I said.

Peggy put the notebook down and started slowly rocking back and forth in her chair, a nervous habit that made the plastic squeak. "Because he liked me, I guess," she said.

"Why?" I asked.

"I don't know," she said. "He just likes me. Is it so hard to believe that someone could like me?"

"Not at all," I said. "It's just hard to believe that this guy could be that someone. I mean, there are a million things to like about you. You're kind, you're generous, you're . . . good at heart. You're probably the only person I've ever *met* who's good at heart. Everyone I know spends all their time putting other people down. The best part of their day comes when bad things happen to the people they hate. You're the only person I know who's not like that."

"That's not true," Peggy said. "Lots of people are—"

"Maybe so," I interrupted. "But I wouldn't know. Maybe I know a lot of people like that, but not well enough to know that they are. Did that make any sense? Look, here's what I'm saying. To tell if someone's good-looking or not you just have to look at them. To tell if they're smart and funny and interesting you just have to talk to them. But to tell if someone's a good person, well, you have to know them for a while. I know that anyone you go out with is lucky to be spending time with you, but does this guy? At best, he asked you out because he thought you seemed sort of nice. Most likely he just asked you out because of your—because of the way you look."

It was on the drive home from King of the Juice that it occurred to me that Fringie was the first of Peggy's boyfriends for whom this argument didn't apply—he had been a long-standing acquaintance at age twelve, though as far as I knew he and Peggy had never talked much when he lived on our street. I also wondered what Peggy's transformation must've looked like to Fringie, having skipped not just from June to September like me, but from June to three Septembers later. But then, Fringie had undergone his own metamorphosis in that time, and knowing Fringie, chances were that he was far too impressed with himself for anyone else to have caught his attention.

But she'd caught his attention now and Fringie had eased himself into the 94 spot, which would've come as quite a surprise to Peggy back when she was convinced she'd never go past one. And in retrospect, Joel had a lengthier run than most: he lasted almost three whole weeks. I came over one evening to find that Peggy had barricaded herself in her room and wouldn't come out, and Kelly told me of the breakup. I asked her what she thought of the whole episode. "Like, whatever," she said. "He only liked her 'cause she's got, like, boobs and stuff." I thought that was a fairly accurate diagnosis.

I didn't learn what had happened till more than a year later, when the embarrassment had worn off enough for Peggy to tell me the details. It seems she'd gone to Joel's house after school, and they'd been making out on the couch; before long he'd started tugging at her sweater. "At first I thought that maybe he just liked acrylic a whole lot," she explained, but soon she'd taken a timeout and asked, "What are you doing?"

"Gettin' it on," Joel had explained.

"It's already on," Peggy had replied, confused. "Maybe we should—"

Joel never found out what Peggy thought they should do, because he chose that moment to stick his hand up her skirt. Peggy slapped his hand away. "What are you *doing*?" she demanded.

"Come *on*," Joel wailed. "I thought you were supposed to be easy."

"What?" Peggy said.

"Aren't you gonna put out?" Joel asked. "Everyone at school says you do."

"They *what*?" Peggy said.

"Look, if you're not gonna put out, beat it," Joel said. "I got better things to do." And thus ended Peggy's introduction to the dating scene.

Peggy didn't mourn for long, though: by the end of the week she'd covered the back of her math notes with the name "Meg Kiley." That is, until she got to the bottom of the last page, at which point she'd reverted to "Peggy Kiley": "The Meg thing just isn't catching on," she explained.

"But where did you get 'Kiley' from?" I asked.

"Sean Kiley," she said. "He's my boyfriend."

Sean Kiley's tenure as #2 was cut short a couple weeks later when he grabbed Peggy in a sadly predictable place; the relationship's fate was sealed when, as Peggy retreated in shock, Sean asked, "Come on, can't I at least *see* 'em?" Upon being denied, he dropped Peggy with nary a moment's thought.

But when it comes to really demonstrating the caliber of Peggy's various swains, there's no getting around #67, Francis Gary Patrick. I met Gary on a balmy Saturday afternoon in October when I happened to be hanging out at Peggy's house, helping—okay, watching—the Kaylins clean out their garage. Then, with a roar of a deliberately removed muffler, a black convertible came skidding up to the curb and out hopped this guy with a rippling physique and a ridiculous blond pompadour. "Hey, Pops!" he said. Mr. K. bristled. Cheese, on the other hand, was clearly awestruck. Gary punched him in the shoulder. "How's it goin', chief?" he asked.

"It's going good," Cheese said, his voice cracking.

"Glad to hear it," Gary said. "Hey, you people mind if I grab something to drink? I'm as thirsty as a, a really thirsty guy." Without waiting for an answer he breezed into the house. Peggy followed him, and I followed her. Kelly was sprawled on the living room carpet, wearing her Vista de la Vista cheerleading uniform. As I came in she jumped up and stuck her foot up on an end table.

"What are you doing?" I asked.

"Stretching," she said. "I have to go cheer at a game and like, you're supposed to stretch first 'cause if you don't you'll, like, tear your ulterior crucial ligature or whatever."

Gary emerged from the kitchen with a soda. "Hey, brother," he said to me, grabbing my hand and crushing my fingers into a fine paste. "Francis Gary Patrick. I play beach volleyball for a living. What do you do?" He chuckled. "Or are you still in high school?"

"I'm fourteen," I said. "That'd seem like a reasonable place for me to be."

"Maybe," he yawned. "Maybe not. I never finished, myself. See, I was kicking back with my good friend Bart Bialy"—he carefully enunciated each syllable of the name to make sure none of us missed it—"and Bart said I was good enough to leave early and turn pro, and I never looked back." He flopped down into a chair, which wasn't designed for flopping and promptly cracked. "Kind of a shame, I guess," he continued, "since when I was in school they had me read the morning announcements, since I've got such a great sense of humor, see, and I'd throw in little jokes and shit, like, it'd say the Spanish Club was meeting in Room 103, and I'd say, 'The Spanish Club is meeting in Room 103, and the Fat Chicks Club is meeting in the cafeteria!'"

With that, Gary burst into uproarious laughter—it took him close to a minute to regain his composure. "Anyway," he said, wiping his eyes, "it's too bad I left 'cause now they probably just have the principal do 'em. But when Bart Bialy says you should turn pro, you turn pro. Three years on the tour and I'm up to my ass in cash. Not as much as Bart Bialy, but enough for plenty of nice toys."

"I take it that's another volleyball guy?" I said.

"Anoth— You really don't know who Bart Bialy is?" he gaped.

"Only from context," I said.

"Man, what planet have you been living on?" he asked. "He's only the best beach volleyball player on the planet. Don't you know anything about volleyball?"

"Not really," I said. "My sister's always been the athlete of the fam—"

"Your sister?" Gary laughed. "What's she do, jump rope?"

"Hockey and baseball," I said. "At least she—"

"Hockey and baseball?" Gary repeated, shaking his head. "See, this is the problem with sports these days. It's chicks. There's only one place I want to see chicks in sports—cheerleading! That's their natural place. Right, Kell? Kell knows the score."

"Like, get real," Kelly said. "You're like one of those male Jehovah's pigs or something. Girls rule, boys are stupid."

"Oh yeah?" Gary said. "Well you're proof it's the other way around!"

"I take it that's some more of that great sense of humor in action," I said.

Peggy sighed and took Gary's soda can into the kitchen. "Hey, I'm not done with that!" he said.

"Yes, you are," she said. "Good-bye, Gary. Don't call me again."

"What?" Gary sputtered.

"You heard me," Peggy said quietly. "I don't want to see you again. Nobody comes into my house and insults my sister and that's all there is to it. Good-bye."

"But—you mean I don't even get to *see* 'em?" Gary protested.

Peggy held the door open. "Get out," she said.

Gary stormed out and Peggy closed the door behind him. "You know," I said, "I may not have known who Bart Bialy is, but I bet I know one thing about volleyball Gary doesn't."

"What?" Peggy asked.

"How to spell it," I said.

Kelly said something but it was drowned out by the roar of Gary's convertible tearing off around the corner. "What did you say?" Peggy asked.

"Can you go get my pom-poms?" Kelly asked. "They're, like, up in my room."

Peggy went upstairs and Kelly switched feet on the table. I shook my head. "Wow, that was something," I said.

"Yeah, Peggy loves me," Kelly said matter-of-factly. "Everybody does."

This may well have been true. Nevertheless, as I pulled into my driveway on my trip home from the juice shop, an odd thought occurred to me. When Peggy had been Kelly's age, her boyfriends already numbered in the fifties; Kelly's, however, you could count on your fingers—after chopping both your hands off. Despite having almost palpable advantages in beauty, pheromones, and popularity, Kelly had never gone steady with anyone, never even had a date as far as I knew. She was stuck at zero. I found this both puzzling and tremendously cheering.

And Peggy was up to 94. Late one night a few years earlier I'd been sitting up talking to Echo, and just this subject had come up. Echo and I used to do that a lot, just lie in our beds staring into the darkness and talk till the middle of the night. It was a better deal for her than for me, since it didn't make any difference to Echo whether she slept from ten to one or one to four, while I'd end up so tired that I'd take catnaps on lawns I passed on the way to school; still, it'd been fun, and I missed it. This particular night I'd done most of the talking, ranting about Peggy. "I don't get it," I'd said. "She's been dating for, what, three months now. Maybe even a day or two less. And she's already had five boyfriends? Going on six, from what I've heard? By the time she turns thirty she'll be on number, what, something like—"

"Three hundred fifty-two," Echo had shot back instantly.

As I walked into the house, I did some mental arithmetic. Not being Echo, it took me a minute or two, but the conclusion was clear: Peggy was ahead of schedule. At her current rate she'd overshoot #352 by a significant margin. I really hoped she wouldn't linger on #94 to try to get back on track.

Someone call Guinness

I wasn't the only one preoccupied with numbers around this time. One afternoon a few days after visiting Peggy at work, I was heading to the *Iliad* room for lunch when I could've sworn I heard Sluggo the water polo player counting out loud: "Forty-two, forty-three, forty-four . . ." I was impressed—he wasn't leaving out any or getting the order wrong or anything, quite an accomplishment for the ol' Slugmeister. I wondered what he was counting. As I opened the door, I learned at least part of the answer, as he declared, "Fifty-seven, fifty-eight, fifty-nine—four minutes." So he was timing something. But what?

Whatever it was, it had attracted quite a crowd: I soon found that I could not only not see what it was, I could barely even get into the room. The place was packed with water polo players–not just Sluggo, but Lemming, Skippie, Grungie, the lot of them. Even Kevin Love stood off in the corner, eyes hidden. And in the back sat a bunch of the *Iliad* editors, looking quite unhappy; I assumed they'd been sitting eating lunch when fifty thousand water polo players had come in and trapped them there. I didn't see Speedy Wilkins till he jumped up on the table.

"Hey, back off, everyone," he said. "People need room to breathe."

"That's cheating!" Sluggo shrieked. "You can't order people around. Eleven, twelve, thirteen . . ."

Nevertheless, the crowd backed off a little and I could finally see the object of everyone's fascination: Fringie sitting in a swivel chair, Peggy on his lap, the two of them apparently attempting to swallow one another. What was worse, Peggy had this meltingly blissful look on her face, as if there were no place she'd rather be than making out with Fringie while Sluggo hovered over them with a stopwatch barking out the seconds. "Twenty, twenty-one, twenty— Hey! That's a break! I win! I win!"

"Oh, there was no break," Speedy said. "Give it up."

Sluggo simpered and went back to his counting. As the five-minute mark approached, his voice trailed off: "Fifty-four, fifty-five, fifty-six . . . crap."

"Five minutes," Speedy declared. "Pay up." Sluggo dug a ten-dollar bill out of his pocket and handed it up to him. "You guys can break that clinch now," Speedy said. "The point has been made."

"I still don't get how anyone can go that long without coming up for air," Sluggo grumbled.

"Who said they were holding their breath?" Speedy said. "Just 'cause you're a mouth-breather doesn't mean everyone else is." He pocketed the cash, hopped off the table, and strolled off down the hall, whistling.

Fringie picked that moment to finally pull his tongue out of Peggy's throat and they disengaged with a lovely wet slorping sound. Peggy looked a bit sheepish but unrepentant; I tried to catch her eye to sort of ask her with my expression what the hell she'd been thinking, but she avoided looking at me. Fringie squinted and put his glasses back on. Then he looked straight at me and flashed me a smug, possessive smile. He stroked Peggy's hair and then pulled some of it back to reach her ear. "C'mon, babe, let's go," he murmured, loud enough for me to hear.

"Well, *that* was a thoroughly disgusting display," Holdn said after Peggy and the water polo players had finally left. "Am I the only one who thinks that we ought to get some kind of federal injunction to keep mushroom-head away from Kaylin? The guy is plankton."

"Jealous?" Hayley said. "What, is Peggy 'shiny'?"

"No," Holdn said, "but she's nice. Close enough."

"Nice?" Cat asked. "You just like her because she's got the biggest breasts in the whole school."

"That's not true!" Holdn said. "One, that's not why I like her, and two, she *doesn't* have the biggest breasts in the whole school, just the most obvious ones. I mean, Kerensky's are just the same and you don't see anyone obsessing about hers."

This was a rather startling assertion and naturally everyone's eyes flew to Hayley's chest to investigate; as it turned out, Holdn proved absolutely right. "Hunh," said Anton, the news editor. "I never noticed. Quite impressive. I wouldn't have thought that wearing looser clothing would make such a difference."

"It doesn't," Hayley said. "I think the difference is that everyone knows I'm taken, so no one ever bothered to 'check me out'—except apparently Holdn, God knows why. Peggy Kaylin's a different story. Even when she's taken, you know she's going to be back on the market in a week or two." She looked around. "You all can feel free to stop staring at my breasts now," she said.

The problem was, it was beginning to look like Hayley's theory was quickly becoming obsolete. A week passed, then two. Usually by the third week Peggy's boyfriends would be visibly itchy and anyone could see that it wouldn't be too long before Peggy would end up spending another night crying in her room. But Fringie was different— he seemed to simply be enjoying the pleasure of her company. This was unprecedented. And I began to worry that it'd have an unprecedented ending: that he'd make his move, and Peggy would go along with it—and *then* he'd dump her. I didn't know whether Peggy'd be able to handle that. It worried me.

The water polo players had another worry altogether: that their fearless leader might be losing his touch. I overheard a lot of snippets of conversations to this effect, as Fringie would often swing by the *Iliad* room to pick up Peggy and his acolytes would follow him. The most chilling talk came one afternoon during layout week when Peggy was in Benito's room looking over the pasteup boards and the water polo players were milling around Fringie as he waited for her out in the hall.

"You gonna score tonight?" Sluggo asked gleefully.

I peeked through the *Iliad* room window to see Fringie shoot Sluggo a look of utter contempt. "Don't be crude," he said. "If the penis is to be sated tonight, as well it may, Peggy Kaylin will surely have no part of it. She is unique. I must proceed very delicately with her, and the penis understands that. For while patience is not among its cardinal virtues, the penis is not about to squander that which it has so long sought now that the moment of triumph has finally drawn near. We will wait for a moment of supreme vulnerability to strike."

I tried to relay some of this information to Peggy, but she refused to hear any of it. "I wish you wouldn't say mean things about Carver," she'd tell me with a mournful look in her eyes. "I thought you'd be happy for me now that I've finally found someone who really cares about me. Maybe you're not such a good friend after all." And then I'd end up spending the rest of the day apologizing.

And so Fringie's plan proceeded according to schedule.

Six

It was three weeks after I'd found her kissing Fringie that Peggy showed up at school wearing a bulky black leather jacket that could have comfortably housed a small family. The zippers alone were enough to set off metal detectors at airports hundreds of miles away. When she came in for journalism class Hank gasped and rubbed his eyes. "Whoa!" he said. "For a minute there I thought you were the Fonz."

"What on earth is that?" I asked.

"It's my new jacket," Peggy beamed. "Carver got it for me. Isn't it the coolest?"

"But you don't wear leather," I said.

"Sure I do," she said.

"No you don't," I said. "After you saw that documentary about the leather industry you got so upset that you refused to wear the patent leather shoes that came with your uniform and your mom had to special-order new ones made out of some space-age polymer. You haven't worn a speck of leather since."

Peggy turned crimson. "I changed my mind, okay?" she said. "I'm not in Catholic school anymore. I can wear what I want." She turned around and stormed out.

I followed her to Benito's room. "What?" she said. "Quit following me."

"Look, I'm sorry if I upset you," I said. "It just seems a little weird to me that you'd be happily wearing a jacket that probably depleted most of some rancher's herd after making such a big deal about not wanting to wear leather."

"But that was eight years ago," she said.

"Still," I said. "Tell me the truth. Are you wearing it because you like it? Or because Fringie does?"

"Are you kidding?" she said. "I *love* it. This is the first day in the last four years that I've been able to walk around without people staring at my breasts. I'm never taking it off. Now leave me alone."

Catch the .WAV

I was still fuming when I got home after peer counseling. When I got to my room I found that Echo had her goban out to practice her tesuji; luckily, all this involved was placing little black and white stones on a piece of wood and not, say, hacking people up with swords. I'd started to recount my exchange with Peggy when Echo cut me off. "I know," she said. "I was right there in the room, remember?"

"Oh," I said. "Anyway, you know what the worst part is? A few weeks ago Peggy never would've said she was 'able to walk around without people staring my breasts.' She'd wouldn't have been able to spit out the last word."

"This is a good thing?" Echo said. "That's one of the more insipid faults I've heard about lately. You should be glad she's rid of it."

"But I *like* her faults," I said. "They're part of what makes her her."

"That's ridiculous," Echo said. She glanced down at her board. "Hey, as long as I've got the equipment out, would you like to play? I'll give you a nine-stone handicap."

"Are you serious?" I said. "Echo, you're a two-dan. I barely know the rules."

"Fine," she said. "I'll give you thirteen stones."

"You could give me an entire quarry and it wouldn't make any difference," I said. "If all you want is the pleasure of giving me a thrashing it'd be a lot easier to just take a swing at me. Can't you find someone to play with over the net?"

"It's not the same thing," she sulked.

Suddenly we were interrupted by a terrible sound from Krieg's room: silence. See, you could always tell when Krieg was in his room by the sound of one of his bootleg Crucified Vomit tapes blasting away inside. This time around he'd been listening to *Please Me, Bitch,* a compilation of early Beatles covers given that Crucified Vomit spin. While I'd been talking to Echo, he'd gotten all the way through "Pus I Love You" and was halfway through "Do You Want to Know a Secretion" when the music was suddenly cut off. That meant trouble. Because Krieg never turned off the music when he was about to leave—he only turned it off when he was about to masturbate.

This in itself wasn't necessarily objectionable. Molly, for instance, was even more of a masturbation enthusiast than Krieg, but she at least had the courtesy to make sure to get the water running nice and loud to drown out any sounds she might make while pleasuring herself. Silence was the key. I took pride in never having once woken Echo up, nor had she ever waked me—though in her case it was to abstinence rather than technique that she owed her track record. But Krieg practically made a point of making sure we all could hear him. Apparently if he didn't turn the music off he couldn't concentrate on the task at hand.

The air filled with the sound of some sort of harpsichord étude, which was Molly's idea of taking preventative measures. Echo and I were older and wiser than she, however, and knew better. "Down-stairs?" I suggested.

"Of course," Echo said.

Before I could get more than a couple steps down the hall, how-ever, I heard something that stopped me in my tracks. Echo heard it too, if her stunned look was any indication. It was as if we'd passed the scene of an accident expecting to find that a couple of cars had crashed into each other and found instead that the cars were being eaten by a giant monster chicken or something. For though Krieg's trademark grunting noises had started up right on schedule, this time they were answered in kind by a female voice.

"This has got to be a sick joke," Echo said.

"Of course it is," I said. "He probably just got Jerem to play him some porn audio clips. I mean, who'd risk exposing herself to Krieg's semen? That's got to be a level-three biohazard at least."

This seemed perfectly logical at the time, but it didn't account for the girl who came stumbling out of Krieg's room a couple minutes later (a longevity record for the Kriegster). She had long stringy unwashed hair and wore black eyeliner and smudged black lipstick and black nail polish. She also wore a long black T-shirt. Having just recently finished having sex with Krieg—and even now, I'm tempted to add a row of exclamation points after typing that—she naturally wore nothing else.

"Hi," she said.

"What the hell is wrong with you?" Echo asked.

Daised and confused

"I can't really talk now," the girl said. She disappeared into the bathroom to clean up. A moment later Krieg himself emerged from his room. He'd thrown on a pair of jeans but was shirtless, revealing undiscovered continents of ketchup-and-mustard acne extending across his shoulders and probably all the way down his back. The rest was just bloated white flesh the consistency of batter—Krieg weighed in at something like 85 percent bodyfat.

"Hey!" he barked. "Don't fuck with my bitch or I'll fuck you up good."

Echo glared at him. Krieg whimpered and retreated back to his room.

A couple minutes later I heard a car horn honk outside our house. Krieg, now fully clothed, pounded once on the bathroom door and headed out to the driveway; his little friend, her postcoital ablutions apparently complete, grabbed the rest of her clothes from his room and followed him downstairs. I waited till I heard the car speed off before I went into Krieg's room myself.

I probably should've waited longer: Krieg's sweat was visibly condensing on the walls and the room smelled as if generation after generation of small woodland creatures had crawled under his bed to die. A row of mushrooms grew along the edge of the carpet where it met the far wall. I was reasonably sure I was going to be sick but I made a mental note to put it off till later. I knocked on the open door. "Jerem?" I said. "You in here?"

He didn't answer, but I heard him typing so I pulled back the curtain around his bed. He blinked and took off the headphones he was wearing. "What?" he said.

Coming out of the headphones was nothing but a random series of bloops, bleeps, and blorps. "What on earth are you listening to?" I asked.

"Music," he said.

"But it's just a random series of bloops, bleeps, and blorps," I said.

"My generation's music has passed you by," he said. He started to put the headphones back on.

"Wait," I said to the back of his head. "I need to ask you something. Do you know anything about Krieg's, you know, his . . ."

"Bitch?" Jerem suggested.

"No," I said. "But his girlfriend, if that's what she is."

He sighed. "Her name's Daisy Warner. She met Krieg through her brother, who lives around here with their father. She herself lives with her mother in Buena Park. She's in eighth grade. That's all I know. She doesn't interest me. Please close the curtain and leave now." He put his headphones back on and waved me away.

"Jerem's a creep," Daisy said. "I don't like him. You know why?"

It was a couple days later and I'd wandered downstairs to grab some ice cream before bed only to find Daisy Warner raiding the fridge. She'd slept over the night before, though from the sound of it there hadn't been much sleeping involved—every time I was just about to settle into that phase of sleep where nothing short of an air-raid siren can drag me back to the land of the living, I'd be woken up by Krieg and Daisy enjoying another forty-five seconds of hardcore penetration. This was the first time I'd had a chance to talk to her, though. I wasn't even sure she knew who I was.

"The problem with Jerem is he's not in touch with the earth at all," she said before I could answer. She grabbed a box of veggie fried rice and threw it in the microwave. "He's completely dependent on his machines. In a state of nature he'd be totally lost. Not me. I don't need any machines." She set the microwave to two minutes and started it up. "Molly doesn't need machines either," she continued. "I dig Molly. She's all skyclad and pagan. I told her about the Earth Goddess and she was into it. She doesn't need civilization."

"Right," I said. "Of course, without it she'd get sick and die in a matter of hours. Um, I don't think we've actually—"

"So what's your name?" she asked.

"Allen," I said. "I take it—"

"Krieg's said that he has brothers and sisters but he's never told me any of your names," she said. "My name's Daisy. I think names have magical powers. Don't you? I do."

"They seem pretty arbitrary to m—"

"Do you know how long you're supposed to cook this stuff?" she asked.

"Not really," I said. "So you and Krieg—"

"We're lovers," she said.

By this point I was well aware that if I tried to stretch my next question over more than three syllables tops I'd get cut off. "But why?" I asked. I decided to try to push the envelope. "Why h—?"

"Why him?" she interrupted. "Because he's so . . . basic. It's like civilization hasn't touched him. When he wants to eat, he eats. When he wants to fuck, he fucks. When he wants to destroy something, he destroys something. He's like man boiled down to its essence, man in a state of nature. He's *primal*." The microwave beeped.

"So basically he turns you on because he's a Cro-Magnon," I said.

"Plus he's got a really big gig," she said.

"There is that," I said.

"So how did he get like that?" she asked, shoveling rice into her mouth with her fingers. Her nails were filthy and flecked with black nail polish.

"How did he get a big gig?" I asked.

"No," she said. "I mean how did he turn out the way he turned out?"

"Good question," I said.

Krieg and remembrance

Echo and I were none too pleased about the addition of Krieg to our family. It wasn't jealousy: it was just that once he was old enough to walk, whenever we were playing by ourselves he'd come stumbling over and start hitting us for no reason. If we were playing with a toy we'd give it to him, but he'd just toss it aside and keep hitting us. Eventually Echo would shove him to the ground, and he'd cry. Oddly, I was usually the one who got in trouble during these exchanges.

One time when he was three and we were four, Krieg had come in for dinner with his toes mangled and bleeding. As my dad was cleaning him up and bandaging his feet, he'd asked what had happened. Krieg said he'd been kicking the tree in the backyard. After two or three kicks it had started to hurt, but he'd kept on kicking it—apparently it hadn't occurred to him that he could simply stop. Dad finished putting on the bandages and went to make an appointment to get Krieg's toes x-rayed. While he was busy on the phone, Krieg slipped outside and went back to kicking the tree.

When Molly was old enough to make the big move from her crib to a regular bed, the plan was for her and Echo to share one room and me and Krieg to share another. I thought this was just about the worst idea I'd ever heard of, and I swore I'd find another family to live with if they put this plan into effect. Echo threatened to jump out the window, several times if necessary. Mom and Dad consulted with one another and decided it'd be cruel to split us up. So they put Molly in Krieg's room. That night as we were getting ready to go to bed we heard a high-pitched squeal that suddenly got cut short. Mom and Dad and Echo and I ran to Krieg's room to find him holding Molly's nose and mouth closed, banging her head over and over again into her pillow. That night Molly slept in Echo's bed and the next morning Dad moved her bed and toys and clothes (which, even then, she refused to wear indoors) into the little room in the corner, which became her room from there on out.

That incident was enough to convince Mom and Dad that something was seriously wrong with Krieg and that they'd better get him put on some medication. And it worked, sort of. It curtailed his violent streak, but it did so by keeping him under more or less constant sedation—he'd lie around on the couch watching TV all day without even the energy to push the buttons on the remote. Eventually he snapped out of it and was back to his usual self. Dad thought that he'd built up a tolerance, but I later found out that he'd actually just been pocketing his pills and selling them to older kids before school.

For his seventh birthday, Bobbo gave Krieg a BB gun. It was the latest in a long string of poor gift choices on Bobbo's part—a few years earlier for our birthday he'd bought a toy truck for me and, for Echo, one of those cheap plastic dolls that talked when you pulled the string. We ended up playing a game where my truck repeatedly ran over the doll and then when we were done both toys were consigned to the garage, never to be seen again. But this time Bobbo had done good, at least as far as Krieg was concerned; his joy at receiving a genuine firearm was only slightly diminished when he discovered that the ammo consisted only of BBs and not hollow-point armor-piercing shells. Dad was less than pleased, however.

"This is the most irresponsible thing you've ever done," he told Bobbo. "Giving a rifle to a child? And to *him* in particular?"

"Hey, relax," Bobbo said. "Take a chill suppository. One, it's not a real gun. Two, it'll be a good outlet for his violent urges. If he feels like beating someone up he can go out back and blow away a couple cans instead. I had a gun back in Pennsylvania when I was his age and I turned out okay. I'll even show him how to use it."

Dad grudgingly gave him the okay and later that afternoon we were all hanging out in the backyard watching Bobbo set up a pyramid of soup cans on a cheap folding table from the garage. All the activity seemed to be riling up Dooj's dog, which was running around and around and around at twice its usual speed. "Um, aren't those supposed to be *empty* cans?" I asked.

"Whatever," Bobbo said. "Okay, Craig, here's what I want you to do. First, you have to visualize a specific target. Don't say 'I want to hit one of those cans' and start firing away—pick the exact spot on the exact can you want to hit. For stability you'll want to drop to one knee—yeah, that's right—and use your left hand to keep the gun steady while you pull the trigger with the right. Okay, got your target in mind? Then you can fire when ready."

Krieg took aim, paused for a moment—then got up, turned around, ran over to the wrought-iron fence, and started taking shots at Dooj's dog. Echo managed to tackle him, but not before he scored a very palpable hit: Dooj's dog went *"Yipe!"* and scrambled into its doghouse for, as far as I knew, the first time ever. A minute later Dooj himself came out to see what was the matter and Dad had a lot of explaining to do, especially since Bobbo took advantage of the commotion to quietly slip out to his car and hightail it back to his apartment. It took a great deal of effort on Echo's part to wrestle the gun away from Krieg, who actually resorted to biting her fingers to keep her from prying it out of his hands.

That was a lovefest compared to the next time they tangled. We were all in high school by then, and while the long midnight conversations between Echo and me had gradually grown less and less frequent and eventually stopped altogether, we'd occasionally hear Krieg delivering a tirade about something or other to Jerem (who may or may not have been listening from behind the curtain around his bed). Usually these centered around elaborate revenge schemes to get back at someone who Krieg had decided had done him wrong—"I'm gonna fuck that fuckhead up so fuckin' bad he won't even be able to fucking fuck"—but on this particular day, not long after I'd been called to the office to read his personality profile, he was serenading Jerem with a disquisition on the fairer sex. "Bitches," he said. "If there's one thing I know about bitches, it's that you gotta fucking show 'em who's boss or they'll fucking jerk you around. I tell you, some bitch doesn't wanna fuck me, I'll fucking *make* her."

Echo threw back her covers with a sound like she was ripping the air in half, yanked open the door nearly hard enough to pull it off its hinges, stormed into Krieg's room, dragged him into the hall, and set to the task of strangling him. Krieg wriggled furiously like a dung beetle flipped onto its back, but he couldn't get any leverage—Echo had a knee firmly planted on his chest. I stumbled out into the hall, rubbing my eyes. "Hey, what're you doing?" I asked. "Eck, you're killing him."

"That's the idea," she said. Krieg's face was a deep shade of burgundy and his tongue, thick and swollen, was sticking out of his mouth. "It's obvious that the world will be much better off without him."

"Come on, you can't just *kill* him," I said. "This is ridiculous. Echo, come on." I grabbed one of her elbows to try to pull her hands off his throat but she shrugged me off easily. There was a click and Molly's door swung open. She let out a shriek and tugged at Echo's sleeve with similar results.

"Echo, stop!" Molly said. "Don't—"

"Don't you understand?" Echo said. "I'm saving some poor girl from being *raped* by this, this *cockroach*! I'm saving *lives*!" She turned to look Krieg in his bloated purple face, his eyes rolled back into their sockets. "Convince me I'm not," she hissed. "Convince me I'm not condemning more people to death by letting you go than by finishing the job."

And at that point, Krieg came up with the only word that could have saved him. That word was ". . . agaaahh . . ."

Echo gasped and let go. Krieg's head fell to the carpet with a muffled thud. "Oh my god, I'm sorry, I'm so sorry," she said. "I don't know what—oh my god, oh my god—"

"Get the fuck off me," Krieg wheezed. Echo sort of fell backward into Molly's arms, tears streaming down her cheeks. Krieg lay on his back and panted for a moment or two before struggling to his feet. He kicked Echo in the side, which just made her cry harder. "You fucking *cunt*!" he spat, in what would have been a scream if his windpipe hadn't just come close to being crushed. "If you ever come into my fucking room again I'll kill you. You hear me, bitch? *Kill* you!" He backed into his room and gave the door a vicious slam.

Echo lay curled up in a fetal position on the carpet with Molly softly stroking her hair. "I'm sorry, I'm so sorry," she whimpered. "I didn't—I mean— My god, what's wrong with me?"

"Shh," Molly said. "Shhhhhhh."

Bobbo's door opened and he stuck his head out into the hall. "Hey, what's going on down there?" he asked.

"Pillow fight," I said.

Fringie gets a yellow card

That fight was sort of moot now, though: Daisy seemed consenting enough, and as the week progressed, I found it increasingly difficult to understand how she and Krieg managed to avoid dropping dead of exhaustion. They seemed to be going at it nonstop all afternoon, all through the night, and judging from the recorded messages we got every day from the Ilium attendance office, probably most of the morning as well. School offered a respite from the sounds of their frenzied copulation, but that just meant I had nothing to distract me from the sight of Fringie clinging to Peggy like he was about to ram his ovipositor down her throat. My only consolation was that Peggy's jacket was thick enough to ward off an artillery shell, so any groping on Fringie's part must've been like trying to cop a feel through a sheet of vinyl siding.

Or so I thought. But then, I didn't have Holdn's practice at these things and so didn't know what to look for. At one point I'd been eating lunch in the *Iliad* room, thinking that Peggy and Fringie seemed uncharacteristically standoffish—they were sitting in separate chairs for once, Fringie reading Machiavelli's *Mandragola* while Peggy looked over that issue's layout sheets—when Cat and Hank and Holdn came in. Holdn glanced at Fringie and scowled. "Where's the other hand, Fringie?" he said.

Fringie looked up from his book. "Hmm?" he said.

"The other hand," Holdn said. "One's holding the book. Where's the other?" He followed Fringie's arm with his eyes till it disappeared into Peggy's jacket. "Very nice," he snapped. "Give me that hand."

"What?" Fringie said.

Holdn yanked Fringie's hand out of Peggy's jacket, grabbed a ruler off the layout table, and smacked Fringie's knuckles with it. "I don't want to see that again, you hear?" Holdn said. "As far as you're concerned, she's a soccer ball. You're not to put your hands anywhere near her. Got it?"

Fringie yawned. "Grow up," he said.

"And you," Holdn said. He hunched over to look Peggy straight in the eye. "Zipped up to the top at all times, okay? Good girl." Peggy obligingly zipped up her jacket an extra few inches.

"Don't listen to him," Fringie said.

"I like it zipped up," Peggy said.

"Damn straight," Holdn said. "Hey, I think I hear Benito calling you."

"Really?" Peggy said. "I'd better go see what she wants." She got up and went over to Benito's room.

Fringie sighed and slammed his book shut; being a paperback, it only made a feeble little rustling sound instead of a nice solid *thap*. "Very mature," he said.

"Oh, I know it's childish," Holdn said, "but I just can't help myself around you. You make me feel things I've never felt before. We were meant to be together, can't you see that?" He hopped up into Fringie's lap and started licking his face.

"You're a riot," Fringie said. He shoved Holdn off his lap. "There. You've had your fun. In the future, I strongly suggest you keep a lid on the bullshit if you know what's good for you. You won't get another warning." He got up and calmly walked out, passing Hayley on the way in.

"What was that all about?" she asked.

"Nothing much," Holdn said. "Fringie makes cheesy threats, I try to keep from wetting myself. I mean, I enjoy splittin' the kitten as much as the next guy, but you've gotta be really low to run a scam on Kaylin."

Brace yourself

I agreed. Especially considering that a big part of that scam seemed to be making sure I always got the brush-off. Every time I'd run into Peggy on campus or during journalism class she'd give me a "Sorry, don't have time to talk now" and walk away. Clearly, we still had issues to discuss. So Saturday afternoon I headed over to the Kaylins' house to see if we couldn't straighten things out. Grant answered the door. "Is Peggy here?" I asked.

"Uh, yeah," he said. "She's upstairs."

"Come on in, Allen," Mrs. K. called from the kitchen. "The kids are in the TV room. Grant, go tell Peggy that Allen's here."

I went down the hall to the TV room, where Kelly was sprawled on the couch staring at her own left hand and listening to a talk show on TV. The topic: "I'm Not Wearing Any Pants!" It was a topic Kelly could relate to: her outfit consisted of a long pink T-shirt with kittens puffy-painted onto it and a pair of paisley boxer shorts. "Hey," I said.

"Uh-huh," she said absently.

Cheese ambled in from the kitchen, cramming the last piece of a brownie into his mouth with his palm. "Hey, gimme the remote," he said through gooey brown teeth.

"I'm using it," Kelly said.

"No you're not," he said. "You're just laying on it."

"'Lying,'" I said.

"I'm not lying," Cheese said. "Look, she's not doing anything with it."

"I'm keeping you from changing the channel," Kelly said, batting her eyelashes at him. "I'm watching this."

"No you're not," he said.

"Am so," she said.

"No fighting," Mrs. K. called from the kitchen.

"C'mon, gimme it," Cheese snapped. He made a lunge for the remote but Kelly sat up and snatched it away and left Cheese with a faceful of cushion.

"Real swift," Kelly said. Cheese made another grab for it but this time Kelly held it over her head and he ended up grabbing her breast instead. "Perv," she said. Cheese's face went bright red and he punched her in the face.

"MAH-AHM!" Kelly yelled. "CHEESE GRABBED MY BOOB AND PUNCHED ME IN THE FACE!"

Cheese looked at his fist in horror and then dropped the remote he'd just grabbed and ran upstairs. Mrs. K. came in from the kitchen as Cheese's bedroom door slammed. "What happened?" she asked. "Are you all right?"

"I'm okay," Kelly said. "He didn't hit me hard. Cheese is a wimp."

"Kelly," I said, "your mouth's all bloody."

"Huh?" she said. She poked the inside of her cheek with her tongue. "Hey," she said. "My cheek's all like shredded and stuff. 'Cause of, like, my braces. Cool."

"Doesn't it hurt?" I asked.

"No," she said. "It feels all tingly. Like when you chew on foil. Wow, that's cool."

"I'll get some ice," Mrs. K. said.

"Maybe I'd better come back later," I said. I retreated back down the hall but just as I reached the door Peggy finally came downstairs.

"What?" she asked.

"Your—your hair," I stammered.

"You came to complain about my hair?" she asked.

"No, I didn't know about it until just now," I said. She'd dyed it glossy black, the same color as Kelly's. "When did you—"

"Just now," she said. "What do you want?"

"Oh," I said. "Uh, well, I've been getting the sense that there's something wrong, and I was wondering—"

"Sorry, Al," Fringie said, appearing on the stairs behind her. "We were just on our way out."

"I wasn't talking to you," I said.

"Hey," Fringie said. "What's up?"

That seemed like a weird thing to say but then Kelly came careening into the foyer and I realized he wasn't talking to me. If he was talking to Kelly, though, she didn't seem to realize it—she just stared at Fringie blankly. "Anyway," I said, "I guess I was just leaving."

"You sure were," Fringie said. He and Peggy went back up to her room and closed the door.

As I walked home I felt like punching someone in the face myself, preferably Fringie. I would've been *really* pissed if I hadn't been so perplexed. No one was allowed in Peggy's room; that was private. Yet Fringie had been up there. It didn't compute. If I'd been one of those hyperintelligent supercomputers I'd've been blowing out circuit boards and refusing to open the pod bay doors trying to wrap my mind around this.

I got home to find Molly in the living room, staring intently at a candlestick on the end table; I thought that maybe she was trying to hypnotize herself until I saw she had a sketch pad in her lap and was trying to draw it. "What's up?" I asked.

"Do you know what you want to do with your life?" she asked.

"My life?" I said. "Uh, I dunno. I kind of assumed I was doing it now."

"I really think I want to do something with art," Molly said. "I'm in that art class they make us take and I'm getting totally obsessed with it. All I want to do lately is draw stuff. I *really* want to draw people but I don't know how you get people to pose for you. Do you?"

"Are you kidding?" I said. "I can barely get people to stay in the same room as me these days."

The door flew open and one of Krieg's dreadnok friends sauntered in. He started up the stairs, then caught a glimpse of Molly from the staircase and just stood and stared. "Excuse me?" I said. "Have you been helped?"

"I'm here to get Krieg and my sister," he said. "We're going to the Crucified Vomit show."

"Your sister? You mean Daisy?" I said. Suddenly I made the connection. "Wait, I remember you. You're Mark Warner. We had a peer counseling session."

"Warder," he spat. "My name is *Warder*."

"Sorry," I said.

"Good," he said, brushing his hair out of his eyes. "You know, I've been meaning to thank you and that pod chick," he said. "I read that pamphlet and I think I learned a lot. I don't cut myself anymore."

"Really?" I said. "That's good."

"Yeah, now I cut other people," he said. He went upstairs and a minute later he and Krieg and Daisy piled into Warder's car and drove off.

I sighed. "So Krieg's off for a night on the town and I get to stick around and maybe hang out on the net talking to fifty-year-old men pretending to be cheerleaders. This sucks. Ever since Peggy started seeing that Fringie guy we never do anything anymore."

"When did you in the first place?" Molly said.

"What?" I said.

"Have I been missing something?" she asked, still working on her sketch. "I didn't know you ever went out and did stuff. I thought you just went and hung out at her house sometimes. Like the goofy neighbor kid on a sitcom."

"It's more than that," I said. "She's my best friend in the world—or *was*, till Fringie got hold of her. We used to do stuff all the time."

"When was the last time?" Molly asked.

"What?" I said.

"The last time you went out to some event together," she said. "Even just seeing a movie or something."

"Well, just a few weeks ago I went over and Cheese had rented *Mohan Tadikonda: Master of the Martial Arts* and we all watched it," I said.

"Rentals don't count," Molly said. "Or visits to work, or school field trips, or anything like that."

"Whatever," I said. "Look, maybe I don't remember the most *recent* time, but there are lots. We played miniature golf once—"

"What color ball did you get?" Molly asked.

"Blue," I said. "Why?"

"And Peggy's?" she said.

"Orange," I said.

"Who won?" Molly asked.

"She did," I said. "Fifty-one to fifty-five."

"You remember all that and you don't remember the last time you did something together?" she said.

"That's a nice cross-examination," I said, "but that's not really what our friendship is about. I mean, anyone can get in a car and drive somewhere. Not everyone can have a real conversation."

"Okay, when was the last time you and Peggy had one of those?" she asked.

"Go away, kid, ya bother me," I said.

Late bloomer

But Molly had got me thinking and I had to admit that Peggy and I had been drifting apart, even before she'd started dating Fringie. Okay, so I was never going to be #95. Fine. But I also wasn't going to be her friend for much longer if things kept going the way they'd been going. I knew for a fact that Fringie was so predatory that he probably chased herds of antelope around for fun. I knew that he was going to seriously hurt Peggy at some point in the near future. I also knew that I'd done everything I possibly could to warn her, and she wouldn't listen. That being the case, I wasn't being much of a friend by continuing to harp on the evil that was Carver Fringie. Better not to mention it at all and just be ready to help her out when he finally did throw her over.

I went over to the Kaylins' the next morning set on putting this new policy into effect, but no one was home. I looked at my watch and it occurred to me that they were probably at church. As I headed back down their front walk I happened to glance over at the school and was surprised to find eight big white trucks parked out front. I decided to go investigate. It wasn't like there was much else to do, and hey, you know, big trucks.

Even from across the street I could hear Doctor Todd barking out orders through his megaphone: "Abatement insufficient! Slogans remain visible! Repeat abatement process!" When I got to the wheel the first thing I noticed was the crew of guys with sandblasting equipment and heavy-duty paint sprayers hard at work everywhere I looked. Then I saw what they were cleaning up. Every visible surface—the lockers, the walls, even the wheel itself—was covered with graffiti in letters six feet high. "FUCK NIGGERS." "GAS THE JEWS." "SPIX GO BACK TO MEX-ACO." "KILL FUCKING FAGS." These were among the more pleasant examples. There were also swastikas aplenty and enough schematic diagrams of male genitalia to make Freud blush. But then I looked over at the tower, and that's when I felt a cold weight in the pit of my stomach like I'd swallowed a rack of pool balls. For scrawled in little Magic Marker letters at the base of the tower was the legend

CRUCIFIED VOMIT RUELS

I walked over to where Doctor Todd was scowling at his megaphone. "I've got a pretty good idea who did this," I said.

"Do not attempt to defend brother," Doctor Todd said. "Prime suspect. Only suspect. Will summon to office tomorrow morning. Am confident of guilt."

"Me too," I said. "Actually, I think if you could get him shipped off to Juvie it'd be a really good idea all the way around. Is there any way I can help clean this up?"

"No," Doctor Todd said. "Possible accident. Cannot afford lawsuits. Return home."

I hopped the fence back to my street intent on dragging Bobbo out of bed and getting him to do something about Krieg's latest stunt, but then the Kaylins' van turned the corner and pulled into their driveway and I pretty much forgot all about it. Cheese and Grant jumped out first and sprinted inside. Kelly and Peggy followed at a more measured pace: Kelly dart-eyed and flouncy in a pretty, frilly dress, Day-Glo orange and vanilla like a Creamsicle; Peggy sullen, jet-black hair hanging in her face, hands jammed in her pockets, wearing her black leather jacket over a canary-yellow dress I'd watched her sew for herself the summer before. "Hey," I said.

Peggy looked over at me and frowned as Kelly skipped inside. The front doors of the van opened and Mr. and Mrs. Kaylin climbed out. "Don't mind Peggy, Allen," Mrs. K. said. "She's just sulking because we wouldn't let her wear her jacket into church."

"Don't talk about me like I'm not here," Peggy muttered under her breath.

"I guess we ought to be grateful, really," Mr. K. chuckled. "We managed to get four extra years out of her before the teenage rebellion set in."

"What are you *talking* about?" Peggy snapped. "First of all, it's not 'rebellion' just because I wanted to wear my *jacket*. I don't wear it because I want to make *trouble,* I wear it because I *like* it, okay? And where do you get this 'four years' thing from? Why does everyone assume that as soon as you become a teenager that you're going to start going against your parents and getting into trouble? When have I ever done a *single thing* that was bad? I've been good, haven't I? Haven't I been good? *Haven't I?*"

"Sure, honey—" Mrs. K. began.

"Then DON'T CRITICIZE!" Peggy said. Her voice echoed up and down the street as she ran into the house and slammed the door.

"It was just a joke," Mr. K. said.

"When was the last time you remember Peggy not being wounded by a joke at her expense?" I asked. "Besides, she's right. I mean, you lucked into one of the best kids in the history of the species and she doesn't deserve to be talked about like she was a used car."

"I'll keep that in mind," Mr. K. said, a little frostily. They went inside. I didn't appear to be invited in. I went home.

The part where I stop beating my wife

When Bobbo woke up I told him about Krieg's latest opus in the hate-spew genre, but he was skeptical. "A little graffiti never killed anyone," he said. "I tagged my share of bathroom walls when I was his age. 'Here I sit, all broken-hearted'. . . Heh heh."

"But this stuff was just *vile*," I said.

"Oh, come on," Bobbo said. "Do you have to exaggerate everything? You see a tall guy and he's the size of the Washington Monument. You see a fat guy and he weighs the same as a Mack truck. So maybe it was a little off-color. Big deal."

"I think 'KILL FUCKING FAGS' in letters six feet tall is more than a little off-color," I said.

"Besides, how do you know it was Krieg?" Bobbo said. "You're just picking on him because he's the only normal one out of the five of you. Look, you want me to talk with him, I'll talk with him. Where is he?"

A quick search of the house revealed that he was nowhere around and hadn't been back since leaving for the concert the evening before. Chances were that he was in Buena Park humping Daisy in Warder's bed while the gentleman of the house hung around outside trying to stab the passing neighborhood kids. He didn't return that afternoon or evening, and when I woke up on Monday, he still wasn't back. When I got to school on Monday, I was pleased to find all the graffiti was gone, though the workmen hadn't entirely covered their tracks: all day I heard people asking, "What's the deal? Why'd they repaint everything if they were gonna do such a crappy job?" and "What's all this powder everywhere?" When people asked me about it as I signed their red tickets for them I tried to change the subject.

I spent so much time signing tickets at lunch that when Peggy came into the *Iliad* room I almost asked what her ticket was for. "Uh, hi," I said.

"My mom told me what you said yesterday," she said.

"Oh," I said. "Uh, I didn't get you in trouble, did I—?"

"No," she said. She shoved her hands into her jacket pockets and looked at the floor for a minute, then looked me right in the face. "Why did you stick up for me when you don't respect me?" she asked.

"What?" I said. "Of course I respect you."

"You don't," she said. "Or else you hate me. Which is it?"

"What?" I said.

"I was talking with Carver about why you keep telling me I shouldn't see him," she said. "And he said that either you don't respect me enough to think that my judgment could *possibly* be right, or you secretly *hate* me and want me to be miserable and alone. I thought I'd be nice and give you the benefit of the doubt that it's the first and not the second."

"Look, if you don't want me to talk about Fringie anymore, I won't," I said. "I'll never mention him again. But I don't hate you and I do respect you. I'm just concerned is all."

"Why?" she said. "What's to be concerned about?"

"Because one of these days he's going to turn out to be like all the others and if you get too invested in this guy you're going to get hurt," I said. "I've heard him discussing his master plan about how he's going to bed you."

"You're lying," she said.

"I'm not," I said.

"You're lying or you totally misunderstood," she said. "Everyone else tried to pressure me into sex when I wasn't ready. But Carver and I already got that out of the way. He asked me what I thought about it and I said that I wasn't ready to share that much of myself at this point in my life, and that it went against everything I believe to do that without more of a commitment, and he said that he totally respected that and that he was glad we could discuss the issue like mature adults."

"He's just trying to get your guard down," I said.

"See?" she said. "*See?* You don't respect me! You act like I'm totally weak and helpless and *stupid* and that I'd never see if he was trying anything funny or make him stop if he did. Isn't that exactly what I've done ninety-three times already? Isn't it? Part of me—part of me—" She balled up her fists in her pockets. "Look," she said, "it's not a matter of not being tempted. I'm not—it's not—I was brought up to believe certain things, okay? And so was Keith, and Kelly, and Grant. And maybe it's old-fashioned, and maybe Zab and people make fun of me—I know it—but that's just who I am. That doesn't mean I—doesn't mean I haven't—I—" She sighed. "I know what I'm doing, okay? No one can trick me or convince me or bully me into doing what I don't want—what I don't *believe* I should do. Even if I w—even—no matter what. I'm not a little kid."

"I know you're not," I said. "But that doesn't mean that you're a 'mature adult.' You're not. And I'm not, and Fringie's not, none of us are. You just don't *go* from being a kid to being an adult. It just doesn't *work* that way, not at thirteen, not at eighteen, it just doesn't. Just like you don't go straight from being a baby to being elderly. There are steps in between. We're *adolescents*. That's different from being kids, and different from being adults. Some people, like my sister Molly, are making the change from being kids to being adolescents. Some people, like Hayley maybe, are turning from adolescents into adults. But being adolescents means that we suddenly have to take a lot of responsibility for running our own lives, but we're new at it and none of us really has good judgment. I sure as hell don't, not yet. If I did we wouldn't be having this talk. If I've been acting like a jerk lately it's not because I don't respect you, or don't care about you—it's because I'm completely selfish. Because I don't want you to make a mistake, because I don't want to see you get hurt, because if you get hurt then I get hurt, because nothing could hurt me worse than something bad happening to you. Did that make any sense?"

"Not really," Peggy said.

"Fine," I said. "Here's the short version. I'm an idiot. I'm sorry. I still think Fringie's a creep but I'll trust your judgment and never bring it up again. Okay?"

"Okay," she said. She turned around and walked out.

Whatcha gonna do when they come for you?

When I went up to the office for peer counseling that afternoon Doctor Todd waylaid me as I headed into the conference room. "Where is brother?" he asked. "Absent. Illness?"

"If so, it's only mental," I said. "I have no idea where he is. He hasn't been home in days."

"Very well," Doctor Todd said. "No choice. Must notify police. Police will apprehend."

"Sounds like a plan to me," I said.

Apparently tracking down vandalism suspects was low on the Fullerton PD's agenda, since I found Krieg before the police did. Or maybe "found" isn't the right word, since I wasn't actually looking for him—I was up in my room doing my homework when I heard a screeching sound outside and looked out the window to find two cars come squealing into our driveway. Krieg and Daisy hopped out of one, Warder out of the other, and they went running into the garage; when they came out they were all holding long metal pipes and went to work bashing in the windshield and windows of the car Krieg had been driving. I called the police.

As I hung up a third car came screaming onto our street, but it wasn't a police car. Two dreadnoks jumped out and I was sure that the automatic weapons would soon be making an appearance but Krieg just looked up and waved his big metal pipe at them. "Next time it won't just be your fucking *car*, got it?" he sneered. "Now get out of my town! Get the fuck out of my fucking town! If I ever see you in my fucking town again, the next town you'll be in is the one you'll be fucking buried in!"

The dreadnoks retreated back to their car and drove off; Krieg got into the wrecked car and took off after them, with Warder and Daisy following behind. This struck me as a lucky turn of events—surely the cops could take time out from manning the microwave at the 24-Seven to chase down a stolen car with a shattered windshield hurtling through traffic with its lights off. About ten minutes later a cop car came to the house and I went downstairs to fill the police in on what had happened. This being the second call they received concerning Craig Mockery in a matter of hours, they'd said they'd get right on it. And if you define "getting right on it" as spending an hour looking for Krieg with no success and then calling the house to ask if by any chance he'd happened to come back, then getting right on it is exactly what they did.

As it turned out, I was the one who finally tracked down Fullerton's favorite fugitive. Doctor Todd stopped me on the way to peer counseling and told me that if I found Krieg I should call his office immediately. "I will remain in office until vandal is located," he vowed. His vigil didn't last long, though—the first thing I heard when I walked in the door to my house was Krieg and Daisy noisily going at it in the room where my mom's old office had been. I called Doctor Todd, and a few minutes later a cop showed up at the door.

"Hi, I'm Officer Cowen," he said. "I'm a friend of Dennis's."

"Dennis . . . ?" I said. For a second I thought he meant the kid who used to live next door to Peggy. "Oh, Doctor Todd."

"Right," he said. He came in and I shut the door. "Now, don't be alarmed by what's about to happen," he said. "We've found that one of the best ways to make kids stop getting into trouble is to scare 'em straight—that means cuffing them, taking them downtown, printing them, letting them sit in a holding cell for a while. Puts the fear of God into 'em, and they turn out fine. You coddle 'em and you'll coddle 'em right into the state pen. I'll give your mom and dad a call when he's ready to be picked up."

I didn't bother to correct him. "He's in that room there," I said, pointing. "Oh, and unless she went out the window, he's with his girlfriend . . ."

"Fine, we'll scare her straight too," he said. "Nothing new to me—half my job is pulling loose girls out of the backs of cars." From the way his eyes lit up, he might as well have added, "And that's the part of the job I LOVE!" With that, he pulled out his gun and threw open the office door. "FREEZE!" he bellowed. "You're both under arrest!"

At that point it suddenly occurred to me that it wouldn't be a good idea for me to be standing there smirking as Officer Cowen led a cuffed Krieg and Daisy out the door—the last thing I needed was Krieg attacking my car with a crowbar. I hurried up to my room and closed the door. A couple minutes later I looked out the window to see Krieg being shoved into the back of what I assumed would be the first of many police cars he'd have a chance to ride in over the course of his life of crime. Through the glass I could hear Krieg saying a number of things that could and would be used against him in a court of law, most of them beginning with the word "fuck." "What's going on?" Echo asked.

"Krieg's going to jail," I said.

"About time," Echo said.

A dish best served cold, and spelled correctly

The next afternoon Doctor Todd was fuming. Things hadn't gone well. "Perpetrator released," he growled through clenched teeth. "Denied everything. Fellow miscreants provided alibi. Career center worksheet proved alibi false. Worksheet matched graffiti. Case closed. But police deemed evidence insufficient. Cannot even suspend now. Potential lawsuit. Farcical."

That wasn't all—the car Krieg had stolen and trashed seemed to have vanished, so before too long, Bobbo had been called to pick Krieg up from the station. Molly had gone along because she wanted to see what a police station was like. "It was great!" she said. "They had these age-progression programs so you could see what you'd look like in the future, you know, so if you were kidnapped ten years ago they'd be looking for what you looked like now instead of what you looked like as a little kid. We had to hang around for a while since Bobbo was busy picking up on Daisy's mom and I got mine done. Want to see what I'll look like when I'm thirty? I got a printout."

Krieg and Daisy came in before I had a chance to answer. "Those fuckers," Krieg was muttering. "When I find out who turned me in I'm gonna—"

"Don't worry," Daisy said. "We'll get our revenge. We'll get our revenge this week. They'll see. We'll show them. We'll show them all." They went upstairs.

"Do you want to see my picture or not?" Molly asked.

"Sure, sure," I said. "That just . . . didn't sound good."

In fact, every morning for the rest of the week as I walked to school I fully expected to find it engulfed in flames. I warned Doctor Todd that some sort of retribution was probably on the way but there wasn't anything else I could really do about it short of having Echo pick up strangling Krieg where she'd left off. But then on Thursday morning I opened my locker and a folded sheet of goldenrod paper fluttered to the ground. I picked it up. It bore a message:

PEOPLE OF ILIUM

You should know that some of those who live among you are being persacuted by the adminastration of this school, namely by one "Doctor" Dennis Todd, who has waged a **CAMPANE OF TERROR** against us charging us with crimes we did not commit. He will do the same to you if you do not join us now and overthrow the adminastration. **FIGHT THE**

POWER! DOCTOR TODD IS A FACIST AND WE'RE GONNA BURN HIM DOWN!

The reason we are being persacuted is clear. They fear us because we have shown them a better way. They force us to go to they're school so they can "teach" us to be good little sheep like them but **ARE WE GOING TO LISTEN? NO! WE DON'T NEED NO THOUGHT CONTROL!** You are being **X-PLOITED** by the government so that you will grow up to be "a good citazen". But we don't want to live that kind of life. We want to live with the earth. We don't need they're computers and they're laser printers and they're copy machines and they're nuclear bombs. **YOU CAN'T HUG A CHILD WITH NUCLEAR ARMS.** The **EARTH GODDESS** is coming and we will all be happy and naked in the sun as we once were. **ARE YOU READY?**

As Wilhelm Krieger lead singer for **CRUCIFIED VOMIT** says, "Killed my mom and killed my dad, best idea I ever had, and I am still mad, so I'm gonna kill you next." We are people of peace but there can be no peace until we overthrow civilazation and return to the earth. **ARISE AND REVOLT!**

Love,

Krieg & Dazey

This last line I doubted very strongly: the chances that Krieg had written a single word of this were about the same as the chances that he had secretly ghostwritten Shakespeare's sonnets. This was clearly Daisy's handiwork, and I found it rather cheering—partly because it meant that their oh-so-ominous revenge scheme was perfectly harmless, and partly because her manifesto was so heartfelt (if not brainthought) that I couldn't help but wonder if maybe she really *hadn't* had anything to do with the graffiti attack and it'd just been Krieg and Warder working alone.

In any event, class hadn't even started before Uta Himmler, acting on the orders of one pissed-off walkie-talkie, was systematically opening locker after locker and removing the offending agitprop (not to mention the occasional bag of roughage or pornographic magazine). This did nothing to prevent people from reading Daisy's cri de coeur, however, since there were enough copies floating around that if you didn't get one you could always look at someone else's. And Uta was only able to grab about half the flyers anyway—she couldn't reach the top row of lockers.

Most of the goldenrod sheets ended up wadded up in the trash or, more frequently, on the ground, but the glee among the *Iliad* staffers was irrepressible. "I am *definitely* running this as a letter to the editor," Zab said. "No *question*. Finally we get something *interesting*."

"Interesting?" Hank said. "*Interesting?* This isn't 'interesting'—it's THE GREATEST PIECE OF LITERATURE IN AMERICAN HISTORY. When I get home it's going in big block letters on the side of my house."

Right then Echo came into the *Iliad* room to drop off the corrected copy for next week's edition. Though to say that she "came in" is an overstatement—she stuck her hand in just far enough to drop the papers on the front desk, and was about to close the door when Hayley stopped her. "Hey, wait," she said.

Echo stood there holding the door frame but didn't say anything. "What are you doing?" Hayley asked.

"Dropping off the copy," she said, and started to close the door again.

"No, I mean, are you doing anything?" Hayley said. "After school. The bell's about to ring. Do you want to go get some coffee or something?"

"What?" Echo said.

"Coffee," Hayley said. "It's a beverage."

"I don't drink coffee," Echo said.

"Then get something else," Hayley said. "Look, I don't want to make a big production out of this. I just thought that since you couldn't make it to the *Ashley* set, maybe we could grab something to eat and talk for a while."

"Why?" Echo asked.

"Hang on," I said. I shouldered Echo back out into the hall and closed the door. "What the hell is wrong with you?" I asked. "She's trying to be nice and you're living up to everything Zab's ever said about you."

"I was just waiting for the punch line," Echo said. "But I guess it comes further along in this farce than I thought."

"Oh, give me a break," I said. "Stop being so paranoid and let her buy you a damn scone."

Echo grumbled and went inside to patch things up with Hayley. My work was done. The bell rang and I went up to the office.

Doctor Todd was practically doing cartwheels when I arrived. "Fatal mistake," he said, waving one of the goldenrod manifestos around. "Signed statement. Cannot deny authorship. Two separate offenses in one. Tampering with lockers. Insertion of paper suffices. Punishable by suspension. More important offense. Distribution of an unlicensed publication on school grounds." Doctor Todd's eyes lit up like he'd heard paddling was being reintroduced to the public school system. "This offense," he said, "punishable by EXPULSION!"

"Wait, just a minute," I said. "Look, we both know he was behind the graffiti attack. But this is just a pretext. For one, you know he's not capable of writing something this eloquent—he can barely form complete sentences." Doctor Todd scowled—apparently I'd inadvertently hit a nerve. Oops. "Daisy probably just signed his name to it without him even knowing about it. But what's more," I said, "if this rule really is on the books it's ridiculous and I can't believe you'd actually enforce it. 'Unlicensed publication'? What ever happened to free speech?"

"Inapplicable," Doctor Todd said. "Only licensed publications on school grounds. *Iliad.* Yearbook. Club newsletters as warranted. Flyer unlicensed. Violates rules. Nonenforcement promotes anarchy. Official hearing tomorrow. But expulsion guaranteed. Guaranteed!"

When I got home Bobbo's car was already in the driveway. Molly was lying on the couch in the TV room reading the newspaper. "I guess Bobbo heard that they're kicking Krieg out of school," I said.

"Yeah, they called him at work and he came straight home," Molly said. "He said that Krieg was entitled to legal representation at his hearing tomorrow and locked himself in his room to work on the case."

"Well, that's disappointing," I said. "The whole walk home I was looking forward to breaking the news and now I find it's already been broken."

"That's not the only thing that's broken," Molly said. "Doctor

Todd wanted to talk to Krieg personally and Krieg threw the phone at the wall and they both broke." She pointed at a big dent in the wall with a dead phone lying on the floor beneath it.

I heard the garage door open and swing shut. It was Echo. "Why isn't Bobbo at work?" she asked. "Did the coffee machine break?"

"He's preparing for Krieg's hearing tomorrow," I said. "It looks like Krieg's getting kicked out of school."

"I thought you said he was going to jail," Echo said. "This is nowhere near as good. So when's the hearing?"

The hearing on Krieg's expulsion for distributing an unlicensed publication was held at one-thirty Friday afternoon at the district office. Present were Krieg; Bobbo, acting as Krieg's guardian and legal counsel; Daisy; Daisy's mom, whose fling with Bobbo was already a thing of the distant past; the principal of Daisy's middle school; the principal of Del Rio Continuation High School; Doctor Todd; some suits from the school board; and Ilium principal Chuck Marzipan, who was no doubt pissed that this hearing was cutting into his golf time. Note who does not appear on that list: yours truly. I heard about it secondhand.

The first person who told me about it was Doctor Todd, that afternoon. "Expulsion complete," he said gleefully. "Girl cracked immediately. Confessed perpetrator's involvement. Gave hour-by-hour account of whereabouts for previous week. Perpetrator refused to provide alternate account. Did little except curse at girl. Pity colleague at continuation school."

Later that evening I heard Bobbo's side of the story. "Well, things were going fine until that girl turned on the waterworks," he said. "All of a sudden she starts bawling that it wasn't her idea and all she did was fix some of the grammar because she was scared he'd hurt her if she didn't and on and on and on. After that it was hopeless. No one's gonna believe a guy over a crying girl. If not for some legal maneuvering on my part things could've been really bad."

"What do you mean?" I asked.

"I managed to sucker them pretty good," Bobbo chuckled. "I talked them down from an expulsion to a transfer. So instead of actually getting kicked out he'll just be going to this continuation high school instead."

"Um, Bobbo, that's what an expulsion *means,*" I said. "Of *course* they're going to make alternate arrangements. He has to go to *some* school. Either a private school, or one in some other district, or the continuation school. Sounds like you jumped on the worst of the three. Not that they'd let him stick around more than a week any- where else."

"Oh," Bobbo said. "Well, whatever. It beat going to work."

And then of course there was Krieg's own take, which I heard him relating to Jerem that night. "That fucking bitch sold me out," he snarled. "Sold me way the fuck out."

"Why do you care if you got kicked out if you never go to school anyway?" Jerem asked.

"Because *nobody* fucking tells me where I can go and where I can't," Krieg said. "I'll go wherever the fuck I want. They'll see. I'm gonna put every one of those fuckers in the fucking *ground*."

Two months later Krieg would be dead of multiple gunshot wounds.

I never saw Daisy again.

Seven

That Sunday was Easter. Easter was always a big day at the Kaylins': every year they held a huge lunch for friends of the family, followed by an Easter egg hunt for the kids. It was always kind of weird seeing Peggy with all her Catholic school friends who I only ever saw at these same Easter lunches, but Mrs. K.'s macaroni salad more than made up for any social discomfort and I'd never missed a single year. Besides, each year since Peggy had made the jump to public school the number of her former classmates who showed up had steadily dwindled, and as it turned out, when I showed up this time around I didn't see anyone I didn't recognize.

Goo goo ga joob

Or, rather, I didn't see anyone our age I didn't recognize. The TV room and backyard were full of little boys around Grant's age—he must've invited every fourth-grader from every school in the state. Cheese and a couple of his buddies hovered around the television watching a basketball game and gobbling down paper plates heaped with roast beef; Peggy and Fringie sat on the freshly wrapped couch, Fringie in a pressed shirt and tie reading Kierkegaard's *The Sickness Unto Death,* Peggy in her black leather jacket wincing every time one of Grant's friends spilled something on the plastic sheet covering the carpet. And Kelly stood by herself out on the patio blinking in the bright sunshine. "Hi," I said to Peggy.

"Yeah, hi," she said.

"Hey, Al," Fringie said, casually throwing an arm around her.

"Weren't any of Kelly's friends invited?" I asked. "No one from the cheer squad or anything? She looks kind of adrift."

"She said she couldn't think of anyone who'd want to come," Peggy said.

"Hunh," I said. "Okay, I'm gonna go get something to eat before my stomach digests itself. See you in a bit."

I slid open the screen door, slipped through the crowd of adults to the folding tables Mr. and Mrs. K. had set up at one end of the back-yard, and grabbed a plate of food. Then I tracked Kelly down—not hard, since she hadn't moved. "Hey," I said. "Aren't you going to get anything?"

"Like, not even," she said blearily. "I've been sick, like, all week. If I tried to eat something I'd, like, spew it. I only got up so I could get eggs."

"Really?" I said. "Aren't you kind of old for that?"

"People only say that when they're, like, not good at getting eggs anymore," Kelly said.

"Fair enough," I said. "I hope you feel better soon." I went inside.

Cheese and his friends slipped out into the hall as I closed the screen door behind me; a drum salvo a moment later made it clear why they'd left. Fringie's lip curled in disgust but he quickly regained his usual placidity. I resisted the urge to point this out as positive proof of his essential villainy. "So, uh, how's life?" I asked.

Peggy shrugged. Fringie put down his book. "Hey, hon, I'm going down to apply for that lifeguard spot next weekend," he said. "Still want me to sign you up?"

"I don't know," Peggy said. "Maybe. I doubt it, though."

"Would they let you wear the jacket?" I asked.

Peggy shot me a tired look and I turned my attention back to the arti-choke dip. I went back for seconds and lingered in the backyard to see if any of the grown-ups were talking about anything interesting, but most of their conversations prominently featured the phrase, "So, Frank, I hear you're thinkin' about gettin' yourself a boat." Mr. and Mrs. K. set to clearing off the tables and folding them up in preparation for the egg hunt. I helped them—it was something to do, at least. As I carried the pots and dishes back to the kitchen I couldn't help but envision this scene twenty years into the future: a yard full of generic suburbanites, the vague people from the *Iliad* all grown up; Peggy bustling from room to room, checking on the squash casserole, making sure the toddlers didn't play with the electrical sockets, refreshing people's punch cups; me pretending to be remotely interested when Fringie talked about the boat he was getting and pulling nickels from behind the ears of his and Peggy's kids. It was almost more real to me than the party in progress. And maybe it wasn't the best future I could've dreamed up, but it was tangible—it had a substance to it that, say, Molly's age-progression por-trait didn't. Molly at thirty was a laughable notion—I was still getting used to Molly at thirteen. But Peggy at thirty, Peggy at sixty, these were people I felt like I knew already. I've already told you that whenever I looked at Peggy I saw her through ten years of history, but that's only half the truth. I saw her through ten years of history in one direction—and seventy in the other.

I dropped off the last set of dishes and returned to the TV room. "Hey, where's Fringie?" I asked.

"He went to go help Mom with the baskets and make Keith stop drumming," Peggy said. The drums obligingly stopped short. A cou-ple of Grant's friends got into a shoving match over by the coffee table. "Hey!" Peggy said. "No fighting."

"Can I ask you a weird question?" I asked.

"I guess," she sighed.

"Where do you see yourself in twenty years?" I asked.

"You mean like what city?" she asked.

"Not really," I said. "I mean, imagine it's twenty years from now. You're thirty-seven. What are you up to? Who are you with? What have you accomplished?"

Peggy shrugged. "That's not up to me," she said. "That's up to God. As long as I live an honest happy life and leave honest happy kids behind me I don't really care about any of the details. And I don't really feel like talking about this kind of stuff now."

Cheese and his friends came crashing downstairs, followed by Mrs. K. and Fringie carrying a bunch of little wicker baskets. The kids crowded around with outstretched hands and the basket distribution went without incident until Kelly glanced inside and saw what was going on. "Hey!" she cried. "Me! Me!" She shoved her way through the crowd and grabbed a basket out of Mrs. K.'s hands. "Like, I'm gonna need a bigger basket than this," she said. "I don't think you understand how many eggs I'm going to get."

"Kelly, don't be rude," Mrs. K. said. Kelly pouted and stomped off—then suddenly swayed on her feet and sank into a chair.

"I didn't touch her!" Cheese protested.

Peggy's eyes went wide. "Are you okay?" she said. "Maybe you should go back to bed."

"No way," Kelly said woozily. "I'm good. It's just, like, the air or something . . ."

Mrs. K. hadn't noticed this little exchange—she'd been too busy handing out the rest of the baskets. "Okay, now listen to the rules, everyone," she said. "There are no Easter eggs inside the house, and none outside our property—at least, not any of ours. That means don't go into anyone else's yard, and don't mess with any of the rooms—there aren't any eggs there. So everyone out into the back-yard, and we'll start when I blow the whistle."

The majestic herd of undomesticated fourth-graders swept out into the backyard. Kelly got up and stuck her foot out on the patio; the minute the whistle sounded, she spun around, ran through the house and sprang for the front door. Peggy sighed and headed into the kitchen. Fringie followed her.

"What's up?" I heard him ask.

"You'll see," she said. I heard her open the refrigerator. I went out to the front yard.

Kelly's basket was already close to overflowing by the time I reached the door. It was quite a sight to behold, the way her hands darted expertly into the foliage lining the front walk—she collected over a dozen eggs in under a minute. She sprinted down the driveway to the mailbox, opened it up, and pulled a particularly beautiful pink-and-orange-swirled egg out. "They always put one there," she explained.

By this time a couple of intrepid fourth-graders had followed her out to the front of the house, but they'd come far too late—Kelly had cleaned the place out. Almost. One boy spotted an egg left on the windowsill, but Kelly vaulted over him, grabbed the egg, and darted back into the house. The boy burst into tears.

"I think she missed a few," Peggy said from the other side of the yard. "Look, there's one." She pointed. As the boy bounded over to grab the egg, Peggy wandered over to the front walk, taking eggs out of the carton she was carrying and slipping them into the shrubbery. "I have to do this every year," she grumbled. "Sometimes she can be so—"

A chorus of shrieks exploded from the backyard. "What the hell was that?" I asked.

There was a frantic scramble of feet through the kitchen and Grant came bounding out onto the driveway, his eyes the size of Frisbees. "Peggy," he gasped, "Kelly—she—Kelly—"

"What?" Peggy said.

"She's *dead*," Grant wailed.

Think I'll go for a walk

Mr. K. had carried Kelly's limp body to the couch and Mrs. K. had called for an ambulance by the time Peggy and I made it to the TV room. I felt a much too familiar calm and clarity settle over me. "What can I do?" I asked. "How can I help?"

"Just be quiet," Mr. K. said brusquely. "We're still getting organized."

Peggy rushed through the crowd of thunderstruck fourth-graders to the couch and stroked Kelly's face. "She's not dead," she said. "She's breathing."

"What happened?" I whispered to Cheese.

"Dunno," Cheese whispered back, his face as white as if Kelly were up and about and *he* were the one who was dead. "She just dropped her basket and fell on her face . . . and her eggs broke . . ."

Peggy started crying softly and Mr. K. herded the rest of us out into the foyer, save for Fringie, who got to stay behind with Peggy. "Here, you want to help?" Mr. K. said. He handed me a set of house keys. "Make sure everyone goes home and lock up." It wasn't all that different from my peer counseling job—I didn't even have to arrange rides for people, just convince them that the best way for them to help the Kaylins would be to clear out. Most everyone was gone by the time the ambulance arrived.

The rest of the day I waited for a call with some kind of news on Kelly's condition, but none came; after night fell I went over to the Kaylins' house a few times to see if the lights were on, but they weren't. If the Kaylins ever came home, they must've gone straight to bed. I knew that whatever it was it had to be serious, because not only did Kelly not show up for school on Monday, Peggy and Cheese didn't either. This prompted one of Benito's rare forays into the *Iliad* room. "Whoa!" Cat said. "Il Duce in da hay-oose!"

"Where is Peggy Kaylin?" Benito asked. "She's supposed to be supervising the last three issues."

"Her sister's in the hospital," I said.

"And?" Benito said.

"And?" I said. "And she's probably there with her."

"She has responsibilities here," Benito said.

"Um, hello?" I said. "Have you been listening? I said her sister's in the *hospital*. You know, the big building with all the really really sick people? I think the last thing on her mind is a stupid high school newspaper."

"Then she shouldn't have agreed to become editor-in-chief," Benito said. "I can find someone else if I have to." She turned around and skulked out.

"What's her sister in the hospital for?" Hayley asked.

"I'm not sure," I said. "She just collapsed at lunch yesterday."

"Did she OD on something?" Cat asked.

"What?" I said. "No, of course not."

"How do you know?" Hayley asked.

"The same way I know that Benito isn't going to be named as Holly Madera's replacement on *Ashley: The Early Years*," I said. "I'll be back in a bit."

An idea had occurred to me. I headed over to the gym and called April Young out of cheer practice. "What?" she asked.

"Hey," I said. "I was basically just wondering if you knew more about Kelly's condition than I did."

"Condition?" she said. She looked around. "Um, I noticed she wasn't *here,* but I thought she'd just skipped school . . ."

"She's in the hospital," I said.

"Did she OD on something?" April asked.

"You're the second person who's asked that in the past five minutes," I said. "I'm not sure *what* happened. I thought her friends might know."

"Sorry," April said. "We're not that close. I don't think any of her friends actually go here. I've met some of them at parties but that's about it."

"Really?" I said. "I've been working most of the bigger parties around here for the past couple of years and I've never seen Kelly at any of them . . ."

"No, not in *Fullerton,*" April said. A couple of the other cheerleaders emerged from the gym and started forcibly dragging her back inside. "We'll visit her or something," she said.

"Swell," I said.

By this point I was desperate for any kind of information, so when I looked out the window of the peer counseling room and saw Grant riding around on his bike out in front of the school, I decided to let that afternoon's session start ten minutes late. I rang the Kaylins' bell and Cheese let me in. "You're home!" I said. "So she's okay?"

"Kelly's still in the hospital, honey," Mrs. K. called from the kitchen. She came out to the foyer, wiping her hands with a dish towel. "Bob's still over there with her but the boys were getting restless so we came home. There's not much we can do now but wait."

"So Peggy's over there too?" I asked.

"No, Peggy's at church," Mrs. K. said. "I think she's due home soon . . ."

"I actually have to get back to school in a minute," I said. "So, uh, what was wrong with her? She didn't overdose on anything, did she . . . ?"

"What?" Mrs. K. said. "No, her appendix burst. It—"

"Her appendix!" I said. "Oh, good. I mean, not good, but—oh, you know what I mean. Okay, I'll be back soon."

As it turned out, "soon" meant a little after five o'clock: Mrs. Handey had scheduled three separate sessions in a row. When I got back to the Kaylins' house I found Mrs. K. grabbing her purse and Cheese and Grant macking out on Chinese food. "Oh, hi, Allen," she said. "Peggy got back from church so I was going to leave her with the kids and head down to the hospital. Do you want me to go get her for you?"

"Um, sure," I said.

Mrs. K. went upstairs and knocked on Peggy's door. "Honey, someone's here to see you," she said. I couldn't quite hear Peggy's reply but I was pretty sure I could make out the phrase "see me like this" somewhere in there. "It's not Carver, it's Allen," Mrs. K. said. "Okay, take your time." She came downstairs. "Peggy'll be down in a few minutes," she said. "Help yourself to some Chinese food—we got way too much."

I had some fried rice and waited for Peggy to come downstairs; I was kind of skeptical about whether she would, but after a few minutes I heard her tread on the staircase. Apparently the fact that she cared more about what Fringie thought about her than what I did worked in my favor for once—she didn't care if I saw her all disheveled, which, in fact, she was. Her hair was a mess and she was wearing a thick flannel robe with her leather jacket over it. "What?" she said.

"Um, hi," I said. I got up from the table and went over to the staircase. "So, uh, how are you?" I asked.

"How am *I*?" she said. "Who cares about how *I* am? I'm not the one who's sick. Did Mom tell you what happened?"

"To Kelly, you mean?" I asked.

"Her appendix blew up," Peggy said. "But not yesterday. It wasn't like it blew up and she fell down. It happened a week ago. Maybe more. You know how she said she'd been feeling queasy all week? That's because she had all these *poisons* inside her. And everything got all *infected* and if we hadn't taken her to the hospital right away she would've *died*."

"Um, wow," I said.

"Even as it is," Peggy said, "it's pretty bad." Her voice was shaking. "It damaged her insides. Her stomach, her kidneys, her—she can't have kids now. She still has eggs and stuff but she can't carry a baby because her uterus is all scarred up. They had to cut her open and drain out all the fluids and stuff and that's not even all—she's going to have to have a whole bunch of other operations to keep the scar tissue from building up. And the pain—they say that as the scar tissue builds up the pain'll get worse and worse till it's like being in labor every minute of every day till the next operation and then that's just setting the clock back for the next one. They can't even put her on painkillers because it's a chronic thing and she'd get addicted. And it's all my fault."

"Say what?" I said.

"I've been having bad thoughts," Peggy said.

There was only one thing I could say to that. "Huh?"

"This is what happens when you have bad thoughts," Peggy said. "If you sin in your heart it's as bad as if you sin in real life and now look what's happened."

"Peggy, people get sick all the time," I said. "It's completely arbitrary."

"It's not," she said. "You don't know. You don't know what I've been thinking about. This was bound to happen. It was *bound* to."

"Don't be—I mean, think about what you're saying," I said. "You're saying the reason that your *sister* landed a ruptured appendix is that *you've* been 'having bad thoughts'? How much sense does that make?"

"It makes lots of sense," Peggy said. "It makes lots. If *I* got sick then I'd be suffering, and that'd mean I was serving my punishment and being absolved. But I'm *not* absolved. I went to confession a whole bunch of times and I explain what's happened and no one'll tell me what I need to do for forgiveness. They say it's because I haven't done anything, but I know how it works. I just don't *deserve* forgiveness. I don't."

"Peggy, don't talk like this," I said. I made a move to hug her but she slapped my hand away.

"Don't *touch* me," she hissed. "Don't you even *dare*."

"What can I do?" I asked.

"What?" she said.

"How can I help you?" I asked.

"You can't," she said. "I'm not worth it." She turned around and trudged upstairs.

Five is right out

It occurred to me that I hadn't visited Kelly yet myself. I thought about dropping in on my own, but decided against it—it'd be kind of weird, and I didn't even know if hospital policy allowed it, considering that I wasn't a member of the family or even a close friend, really. So I talked to Mr. and Mrs. K. and they brought me along on their Wednesday visit.

Peggy didn't come along, ostensibly because she had to stay behind and take care of Grant. I suspected that she wouldn't have come in any case, given her mental state. And then there was the sheer creepiness of the hospital to take into account. As soon as we stepped through the sliding doors I felt like there were earthworms crawling up and down my spine; it made me want to shiver but I couldn't because I wasn't cold. It sort of surprised me, since I hadn't thought I had any kind of phobia about hospitals. Then, on the elevator ride up, it dawned on me: it wasn't hospitals that made me squirm, it was *this* hospital. I'd been here before.

My mom had always been kind of a flake. She had a knack for disappearing for weeks at a time: my dad would wake up in the morning, find that he was the only one in bed, go downstairs to find a note reading only WENT HOME. SUSAN, call up her parents' house in Santa Fe, and find her there having breakfast and saying she'd be back when the mood struck her. Echo and I had taken one of these trips with her: we were negative two months old at the time. Once we were born, she tended to treat us kids like strange short people who happened to live in her house but didn't really have any connection to her—but once or twice a year there'd be an exception. Back when I was just starting school, my bedtime was around seven o'clock; on these rare days, though, just as I was drifting off to sleep, I'd hear a sharp "Psst! Hey. Kid. C'mon, get up. Let's shop." and my mom and I would hit something like eighty thousand toy stores and anything I wanted was mine for the asking. The next day at breakfast I'd thank her. "Huh?" she'd say. "Oh, yeah, sure." She'd turn to my dad. "Can you get these people fed and off to school? I'm going back to bed. It's too early."

"Susan was just a freaky chick," Bobbo never tired of telling us.

"Hate to say it, but it's true. Even back in college, when she and your dad had just started going out. There'd be weeks when he couldn't get away from her—they'd go to parties and stuff and she'd literally cling to him. And then sometimes he'd call her place and her roommate would give him the number she'd left, and when he'd call that number he'd get some strange guy's apartment. Same thing for me, man. Back when you guys were just babies, some days I'd come over to visit and she'd practically stick her tongue down my throat kissing me hello, and then other days she'd walk right past me and drive away somewhere. It makes sense, when you think about it. Susan was . . . well, she was a supreme hottie. And Andrew—I mean, I guess he was okay for an egghead, but he was not the kind of guy who made a habit of scoring A-list chicks. So he put up with her precisely because she was an A-list chick and she stuck with him because he was the best guy she could find who wouldn't eventually drop her for being such a headcase."

I don't really have a good mental image of my mother; I was only six when she died, and my memories from those years are crayon drawings, not the digitally crisp mental movies from the years thereafter. But there's one moment I do remember like a snapshot: Echo's and my sixth birthday party. My dad, as always, had organized the festivities, but Mom was at least there, and that's how I remember her: a white dress over dusky skin, long ebon hair flecked with white confetti, standing in the door frame eating a piece of chocolate birthday cake with vanilla icing, while Echo and her legions of friends played hockey in the backyard and I watched them from the patio and wished some girls would move into our neighborhood. All my other memories of my mom have been colored by that image: even when I know she didn't have any, I always see her with confetti in her hair, even in the hospital bed where she died.

The day I turned six years old my mother was two months pregnant. When Mom went into labor that September, Dad hopped on the phone and roped Bobbo into watching us all while he and Mom went down to the hospital. That was shortly before breakfast. Soon night fell. Molly had gone to bed hours earlier, Krieg was flat on his back snoring in the middle of the room, and I was groggy beyond words; Echo was up reading a book, but then, she pretty much never slept.

"What is this shit?" Bobbo grumbled. "How long can it take to spit out a kid? I've got a hot date tonight. Shit." He got his answer before too long: Dad stumbled into the house, looking like he'd slept in his clothes every night for the previous eight years. "About time," Bobbo said. "What kind of kid did you get?"

"Shut up," Dad said. "There've been complications. Help me pack. I've got to get back to the hospital in twenty minutes."

This sounded bad. But I was too tired to give it much thought. I was asleep before Dad and Bobbo got back downstairs.

That night I dreamed that I was wandering around a mall killing people by zapping them with a cell phone: I'd hit a certain button and a bolt of lightning would shoot out the antenna. The phone started ringing and I was sure that it was the cops calling to arrest me. I hit the TALK button but it kept ringing. That was when I realized that I'd fallen asleep on the couch and the kitchen phone was ringing. Echo picked it up—she'd been up for hours.

"Who is it?" I asked.

Echo waved me off till she hung up. "It was Daddy," she said. "At the hospital. He said there were problems with the delivery but it wasn't that big a deal and that all it meant was a couple extra nights in the hospital just to make sure. By the way, we have another brother now."

I grunted. Even then I knew that another boy in the world was hardly cause for celebration. "Yeah, I know," Echo said. "Too many kids. They should've stopped with two."

Dad brought the four of us kids to visit the day after that, right after we got home from school. It wasn't the nightmare you'd expect: Molly was very small but nonetheless well-behaved, and Krieg was still on medication and didn't do much but sit around. Mom looked fine, if you don't count the fact that her hair looked like it hadn't been washed in a while. When I think back on that visit, the main thing I remember is intense boredom. The room was basically a blank office cubicle with a bed and a TV in it; there being absolutely nothing to do, after a few perfunctory hellos we each picked out a spot on the wall and set to the task of staring at it. Molly asked if Mom had had a chance to hold the baby; Mom said she hadn't. I couldn't really think of anything to say and spent most of my time flipping through the only reading material in the room, a battered TV guide left over from the Sunday newspaper. "Hey, Mohan

Tadikonda's gonna be on *Straight Flush* tonight," I finally said. "He's the Master of the Martial Arts, you know."

If at some point in your life you have the opportunity to say a few last words to your mother a few hours before she dies, these are not the ones I would suggest.

I've gone over that visit in my head about eight hundred thousand times—not a fun task, given that, as mentioned, it was really boring. And every time I do so I try to conjure up a "good-bye" I might have mumbled, or an "I love you," or even an "I have to go to the bathroom." No such luck. After announcing Mohan Tadikonda's guest shot, I didn't say another word until the car trip home. And the next morning my mommy was dead.

Dad got the call early in the morning, early enough that none of us had gotten up for school yet except Echo. I was woken up by the sound of my dad roaring at Bobbo over the phone to get over to the house immediately, and then with a slamming of doors and screeching of tires, he drove off, leaving us alone in the house. I opened our bedroom door to find that Molly had come wandering out into the hallway, rubbing her eyes; I beckoned her inside and had her go back to sleep in Echo's bed. Echo herself came upstairs a minute later. "She shouldn't be in here," she said.

"What's going on?" I asked. "What's all the noise?"

"I can't tell you with her in here," Echo said.

"She's asleep," I said. "She fell asleep half a second after she got in bed."

Echo sank to the floor—not a swoon, since she sat down naturally enough, but it sure looked like her legs had buckled under her. "I don't know what to do," she said. "Daddy said Mom's dead."

"What?" I said.

"Daddy said I'm in charge till Uncle Rob gets here," Echo said, her voice thick and hoarse. "How can I be in charge? I'm six."

I doubt I could've answered that question even had I registered it.

Luckily, there wasn't all that much charge for Echo to be in—Bobbo showed up a few minutes later. "I just *did* this," Bobbo said. "It's five-thirty in the damn morning. What, is it twins three days apart this time? What the hell's going on?"

Echo told him.

"Oh," Bobbo said. Four seconds later it hit him. "Oh, *shit*," he said.

"I don't know what to do," Echo said, mainly to herself.

"I better get down there," Bobbo said. "Shit. *Shit*. Are there any neighbors you all can stay with?"

"We could go to Peggy's house," I suggested.

"Is that close?" Bobbo asked.

"Two doors down," I said.

"Okay, then we have a plan," Bobbo said. Molly came downstairs to see what the new burst of noise was about. "Oh, for God's sake, someone put some clothes on that kid," Bobbo said.

I dressed Molly and Echo got Krieg out of bed and Bobbo called over to the Kaylins' and within a couple of minutes we'd completed the handoff. Mrs. K. said she'd put Krieg and me in Cheese's room, and Echo and Molly in Kelly's; this was ostensibly to avoid completely splitting us up, but I strongly suspect that even then, Peggy had declared her room off-limits. She was also the only one of the Kaylin kids who was awake. "What's going on?" she asked.

"My mom died," I said, once Krieg and Molly were out of earshot.

"You mean your gramma?" Peggy asked.

"My mom," I said.

"But your mom's not old," Peggy said.

"Peggy, hush," Mrs. K. said.

Bobbo was out on the front porch talking to Mr. K. They shook hands and it looked like Bobbo was about to leave for the hospital. "No!" Echo burst out. "I want to go too! I can help! I can help Daddy!"

The idea of going to the hospital with Bobbo hadn't even occurred to me, but Echo's idea suddenly seemed to me to be very . . . brave, I guess. "Yeah, me too," I said.

"You're not old enough," Mr. K. said.

"I was old enough for Daddy to put me in charge," Echo said.

"Yeah, I'll take 'em, I guess," Bobbo said. "Not the two little ones. But these two. Come on." Around this time Bobbo was driving an old Volvo my dad had given him and on which Bobbo had subsequently

put racing stripes; Echo and I climbed into the back and buckled ourselves in, and Bobbo drove us to the hospital.

This may not have been the brightest move. When the elevator
doors opened we found Dad sitting lifelessly in a chair; Echo went
running up to him, and while he didn't fend her off, he didn't exactly
sweep her up into an embrace of filial love either. He just sort of let
her stand there. "Daddy!" she said. "What happened? Why didn't
you bring us?"

"I told you to stay with the children at the house," Dad said, glar-
ing at Bobbo. "That was all of half an hour ago. What could *possibly*
have motivated you to bring them here? What were you *thinking*?
Were you thinking?"

"I, uh, thought it'd cheer you up," Bobbo said.

"Cheer me *up*?" Dad said. "My wife *left* me, Robert. How is
bringing over someone who looks like her supposed to cheer me *up*?"

"She didn't *leave* you, Drew," Bobbo said. "She died."

"She left me," Dad said. "There was nothing wrong with her.
She'd recovered completely. But that taste of oblivion was too sweet
for her to resist. She took off and left me here."

"Right," Bobbo said. "Look, uh, I don't exactly know what to say
here . . ."

"Of *course* you don't!" Dad said. "You're a cretin!" He grabbed
him by the collar and shoved him up against the vending machine.
The impact knocked a couple candy bars off the rack. Dad looked
like he was about to put his fist through the wall but stormed off to
the restroom instead. Echo put her hands over her eyes and cried.

"Uh, are you okay?" I asked Bobbo.

"Yeah, sure," he said. "Come on, maybe we better go."

Not everybody hurts

The same vending machine was still standing by the elevator as we
headed out to visit Kelly. Kelly herself was a mess: her hair looked like
it hadn't been washed for days, she didn't appear to have slept very
well if at all since the weekend, her hospital gown looked sticky and
clung to her, and none of this dissuaded me in the least from wanting

to climb into bed with her. If anything, it made her more delectable than usual. Which made sense: it meant she'd spent several days doing nothing but stewing in her own pheromones.

"Hi, honey," Mrs. K. said.

"Hi," Kelly said woozily. "Did you bring ice cream?"

"What?" Mrs. K. said.

"Ice cream," Kelly said. "You said after the operation I could have ice cream . . ."

"That was for if you got your tonsils out," Mrs. K. "And we decided against that eight years ago."

"You mean all these operations and I still have tonsils?" Kelly said.

"Afraid so," Mr. K. said.

"I hate tonsils," Kelly said.

Cheese picked up an old TV guide and started thumbing through it. I surreptitiously jabbed him in the ribs. "Tell her you love her," I whispered.

"What?" he said.

One of the doctors came in and stopped short. "Oh!" the doctor said. "I didn't know you were expecting more visitors."

"More?" Mr. K. said.

"Like, the cheer squad came yesterday," Kelly said. "Some of them, anyway."

"Right when we were about to run some tests," the doctor said.

"What kind of tests?" Cheese asked.

"Keith!" Mrs. K. said. "That's none of your business. Especially given the . . . kind of sickness she had."

"Don't worry, this isn't remotely embarrassing," the doctor said. "We're trying to diagnose how it is that Kelly could have somehow not noticed a case of appendicitis, or why when we allowed her to self-medicate she only ended up giving herself one dose the entire time she's been here—in a case like this it'd be more reasonable to expect her to be hitting the painkiller button every three minutes."

"The button didn't do anything," Kelly said. "It doesn't hurt, anyway."

The doctor turned to Mr. and Mrs. K. "How long has she been like this?" he asked. "Has she *ever* come to either of you complaining of being hurt?"

"She must have," Mrs. K. said.

"Can you remember a specific instance?" he asked.

"I can!" I interrupted. "Uh, sorry. But I remember she cried when she was five and Cheese pushed her off a swing."

"But that could have been just the shock of the impact," the doctor said. "Or even just a desire to get her brother in trouble. Has she ever had a headache, an earache? A sore throat? Menstrual cramps?"

"Out!" Mr. K. ordered Cheese and me.

Ugly butterflies

On the trip home Mr. and Mrs. K. wouldn't say anything about how the discussion had proceeded from there, no matter how much Cheese whined about it. But I was pretty sure it wasn't a congenital condition. That left only one possibility I could think of—one that would've seemed impossible a week earlier, but which the responses of Kelly's friends to her hospitalization all pointed to.

The next afternoon before our peer counseling session I went to the closet where our big three-ring binders were kept and grabbed the one labeled DRUGS. To my surprise, the one on STDs was missing—September was sitting at the long table flipping through it. "What're you looking up?" I asked.

"HPV," she said.

"Eww," I said. "That's papilloma, right? Warts? Is that what our first case is about?"

"No," September said. "I haven't even seen the schedule. This is . . . personal."

"Oh," I said. "You mean April?"

"She's such an idiot," September said. "Oh, some people have signed up to have us work their parties. One of them's at Greg Garner's. Can you take that one? That's way out of my way."

"I suppose," I said.

"Great," September said. "Also, can you go pick up the schedule?"

"Sure, just a minute," I said. I flipped to the last section in the folder, the one on designer drugs. I'd only read this section carefully once, and that'd been a year and a half earlier; since then I'd only scanned through it when I was looking up something specific. But one detail I'd encountered had stuck with me. I'd started a little too far back, and flipped toward the front, past superchick, past squeak, and then there it was before me, in black and white and encased in plastic:

SCRATCH

The common name for the blue crystalline amphetamine typically printed onto thin pieces of cardboard resembling business cards and coated with a polymer, which, when scratched off, allows the user to place the substance in direct contact with the tongue, producing an effect that, depending on the strength of the substance, can range from a pleasant sense of well-being and heightened libido to intense euphoria with the possibility of hallucinogenic effects. This substance is not believed to be addictive, but has been known to cause cardiac and respiratory failure when taken in a large dose, and to inhibit sensitivity to pain when used chronically over an extended period, particularly when that use was initiated in childhood or adolescence.

This was the part that confused me. Much as I hated to admit it, it was certainly not out of the question that upon reaching high school Kelly had fallen in with the wrong group of friends, started experimenting with roughage, moved on to scratch, maybe even made a habit of it . . . still, I couldn't see how even fairly heavy use over such a limited period could produce such a dramatic effec—

"Allen?" September said. "Can you get the schedule now?"

Peggy ended up missing the entire week of school, but when I went to her house at lunch to visit her, she was in the best spirits I'd seen her in all week. "Kelly's coming home tonight," Peggy said. "So that's good. I finally feel like I'm up to doing some work, too—I've spent the whole morning catching up on all my classes. That reminds me—can you get me this week's *Iliad* copy? I'll send Keith after class to pick it up."

"I can just bring it over after school," I said.

"That's not a good idea," she said. "I have a date."

"A *date*?!" I didn't say. "You've been locked in your room all week refusing to see anyone and you still have a *date* lined up?!" I didn't add. But I thought it. What I actually said was, "Really? Oh, okay."

That afternoon I was surprised to find out that the person she was going on the date with was just as unaware of this fact as I'd been. Water polo season was under way, and Fringie and Skippie and Grungie and Buddie and Lemming had come by the *Iliad* room to collect Sluggo before heading to the locker room to change for that afternoon's game. This looked to be a long-term project, since Sluggo had taken off his shoes and now couldn't find them. Fringie glared at him with near Echo-like intensity. "Sorry," Sluggo said. "They were here a minute ago, I swear—"

"Your shoes are the least of my concerns," Fringie said. "The penis is extremely displeased."

"Say what?" Sluggo said.

"I have had no contact of any kind with Peggy Kaylin since Sunday," Fringie said. "She is shunning me. The penis senses its window of opportunity closing. I can now see that I left a factor out of my calculations: Peggy Kaylin's caprices."

Hurray for caprices! I thought.

"Peggy Kaylin's receptivity is in a state of perpetual flux," Fringie said. "This indicates that any opportunity must be seized. Solvency must be achieved as soon as possible."

The other water polo players cheered and clapped him on the back. My immediate inclination was to give up waiting for Cheese and run to the Kaylins' house to warn Peggy, but I remembered that I'd promised to stop doing that. In any event, Cheese showed up a minute later. But instead of coming inside, he stopped to talk to Fringie.

"What is it?" Fringie sneered.

"Uh, hi," Cheese said, shuffling his feet. "Um, Peggy said she wanted you to come over tonight. We're going to be picking Kelly up from the hospital but she wanted to stay behind and, like, talk and stuff."

Fringie's face lit up like the sun coming out from behind a cloud of airborne toxins. "Excellent!" he declared. "Excellent! Now is the winter of our discontent made glorious summer by this sullen dork. Tonight's the night."

And Peggy wasn't the only one with a date lined up after school.

Echo didn't get home until dinnertime, and as she came in I could see Hayley's car backing down the driveway. "Man, this chews," I said. "Even my sister gets more chicks than I do."

Echo gave me a look that could've put me in the hospital. "Kidding, kidding," I said. "You guys went to get some more coffee, I take it?"

"You know I don't drink coffee," Echo said. "We went to her house and she showed me some of the leftist magazines she used to collect when she lived in Seattle."

"Oh, that's the oldest scam in the book," I said. "'Hey baby, why don't you come up to my room and I'll show you my communist propaganda.' That's just a step above asking you to come see her stamp collection."

If the last look Echo had given me could've left me in need of medical attention, this one could have simply made my head burst into flames. "Still kidding," I said. "I think it's great that you're hanging out together. Really. Hayley's terrific. She's really smart and she's not childish. Which is more than I can say for your *last* bunch of friends."

It marks the spot, you know

When Echo and I were in elementary school, it was never more than a couple minutes after we'd get home in the afternoons that every kid in the neighborhood and more than a few kids from other neighborhoods would be banging on our front door. I'd come downstairs to find several thousand ten-year-old boys huddled on the porch, resplendent in their long flowing manes, which was the style at the time—not that I had much room to talk: I was sporting quite the fro my own self. Only Echo was ahead of the curve, keeping her hair just barely long enough to run her fingers through. And that was who they always wanted: the second I'd open the door it was Prime Minister's Questions out on our porch. "Is Echo home?" "Can Echo come out?" "Where's Echo?"

In the early days, the sport of choice was baseball, or an approximation of it: not many of the kids had bats or baseballs, but every house had half a dozen tennis racquets lying around, and tennis balls lined the gutters, so they just used those. This rendered strikeouts relatively rare—a good thing, too, since they didn't have a backstop. First base was Dooj's mailbox; second was the sewer cutaway at the end of the cul-de-sac; third was the fire hydrant in between the Fringie and Monihan residences; and home plate was the manhole cover near the intersection. Those who attempted sliding were generally rewarded with deep bone bruises and tetanus shots.

But once the kids discovered hockey, it was love at first sight: unlike baseball, you got to run around for the entire game and smack into other people with impunity. You even got a big stick to smack them with. And if you were on Echo's team, you got to win. Echo tended goal. She was rather good at it. No one had ever scored against her. They'd play twelve-on-three and Echo would block every shot. After a while, the shots on goal became increasingly half-hearted. See, every shutout magnified Echo's legend, and this imparted a certain status to the people she hung around with. But the fact that she'd never been scored on, not even once, lent a fragility to her status as hockey god. Had she merely been extremely good, the way she was as a soccer goalie, her celebrity could survive the occasional mistake; but since her aura hinged on her absolute invincibility, one goal allowed could shatter her rep completely. After all, pretty much every neighborhood had a *good* goalie; but only the kids who played on Hyacinth could show up at school and boast that *their* goalie was *perfect*.

I never had any interest in joining in, myself. For one thing, aside from Echo, they were all boys. More to the point, they were all asses. There was Vance Judden and the way he'd shout "Judden is great! Judden is great!" even when he hadn't done anything—part of the reason I wanted to take up the guitar was to drown him out. There was Jay Kyeutter, whose vocabulary was comprised entirely of the word "cocksucker" and the phrase "haw haw haw haw!" There were Christian Variola and Min-Hsun Lee, a couple of thugs who left the street covered in spit after the game. And there were Neil, Ryan, and Clement Campbell, who may well have been the worst of the lot: they got their kicks out of tormenting Peggy. One incident that stands out was the time that there was a knock on the door, and when I opened it I found not a horde of jocks-in-training but Peggy, tears streaming down her face. "Clement Campbell said there was a surprise for me at his house," she sobbed, "and I went down there, and there was a big X on the driveway, and he told me to stand on it, and then Ryan and Neil threw acorns at me from a tree till their mom made them stop!"

"Why didn't you run away?" I asked.

"Because they told me to stand on the X!" she wailed.

There was a knock at the garage door. I looked at my watch; it was a little before ten. That meant it was probably a pizza for someone. I hadn't ordered one, so I let it pass—till the knock came again, harder this time, more of a pounding than a knock. I went to investigate.

It was Peggy, tears streaming down her face. "Oh my god," I said. "What's wrong? Come in, come in, what's wrong?"

"Carver," she said. "He—he—"

"He threw acorns at you?" I asked.

"He tried to rape me," she sobbed.

A brick through the window

So that's when I took my Tec-9 and killed Fringie.

No, not really. The first thing I did was usher Peggy into my mom's old office and sit her down on the couch. She was still crying pretty hard so I tried to hug her but she shrugged me off. "Okay, I'm going to go call the police now," I said. "Can I get you anyth—"

"No!" she said. "No police."

"But—" I began, then caught myself. It occurred to me that Peggy's definition of rape and the state of California's definition might differ significantly, and that before pushing for a police report, or even debating the meaning of the term, I should find out what had happened first. Only the fact that Peggy had triggered the emergency mode in my brain kept me from making an ass of myself—normally I would've just asked, "Well did he try to rape you or not?" and would only come up with a tactful and logical way to approach the situation fifteen minutes later, after she'd already run from the house. "So, what happened?" I asked. "Can I get you anything? Some hot chocolate or something?"

"No," she sobbed.

I gave her some tissues and let her huddle in her thick leather jacket and cry for a few minutes. My mom had a clock up on the wall that hadn't had a new battery put in since she'd died, the hands frozen permanently at 9:07; I ducked out to the kitchen, grabbed a battery from the junk drawer, and put it in. The regular ticking seemed to soothe Peggy a bit, and soon she was able to hold back her tears.

"Do you want to talk about it?" I asked quietly.

"Not really," she said, sniffing.

The phone rang, so I picked it up. The line was dead. By the next ring I realized that it was all the other phones that had been ringing—the one in the office was hooked up to a different line, which had been turned off eight years ago. I decided not to bother running out to get it; I didn't want to leave Peggy, and I was sure someone else would pick it up. Sure enough, the ringing stopped, and a minute later the door opened and Molly poked her head in. "What're you doing in here? It's for you."

"Thanks," I said. "I'll be right back," I told Peggy.

Peggy's eyes went wide. "She still doesn't wear anything?" she said. "I thought she'd grow out of that when she started, you know—"

"Nothing to grow out of," Molly said from out in the hall. "I just grow." Peggy blushed. I went to answer the phone.

It was Mrs. K. "Hi, Allen," she said. "Is Peggy over there? She ran out of here in an awful hurry. Carver said that they'd had an argument."

"An argument?" I said. "Uh, so, did you want to talk to her? I mean, she did come over a few minutes ago, yeah. Should I put her on?"

"That's okay," Mrs. K. said. "I just wanted to make sure I knew where she was. She didn't take the car so I didn't think she could've gotten far. 'Bye, Allen."

"'Bye," I said.

I went back to my mom's office and told Peggy about the call. "An argument?" she said. "He said it was an argument?"

"So what did happen?" I asked.

"Okay," she said. She sighed.

"It started when Kelly got sick," she began. "Right away I remembered what I was doing the second that she fell down. I was saying something bad about her. Remember? I was having bad thoughts about my own sister. And before that I was having all kinds of bad thoughts about my parents, in *church*. That was two bad things in one—not honoring my father and mother, and at the same time not thinking about God at the one specific time I'm supposed to be doing nothing but thinking about Him. I was just being a bad person all the time. And the *reason* was that I was spending all my time thinking about Carver and what we were going to do that afternoon and that weekend and for our twenty-fifth anniversary. So this week while Kelly was in the hospital I spent a lot of time thinking about our relationship."

"And you decided to dump him?" I asked.

"No," she said. "I just thought we needed to *talk*. He'd been calling all week and I wasn't ready to talk yet and when I finally was ready I had Keith ask him to come over. He had a water polo game so he didn't get there till everyone else had already left. So I said we needed to talk and he said why didn't we go up to my room where we could have some *privacy* and I said that no one was home so there was just as much privacy in the living room as anywhere else and that besides no one except my family was allowed in my room anyway."

"Really?" I said.

"Of course," she said. "*You* know that."

"Hasn't he been in your room before, though?" I asked.

"And look what happened to Kelly," Peggy said.

"Okay," I said. I still thought this was pretzel logic at its finest, but this wasn't the time to pick a fight. "So what happened next?"

"So I told him what I thought up to tell him," Peggy said. "I said I'd been thinking about where I was in my life, and that he was the best boyfriend that I'd ever had, and that I was really happy with where our relationship was, and that I thought it'd be a good idea to just keep it at that level for a while, because I'd been spending all my time trying to be a good girlfriend, but I wasn't being a very good daughter or a good sister or a good Catholic."

"I take it that didn't go over well," I said.

"It went great," she said. "I thought. He didn't seem mad or anything. He even said, 'That sounds fine, it sounds like you've given this a lot of thought, I respect your decisions,' that kind of thing . . . we started kissing . . . and then . . . I couldn't move."

"What?" I said.

"He pinned me to the couch," she said. "It wasn't like he was holding me down, because there wasn't any pressure . . . and it wasn't like I was struggling against him, because the way he was holding me I couldn't even move enough to struggle, my brain would tell my arm to move and it just wouldn't do anything, and he wouldn't even let me talk, he didn't stop me from talking, it's just that whenever it even looked like I was about to start saying something he'd kiss me again . . ." Her breathing started to get heavy. "And I didn't even *notice* at first. I thought it was *me*. Because we weren't doing anything we hadn't done before, so even though I decided to start drawing the line earlier, I thought maybe I was chickening out about telling him to stop . . . but then he started stuff we *hadn't* done . . ." The tears started flowing once again. "Why?" she wailed. "Is it me? Am I so *stupid,* so *uninteresting,* so WORTHLESS that you can know me for *ten years* and tell me you *love* me and that we're going to spend our *lives* together and *still* only be interested in getting to SECOND BASE?" I took a step toward her. "*DON'T TOUCH ME!*" she cried, her fists balled up tight. "Why would you want to touch me? What, were you going to hug me? I'm not worth it. Unless you wanted to feel me up. Is that what you wanted? Then go ahead. That's all I'm good for."

"Okay, I've heard enough," I said. "This case is as clear-cut as they come. We're calling the police."

"*No!*" Peggy seethed. "I'm not going through that. It'd just be my word against his. I don't want to think about this anymore. I just—I just—I don't know. I don't know why I came here. I just couldn't be in the house right then." She swallowed. "I trusted him. I *trusted* him. Ten years . . ." She looked up at me and her face changed. "I'd better go. I've got to go . . ."

That scared me, but the last thing Peggy needed right then was to be kept somewhere she didn't want to be. "Okay," I said. "You'll be okay, right? You're not going to . . . do anything . . . ?"

She shrugged and opened the door. "I love you," I called after her. She didn't react. A second later she was gone.

immune deficiency

As you can probably guess, I didn't get a whole lot of sleep that night. At first I was up trying to figure out if there was anything I could do to make things easier for Peggy, but that soon passed and all my energy was directed toward coming up with ways to get back at Fringie. And then I had to decide what country to flee to after Fringie was out of the way. I'd narrowed it down to Switzerland and Costa Rica when at long last I finally fell asleep. You'll note that I never said that I wasn't tired—once I did get to sleep, I didn't wake up until well into Saturday afternoon. I went over to Peggy's house about five seconds later.

I arrived just as Peggy was putting a cake in the oven. She was still wearing the jacket Fringie had given her, but on the bright side, I was pleased to see that instead of locking herself in her room as usual she had elected to sublimate her sorrows in the preparation of baked goods. "Hi," I said. "What's the cake for?"

"It's for Kelly," Peggy said. "Now that she's home again. I was going to make it last night, but, but stuff came up."

"Right," I said. "Listen, have you given any more thought to filing a police report? I'd be more than happy to go in with you to tell them what I heard him s—"

"*No,*" Peggy said. "I don't want to think about that anymore. It probably didn't happen the way I thought anyway. I probably just misunderstood what was going on. There's probably a simple explanation. I just don't want to think about it. It's not important."

"Say what?" I said. "Not imp—"

Peggy put her hands over her ears. "I'm not going to talk about this," she said.

"Wait," I said. "At least tell me you're not going to see him anymore. You're not, right?"

"I'm not going to see anyone anymore," Peggy said. "I give up. I almost gave up two months ago but *you* convinced me that I should see someone that I already knew really well. So now I know that if I date people I meet at school or at work or at church or just walking around that they'll turn out to be not decent, and if I date people I've known for my whole life then they'll turn out to also be not decent and I just didn't know it. The only decent people I know are my mom and my dad and my brothers and my sister. And I can't date any of them so I'm not going to date anyone ever again. I'll live here, and if my parents ever sell the house and get a smaller place just for them, then I'll live with Kelly and her family, and if they can't find room for me, then I'll join a convent."

"Sounds perfectly sensible to me," I said. "So, uh, if you're not seeing Fringie anymore, how come you're still wearing the jacket?"

"It's my jacket," she said.

"Yeah," I said, "but—"

"It's mine," she said.

"Noted," I said. Peggy took a box of sugar and a bottle of vanilla from a cabinet over the stove and then collected some cream cheese and eggs from the fridge. "What're those for?" I asked.

"Frosting," she said.

"Really?" I said. "You're making frosting? I've seen you make a million cakes. You never made—"

"Kelly likes homemade frosting," Peggy said, "so that's what she gets."

"Is she around?" I asked.

"She just got up," Peggy said. "She was in the shower a couple minutes ago."

I hadn't been aware of any water running, but when I flashed back over the previous few minutes, there it was—the water had shut off while Peggy had been busy detailing her future housing plans. And now that I'd actually become conscious of it, the sound of running water had its predictable effect. "She's not the only one who just got up," I said. "I came right over. I mean *right* over. I'll be back in a minute."

I ducked out of the kitchen, went to the end of the hall, and tried the bathroom door, but it was locked. "Busy!" Grant hollered from inside. He sounded all happy about it. I thought about running home but decided to just go upstairs instead. I took the long treacherous stairway in four jumps, turned right, and tripped over Cheese.

"*Yahh!*" he yelped. From the panic in his eyes you'd think I'd come to stuff him in a pet carrier and haul him down to the vet to be fixed.

"What's going on?" I asked. He'd been kneeling in the hallway peering at something; I turned to look just in time to see Kelly pull on her T-shirt—she'd left her door cracked open. My reaction was immediate: I got Cheese in a headlock and dragged him down to the end of the hall. It wasn't until later that I realized he outweighed me by a good fifty pounds and I shouldn't have been able to do this.

"Don't tell my parents, man," he mewled. "My dad'll send me to military school. I didn't mean to. I was just passing by and saw the door was open and looked in and—and—"

"This is pretty low," I said. "Spying on your *sister*?"

"I know, I know," he whimpered. "But—I mean—*you* know what she's—I mean—every day, she's skipping around and stuff, and, and I can't do anything—*you* know—"

"But she's your *sister*," I said. "Aren't you, you know, immune?"

"To *her*?" he said. "You've gotta be kidding."

It was a tough call. On the one hand, this was thoroughly creepy, even creepier than when that Warder guy was staring at Molly, because at least I knew that Molly didn't mind. Part of me thought that the right thing to do would be to inform Mr. and Mrs. Kaylin and let them decide what the consequences should be. On the other hand, I had to admit that had I glanced in Kelly's room half a second sooner I wouldn't have enough blood left in my brain to be thinking about this at all. "All right," I said. "I'm not going to tell your parents—as long as *you* tell Kelly herself. Right now. And *knock first*. Got it?"

"Okay," he said. He knocked on the door. I'd planned on waiting around to make sure he followed through, but I really, *really* had to go to the bathroom. I came out a minute later to find Cheese rubbing his jaw. "She punched me in the face!" he lamented. He slunk back to his room and started pounding on his drum set.

"That's just for when *you* punched *me*," Kelly called after him. "You're still gonna get it for spying on me. I'd, like, take a picture of you in the shower or something and show it to people except if I saw you naked I'd be too busy throwing up to work the camera."

What came next happened so quickly that at this point I can only reconstruct what I must've been thinking. I know that I was headed downstairs to get back to Peggy when, as I passed Kelly's door, it occurred to me that I hadn't told her welcome back or anything. I'm not entirely sure why I was moved to actually knock on her door instead of waiting for her to come downstairs, but when I did, I discovered that the door wasn't latched completely, as it swung open. And that's when I saw something I really didn't want to see. No, not Kelly in a state of undress—that I had absolutely no problem whatsoever with seeing. Instead, I found Kelly gently placing a scratch card on her tongue. She shivered, blinked hard, and then realized I was standing in the doorway.

"Um, like, you didn't see that," she said.

"Is that a question or a statement?" I asked.

She shivered again. "A statement," she said, an odd twist playing over her lips. "If you don't believe it, c'mere and I'll, like, convince you."

I cannot possibly put into words how much I wanted to be convinced. I had spent every single night of the previous three years dreaming of being convinced by Kelly in every way imaginable and quite a few unimaginable ways as well. And on any other day—a day earlier, a day later—I doubt I would've been able to hesitate for a second before letting this luscious creature have her way with me. But Peggy had just told me that she'd decided she couldn't trust anyone outside her family, not even—perhaps even especially not—the people she'd known for practically her entire life. I was determined not to be Fringie. No matter how much the penis wanted to be.

"Uh, gotta go," I said.

I suppose that's also why I didn't tell Peggy or Mr. and Mrs. K. about what I'd seen—I didn't know how Peggy would take it. And at that moment, that was really the only thing that mattered. Or at least that's how I remember it. It was entirely possible that it completely slipped my mind as I rushed home to spend the rest of the afternoon imagining being convinced.

One idiot savant, hold the idiocy

Later, I was surprised to find how little I felt like throwing myself off the nearest freeway overpass. It's true that while some people had goals like getting into med school or making a major league roster, my one goal in life had always been to at some point in my life get it on with Kelly Kaylin; but I'd always envisioned us succumbing to a moment of crazed mutual lust, not arranging some kind of mercenary deal. The more I thought about it, the clearer it became that any encounter the day before would've fallen on the wrong side of the line between glorious sex and weasel sex. This is assuming I'd even understood her right, of course. It's entirely possible that she just would've slipped me a twenty and sent me on my way.

The next day I decided not to stop by the Kaylins' place, even though I wanted to check on Peggy's spirits—I feared the odds that I'd reconsider Kelly's offer would prove too great. And I had a paper for my Non-Western Civ class coming up so I spent a good chunk of the afternoon at the Cal State Fullerton library doing research. When I got home I was about to throw my backpack on my bed when I noticed someone sitting on it. "Hi," Hayley said. "Echo's teaching me how to play go. Which one's your room?"

"This one," I said. "You're sitting on my bed."

"What?" Hayley said. "You mean you share a room with your—"

"That's the second question everybody always asks," I said.

"I'll bite," she said. "What's the first?"

"Have you run into Molly yet?" I asked.

"Nope," Hayley said.

"When you run into Molly, you'll know what the first is," I said. "So where's Echo?"

"She went downstairs to get me a glass of water," Hayley said.

Echo came in a moment later and handed Hayley her beverage. "You know," Hayley said, "unless there's a lot more to this than what you've told me, this doesn't really seem all that complicated. Haven't they fed this into some computer and come up with an unbeatable series of moves? Seems like it'd be easier than chess—"

"Chess is much simpler," Echo said.

"But chess has a bunch of different pieces, and they move around—it seems like it'd be much harder to predict—"

"At the beginning of a chess game there are only eighteen possible moves," Echo said. "And the other player has eighteen possible replies. That's eighteen times eighteen. The goban is nineteen by nineteen. The number of points on which the first stone can be placed outnumbers the number of possible states after *both* players have moved in a chess game. This may seem like a small difference but it's geometric, not arithmetic. Try comparing them directly. We'll even make an allowance for symmetry and say that instead of three hundred sixty-one points there are only fifty-five unique points in relation to the shape of the board. And the center point preserves that symmetry for the first move by White, and the ten other points along the diagonal allow for at least bilateral symmetry. So we'll call it one times fifty-four plus ten times one hundred eighty-nine plus forty-four times three hundred sixty, which is seventeen thousand seven hundred eighty-four. Which means that even considering just one single move by each player, go is fifty-four and eight-ninths times deeper than—"

"Please tell me you have all those stats memorized," Hayley said.

"What?" Echo said.

"What's the square root of a billion and five?" Hayley asked.

Echo blushed. "Three one six two two point seven seven six six eight—"

"Wait," Hayley said. "I have no idea if that's even close to right. Let me borrow your calculator."

"I don't own one," she said.

"I do," I said. "Second drawer of the desk."

Hayley grabbed the calculator. "Okay, what's um, one two three four five six times six five four three two one?" she asked.

"Eighty billion, seven hundred seventy-nine million, eight hundred fifty-three thousand, three hundred seventy-six," Echo replied instantly.

"Okay, how are you doing that?" Hayley demanded. "You couldn't possibly have figured that out that fast."

"I didn't really figure it out at all," Echo said. "I just saw it. Just as if I were to hold up some fingers you wouldn't count them one by one—you'd just see the number."

"That's incredible," Hayley said.

"It's just genetics," Echo said. "It can't be attributed to any effort on my part."

"So how is it that in all the time we've been on the paper together I never found out you could do this?" Hayley asked.

"It never came up," Echo said.

"And what kind of math do they have you in?" Hayley asked. "Probably not Algebra II, I'm assuming?"

"I'm taking topology over at Cal State Fullerton," Echo said.

"I don't even know what that means," Hayley said. "Can I see the book?" She went over to our bookshelf. "Hey, you've amassed quite a collection of go books here. You're really dedicated to this game, aren't you?"

"Not so much anymore," Echo said. "I play over the net sometimes."

"Is there anything like a club where you could play?" Hayley asked.

"I don't go to clubs anymore," Echo said darkly.

"Wait a minute," Hayley said. "Echo, this book is in Japanese."

"A lot of the better books still haven't been translated," Echo said.

"And so's this one," Hayley said. "No, wait. This is *Chi*nese. And this one's Korean!"

"Those are the major go-playing countries," Echo said.

"Please tell me you don't actually speak all these languages," Hayley said.

"I don't," Echo said. "I do speak Japanese. The others I can only read."

But Hayley had already found the shelf with the literature on it. "How about these?" she said. "French, Spanish, German . . . *Russian* . . ."

"I do speak most of those," Echo said. "Those I was able to find tapes for—"

"But how were you able to find time—"

"Reading knowledge usually takes about a week," Echo said. "It's a simple skill—"

"You see the world completely differently from the rest of us, don't you?" Hayley asked. "I can't imagine what it'd be like for mathematics and language to be transparent to me. And Holdn thinks he's special because he finally figured out how to use chopsticks."

"It's just genetics," Echo said. "It can't be attributed to any effort on my—"

"Should I even ask whether you've got any more of these abilities I don't know about?" Hayley asked.

Echo shot me an urgent look, which I promptly pretended I hadn't seen. I mean, I suppose the altruistic thing to do would've been to take some of the heat off her, but I wasn't about to volunteer my little talent. Echo wasn't the only one who'd had her fill of being a circus freak.

And the Ukrainian judge gives it a 5.9

That night I woke up at three in the morning to find myself braced in the door frame. I'd lived in California my whole life: I didn't actually have to be conscious to spring for cover in a quake. Bobbo, however, could not say the same. *"AAAH!"* he shrieked. "Shit! What do I do? What do I do? *AAAH!"*

"Get in the door frame!" Molly yelled from the door frame next to mine. It being well past the time Echo usually got up, she was presumably downstairs somewhere; the door to Krieg and Jerem's room remained shut. "What is this?" Molly asked. "About a six, maybe?"

"Something like that," I said. "Not too hard, but it's taking a while."

"Get out of the door frame!" Bobbo yelled. "I need it!"

"Get your own!" his date said.

"Come on!" Bobbo pleaded. "I've got shit falling on my head here!"

"You do not!" she said.

"But I could!" he protested. The shaking stopped. "Oh, forget it," he said. He stumbled over her and out into the hall. "You guys all right?" he asked. "Hey, have you met Tammy?"

I got up and surveyed the wreckage. Echo had left her go equipment out after her game with Hayley; now half the stones were on the floor. That seemed to be the extent of the damage. Even the books had stayed on the shelves.

Molly knocked on Krieg and Jerem's door. "Are you okay?" she asked.

"Fuck you!" came the muffled reply.

"I'll take that as a yes," Molly said. She yawned. "I'm going back to bed. See you for the aftershock."

"Bed?" I said. "You can't go to bed! We have traditions to uphold! We have to spend an hour listening to quake coverage on the radio and hear about how they felt it in Thousand Oaks and Twentynine Palms, and how it compared to the one in 1971, and how the cat was acting weird all day—"

"Tape it," she yawned. She went inside.

I went downstairs to make sure Echo had made it through the quake okay. Not that I expected to find her crushed under a file cabinet or anything; I just thought that if *I'd* been alone downstairs when a quake hit and no one came to look for me, I'd be looking for a file cabinet to pull onto myself just to make everyone feel guilty. Echo didn't seem to be anywhere downstairs, though. I even looked in places like under the sofa and inside the refrigerator, with no luck. I finally got it into my head to check outside, and though I didn't find Echo in the garage, I did find her bike; since the car was out on the driveway, that meant that she couldn't have gotten far. I hopped into the car to drive around the block a few times looking for her, or rather, started to hop—I revised my plan when I found Echo in the car, her face streaked with tears.

"Echo?" I said. "Eck, what's wrong? What—"

"Don't touch me," she said.

"No one seems to want to be touched these days," I said. "C'mon, what's the matter? This is starting to upset me."

"Just leave me alone," she said.

"I mean, today was a good day, right?" I said. "With Hayl—"

"Please just leave me *alone*," she said.

I shut the door and went upstairs. All I could think about was how I could turn the tables on Echo for being so secretive about whatever was bothering her. I wondered whether Siren Delaney might be willing to teach me how to cry on command. Then I fell asleep.

No more than forty-five seconds later the phone rang. I picked it up. "Huh? What?" I said.

"Allen?" came the voice at the other end. "Allen, it's Peggy. Have you seen Kelly anywhere?"

"What?" I said.

"We all got woken up by the quake and Kelly's not here," she said. "She's not anywhere in the house. She—wait, a car just pulled up. I'll talk to you later." *Click.*

That was just too tantalizing to resist—I had to see how it played out. I went downstairs and out to the driveway just in time to see a Corvette speed off, leaving Kelly standing on the curb in front of her house, resplendent in an outfit none of us had ever seen her wear: a shiny collared shirt two sizes too small, with metallic vertical stripes in burgundy and mustard and forest green, and pale blue jeans laced up the front like a shoe, with bright red laces done a little under halfway up. She was barefoot. Standing on the porch was her entire family. Mr. and Mrs. K. looked upset; Grant looked confused; Cheese looked awestruck; and Peggy looked like she'd just seen Kelly gunned down before her eyes.

Kelly collapsed onto the grass, laughing hysterically.

Das Parfum

Peggy's much-anticipated return to school didn't happen. "That's six straight days of absences for Peggy Kaylin," Benito said. "With this kind of irresponsibility she can consider herself no longer in contention for next year's editor-in-chief."

"Look, a couple things came up over the weekend," I said. "She'll be back eventually. I mean, come on, who else are you going to get? One of the vague people?" The vague people glared at me. "Yeah, you heard me," I told them.

Still, I thought I'd best tell Peggy about Benito's edict, just in case she cared. But when I went over to her house after peer counseling, she wasn't home: "She went to work," Cheese told me. I thought about heading down to the juice shop but I knew Peggy hated being visited at work. So I settled for periodically checking the Kaylins' driveway to see if the Kaylins' van had returned. I checked at eight-thirty, at nine, at nine-thirty, at ten. At ten-thirty I finally rang the bell again and a disgruntled Mr. Kaylin told me that Peggy had called ahead to say she wouldn't be back till later that night. The fact that I kept checking after that owed more to a mild case of obsessive-compulsive disorder than to a burning need to pass along Benito's message. At midnight I tried to go to sleep, but couldn't; at one o'clock I startled Echo by switching the light back on just as she was carefully sneaking out the door to avoid waking me up. Still no van. I took to watching the intersection outside our window to see if any cars turned onto our street. It being the middle of the night, traffic was somewhat less than brisk. Finally at one forty-five a car turned onto Hyacinth and pulled up onto the Kaylins' driveway.

Note that I said "car" and not "van the size of Newfoundland." I still couldn't sleep—I felt like someone had poured a wading pool full of espresso down my throat—so I thought I'd take a little stroll and see what was going on. The car was noisily idling in the driveway as I passed, and the front door to the house was wide open, with light flooding out from the kitchen. Since I was trying to make like I was just passing through—"Don't mind me, I'm just a drifter from Idaho"—I kept right on walking, past Peggy's house, over the fence, across the street, into the Ilium parking lot. I looked around as if to verify that yes, it was indeed a parking lot, and then doubled back. The door was still open and this time someone—Kelly?—was silhouetted in the frame. She beckoned to me and then disappeared inside. I knew it was probably a bad idea but curiosity got the better of me and I went up the front walk past the idling car and knocked on the open door. "Um, did you need something?" I said.

There was no answer, but the kitchen light was on so I stepped cautiously inside. I stared straight ahead, knowing that I stood a much better chance of keeping my cool if I were to remain blissfully unaware of what lay in my peripheral vision (Mr. Kaylin pointing a shotgun at my head, the guy from the car about to clock me with a tire iron, burglars in the middle of ransacking the house realizing they were going to have to dispose of any witnesses—I didn't really care to know). I stepped into the kitchen.

The smell literally knocked me to the ground. The kitchen reeked of sex, thick clouds of it. If you could bottle this scent you'd make a fortune but then you'd spend it all buying up all the bottles. And at the center of it all was Kelly Kaylin, sitting cross-legged on the floor eating a box of cookies. She had on what was in a certain respect one of the most conservative ensembles she'd ever worn, namely, a pair of overalls—at any rate, it covered more square inches of her body than her outfits usually did. On the other hand, to the extent that breast containment is a desirable quality in a garment, it fell short. "Umm, aren't you supposed to wear a shirt or something under those things?" I asked.

Kelly looked up from her box of cookies. "Like, I was," she said. She blinked at me; her pupils were dilated to the point that her irises were completely gone. "It went away," she giggled. It was a good thing that my impromptu trip to the ground had knocked the wind out of me because if I'd had even the slightest chance of catching my breath I doubt anything could've stopped me from having frenzied, seething sex with her right there on the kitchen floor. The scent was just that powerful—it was like mustard gas. Only really, really good mustard gas.

"Uh, if you don't need anything, I think I better go home now," I mumbled. "Should I close the door? It's open . . . there's a car outside . . ."

"What?" Kelly said. "Oh, right . . . I was supposed to, like, get something." She crammed the last four cookies into her mouth and clambered to her feet. She looked around. "Whoa!" she said. "Uh, how did *you* get here?"

"You told me to come in," I said.

"Oh, right," she said. "I thought you were someone else. I was supposed to, like, get something. I think I already said that." She looked around and grabbed a sponge out of the sink.

"A sponge?" I said.

"Yeah," she said. "Raul says I have to wipe the come off the back-seat or it'll, like, stain the vinyl or something."

The pheromone cloud quickly dissolved as Kelly vanished out the door and I was able to pull myself to my feet. The car's engine had been switched off and the windows were fogged up by the time I got back out to the front walk. And it suddenly occurred to me that I'd seen that car before: I'd seen Rachel Monihan get into it once. I wondered whether Rachel was one of Kelly's mysterious friends April had referred to.

But mostly I wondered what it must be like to be this Raul guy, experiencing delights of which even Fringie had only dreamed. And not until the next day did I remember that I never did see the van return.

Swingers

The van was in the driveway when I got back from peer counseling the next day, though, so I ventured a knock on the Kaylins' door. To my surprise, Peggy herself answered.

"Uh, hi," I said.

"Don't tell me, let me guess," she said. "You want to talk. Okay, let's talk. I was just about to call you anyway. Come on, let's go for a walk."

She stuffed her hands in her jacket pockets and started walking. It was left to me to close the door. We hadn't gotten much past Dooj's house when she asked, "So, when did *you* start fucking?"

I probably would've been less startled had Dooj's dog leaped over the fence and bitten my arm off. "Say what?" I said.

"It's okay, you can tell me," Peggy said. "I know all about this kind of stuff now. Kelly told me all about it. So, what was it, sixth grade? Seventh? Or don't you remember exactly because you were leafed up on roughage at the time and the memory didn't stick?"

"Um, you're talking to me, but you're thinking about someone else," I said. "C'mon, you know me better than that."

"Know you?" she said. "*Know* you?" She laughed. It wasn't a pretty sound. "I *thought* I knew the people I worked with, but they've all been doing scratch since kindergarten. I *thought* I knew the kids I've been going to church with for seventeen years, but they've all been sleeping with each other since before confirmation." We crossed into the park. "I've been asking around, and it's the same story everywhere, so you might as well own up to it. You don't have to hide your underlife from sheltered little me anymore."

"Uh, Peggy, you're talking to the biggest deeg in the world," I said. "After I get up, I go to school, and then I do peer counseling for an hour or two, and then I come home and do my homework and watch TV and go to bed. When I go to parties I collect everyone's keys and then lock myself in the pantry. People in iron lungs live wild and crazy lives compared to me."

"I wish I could believe that," she said. We reached the swing set and she plunked herself down into the highest swing. Even that one was perilously close to the ground. I used to have to give her a boost when she wanted to use the high swing. "I really wish I could believe that," she sighed.

"And I kinda wish it were hard to believe," I said. "But the sad truth is that watching the occasional episode of *Ashley: The Early Years* is the closest I get to anything even approaching debauchery."

"Give me a push," she said. I did. Even with the glossy black hair and the leather-and-metal spectacle of her jacket, she bore an almost frightening resemblance to the redheaded girl who'd tried to dissolve the freckles off her cheeks. On the swing back I took a look at her face. If the freckles were still there I couldn't see them. "So," she said. "You'll be glad to know that you were right."

"Right?" I said.

"About the whole God thing," Peggy said. "It's a crock of shit."

"Um, I don't think I ever said—"

"Kelly's appendix didn't rupture to punish me for bad thoughts," she said. "It ruptured because she's been doing scratch every day since fourth grade and it's fried her sensitivity to pain. It wasn't till she was in fifth grade that she started sneaking out of the house in the middle of the night to go to sex parties, though. Kind of a late bloomer on that one. Push harder."

I pushed harder. "I wasn't even totally clear on how sex *worked* till we got it in health class last year," Peggy said. "When *I* was in fifth grade I was still playing with dolls. Kelly was fucking college guys. I thought Kelly was my better self. She was just like me only more beautiful and graceful and intelligent and good—and didn't have bad thoughts like me. Now—now I find out that where Kelly went and what Kelly did every night after finishing her subtraction problems made the most depraved fantasy I've ever had look tame. And this is normal to people. Not one of the girls I work with at the juice shop believed for a second that I didn't put out for all ninety-four of those guys I dated. *That's* freakish to them. Sneaking out the window at three A.M. to go have sex with guys three times your age, though, that's just part of growing up. It's like every single person I've ever met has been slipping down a man-hole whenever I haven't been looking."

"Not everyone," I said.

"Everyone," she said. "Everybody's doing it. I used to complain because everyone just sort of assumed that once you hit your teens, you were going to rebel against your parents and start doing things that you were told all your life were bad—just like flipping on a switch, happens every time. And I *hated* that because I tried as hard as I could to be good and no one seemed to respect that. But now I know why. Because no one believed it, because I was the only one in the world like that. Everyone else who seemed like they were good was just pretending so they wouldn't get in trouble. *Everyone* else. And if you don't believe it, you're just as naive as I used to be."

"But that's just not true," I said. "I've been peer counseling for almost two years now and I've been trying to figure people out for even longer and the one thing I've learned is that really no two people even live on the same planet. For everyone who's out trading sex for scratch cards there's someone else whose every waking moment is devoted to figuring out how to get to level twenty-five in Bloodgnarl. And another's obsessed with finding the perfect pair of shoes and another's organizing a canned food drive for the homeless and another's just trying to manage to get through the day without being hit. You can't say 'everyone else' is doing *anything* because there's nothing that everyone does or doesn't do—we all might as well be different species. Which probably doesn't make you feel any better but it's not just you on one side and everyone else on the other. There are seven billion sides."

"What's Bloodgnarl?" Peggy asked.

"Not important," I said. "So, look, are you going to be okay?"

"Push harder," she said.

"No, I mean it," I said. "I mean, I've never heard you talk like this. It bothers me. I mean, an awful lot of people care about y—"

"Bullshit," Peggy said. "I've talked with some of my so-called 'friends.' They don't care about me. I'm nothing but a big running joke. What's the difference between Peggy Kaylin and an inflatable sex doll? The doll has smaller tits and knows that 'gullible' is in the dictionary."

"Let me guess," I said. "One of Zab's?"

"I don't know," she said. "None of the eight people I heard it from talked about the copyright."

"Peggy," I said, "I think you should talk about this with someone who can help you more than I c—"

Peggy hopped off the swing. "See a psychiatrist?" she asked. "So I can become a well-adjusted member of society and fuck my boyfriends like a good girl should? I think I'll pass." She shivered. "If you want to do me a favor, though, you can."

"Name it," I said.

"Don't visit me again," she said. "Not till I tell you. Promise."

"But why?" I asked.

"That doesn't sound like a promise," Peggy said. "What kind of a friend are you if you can't make a simple promise?"

"Fine," I said. "I promise. But—"

"Good," she said. "Here, I'll pay you back in advance." She leaned forward and kissed me on the cheek. I was pretty sure she was being sarcastic. And with that she turned around and trudged back to her house.

It's all good

At morning break the next day I looked around for Kelly but she didn't seem to be on campus anywhere. I did run into Kim Lasker from the cheer squad and asked if she'd seen her and where she might be. She laughed. "Three guesses," she said.

So a couple minutes later I found myself on the corner of Chapman and State College waiting for Kelly to finish buying her week's supply of scratch cards from some guys—friends of Krieg's, it looked like—hanging out in front of the doughnut shop. She scratched one off and stuck it on her tongue and stashed the rest of them in her sock. "Hey!" she said. "I didn't know you bought from these guys. Want some of mine?"

"No," I said. "C'mon, let's walk." We crossed the street back toward school. "So your parents know, huh?" I asked. "How did that go over?"

"They want to put me in, like, rehab or something," she said. "Whatever. That trick never works. Besides, it's my life. I'm not a baby."

"Well, you might want to give the whole rehab thing a try," I said. "If only for Peggy's sake. Finding out that you've got this whole secret life that she didn't know about hit her pretty hard."

"Well, how was I supposed to know she didn't know?" Kelly said. "Like, I just figured she bought from different people and snuck out at different times and stuff. I *offered* to, like, bring her to the next party, but she just, like, cried."

"How could you think that?" I said. "You've known her even longer than I have. Peggy's as big a deeg as they come."

"I didn't know that meant she didn't scratch up," Kelly said.

"What do you think that being a deeg means?" I asked.

"Your sister's kind of a deeg and she does smack," Kelly said.

"What?" I said. "Echo? Get real."

"No, not Echo," Kelly said. "Like, the other one. Molly. Last year I saw her shooting up all the time. Like, at school and everything."

"Molly?" I said. "Of course you did. She's diabetic. That's not heroin, it's insulin."

"Insulin?" Kelly said. "Can you get high on that?"

"Are you even listening to me?" I asked. "Do you have any idea how important you are to your sister? She was already having a rough time of things thanks to Fringie, and she'd pretty much pinned all her hopes that the world was still a basically good place on you. And now you turn out to have this whole . . . 'underlife,' she called it. She's crushed, Kelly. How does that make you feel?"

"Oh, I'm good," she said.

"Of course you are," I said. "Everything seems pretty much okay, doesn't it?"

"Uh-huh," she said.

"Well, it shouldn't," I said. I started to turn around so I could emphatically walk away but then I remembered that I still had to get back to school. I'm telling you, there's never a dramatic exit around when you need one.

Who will be the King and Queen of the outcasted teens?

At lunch the *Iliad* room was buzzing about prom: ballots for prom court had just been handed out to the upperclassmen. "So, it seems pretty obvious that yours truly's gonna be king," Holdn said. "But who's gonna get queen? Will she be a dream? (Mmm!) Or a dud? (Mmm.)"

"Okay, now on this alternate planet where you get more than your own vote, who would you *want* to be queen?" Cat asked.

"I was just thinking about that," Holdn said. "I'm thinking we break into the attendance computer and enroll Holly Madera from *Ashley: The Early Years*. Then she'll win for sure and everyone's stoked."

"Except Holly Madera," Hayley said.

"Details," Holdn said. "Okay, Nicholls, your turn. Who would *you* want if you could have anyone for queen?"

"For the last time, Holdn," Cat said, "I'm *not* interested in getting in on some girl-girl action and I wouldn't let you tape it if I were. Got it?"

"How about you, Kerensky?" Holdn said.

"Jefferson is my queen," Hayley said.

"Yeah, yeah," Holdn said. "Remind me to gag later. Seriously, of anyone in the world, who do you pick?"

"Jefferson," Hayley said. "I wouldn't be involved with him if I weren't attracted to him."

"Okay, remember when I said to remind me to gag later?" Holdn said. "Forget about the 'later' part. Andreas?"

"Adlai Stevenson," Hank said.

"Oh, right," Holdn said. "Mockery?"

There was a sudden silence. "Hey, Mockery, coma's over," Holdn said. "Answer the question."

"Huh?" I said. "Sorry, I wasn't paying attention. What?"

"Who are you most attracted to?" Hayley asked.

"Hunh," I said. "Well, a week ago I would've said Kelly Kaylin, no contest."

"But?" Hayley said.

"But, I guess I don't know who that is," I said. "I mean, the main thing that creeps me out about people using drugs is that they turn people into parodies of themselves. I'll be working key patrol at a party and I'll see people I know come in seeming perfectly intelligent and come out ceaselessly amused by how fingers and toes are so similar and yet so different. They *look* like the people I know, but they don't *act* like it. And it's always seemed to me that who you are is the way you think and act, and so if you go around changing the only things that make you knowable to other people, it's almost a kind of suicide. If I want to talk to Elroy T. Funbun, and the person in Elroy T. Funbun's body isn't acting like Elroy T. Funbun, then Elroy T. Funbun is effectively dead to me."

"Who's Elroy T. Funbun?" Cat asked.

"Doesn't matter," I said. "The point is, that's *not* the case with

Kelly Kaylin. She's been doing scratch since she was nine or ten—since before she had a personality, really. It's burned out her sense of pain but it's also burned out any empathy she might've developed because she feels good all the time, even when she sees other people suffering. And so I can't say that the scratch is affecting her behavior because I guess I've never seen her behavior when she's *not* affected. There *is* no Kelly other than the sort of dissociated sex bomb who doesn't especially care about other people one way or the other. Who I've discovered I don't like much."

"Yeah, yeah, but who's Elroy T. Funbun?" Cat asked.

Echo came in from Benito's room with some corrected copy. "Hey, Mockery," Holdn said. "It's prom season. Who's your queen?"

"What?" Echo said.

"We were just discussing who we found most attractive," Hayley said.

"How nice for you," Echo said. She started to shut the door.

"No, wait," Hayley said. "Don't you want to answer? There's nothing embarrassing about finding someone attractive. C'mon, you can tell me. I'm curious."

"For you?" Echo said. She sighed. "Fine. I suppose there is someone I've always thought had a certain . . . something . . ."

"Who?" Hayley said.

"Carver Fringie," Echo said.

I'm not entirely sure how to spell my reply. I believe the correct spelling is *"EEEAGH!"*

Eight

"Carver Fringie?" I said. "*Carver Fringie?* Has the whole world gone
MAD?"

Echo looked up from her homework and rolled her eyes. "Okay,
that's just something I've always wanted to say," I said. I threw my
backpack in the corner and flopped onto my bed. "It's still true,
though."

"I hardly think I need to defend myself to someone who tried
courting Siren Delaney," Echo said.

"Um, ow," I said. "Seriously, though, you really need to stay away
from that guy."

"Gosh, I don't know what I'd do if you weren't looking out for
me," Echo said to the computer screen. "But I'm not worried. I'm
sure if he tries anything you'll come beat him up for me."

"Look, I don't doubt that you can handle yourself," I said. "But
Carver Fringie is the definition of vermin. He tried to rape Peggy, you
know."

"Spare me," Echo said.

"I'm serious," I said.

"Which isn't the same as being right," she said.

"What, you think Peggy's lying?" I said.

"Not necessarily," Echo said. "She may believe it. That's no doubt
how she justifies things to herself—she can't handle that she got
thrown over, so she magnifies a moment of miscommunication into

some horrible crime. From what you've told me, these moments of hysteria aren't exactly rare. The fact is that she's simply not of Carver Fringie's caliber."

"Watch it," I growled.

"Why?" she said. "It's true. How they got together in the first place given the disparity in their social standing can probably be attributed to high-mindedness and a lack of concern for high school provincialism on Carver's part. But why they stayed together for even as long as they did is a mystery. What could they possibly have in common? He's lived through childhood illness and the death of his mother—how is Peggy Kaylin supposed to relate to that? Talk about the death of her goldfish?"

"See, the problem here is that you don't know what you're talking about," I said.

"And he's by far her intellectual superior—and the superior of virtually anyone you'd care to name," Echo went on. "Peggy Kaylin, on the other hand, is nothing special. Beyond a certain vapid pleasantness there's not much to recommend her."

"What's there to recommend you?" I shot back.

Echo smirked and went back to her typing.

How unsporting

"So why Carver Fringie?" Hayley asked. "That seems like an odd choice to me."

"That's easy," Zab said. "The answer is seven inches long."

It was layout week once again, and that meant hanging around the *Iliad* room putting the paper together well into the night. Or rather, that's what it had meant before Daylight Savings Time kicked in, back when night fell at four-thirty. Now that summer hours were in full swing, not only was it still light out when I got back to the *Iliad* room from peer counseling, but the place had mostly cleared out: only Zab and Hayley were still hanging around. That I'd sort of expected—they usually tried to get their pages done in one shot. I wasn't expecting Echo to still be hanging around, though. She usually had all the copy ready to go long before layout week started. Even odder was that she was wearing her glasses instead of her contacts. They were a lot like Hayley's, only more elliptical and with silver frames instead of gold. She'd apparently gone home and dug them out of her desk drawer while I was up at the office with September trying to explain to this guy why throwing tacos at Uta Himmler was unacceptable.

"Didn't you say you were leaving?" Hayley asked Zab. "I thought you were finished."

"Oh, I am, luv," Zab said. "I can't wait to hear the Ice Queen's answer to this one, though." This turned out to be literally true: after twenty seconds of watching Echo typing, Zab's gnatlike attention span got the best of her and she got bored and left.

"Okay, she's gone," Hayley said. "So what's the attraction? I mean, he may be more well-read than most, but look at how he spends his time and who he spends it with. He may read a couple pages of Heidegger in his spare time, but his coterie of admirers isn't awestruck by his mastery of post-Kierkegaardian existentialist philosophy. They're impressed because he's captain of the water polo team. What could you possibly have in common with—is something funny?"

"Sorry," I said. "I'm not laughing at you, it's just—you just described Echo six or seven years ago. Carver Fringie was the one huddled on his porch with a blanket and a book all the time and never really talking to anyone. Echo was the jock supreme. Kids came from miles around to bask in her aura."

"Is that true?" Hayley asked.

Echo glared at me. "I don't talk about that," she said. "It was a long time ago."

"But it's not really a secret, is it?" Hayley said. "You've lived here your entire life, right? Most of the people who go here know all about this because they've known you for years. So I'm practically the only one who doesn't know."

"There's nothing really to tell," Echo said. "I used to play sports. Then I stopped. End of story."

"There has to be more to it than that," Hayley said.

And of course there was.

One evening when Echo and I were nine, we were all sitting around eating dinner—something she and Dad had thrown together with rice and lentils and eggplant and stuff—when Echo announced, "The baseball league all my friends are in is having tryouts in a couple weeks. I think I'd like to sign up."

"Certainly," Dad said. "Why the change of heart, though? When the soccer season started up a few months ago you said you weren't interested in playing in an organized league."

"That was soccer," Echo said. "They segregate by sex. I would've been stuck in a girls' league and couldn't play with any of my friends. The baseball league's integrated. So's hockey, though that doesn't start till the end of summer."

"Wouldn't it be cool to be in the girls' league, though?" I said. "I mean, you'd totally dominate. In the boys' league you'd just, uh . . . well . . . totally dominate, I guess. Okay, I'm an idiot."

The tryouts were somewhat less official than I'd anticipated. It was basically just a couple dozen kids running around the Vista de la Vista baseball diamond while the usual bunch of generic middle-aged men took time out from contemplating boat purchases to squint at the chaos and come up with deep philosophical insights like "That one's got good speed, but not much of an arm." Echo, of course, had both, and was the first kid picked. There were games pretty much every Saturday afternoon: Echo's team was called the Angels, and she got a cheap replica Angels jersey with the legend "MOCKERY 25" on the back. The coach put her in center field, since she was the only one who could get the ball back to the infield without having to run three-quarters of the way there. She was also usually good for at least a base hit every time she came to the plate. Unfortunately, the coach insisted on having his son pitch, so virtually every player on the opposing team ended up hitting even better than Echo did. Her team ended up winning less than half their games.

Of course, that didn't work against Echo's celebrity any more than the Ilium water polo team's abysmal record worked against Fringie's. She still always had an ambush of would-be teammates waiting outside the classroom door when the bell rang for recess; in fact, Echo was one of maybe two or three kids, tops, in the gifted class who hung around with the regular kids. To the rest of us, the non-gifted kids were pretty much just standard-issue vague people we never had any contact with. But at the beginning of the school year Echo wore her Angels cap and jersey to school a couple of times a week, and that gave the regular kids an opening to strike up conversations with her, at least to the extent that "You played on the Angels? Their pitcher sucked!" can be considered conversation. Before long they had games lined up every afternoon. And that's really the only thing that kept Echo sticking around: Mrs. Wu wanted to have her start spending the bulk of her school day at Ilium—"We just don't have anything to teach you here," she said—but Echo refused. "I'm not leaving my friends," she said.

"But you could still see them as much as you like after school," Mrs. Wu argued. "Most of the children you play with aren't in our class, after all. You only associate with them for extracurricular activities. There would hardly be any difference."

"Yes, there would," Echo said. "I fit in here. I may not see a lot of my friends in class, but they still accept me as a peer. That would scarcely be the case if I were to go to high school now. I'd be an outsider there by virtue of my age and I'd be an outsider here by virtue of my absence."

"But these children aren't your peers, Echo," Mrs. Wu insisted. "How many nine-year-olds do you hear using words like 'scarcely' and 'by virtue of' in casual conversation?"

"But you can restate that the other way: how many people who do use those words are nine?" Echo countered. "Even if I were to skip some grades and spend time with people with the same vocabulary as me, what could I possibly have to say to people twice my age? I'm not lacking for intelligent conversation or intellectual challenge as it is—I have my dad, I have the net, I have books. It's true that I don't have much to say to kids my age on a social level, but moving to high school wouldn't remedy that—quite the opposite. And companionship is companionship. I have some here, and I'm not going to give it up. Even if it is predicated on the fact that I can hit a baseball."

Of course, Echo's place among our coevals wasn't quite so fragile as all that: her friends wouldn't simply abandon her if one day she woke up unable to swing a bat. Not so long as she could still stop a hockey puck. Or at least those bright orange things that passed for pucks in street hockey. And when she showed up at school wearing her youth league hockey jersey with "KINGS" on the front and

"MOCKERY 66" on the back, no one took her to task over how much the team sucked, because Echo's team was undefeated. Which isn't to say they'd won every game—they'd racked up a lot of scoreless ties—but moving up a step from the competition to be had on Hyacinth Avenue hadn't tarnished her record any: Echo still had yet to allow a single goal.

I actually kind of enjoyed going to Echo's hockey games on Saturday afternoons: unlike the baseball games, where entire innings would go by where Echo never came to bat and never had to catch a ball, the hockey games had her fending off shots on goal every couple seconds, it seemed. It was nonstop Echo kung-fu action. On the other hand, it wasn't quite so much fun when her team had control of the puck and I had to hear Vance Judden warbling, "Judden is great! Judden is great!" every time he took a lame shot at the opposing goalie—I usually rooted for the opposition whenever they weren't actually firing at Echo. To me there was no outcome so satisfying as the scoreless tie: Echo got the satisfaction of another shutout, and the other little dolts on the team were denied the satisfaction of a win. "A tie is like kissing your sister," Christian Variola would lament, who, having no sisters, was singularly ill-informed on the topic. The fact that he always said it with a thick Canadian accent indicated that he'd probably picked up that little chestnut watching NHL games on his satellite dish.

Their rhetoric got more and more unbearable as the season progressed. Unlike in baseball, where they were split among four or five different teams, hockey in Orange County still had a small enough draw that all the kids from our neighborhood ended up on the same team, and all the little dweebs seemed to think that they were somehow responsible for the team's success. When playoff pairings were released that's what all the street chatter was about for a week. "Like La Habra could beat *us*!" Vance Judden sneered. "Yeah, right!"

"Yeah!" said Jay Kyeutter. "We'll kill those cocksuckers! Haw haw haw haw!"

"No shit we'll kill 'em!" Neal Navarre chimed in. "Echo, you with us?"

"Come on, we need to practice," Echo said.

Echo's team won their first playoff game one to nothing. Her teammates pointed and laughed at the kids from La Habra after the game and made them cry. It made me sick. "Look, Eck, you know I don't have anything against you personally," I said when Echo got back from the postgame pizza party. "But now that they put in tiebreakers for the playoffs I can't root for your team anymore. I want to see those little dirtbags miserable and crying. Can't you let in a goal or two? They'd never make up the deficit—they're awful."

"Don't be ridiculous," Echo said. "I'm not throwing games."

"Don't think of it as throwing games," I said. "Think of it as secretly defecting to the other team."

"What makes you think the other teams are any better than ours?" Echo said. "My friends aren't any different from anyone else."

"That's just not true," I said. "You've just grown accustomed to people who are stupid and, probably not incidentally, male. No one I hang out with talks like those cretins."

"And no one *you* hang out with plays hockey," Echo said. "I'm not really interested in their conversation. I just want to play. And these are the guys I've always played with. Maybe they aren't going to be making any all-star teams anytime soon, but we know all there is to know about each other and that's more important—I can predict where they're going to be and what they're going to do. Ninety percent of my job as a goaltender is done right there."

And 90 percent was way more than Echo needed in the next couple rounds of the playoffs: her team won both games three to nothing and that put them in the league championship game against the Placentia Ducks. The game was held right at Ilium, as part of a package of four straight championship games for different age groups. Echo's game was up second; Dad and Molly and I showed up at the end of the first game while Bobbo stayed home with Krieg and Jerem. I was impressed. Not only did they have bleachers set up on the blacktop so we all could sit instead of standing around like in the regular-season games, but they had a PA system too. After they'd shepherded the toddlers off the blacktop, they brought out the eight-to-ten-year-olds, and instead of plunging right into the game, they started with player introductions. First they announced the names of the Placentia Ducks' starters, and then those of the Fullerton Kings:

"At left wing, number one: Michael Donner!

"At right wing, number three: Neal Navarre!

"At center, number two: Vance Judden!

"At defense, number four: Min-Hsun Lee!

"At defense, number five: Christian Variola!

"And at goal, number sixty-six: Madeleine Mockery!"

"How come they said Echo's real name?" Molly asked.

"This is a special occasion, honey," Dad said.

"We have a delay of game warning against the Kings," the announcer declared. "Please take your positions for the face-off."

The game started.

Original or extra crispy?

It wasn't long after Molly had started talking in complete sentences that she hit Dad with the question. "How come you call Echo 'Madeleine'?" she asked.

"Because that's her real name," Dad said.

"What's my real name?" Molly asked.

"Molly *is* your real name," Dad said.

"Then how come everyone calls Echo 'Echo' if it's not her real name?" Molly asked.

Dad scowled.

I'd heard the story before—both Dad's and Bobbo's versions of it—and so had a pretty good idea of the answer. Naturally, I can't claim to be repeating this conversation verbatim, since I was a fetus at the time and my sense of hearing wasn't what it could've been.

"So what are you gonna name the kid?" Bobbo asked.

"We haven't made any decisions yet," Dad said. "I suppose we probably should. Do you have any preferences?"

"How about Rob?" Bobbo said. "Rob's a good name."

"I was talking to Susan," Dad said.

"I don't care," Mom said.

"What?" Dad said.

"Name the kid whatever you want," Mom said.

"I can't name *our* child by myself," Dad said.

"It really doesn't make any difference to me," Mom said. "Whatever you want to call the brat is fine by me."

"I'd call that a vote for Rob," Bobbo said.

"Shut up," Dad said.

Eventually Dad came to a decision, or at least half of one. "If it's a boy, I think it'd be a nice gesture to name him Allen after my mentor," he said. "Virtually everything I've accomplished in academia I owe to Allen McLaughlin. His work is never less than brilliant."

"What if it's a girl?" Bobbo asked.

"If it's a girl, then I was thinking maybe 'Susan,'" Dad said.

"Oh, come off it," Bobbo said. "All that'd do is cause problems. You couldn't keep them straight."

"Wouldn't naming the child Robert cause the same problems?" Dad asked.

"Whatever," Bobbo said. "How about Elaine? That sounds like Allen."

"Don't be absurd," Dad said. "Hmm. I do like 'Madeleine,' though . . ."

"What would you call her for short?" Bobbo asked. "Maddie?"

"No, we'd call her Madeleine," Dad said. "It's three syllables. Is that so difficult?"

"Yeah, *that's* gonna last," Bobbo said.

It lasted for about a year and a half. Madeleine crawled first; she walked first; she talked first; eventually, she got her period first, though I suppose that was to be expected. Nevertheless, she was the one who got tagged with the name "Echo." Not because she copied me or anything, because really she didn't. It just so happened that one day Mom was watching *Poppyseed Park* with us and one of the bits was this little girl and this enormous talking chicken trying to figure out how to count to ten. First they introduced themselves to each other. "Hi there!" the chicken said. "I'm Chigantic Chicken! What's your name?"

"Echo," the girl said.

"Echo!" Mom echoed. "Wow, that's beautiful! Hey, which one of you's the girl? You? C'mere." Madeleine toddled over. "You want to be my Echo? Hmm?" She kissed her half a dozen times. Echo seemed rather nonplussed. "Echo it is. Okay, go watch the counting part." I suppose I should consider myself lucky that Mom's interest in the program waned at that point or I could've ended up named after the chicken.

Dad, of course, knew nothing about this until a couple of days later when Mom called us for dinner. "Allen! Echo! Food's ready!"

"'Echo'?" Dad said.

"Yeah, I named the girl one Echo," Mom said. "I didn't get to name them before so I'm doing it now. It's pretty, it's short—"

"It's cruel," Dad said. "You can't name a twin 'Echo.' She'll get an inferiority complex."

"It's better than Allen and Mad-Allen," Mom countered.

Dad paused. "I hadn't considered that," he said. "Still, I wish you'd brought that up when we were first naming them. It's rather late in the game to be—"

"Oh, they don't know their names yet," Mom said.

"What?" Dad said. "They're not goldfish, Susan. They're children. Almost two years old. Exceptionally bright for their age, too. Of *course* they *know their names*." He sighed. "If you feel you've been left out of the naming process—and you *opted out,* Susan—you can rename the baby. He actually *is* too young to—"

"No," Mom said. "I like 'Echo' and it's a girl's name and we only have one girl. On the other hand," she purred, "I wouldn't be averse to making another one. Hmmm?" She started undoing her buttons.

"Not now, Susan," Dad said. "The children—"

"Oh, they don't know," Mom said.

"They're not *goldfish,*" Dad sighed.

I'd like to thank the Academy

Echo seemed rattled as the game started. Inside of two minutes the Placentia Ducks had faked her out of the box and made a quick shot that missed the tip of her glove for a goal. Clearly, something was wrong. Of course, I suppose it's possible that the Ducks were just the first team Echo had encountered good enough to score on her—they *had* made the championship game, after all. Or maybe she didn't get enough defensive help. At any rate, for the first time ever, Echo had to turn around to look at the bright orange ball entangled in her own net. It was a good thing they played on asphalt and not ice, because if Echo had been wearing skates, she looked like she would've slashed her wrists with them right there.

The Kings somehow managed to score a goal of their own before time expired, and for a second I thought the two teams were going to have to share the championship; then I remembered that this was the playoffs, and ties weren't allowed. The game went to overtime. The Ducks pelted Echo with shot after shot, and she somehow managed to deflect them all—and remained visibly furious with herself even as she did; at long last, on one of the few scoring chances Echo's team had all afternoon, Clement Campbell came off the bench and managed to slip the puck past the opposing goalie, and Echo's team won the championship. The team received a double-decker four-post trophy, and Echo got a smaller one as Most Valuable Player. Molly and Dad and I cheered, but the rest of the people in the stands were fairly quiet and Echo's teammates seemed actively pissed. "Clement was robbed," Judden complained as the players were cleared from the blacktop to make way for the eleven- and twelve-year-olds. "*He* won the game."

The coach tried to round up all the kids on the team for the traditional postgame pizza party, but most everyone begged off. Once it started to look like there'd be one or two attendees at best, the party was canceled. We headed back to the house and Echo put the trophy up on the dresser. We both stood back and looked at it for a minute. "Looks pretty sharp," I said. "You know, I still think that giving out awards to a bunch of stooges running around with sticks is pretty dumb, but I have to admit, there is something very cool about the Triumph of Echo."

"I don't deserve it, though," she said. "I let in a goal. I let the team down. You could tell."

"The team can bite me," I said. "They wouldn't have won a single game without you."

"I don't know," she said. "Maybe we could all share it. I don't need it. It's not that big a deal."

Of course, that was like saying that Jupiter wasn't that big a planet. I went downstairs for some juice and when I got back Echo was sitting on her bed holding her MVP trophy, stroking the little gold hockey player's face; the rest of the day, every time I left the room I'd come back to find the trophy in a different place, usually with Echo admiring it while trying to look like she wasn't admiring it. "You know, it's okay," I said. "Go ahead and stare. Exult. All that good stuff. You earned it. You done good, sis."

She put the trophy back on the dresser. For a minute she just stood there like someone had put the world on pause. "Thank you," she finally said.

The next afternoon I went over to the Kaylins' to find Peggy in the backyard collecting dandelions. "What's this all about?" I asked.

"It's for math," she said. "We're doing averages. The worksheet says we have to either get the average number of sesame seeds per bun for a bag of hamburger buns, or petals per dandelion for the dandelions in your backyard, or some others, or you can choose your own if you ask the teacher, but I wanted to do the dandelion one."

"Cool," I said. "Can I help?"

She thought for a moment. "Okay," she said. "You're not allowed to do any of the math part, but it's okay if you do some of the counting part. Here." She handed me half a dozen dandelions and we went inside.

We sat down at the kitchen table and started counting. I'd made it about halfway through the first one when Peggy looked up and shrieked. "What?" I said.

"You're ruining it!" she said. I'd been plucking the petals as I went so that I didn't count any of them twice, or skip any; on the table in front of me was a little pile of cheerful yellow dandelion remains.

"Uh, sorry," I said. "But, I mean, the dandelions have already been cut. You can't replant them. Might as well—"

"So?" Peggy said. "Does that mean it's okay to rip a baby apart as long as you cut the umbilical cord?"

"Eep," I said. "That's kinda morbid."

"What's morbid?" she demanded.

"What you just said," I said. "Ripping up babies . . ."

"No, what's 'morbid' mean?" she asked.

"Never mind," I said.

As I headed home later that afternoon I was blindsided by a vicious cross-check from Jay Kyeutter. "Haw haw haw haw!" he said as I picked myself up off Dooj's lawn. "Sorry, thought you were on the other team. Haw haw."

I flashed Echo my usual these-people-are-idiots look, only to discover that it wasn't Echo tending goal. When I got back to my room I found her sitting in bed reading a go book. "Finally had your fill of hockey, huh?" I said.

"What?" she said.

"Nothing," I said. "It's just that there's a game on and you don't seem to be doing a very good job of minding the net."

Echo looked out the window. "Krieg must've chased them away before they had a chance to ring the bell," she said. She pulled off her T-shirt and dug her hockey jersey out of the closet and slipped it on. "Back in a bit," she said. She grabbed her stick and went downstairs.

A couple minutes later the door opened and she came back in. "Forget something?" I asked. She looked over at me, her gray eyes somehow opaque; then she took the trophy off the dresser. "Oh, you can't be serious," I said. "They actually want you to give that other kid your trophy?"

She stared at the trophy for a moment. Then, before I knew what'd happened, she snapped it in half and sank to the floor, the two pieces slipping out of her hands as she burst into helpless sobs. It'd broken at the weakest point: the figurine's ankles. "Echo!" I said. "What happened? What happened?" But she didn't answer. She just lay balled up on the carpet shaking and crying.

"One goal?" Hayley said. "They stopped playing with you just because you let in one goal?"

Echo didn't say anything for a long moment. Then, slowly, she shook her head.

After the player introductions the two teams had huddled up. The Placentia kids had repeated a few motivational slogans, put their hands together, and shouted, "Go Ducks!"; in the Kings huddle things were more contentious.

"Why did that guy call you 'Madeleine'?" Christian Variola demanded.

"Because that's my real name," Echo shrugged. "Same reason they called Mikey 'Michael' . . ."

"But that's a *girl's* name," Mikey Donner said. "How come you got a *girl's* name?"

"Because I'm a girl?" Echo suggested. "What are you talking about? 'Echo' is a girl's name too."

"No it isn't," Variola insisted. "It's just a kind of *sound*."

"We have a delay of game warning against the Kings," the announcer declared. "Please take your positions for the face-off."

"Come on, the game's starting," Echo said.

And Echo honestly seemed to think that was the end of it. In fact when the other kids started taking down the nets as soon as she walked outside the next day, her immediate response was, "What? What's wrong? Are you mad at me or something? Because I let that goal in? Do you want the trophy? I'll give you guys the trophy if that's what you want."

"Fuck the trophy," Vance Judden said. "The trophy's got nothing to do with it."

"Then what?" Echo said.

"Show us your dick," said Christian Variola.

"What?" Echo said.

"You heard me," Variola said. "What do we look like, *fags*? We don't play with *girls*. So either show us your dick or get the fuck inside, bitch."

"But—I thought you knew," Echo said. "How could you not know?"

"I'm wondering that myself," Hayley said. "Not to interrupt your story, but here's what I don't get. I can buy that you *looked* like a boy. I can buy that you *sounded* like a boy. I can buy that they might have *thought* you were a boy. But that being the case, didn't you hear them referring to you as 'he' and 'him'? Didn't you correct them?"

"It didn't seem important," Echo said, almost under her breath. "I just wanted to play. I wasn't trying to deceive anyone. I thought it was just an occasional slip of the tongue. After all, everyone in my *class* knew I was a girl. And the kids who actually lived on my street. Dennis knew. Angus knew. And Carver . . ."

"Oh, that's right," Hayley said. "Carver Fringie used to live in Cat's house, didn't he?"

"He used to watch the games all the time," Echo murmured. "Enough that when the other kids found a different street to play on, he asked me why the games had stopped. And I told him, and he was appalled. He apologized for his entire gender. Carver was very sweet to me." Echo glared at me. "He was very sweet."

"Wow," Hayley said. "Well, I suppose that's the silver lining, isn't it? It probably wasn't fun to live through but if the two of you ever do get together, you have a great story to tell."

Echo's face went dark. "That's never going to happen," she said.

That, of course, was *my* silver lining. Right up till the day Fringie asked Echo to the prom.

I don't know art, nor do I know what I like

As you know, the summer that Peggy developed her figure, the Mockery clan was down on the farm in Pennsylvania. But we didn't spend the entire trip milking the chickens and whatnot. A full week of the trip was spent touring New York City, or at least the 3 percent of it that didn't leave us consumed with terror at our imminent violent deaths. One of our stops was the Museum of Modern Art, though I use the term "our" loosely here: Bobbo and Krieg and Jerem stayed back at the hotel raiding the mini-fridge while the rest of us made our excursion.

It was an interesting trip. Molly was absolutely captivated. *"Cool!"* she'd say with each new painting. Then would come the questions. "So did he just drip the paint onto the canvas? Was the canvas on an easel or on the floor? Did he have a plan when he started or did he just see what happened? Did he use oils? Are acrylics the same as oils? Can I get some oils? Is this one by the same painter? *Cool!*" While Dad enthusiastically answered Molly's questions, Echo's cheeks grew steadily more and more flushed; by the time we got to the Mondrian exhibit (which sent Molly into peals of rapture) her eyes were burning with frustration.

"Everything okay?" I asked.

"I don't get it," she hissed through clenched teeth. "There *must* be a pattern here. Some kind of organizing principle. But I don't see it. I don't understand what I'm seeing."

Molly skipped over to where we were standing. "Doesn't it look neat, though?" she asked.

"I don't *know*," Echo said, her voice cracking.

It was precisely that blend of panicked, frustrated bewilderment that Echo radiated when she told Hayley and me that Fringie had asked her to the junior prom.

"Hey, congratulations," Hayley said. "So why don't you sound thrilled? I thought this was what you wanted."

"But it's bizarre," Echo said. "We haven't spoken since we were children. *No one* speaks to me here at school, except you. When he asked me how I was, I was taken aback. When he asked me if I wanted to go with him to this dance, I started looking for the hidden camera. What do I say? I can't say that I even *know* him."

"Well, before I hooked up with Jefferson, my criteria when random people hit on me were: is he cute, and not a cretin?" Hayley said. "If so, then say yes."

"Of course, since Fringie *is* a cretin, the whole point's moot," I said.

"This must be someone's idea of a joke," Echo said. "Zab was doubtless waiting in the wings to point and laugh if I'd said yes."

"I wouldn't jump to any conclusions," Hayley said. "Would it surprise you if I were to say that I put in a good word for you?"

"Really?" I said. "Are there finders' fees involved when you go scouting for rapists?"

"You're not helping," Hayley said.

"I am helping," I said. "I'm helping my sister avoid ending getting screwed over by this guy like Peggy did."

"Well, Peggy Kaylin is never going to win any awards for stability," Hayley said. She turned to Echo. "I'd say go for it," she said. "Of course, I'm biased. Since I'm in a committed relationship and am going to be in one for the foreseeable future, the only way I get the thrill of hooking up with some exciting new guy is to do it vicariously."

"But Fringie's not new," I said. "He's been around as long as I can remember. And unless 'exciting' is doing double duty as a synonym for 'nauseating' these days—"

"Do you mind?" Hayley said. "Butt out. This is girl talk."

"Alligator," I said.

"What?" Hayley said.

"I thought you said this was girl talk," I said. "I'm better at it than either of you. Wait, wait—I can't say that for sure. How about a test? Tell me, Hayley, what kind of 'girl talk' would you have used on Peggy if she'd come to *you* with tears streaming down her face the night Fringie pinned her to the couch and tried to force himself on her? Hmm?"

Hayley rolled her eyes. "Don't be so melodramatic," she said. She looked around. "Hey, where'd Echo go?"

Echo seemed to have slipped out somehow. We hadn't even seen her leave.

Later on I was up in the conference room doing peer counseling when way off in my peripheral vision I caught a glimpse of Fringie and an indistinct black shape—Echo, no doubt—cross past the six-inch-wide window. "Hey, can you finish this up?" I asked September. "Emergency. Sorry about this." I took a hard right outside the conference room and caught up with Echo a minute later. By that point Fringie was long gone. "What was that all about?" I asked.

"Carver asked me if I'd given any thought to going with him to prom," Echo said.

"And?" I said.

"And I said I had," she said. "And that the answer was yes."

"And he said?" I asked.

"He said, 'Excellent. I'll see you then.'" Echo said.

"Does that sound like someone who's smitten?" I said.

"What do you expect?" Echo said. "A Pee-Chee folder with 'Carver-n-Echo 4-ever' doodled all over it? So he's mature about this kind of thing. That's an asset, not a liability."

"I don't suppose there's anything I could say to change your mind," I said. Echo gave me a deadpan stare. "Fine," I said. "Then let me just say this. It's going to sound inappropriate now, but when it does become appropriate, it'll be a bad time to say it. So here it is."

"What?" she asked.

"'I told you so,'" I said.

Midnight census

"So what are you going to wear?" Hayley asked the next afternoon.

Echo shrugged. "I'll find something," she said.

"I have some dresses you can borrow," Hayley said. "You might have to have them, uh, taken in a bit, but come to my place and if there's one you like you can keep it."

"Thanks," Echo said. "That shouldn't be necessary—"

"You probably ought to wear your contacts, too," Hayley said. "I notice you've been wearing your glasses lately but even I don't wear glasses to go dancing. Hey, as long as we're on the subject, how come you always wear those black sweats? Is there some significance there?"

You may be thinking that Hayley was just being dense here, given the story Echo had told her not too long before; but as it happens, it wasn't being rejected by all her friends that had prompted her change of wardrobe. If anything, she became more insistent on wearing her usual baseball jerseys and hockey sweaters: she'd wear different T-shirts underneath, of course, and different jeans, but on top, it was always either "MOCKERY 25" or "MOCKERY 66." It was like Peggy with her leather jacket. "I don't get it," I told her at one point. "Doesn't wearing that stuff just bring back a lot of bad memories?"

"Yes," Echo said. "It's meant to."

This lasted for a couple of years, up until our trip to the East Coast. Living in the farmhouse could hardly have been more different from life in our house on Hyacinth. Okay, that's an exaggeration. Becoming nomads in the Sudan would probably qualify as a somewhat greater change of pace. But it was strange, having no neighbors within view of the house, with trees all around that hadn't been placed there by a landscaping crew, and on top of that, there were the rhythms of summer: nothing to do, nowhere to go, all the time your own. Bobbo was absolutely miserable, sitting in the living room watching baseball games on TV through a haze of static: "Look at this!" he cried. "The reception's even crappier than it was when I lived here! Dammit, there's a *reason* I moved to California. Shit." Molly, on the other hand, was in love with the place: it was the first time since she was a baby that she'd been allowed outside without having to put on at least her kimono. We couldn't keep her in the house. Dad and Bobbo were staying in their old rooms, and their parents' room was off limits while Dad collected their things and tried to get the family's affairs in order, so the five of us kids were left to divvy up a fold-out sofa and a couple of makeshift cots; every morning Molly would wake up, climb over the rest of us, take a shower, grab a blanket, spread it on the grass out in a backyard the size of a golf course, and wouldn't come in till it was time to go to sleep again. She'd read, or draw, or just sunbathe: it was a permanent picnic as far as Molly was concerned.

And something in the air seemed to have infected Echo, too. Our first day in Pennsylvania, she wore her hockey jersey; the second, her baseball one; and on the third, I woke up to find her setting the kitchen table in a loose white dress, with lace at the sleeves and neck and hem. "What on earth is that?" I asked.

"It's a dress," she said.

"But I've never ever seen you wear a dress before," I said. "I mean, that's girl stuff."

"And I'm a girl," she said. "Funny how that works out, huh?"

The dresses went back in the drawer once we returned to California, but the next summer they came out again. And the sports jerseys were consigned to the closet. "They said something about who I was," she explained, "but I'm a different person now. Which normally wouldn't matter, since I threw in with the wrong clique and ended up without any friends after I got bounced. But we're heading into middle school now and all the lines get redrawn. Half the kids won't have any idea who I am. By the time the word gets around that in a former life I used to be a jock whose teammates couldn't handle being bettered by a girl, it'll be nothing more than a curiosity." She looked in the mirror above the dresser. "Maybe I'll let my hair grow out some more," she said.

"Are you going to get your ears pierced?" I asked.

Echo rolled her eyes. "I said I might let my hair grow," she said. "That doesn't mean I'm going in for ear-piercing and face-painting and foot-binding. Not every slope is slippery."

As it turned out, Echo's analysis seemed to be more or less dead-on. Her old clique continued to hiss nasty comments at her when they passed her in the quad; the kids who'd had nothing to do with her in elementary school continued to have nothing to do with her; and the kids from other schools that she met in her classes treated her fairly decently. On the first day half a dozen of them invited her to sit at their table during lunch, which I thought was fairly cool. For my part, I discovered that unlike in third grade, in seventh grade when you tried to strike up a conversation with a girl she was less inclined to assume you were trying to be friendly and more inclined to assume you were hitting on her. This shot to the top of my list of disadvantages of growing older.

One of the advantages was that with Echo and me now twelve and a half, Dad finally felt comfortable leaving the five of us alone in the house without dragging Bobbo over to babysit. This didn't mean he left us unattended—whenever he went to a conference, or just had to stay late on faculty business, he sent grad students at regular intervals to check up on us. That struck me as bordering on an abuse of power, but when I asked Grad Student Danny about it he just laughed. "Don't worry about it," he said. "Other profs have their grad students picking up laundry from the dry cleaners, washing cars, mowing lawns, performing sexual favors—we get off light."

The first time this happened during the school year was at the end of our first week of classes: there was a conference called "Cartography, Community, and Culture" or some such up at Claremont, starting Friday afternoon and concluding Sunday evening. It was close enough that Dad was able to commute but far enough that he wasn't expecting to be able to get home until well after dark. Grad Student Katie came over at eight; Grad Student Danny dropped by at ten. Krieg and Jerem went to bed shortly thereafter; the rest of us decided to wait till Dad got home, since it was one thing to be allowed to look after ourselves and another thing to go to sleep with just us kids in the house—it felt weird. Of course, decision and action are two different things: Molly and I conked out in the TV room pretty much immediately. Only Echo was really awake when the next set of knocks came at the door. "Huh? What?" I said.

Echo put down the newspaper section she'd been reading. "I'll get it," she said.

Molly rubbed her eyes. "What time is it?" she asked.

"It's—jeez, it's one," I said.

"Who is it? Is it Danny?" Molly asked.

"I dunno," I said.

Echo popped her head back into the room and threw Molly's kimono at her. "Put this on," she said.

"Why?" Molly said. "Danny doesn't care."

"It's not Danny," Echo said. "I looked through the peephole. It's the police."

I followed Echo back to the foyer. Echo opened the door. "Yes?" she said.

"Hello," said one of the cops. "Can I speak to your mother, please?"

"Not unless you know how to conduct a séance," I said.

"Excuse me?" said the cop.

"Our mother died some time ago," Echo said.

"Oh, mother*fuck*," said the other cop.

"Quiet," said the first cop. "Do you have a stepmother?"

"What's this about?" I interrupted.

"No, we don't," Echo said. "What *is* this about?"

"Are there any adults we could speak to?" the cop asked.

Molly poked her head out of the TV room. "What's going on?" she asked.

The cop paused. "How many children live at this address?" he asked.

"Five," Echo said.

"How many adults?" the cop asked.

"One," Echo said. "He's not home at the moment . . ."

"Motherfuck," muttered the second cop.

"Are there *any* adults we can speak to?" the first cop asked. "Grandparents? Aunts? Uncles?"

"There's Bobbo, but he took off to spend the weekend in Vegas," I said. The world slowly started to morph around me: time moved at a calmer pace, objects took on a sharpness and clarity. "What's happened?" I asked. "Has there been an accident?"

"How about neighbors?" the cop asked. "Are you close with any of your neighbors?"

"Sure," I said. "The Kaylins, two doors down. 151 Hyacinth."

The first cop nodded and conferred with the other one for a second. "I'll be right back," he said, and disappeared down the front walk. The second cop stood framed in the doorway. "Don't worry, everything's okay," he said.

"Right," I said under my breath. I beckoned Echo over to where I was standing. "Okay, it looks like there's been some kind of accident," I whispered. "I'm not entirely sure what the procedure is, but we may end up having to go with them down to the station. This means Krieg and Jerem are going to have to be woken up, and both they and Molly are going to need to change clothes quickly, so—"

"Accident?" Echo said, uncomprehendingly.

Echo seemed out of it—drugged, almost. I wondered how long it'd been since she'd last slept. A minute later the first cop came back accompanied by Mrs. K. She was wearing a heavy terry-cloth robe with a white winter jacket on top. "Hi, honey," she said. "It looks like you kids are going to be spending the night at our house—"

"Okay, change of plan," I said. I tugged Echo's shoulder. "We're going to need sleeping bags," I said. "I think we have two in the upstairs closet. We can throw together some makeshift ones out of comforters to make up the differen—"

"It's all right, honey," Mrs. K. said. "We have all those things at home. Just put on some slippers."

"Accident?" Echo said.

Peggy was waiting at the foot of the stairs when Mrs. K. opened the door to let the five of us in. "What's going on?" she asked me. "Mom says you're going to be living at our *house?*"

"I'm not sure," I said. "I'm waiting for things to settle down so I can get the full story." Peggy was wearing a blue-gray bathrobe with a hint of something pink underneath it, and I suddenly couldn't help wondering what she wore to bed and whether I'd be finding out anytime soon. It occurred to me that this was a wholly inappropriate thought given the circumstances. I didn't stop wondering, however.

"Okay, let's see here," Mrs. K. said. "I suppose we'll put Molly in Kelly's room, Echo in Peggy's—"

"No!" Peggy said. For the briefest of moments I thought that Peggy was going to insist that I stay with her, considering that we were the ones who were friends and all. No such luck. "No one's allowed in my room," she said. "That's private. That's the rules."

"We'll just have to change the rules, then," Mrs. K. said.

"No," Peggy said. "Rules are rules."

I glanced over at Echo. She was staring into the middle distance like it was a Mondrian painting. "I think maybe we shouldn't be split up," I said. "We can all stay in the TV room."

"Okay, maybe that's a good idea," Mrs. K. said. Peggy looked relieved. Of course, she wasn't the one with the most to lose had Mrs. K. insisted on her original plan: it being a Friday night, any attempt to have us room with the Kaylin kids would've led to the discovery that Kelly was not snug in her bed but rather out somewhere having highly illegal sex with some thirty-year-old who'd set her up with her weekend supply of scratch cards.

Mr. K. came back in from talking with the cop. "This should only be for one night, kids," he said. "Tomorrow night you'll be back in your own beds."

"So the accident wasn't serious?" Molly asked.

"Wasn't—uh, what've you been told?" Mr. K. asked.

"Nothing," I said. "The cop wouldn't talk to us. Is Dad okay? What happened?"

Mr. K. was silent for a moment. "I can't think of an easy way to put this," he finally said.

That's a mighty long time

So we were orphans. It seemed like such a bizarre word. Like we could all look forward to spending our days as chimney sweeps and our nights begging the governess at the orphanage to let us have just one more bit of blood pudding. That was almost comforting. Since I couldn't connect that image to our lives, it was like it had happened to someone else.

It was a couple of days before I found out exactly what had happened. Dad had called Danny to say he was on his way home from Claremont. A few exits from home, one of his tires blew out. He pulled over, turned on the hazard lights, and got out to change the tire. What happened next was apparently not atypical. "Happens all the time," the cop told Mr. K. "Happened to a couple of my friends, in fact. Pull someone over, get out to give 'em a ticket, and while you're writing it up, BAM! You turn around and someone's smashed into the patrol car. One of the most common drunk-driving accidents. They follow the pretty lights. Don't see that the taillights aren't moving till they've kissed 'em with their own headlights." And that's more or less what happened in this case as well. One of the cars trailing a good ways behind Dad had been a little four-seater containing seven people coming back from (or going to—it wasn't clear) a party. The driver was seventeen years old and had a blood alcohol level of 0.13 percent. And sure enough, he had followed the taillights and crashed directly into the back of Dad's car. Dad had been digging through the trunk looking for the tire jack. The impact nearly cut him in half. He died instantly.

"I can fly," Echo said.

"What?" I said.

Echo was sitting on the Kaylins' couch, rocking back and forth and hugging herself. "I just finished a book about this," she said. "It's called lucid dreaming. This isn't real. This *can't* be real. Look, this isn't even our house. So once you recognize that it's a dream, you can control it. You say, okay, this is a dream, and I want to fly. And you do."

"But you're not flying," I said.

"I choose not to," Echo said.

"Shhh," I said. I tried to move her arms out of the way so I could hug her but she wouldn't budge. I hugged her anyway.

"I had my first period today," she said.

I had no idea how to respond to that. "Uh, really?" I finally said.

"I think so," she said. "That may just be part of the dream. It's hard to say for sure . . ."

"Right," I said. "Look, why don't you try to get some sleep . . ."

"I *am* asleep," she said.

At this point I was completely lost. "I love you, Echo," I said, for lack of anything else to say.

"See?" she said. "That proves it."

The cops tracked down Bobbo in Vegas and he was back in Fullerton by lunchtime. Which was almost kind of a shame, since the morning had shown me that even from catastrophe could come at least a measure of sweetness. Peggy had come downstairs to help make breakfast and while she was getting out the pots and pans she asked, "So why are you all here? I don't understand."

"Our dad was killed in a car crash last night," I said. "We don't have anywhere else to go."

Peggy's face froze, like she just realized she'd accidentally kicked a puppy in front of an oncoming truck. And then she threw her arms around me and held me tight. It was a very different feeling from when she'd been seven. "Oh, I'm so sorry," she said. "You must be so sad."

That wasn't exactly the word I would have picked, but I wasn't about to fault her vocabulary. As it happened, I had been kind of troubled right before she'd come downstairs. I couldn't help but think about Dad's last moments. There must have been just the briefest instant before impact that he realized what was about to happen. Not more, or he would've had time to dive out of the way. But not less. He must have had a moment—if only a tenth of a second—when the lights of the oncoming car were upon him, and he knew it was the end. And what was his last fleeting thought? That he was about to join Susan? No, he'd never bought into any of the usual afterlife myths. Did his life flash before his eyes? Not nearly enough time for that. No, I was sure—and am sure today—that his last thoughts were of us, that he was the only one left to make sure we were loved and provided for, and that now there were going to be five children out there left with nothing and no one. And that upset me. Not because he'd died, but because he'd died distraught, because he didn't know that we were going to be okay. And we were. Standing there in the Kaylins' kitchen with the sun streaming in through the eastern windows and Peggy crying sympathetic tears into my shoulder, I felt more safe, more centered, more secure than I'd felt in years.

"My mom and dad'll adopt you," Peggy murmured.

"Hmm?" I said. I was tremendously pleased that Peggy's decision to start a conversation didn't mean that she was at all inclined to let go.

"They will," she said. "They won't let you get split up and go to foster homes. We'll get a bigger house and you and me'll be brother and sister. And we can sit together in church . . ."

"That'd be great," I said. "Really. But I have a pretty good idea of how this is going to work out. Dad's got to have had some life insurance for us to live off of, and I'm pretty sure they'll probably rope Bobbo into being our legal guardian. Which doesn't mean that I'm not going to need you to stay close. But I think I'm going to be fine."

You'll note that I was speaking in the singular here. Peggy's house had been my second home for years; none of my siblings had ever seen the inside of it, as far as I knew. It's probably a safe bet that they didn't feel quite as sanguine about the situation as I did. I can't say I did much to help, at least not in those first few days: I spent most of my time at the Kaylins' house, and when I was home, I was usually up in my room with the lights out and my headphones on. On the other hand, I was more help than Bobbo, who kept going to get stuff out of his apartment and then coming back empty-handed, saying, "What the hell am I doing? I can't take care of five kids. I can't even take care of a toaster." Molly took to sleeping with Dad's personal effects: first a couple of his books, then one of his shirts (maybe because it was more emotionally charged, or maybe just because it's no fun rolling over onto a trade paperback in the middle of the night). Krieg wouldn't shut up about the accident for days—he just went on and on about it. "You think his guts sprayed on the back of the car? Or maybe he just got squeezed till they all came out his ass! Yeah, his ass!" And Echo . . .

. . . Echo was pretty much impossible to read. For one thing, she didn't say anything. If you asked her a question, she'd start to answer, and then before she could get out the first word, she'd just freeze, as if someone had forgotten to tell her that time hadn't stopped. And when she did freeze, even waving a hand in front of her face didn't help—I actually had to shake her by the shoulders a couple of times to get her to snap out of it, and then she still wouldn't answer, she'd just turn and leave the room. I tried asking Molly for help or advice but she just shrugged and blinked. It was as if they'd both taken a vow of silence. Which meant there was nothing to drown out the sound of Krieg telling Jerem, "Hey, you think when his head hit the ground that he cracked open the back of his head or you think his face got pulped? Fuckin' yeah!"

We didn't go back to school on Monday, though that morning I made appointments with the principals of both the elementary school and the middle school and explained that my father had been killed in an accident and that my brothers and sisters were consequently going to be taking a few days off from school. Dr. Strick down at the elementary school was very understanding—she'd always liked me—but Mr. Fossle at Vista de la Vista didn't quite seem to be following. "Rules are rules," he said. "If you and your sister are going to be absent I'm going to need a note from your parents," he said.

"Um, excuse me?" I said. "Have you even been listening—?"

"Hmm?" he said. "Oh, yes. Death certificate. I'll need a death certificate. Apologies."

As it turned out, we didn't miss much school. I went back on Tuesday, Krieg and Jerem on Wednesday, Molly on Thursday. That left only Echo, sitting in our room staring out the window for hours at a time. Serenading her with the usual clichés like "Hey, sis, it's gonna be okay, really" and "If you want to talk I'm here for you" didn't elicit any reaction so after a while I gave them up. On the other hand, there'd be times when I'd be doing my homework and after an hour of silence she'd suddenly mumble, "What did I miss in history class?", as if she were addressing someone just on the other side of the window and didn't want me to hear.

When I came downstairs for school the following Monday I found Echo downstairs waiting for me. She was wearing dark black jeans and two black sweatshirts. "Are you coming to school today?" I asked.

"Yes," she said.

"Great!" I said. "But, uh, are you sure you want to wear all that? The forecast says it's supposed to get over ninety—"

"Yes," she said through clenched teeth. "It'd be an *insult* to wear anything else."

Our first class of the day was science; as it happened, we had a lab that day. It turned out that my lab partner had somehow never heard of Celsius before, and I was trying to explain why the thermometer said it was only twenty-five degrees in the room when suddenly there was a crash and Echo ran out of the room, sobbing hysterically.

I stuck my head outside to see if I could find her, but she was long gone. At lunch I swung by the house and sure enough, Echo had run straight home. She was even still crying, though it'd modulated from convulsive bawling into a gentle weeping that one could conceivably find rather becoming. "I don't know what's wrong with me," she said. "I just can't seem to stop . . ."

"That's okay," I said. "Take some more time off. No one's going to—"

"No," she said. "I have to go back. You all went back. I just have to be strong. I'm not some, some *cripple.*" She wiped the tears from her eyes with the back of her hand. "What's wrong with me?" she asked.

The next morning I came downstairs to find Echo pulling her black sweatshirts out of the dryer. "I'm going to have to get more of these," she muttered.

"Right," I said. "Um, how long are you planning on wearing—"

"Forever," Echo said.

"Right," I said. "Look, Eck, right now it's barely been more than a week. It's totally appropriate that you be in mourning. I think the rest of us don't seem to feel as strongly about it as you do because we're all still kind of in shock. But, you know, someday things'll look brighter, life'll go on—"

"*NO!*" she said. "I *knew* you were going to say something like that. 'Life goes on.' Life *doesn't* go on! That's the whole *point*! It just *stops,* and then it's lost forever and you can never ever get even an instant of it back." She balled up her sweatshirts under her arm and stormed off into Mom's office to change.

For a while I was under the impression that I'd somehow managed to stumble into saying exactly the right thing: if Echo was furious at me, that might give her something else to focus on. And it worked, at least through first period. Then in English we were right in the middle of identifying comma splices when without any warning Echo buried her face in her hands and started crying helplessly. She stumbled to her feet, knocked over her desk, and fled from the room. Most everyone in class burst into laughter: a lot of it nervous, to be fair, but there were at least a couple people who seemed to think the incident was the height of comedy. Those were the ones who laughed the loudest. It was almost loud enough to drown out the sound of the splash as my heart plummeted into my lower intestine.

This time Echo was ready to agree that returning to school a third time in as many days would be a mistake. "Why should I go back at all?" she said darkly. "I reinvented myself, all right. Now I'm a different *kind* of joke. The crying girl all swathed in black. All I have to do now is get some scars on my wrists and write a couple reams of bad poetry and I'm set for the next six years. No, wait. Throw in an eating disorder and an abusive boyfriend. Then I can really start living the cliché . . ."

"Echo, don't talk like that," I said. "How about when Bobbo gets home I have him get you an appointment with someone you can talk to about all this . . . ?"

Echo started to cry again.

I got myself another appointment with Principal Fossle. "I see," he said. "You realize that if your sister withdraws from school that she'll have to repeat—"

"Oh, please," I said. "You're going to make Echo repeat the seventh grade? Echo's taking graduate-level math. She writes on a level that puts college professors to shame. She took the SAT at the end of fourth grade and got a sixteen hundred without even thinking about it. You're going to make Echo repeat the *seventh grade*? She's humoring you by being here at all."

Mr. Fossle didn't seem to know what to say to that. Thus he relied on an old favorite. "Detention!" he cried.

Echo's session with the psychiatrist Bobbo found didn't go much better. For a couple of weeks she wouldn't even talk about it. Finally I got her to spill. "She wanted to put me on antidepressants," Echo said. "As if it were my *brain chemistry* that was the matter. My *brain chemistry* isn't the problem. The problem is that life is cruel. And the fact that that's a mantra of every angst-ridden teenager in the history of the world doesn't make it any less true."

"So wait," Hayley said. "You mean you still wear all that black stuff—"

"—because life is still cruel," Echo said. "I'll stop when it does."

"How about now?" Hayley said. "I could sort of see your point if you were some kind of pathetic, friendless laughingstock. But you're not friendless, and the most attractive boy at school seems to think you're rather far from a laughingstock. No one's denying that loss is a part of life. But in your case, I'd say that it's starting to be offset. Don't you think?"

Echo blinked. She started to say something, then blinked again. "I'll take that into consideration," she said.

Liniment, please

One afternoon not too long thereafter I came into the office for peer counseling to find Mrs. Kaylin waiting at the attendance desk. "Hi!" I said.

"Hello, Allen," she said.

"Um, how are you?" I asked. "How is everyone?"

"We've been better," she said.

"Right," I said. "I'm sorry. Um, is there something I can do for you here . . . ? Someone you need to talk to . . . ?"

"Whoever's in charge of attendance," Mrs. K. said. "I have to have Peggy and Kelly withdrawn from school."

"So they're not coming back?" I asked.

"Not this school year," Mrs. K. said. "We sent Kelly to this . . . hospital . . . to help her with her . . . problem. By the time she gets back it'll be too late to make up the work she's missing. Peggy . . . we thought about maybe sending her . . . to another place we found . . . but we decided that would be too extreme."

"Peggy? A place?" I asked. "What kind—I mean—is she—"

"She's not doing much these days," Mrs. K. said. "Sleeping a lot. She goes to bed at seven or seven-thirty at night, doesn't wake up till ten or eleven in the morning. She keeps saying she wants to go visit Kelly, but the rules don't allow that . . . Bob and I don't much care for the boys she's been seeing, either . . ."

"Oh," I said.

"I don't understand it," Mrs. K. said. "Something happened to my girls . . ." She shook her head. "Anyway, we got this progress report in the mail, and most of the grades were I for incomplete, but there was one F, and we thought it'd be best if we took her out of school before it goes on her transcript for college . . ."

"Was the F in journalism?" I asked.

"Yes," Mrs. K. said. Right then Doctor Todd came out to talk with her and I was left to go to my peer counseling session. Not that I was really equipped for it—I felt . . . well, emotionally I didn't feel much of anything. Physically, I suddenly ached all over. When I went home I couldn't summon up the strength to jump over the fence back to Hyacinth. I had to walk all the way around. I might as well have driven.

The next afternoon I had a succinct conversation with Benito. "So, you flunked Peggy, did you?" I asked.

"She got the grade she deserved," Benito said. "She wasn't here."

"And you thought that giving her an F would somehow make her more inclined to come back?" I asked. "You thought it'd make things *better*?"

"I don't care what effect it has," Benito said. "That's what she deserved, that's what she got. The grading system was her idea."

"So you don't care what effect it has, huh?" I said. "Then I guess you won't care about this effect: I quit." It suddenly occurred to me that I couldn't afford an F on my transcript any more than Peggy could. "I mean, I'll finish out the year," I said. "But this is an elective class. And as of June, you're not elected. And I bet Echo'll say the same thing. She's even less a fan of capricious cruelty than I am."

"Are you still talking?" Benito asked.

It took an awful lot of effort to restrain myself from grabbing her stapler and stapling her face to the desk.

Admiración

When I was three, I came upstairs one afternoon to find Echo staring at her reflection in the mirror. She looked unhappy. "What're you doing?" I asked.

"I don't get it," she said.

"What?" I asked. "How a mirror works?"

"My eyes," she said. "I can see out of them but I can't see into me when I look into them."

"What do you see?" I asked.

"Just black," she said.

Of course, "just black" was at least a passable description of what most people saw when they looked at Echo these days. And I couldn't help but think back on that little exchange when I found Echo staring at herself in the mirror again on prom night. Once again she seemed unhappy, though this time I was reasonably sure it was for less esoteric reasons. "Hey, Eck," I said. "What's up?"

"Nothing," she said. "Just trying to figure it all out . . ."

"Figure wh—uh, are you shaking?" I asked.

Echo's hands were trembling uncontrollably. Her lower lip too. "I—I'm really nervous," she confessed. "I don't think I can do this."

"Do what?" I asked. "Dance? Don't worry about it. No one—"

"I know how to dance," she said. "I just don't—I mean—I'm sure Carver means well, but this was a bad idea. I can't—I don't know how to act, what to say . . ."

"If you're having second thoughts, you shouldn't go," I said.

"Hayley would be so disappointed," Echo said.

"So?" I said.

"And Carver," Echo said. "It was very courageous of him to jeopardize his social standing by asking someone like me to an event like this. I can't abandon him now. That would be the worst thing I could possibly do." She sighed. "I suppose I'd better change."

I went downstairs and turned on the TV. I was flipping through the channels for the fifth time when I heard Echo's tread on the staircase. "Do I look okay?" she asked.

I turned to look. At which point I said the only thing I could think of: *"¡Dios mio!"*

I had been under a whole series of misconceptions. The first was that Echo had borrowed some long flowing peasant dress from Hayley. This dress was not long and it was not flowing and it certainly didn't make Echo look like anything resembling a peasant. Nor was it frilly or fluffy or poofy or shiny or any of the other qualities one usually associates with prom dresses. It was basic matte black, with simple lines, and of a fabric with some solidity to it: it didn't ripple at all but held its shape. And what a shape it was. The neckline wasn't what you'd call daring, but it certainly wasn't conservative. The hem fell at midthigh. And it was backless. This was not a dress designed for sixteen-year-old sorority-sisters-in-training as they bopped around at the junior prom. This was a dress designed for twenty-five-year-old bombshells as they tangoed with their Argentinian lovers.

And then there was Echo herself. Having been buried under three layers of black for all these years, I'd expected her to be pale as dough. I don't know why I thought this: on an intellectual level I knew that her coloration was genetic, not the product of years of sucking up UV radiation. And sure enough, Echo remained as bronze and glistening as ever. But that was minor compared to my next error. The last time I'd seen Echo wearing something that wasn't baggy enough to make you wonder whether there was a person underneath was during our first few days of middle school. Back then she'd been the picture of coltishness, the last of her baby fat melted away, leaving her all arms and legs but no less lissome or graceful for that; I figured that the best-case scenario would be for her to be lucky enough to stay that way. But I suspected that more realistically, she'd probably grown a bit dowdy, still basically androgynous, with maybe a flaccid feint toward femininity that'd prompted her to stop changing in front of me . . .

I could not have been more wrong.

Though I wouldn't have believed it if you'd told me, I could not deny the evidence of my eyes: Madeleine Eve Mockery was *perfecto y espectacular.* Not in the same way as Kelly Kaylin: where Kelly was invitingly soft, Echo was athletic and hard as marble. I had no doubt whatsoever that had she been so inclined, she could've grabbed me by the shoulders and broken my skeleton into kindling with a flip of her wrist. Not that she was bulky at all—far from it. She was lean and tight, and her tone was just incredible: you could make out all the interplay of muscles in her arms. And somehow this didn't make her a jot less feminine. The dress was the proof, if any proof were needed. That dress had clearly been designed by a consortium of artists and eugenicists to fit the ideal human female and her alone, just in case natural selection happened to produce one. On Echo it looked like she'd been the model for which it had been sewn.

"¡Madre de dios!" Molly cried from the bottom of the stairs. *"Echo?* I heard Allen yelp, but—"

"What?" Echo said, her face flushed. "Should I change? I should change. I look ridic—"

"No!" I said. "You look good."

"Good?" Molly said. *"Good?* Echo, you are so beautiful the only appropriate response is *fear.* But why are you wearing that?"

"It's prom night," Echo said.

"It is?" Molly said. "And you're going? No one tells me anything. Who's your date?"

"Carver Fringie," Echo said.

"The boy who used to live across the street?" Molly asked.

"Yes," Echo said.

"Lucky him," Molly said. "Are you going to have sex with him?"

"No!" Echo said. "I barely even know him. We're just renewing our acquaintance this evening."

"Oh," Molly said. "Well, he's going to be disappointed by that news. I know I would be. Heck, I *am*. I could eat you up like ice cream right here. I wouldn't even need a spoon."

Echo looked mildly alarmed but didn't say anything. She walked over to the couch and carefully crossed her legs; the whole series of movements looked highly artificial, as if she were balancing a crystal vase on her head or something. "You okay?" I asked.

"I feel like if anyone touches me I'm going to shatter into a million pieces," Echo said.

There was a knock at the garage door. I went to go answer it. It was, of course, Fringie. He was wearing a tuxedo with a gray tortoiseshell vest; his mushroom-head haircut had been freshly touched up. "Hey, Al," he said. "She here? Car's running."

"Charming," I said. I'd meant to bash his face in with the door, but by the time the intention translated to action, it'd been diluted from a shocking display of violence down to a lame barb. Molly skittered out into the foyer to see who it was; Fringie's eyes narrowed as he looked her up and down. "Don't even think about it," I said.

I needn't have worried. The second Echo stepped into the room Fringie's eyes were locked on her and her alone. "Echo?" he said. "Oh. My." He coughed. "You're exquisite."

Echo blushed—I could literally feel the heat radiating from her face. Fringie gave her an appraising look. "I must say, I'm very impressed," he said. "To be perfectly honest, I had no idea what to expect. But you make my most optimistic projection look like a Bosch painting."

"Th—thank you," Echo said. She bobbled unsteadily on her feet.

"Hey, you sure you're okay?" I whispered.

"That was supposed to be a curtsy," Echo said under her breath. "I'm out of practice."

"You're more than welcome," Fringie said. He kissed her hand. "Well, I don't see any reason to linger. Shall we be off?"

"Okay," Echo said. She looked at Molly and me. "Um, 'bye," she said.

"'Shall we be off,'" I muttered as the door slammed shut. "Who talks like that?"

"It's a special occasion," Molly said.

"Oh, give me a break," I said. "Am I the only one who sees through this guy? You'd think the register shifts alone would give him away. One second he's monosyllabic, the next it's like someone jabbed a syringe full of chivalry into his neck. And those are just the personae we saw in the forty-five seconds he deigned to grant us. We totally missed out on this evening's installment of Carver Fringie, Penile Philosopher."

"He's really cute," Molly said.

"Cute? *Cute?* What *is* it with you people?" I said. "Come on, this is ridiculous. You and Echo are the smartest people I know. Fringie comes by and now we have to get the floor repaired from your IQs crashing through it."

"Let's get some ice cream," Molly said.

"What?" I said.

"Ice cream," Molly said.

"You can't eat ice cream," I said.

"Sure I can," she said. "They're bound to have *something* without sugar."

"Fair enough," I said. "Go put something on and I'll get you a waffle cone."

"My favorite of all cones!" Molly declared.

The Islets of Langerhans

Molly threw on a pair of bell-bottoms and her favorite T-shirt: it was mainly white, with short red sleeves and a red band around the neck and a big blue "76" on the front. I was about to hop in the car when Molly stopped me. "It's a nice evening," she said. "Let's walk. It's only down by the Video Supercluster." She looked up at the dimming sky, dotted with clouds. "Maybe I should get my rain gear, though," she said. "Just in case."

"Let's not make a big production out of it," I said. "If you want to walk, let's get going before it gets dark."

We didn't talk as we headed down to State College; the only sounds were the cars going by in the distance. "What are you thinking?" Molly asked as we reached the corner.

"I dunno," I said. "This prom thing, I guess. Still seems fishy to me. Echo says she likes Carver Fringie and then out of the blue he asks her to prom? That's like Holly Madera calling me up and asking if I'll take her to the Emmys. And . . . well, to be perfectly honest, if you'd asked me even a few weeks ago who in our family would start dating first, Echo would not have been my first choice."

"But she didn't," Molly said. "Krieg did. Remember Daisy?"

"Oh, great," I said. "So, best-case scenario, I finish third. Of course, now you're probably going to tell me that you've found the boy of your dreams and it's gonna be a fight to the finish between me and Jerem."

"I don't think that's going to happen anytime soon," Molly said. "The kids at school don't really hang out with me much. I think they think I'm kind of weird."

"That's okay," I said. "I know exactly what's going to happen. You'll be an outcast for a while, but then you're going to graduate from Ilium and go off to art school and you're going to fall in with a bunch of kindred spirits and you'll all buy a big dilapidated house on the outskirts of town and paint naked in the backyard and grow your own food and I'll come to visit one day to find you living a life of glorious polyamorous debauchery while I spend my days sitting alone on the floor of my dorm room eating carpet."

"So are you looking?" Molly asked.

"Looking?" I said.

"For a girlfriend," Molly said. "So you don't finish last."

"Well, no," I said. "I can't say I'm actively looking. I mean, sure, I wish I were with someone. But if wishes were dishes the world would be a dinette set."

"You don't sound very self-confident," Molly said.

"Oh, it's not that," I said. "I mean, it wouldn't be hard to find *someone*. All I'd have to do is accept The Lord Jesus Christ as my personal savior and I suspect that September would be all over me. But even without that condition . . . I don't know. I mean, I like her, but I can't ever see myself falling for her or anything. And there's no point otherwise, right? I mean, you can't look for someone to fall for like shopping for a pair of pants. I just figured that one day I'd be hanging out with someone and we'd sort of look at each other and somehow we'd both just *know*. So, no, I can't say I'm looking. But I sure wouldn't mind being found."

"Do you think that's likely?" Molly asked.

"I don't know," I said. "I guess not. I mean, when I got to the age where the kids in my class started pairing off, I thought I was in good shape. You had guys who'd literally never had a single conversation with a girl in their entire lives just walking up to them out of the blue and asking for dates and getting them. And me, I'd been friends with these girls for most of our lives. They weren't alien creatures to me, they were the kids I'd played with at lunch and recess since kindergarten. And okay, maybe I'm not exactly the mayor of Studville here, but I'm reasonably smart and pretty much okay-looking and I try to be a good person and help people out if I can and I figured *someone* would be interested. And— I mean, I've read the surveys. Whenever they ask girls what they look for in guys, number one is always 'sense of humor.' And—"

"And that's your problem," Molly said.

"What?" I said.

"Your sense of humor is pathological," she said. "It's a defense mechanism. Echo's defense is to be insular and antisocial; yours is to crack a joke every twelve seconds. It's the same thing. It's a way of keeping the world at arm's length. People sense you're keeping your distance and so they return the favor."

"Wow," I said. "And here I thought our cable service didn't carry the Bogus Pop Psychology Channel."

"Case in point," Molly said. "It's hard to get together with someone when your defenses are keeping you apart from everyone. And it's not just you. It's everyone. What do you think these things are all about?" She tugged at her shirt. "It's all about keeping people apart, locked away in their own little boxes. That's why everyone's so unhappy all the time. It's all the distance. People aren't allowed to touch anymore. They can't even look at each other. And they get trained to like it that way. Any parent will tell you that there's not a toddler in the world who likes being dressed. But the message that you have to wear clothes whether you need them or not is beaten into them over and over again so many times that soon the idea of being seen naked becomes embarrassing and intolerable. It's backward and stupid. You get forced to put up these defenses when there's nothing that needs defending, and soon you feel exposed without them and so you *do* need them. And it's not just about mental health. The material revolves around the psychological. If we could all just get together and count up what we needed, and figure out what it'd take to produce it, and divvy up the work, no one would have to do without the things they need, and everyone would have a lot more leisure, because we wouldn't waste time working at cross purposes. We have the *physical* capacity to meet everyone's needs, easily, and spend the rest of the time playing and having fun. But from day one we're shepherded into thinking of ourselves as isolated little islands, to *want* to be isolated little islands, and until that changes we'll never be able to coordinate things and make the world a better place. I'll have a scoop of sugar-free vanilla and a scoop of coconut fudge in a waffle cone, please."

We had arrived at the Cone-U-Copia. "Um, the coconut fudge isn't sugar-free," I said.

"So I'll take a bigger shot when I get home," she said. "Look, I can live without insulin at this point. Living without coconut fudge is something else. Trust me, I know what I'm doing."

"Okay," I said. I had barely enough money on me to cover Molly's ice cream so I contented myself with a cup of water. The Cone-U-Copia guy seemed less than pleased by this turn of events. Watching him sneeze into the caramel swirl didn't make me any more inclined to surrender my last dollar. We sat down at one of the little plastic tables and Molly savagely tore into her waffle cone. "So, uh, how do you think Echo managed to get in shape like that?" I asked.

Molly shrugged. "Works out," she said. "Probably at night. She's still only sleeping three hours a night, right?"

"Right," I said. "That's so weird, though. I mean, Echo's never struck me as the gym-going type. Though the crowds are probably smaller at three A.M. . . ."

"Doesn't need a gym," Molly said. "We've got weight equipment out in the garage."

"Since when?" I asked.

"Since always," Molly said. "I thought it was Bobbo's. He's got all kinds of stuff out there. Remember the pasta maker? He stuck it out in the garage when it turned out to actually need ingredients and didn't just summon linguine out of the ether."

"I've seen the pasta maker," I said. "Never noticed any weights, though."

"Not very observant," Molly said.

"Hey, slow down there," I said. Molly had already devoured half her ice cream. "Even if you don't keel over in a sugar coma you'll get a headache if you keep this up."

"Hmm?" she said. "Oh, hey. I guess I was in a hurry to get out of here. Come on, I can finish it on the way back."

And in fact she did consume her ice cream at a much more leisurely pace on the way back. By now dusk had established itself quite solidly and Molly was a dim silhouette against the headlights on State College. Suddenly she stopped like she'd hit an invisible wall. "I'm sorry," she said.

"Hmm?" I said.

"I didn't even think," she said. She held out the stub of her waffle cone. "Want the last bit? It's really good."

"That's okay," I said. "Thanks though."

"You sure?" she said.

"You bet," I said.

"Okay," she said. She popped the tip of the cone into her mouth— and flinched. "Oh no," she said.

"What?" I asked. "Are you okay? Is it the sugar?"

"Raindrop," she said. She looked up; you couldn't see any stars through the clouds. Not that you could usually see any stars anyway.

"Maybe it's just one," I said. I felt a sudden wet chill on my hand. "Or maybe not."

"There's another one," Molly said. She looked around wildly like a cornered cat. We had traffic along one side, a row of cinder-block walls and tall wooden fences on the other. There was no shelter. Molly looked back at the ice cream shop, ahead toward our street, did a quick calculation, and took off sprinting toward the house.

Someone needs a timeout

Molly's water phobia started the day my dad took us all to the beach. We were all still quite young, young enough that Echo was able to get away with borrowing my old swim trunks without getting arrested. It was the predictable fiasco. Krieg immediately set to kicking over sand castles and throwing seaweed at people, and Molly was even more of a nuisance as she tried to pet the seagulls which would fly away, leaving her to run into sunbathers as she chased after them. Then a bunch of neighborhood kids showed up—Echo had told them the day before that we were heading to the beach the next day, and still being in the throes of Echo-worship, they'd nagged their parents into taking them too—so Echo went off with them to throw a Frisbee around. This meant that when one too many people came to Dad to complain about Molly tripping into them, I got elected to distract her from the birds by taking her out into the surf. We walked out onto the wet sand, and before long a wave came to shore; it crashed a good way out, but the foam raced up at us at a fairly alarming rate and lapped at our ankles.

Molly screamed. It wasn't a "Yipes! It's cold!" scream, or a "Whoa! That was unexpected!" scream—this was an "OH MY GOD I'M BEING HACKED APART BY A RUSTY CHAINSAW" scream. She dashed blindly back to our beach towel and collapsed in a heap. "I—I *saw* stuff," she gasped, tears streaming down her face. "Monsters, and—and blood, and—I *saw* stuff."

That was summer. In the fall, we had a rare rainstorm and Molly made the mistake of going out to get the mail in just her kimono—no raincoat, no umbrella. She came tearing back inside a moment later, her golden complexion blanched into something closer to platinum. "It happened again," she panted. "I saw—I saw a gigantic bird swoop out of the sky and rip my heart out and fly away—it's the water, I know it, any water that doesn't come from a house does it, makes me see horrible things . . ."

"Interesting," my dad said when he found out. "This is clearly a case of conversion disorder brought on by some childhood trauma."

"She's six," I said. "What other kind of trauma could she have?"

"Molly, can you remember any unpleasant experiences from your early life involving water?" Dad asked.

"When we went to the beach," Molly said.

"No, from your *early* life," Dad said.

"That *was* from my early life," Molly said. "I was just a kid."

Dad snapped his fingers. "Perhaps it's symbolic," he said. "Not necessarily metaphor, but metonymy. A matter of association. Was it raining the night Susan died?"

"Hey, maybe Mom tried to drown her," I said.

"Allen!" Dad cried. "How dare you even suggest such a thing?"

"What?" I said. "Seems like the kind of thing she'd do."

"Go to your room," Dad said.

The puzzle continued to fascinate him, however. At one point he even brought in a psychiatrist to check her out. I came downstairs one afternoon to find Molly sitting lifelessly in a chair in the TV room while some strange guy muttered something to her. Dad headed me off on the staircase. "What's going on?" I asked.

"We're trying to determine the root of Molly's hysteria through hypnosis," Dad said. "She can't be disturbed."

"That guy's a hypnotist?" I asked. "Great. He'll just say that she drowned in a past life."

"Not everyone trained in hypnosis is a charlatan," Dad said. "Freud himself used it to cure the hysteria of one of his most famous case studies."

"Whatever," I said. "But when Molly starts acting like a chicken, remember that I told you s—"

"Go to your room," Dad said.

When I came back downstairs after hanging out in my room for a bit I found that the hypnotist had left but Molly was far from back to her old self. She continued to just sit in her chair and stare. "She's been left with a posthypnotic suggestion to overcome her fear of water," Dad explained. "Apparently it's taking her some time to process the change. She'll come out of it before long."

And this may well have been true in a geological sense. But when we couldn't get her to snap out of her trance for dinner, or to go to sleep, or the following morning, Dad called the psychiatrist back and had him remove the suggestion. This time when he told her to reawaken feeling refreshed and relaxed, she did so. "So when do we start?" she asked.

Then after a couple minutes she slumped and fell fast asleep. She may have been feeling refreshed and relaxed, but she still hadn't slept in over twenty-four hours. When she woke up that evening, Dad took her to the store to buy an umbrella and several layers of rain gear. And she never got rained on again without protection until prom night.

Back to our program, already in progress

I found Molly huddled in front of the hall closet by the garage door, clutching her knees to her chest. "I saw terrible things," she said darkly. "It's Echo. Something awful is going to happen to her."

"Wait a minute," I said. "Since when did these visions become oracular? I think I missed a couple episodes here."

"I just know," she said. "Something terrible is going to happen. I know it."

"Well, she's on a date with Fringie already," I said. "I can't imagine anything more terrible than that."

It was well after midnight when I got the call. "Can you pick me up?" Echo asked. Her voice was husky and distant. "I'm outside Richard's Market in—"

"You mean Fringie isn't gonna drive you home?" I said. "Why, that's not very sweet of him."

Echo hung up. I punched the call return code and rang her back. "Sorry," I said. "Just give me the directions."

The prom had been held at some hotel in Anaheim Hills; I saw it floating by on the left as I sailed down the freeway off-ramp and onto an empty road that ran past a few shopping colonies and then wound onward into the dark. Once I cleared the gauntlet of condos I found myself in what would've been quite a lovely little area, hills silhouetted against the dusky charcoal sky, moonlight reflecting off a reservoir as I rounded a hairpin curve—would've been, that is, if not for the torrential rains that kept me from seeing anything other than distorted flashes of scenery between the frantic windshield wipers. Richard's Market turned out to be an abandoned convenience store catty-corner from an elementary school perched on the rim of a canyon; the drenched figure slumped by the pay phone out front was, of course, Echo. As she slunk toward the passenger-side door she gave no indication whatsoever that she was aware of the millions of gallons of water crashing down on her head. "Hi," I said. I reached into the backseat and handed her the stack of towels I'd brought. I already had the heat running full blast. "Here," I said. "You can dry off at least a little."

She started to say something but then just threw one of the towels over her head. Her hair was flat and lifeless but took on more of its usual wave as she scrubbed the water out of it. "So what happened?" I asked as I pulled back onto the street. "Are you okay?"

"I don't want to talk about it," she said.

"Molly's really upset," I said. "She had a vision that something horrible was going to happen to you."

"That's ridiculous," Echo said.

"It can't have been too ridiculous if you just spent half an hour standing out here in the rain," I said. "C'mon, talk to me."

She ground her teeth. "What do you want me to say?" she asked acidly. "Are you looking for an abject apology? 'Oh, what a fool I was ever to have doubted you! Truly must I bow to your superior judgment!' Or maybe you'd prefer that I linger over every minute detail of how Carver Fringie pinned me to the seat of his car and put his hands in places where I didn't want his hands—get a little vicarious thrill, hmm?"

"Look, you're wasting your time," I said. "I'm finally on to you. I know you don't really think those are my motives. You're just trying to maneuver me into getting mad at you so I'll kick you when you're down and all that. I'm not entirely sure where you picked up this little masochistic streak of yours but I'm not playing."

Echo glared at me. The ride proceeded in silence, at least for a while. As Echo and her black dress dried out, the car became rather humid and I cracked open the window to let some of the moisture out. The whistle of the wind broke the silence nicely.

Before long we pulled up into the driveway. I got out and headed inside but before I reached the garage door I realized that Echo hadn't gotten out of the car. I doubled back, opened the car door a crack, and stuck my head inside. "Are you coming in?" I asked. She shrugged. "Whatever," I said. "Look, I was asleep when you called, and I'm going back to sleep. If you want to talk, wake me up. Good night." I went upstairs and true to my word went right to sleep. I was really tired.

I'm not entirely sure how long it was after that that Echo finally came inside. I just remember a flash of light from the hallway and then Echo carefully closing the door behind her with a precise click. "Can I sleep with you?" she asked quietly.

"Huh? What?" I said.

"Like before," she said.

When we were little, Echo was plagued by nightmares of every variety. Sometimes it was an earthquake, sometimes the house burning down, sometimes a deadly plague, sometimes nuclear war, sometimes a pack of killer robotic monkeys on the loose, but whatever it was that had scared her on any particular night, she'd end up fleeing to the comparative safety of my bed several nights a week. But that had been years ago. "Sure, I guess," I said.

Echo lifted up the covers and slid in next to me. She was still wearing her prom dress. I thought about saying something about it but the gentle caress of alpha waves proved too enticing and I was about seven-eighths asleep a second or two later. "He was wonderful at first," Echo said.

"Mmrnhrmm," I said.

"It wasn't just that he treated me nicely," she said, "though he did. It was the way he acted as if he'd scored some sort of coup by getting me to come with him. As if *he* were the loser outcast and *I* were the one sought after by every boy and girl at school. Of course, no one else talked to me, but at least it was a different kind of silence this time—as if I were an exchange student just off the plane from Peru. It wasn't hostile, just confused. And Carver seemed to revel in being seen with me. I'd expected that we'd show up early and leave even earlier. Instead we were the last couple to leave. Not that the others had gone particularly far: a lot of people had taken suites for the night at the hotel. Which I suppose was to be expected for some of the more established couples. Why *Carver* had booked one was anyone's guess. He said it was dangerous to drive if you're sleepy, and so it seemed like a better idea than trying to go all the way home at this hour—as if it were hundreds of miles away. I said I wouldn't be sleepy for hours yet and that I was ready to head home—in a cab, if necessary. But he said he'd drive and suggested we take a route past some scenery he liked, which sounded innocuous enough. So he took me along one of these twisty roads up to the crest of a hill and pulled over and we looked down at the lights of the towns below—"

"And flipped them off?" I said.

"What?" she said.

"Nothing," I said. "Flashback."

"And then Carver kissed me," Echo said. "Which would've been nice at our door, but not there. And I tried to explain this to him. That yes, we'd spent the evening dancing, but that this wasn't a *musical,* that dancing couldn't be shorthand for growing intimacy when we still hadn't had a real conversation, and so he started to get very short with me and asked what I wanted to talk about, and things degenerated until he tried kissing me again. Only this time he wasn't seductive about it—he didn't care what I thought about it. And I tried to struggle, but I couldn't get any leverage—he knew exactly where to hold me so that I couldn't apply any force against him, couldn't even seem like I was fighting it. And he started talking in a very clipped manner, saying things like, 'Patience has proven to be a counterproductive strategy in the past' and 'Resistance is nothing more than the first step on the road to acquiescence' . . . anyway, his intentions were more than clear by this point so the next time he stuck his tongue in my mouth I just bit it."

"Excellent," I said.

"That got him to flinch," she said, "and he let me go just long enough for me to get another shot in. I managed to get out of the car before he recovered and I climbed up the hill a little ways away from the road—far enough that he'd have to get out of the car to get at me. Instead he just shouted something at me and drove away. So I waited until I was sure he was gone and walked back to the last pay phone I'd seen."

"So are you going to report him?" I asked.

"Absolutely," she said. "Of course, nothing will happen. The police will just say that they're not in the business of busting every hormone-crazed seventeen-year-old who tries to cop a feel from someone. But at least the report will be on file so that when it happens to someone else they'll be more inclined to pick him up."

"That's exactly what I was going to say," I said. "Alike minds think great, or however that goes. Okay, I'm *really* tired. We can talk more in the morning."

"Okay," she said. "Good night." She paused. "I love you," she added. She sounded as if she were sight-reading a foreign language and wasn't sure she was translating correctly.

"Love you too," I said sleepily.

I drifted back off to sleep but before long I felt a sort of tickling just at the edge of my consciousness and I ducked down out of dreamland for just a second to figure out what it was, the same way that a mysterious noise downstairs will get you to tune in for a moment—not enough to actually open your eyes, but enough to make sure that no one's breaking into your house. Of course, once I did identify what it was, my eyes snapped right open: it was Echo, sort of gently nuzzling at my neck. "Hey, what're you doing?" I asked.

"Shhh," she said. "Go back to sleep."

"I think you'd better go back to your own bed now," I said.

She kissed my cheek. "Shhh," she said.

"C'mon," I said. "Out." I sat up and turned on the little book light clamped to the bed. "I'm going to go get some juice," I said. "When I get back, you know, let's get back to our regularly scheduled planet, okay?"

"But—"

I went downstairs, poured myself a glass of orange juice, gulped it down, had another. When I went back upstairs Echo had returned to her bed, face to the wall. I turned off the light and slept till morning.

The dihydrogen monoxide menace

There are two unmistakable signs that you've crossed the border from Orange County into San Diego County. One is a particular street sign that crops up on the freeway. This sign depicts a man in a sombrero and a woman in a long flowing dress dashing across the freeway with their toddler in tow, both of the kid's feet yanked off the ground as they make their break for it. On the southbound side of the freeway this sign is labeled CAUTION; on the northbound side, PROHIBIDO. The other sign is that one of the region's most recognizable landmarks appears along the shoreline: the nuclear power plant at San Onofre. This plant is comprised of enormous twin round domes, each one capped at the top with a little nipple. The nuclear facility at San Onofre has been called "the biggest set of tits in California" by Bobbo and countless other high-larious comedians, and "the second biggest set of tits in California" by a few people trying to be cruel to Peggy Kaylin.

I parked the car not too far from the power plant and Molly and I got out. We started making our way down a twisting, arduous passage to the sand below. "Explain to me why we're doing this again," I said.

"I already told you," she said. "I have to know for sure what it was I saw. If that means going into the ocean again, then that's the way it has to be."

"Right," I said. "So why did you make me take you all the way to San Onofre when there are miles of perfectly good beach in OC that you don't have to clamber down a hillside to get to?" I asked.

Molly pointed to a sign marking the entrance to the beach: BEYOND THIS POINT YOU MAY ENCOUNTER NUDE SUNBATHERS

"Oh," I said.

With that, she slipped off her kimono, handed it to me, and strolled naked toward the surf. I looked around and, sure enough, there were lots of other naked people lounging on beach chairs and playing volleyball and stuff. About 90 percent of them were male and about 90 percent of them weighed over three hundred pounds. I'll leave it to you to draw the Venn diagrams.

I caught up with Molly as she tentatively knelt down at the tide line. "Um, the ocean's over there," I said.

"It'll get here," she said. A wave came crashing in and the foam raced up the beach—and came nowhere near us before retreating.

"You're right," I said. "It'll get here—when it's high tide again. Shouldn't be more than a few hours."

Molly took a few steps closer to the water and this time when the foam looked like it was going to crash around her feet she hopped back and stuck her fingers in it as it was sucked back out to sea. She winced and looked at her fingertips as if she expected them to have been eaten away.

"Okay, now I'm sure of it," she said. "Something awful is going to happen to Echo, and then she's going to kill herself."

"You're weird," I said. "Okay, let's go."

"Not a chance," she said. "This is the first time since Pennsylvania that I've been allowed out of the house without having to get all bundled up. And I stand a much better chance of figuring out what to do about Echo with my solar cells recharged." She took the kimono out of my hands, spread it out on the sand, and plunked herself down on it. It had a pocket under each dragon and Molly reached into one and pulled out a small bottle of sunscreen. "Want to put my sunblock on?" she asked.

"Uh, that's okay," I said. "I'd say my genetic sunblock and the fact that I'm actually wearing some freaking clothes should do the trick."

"I meant on me," she said.

"Ah," I said. "That would be a no."

"You suck," she said.

After a few hours the sun finally dipped below a horizon littered with aircraft carriers and battleships and destroyers and assorted other deathboats from the neighboring Marine base; Molly gathered up her kimono, shook the sand out, and put it back on. We made the climb back up to the car and merged onto the freeway back to Fullerton. "We definitely have the best ocean," Molly said.

"Excuse me?" I said.

"I guess it's more where we are relative to it," Molly said. "Not completely—you can tell the Atlantic's worse because it's all tiny and warm, like a wading pool that generations of first-graders have relieved themselves in. But I suppose it'd be okay if we lived in Portugal or something so the sun would go down over it. That's the biggest factor. When the sun comes up over the water and goes down over the land it really jars. It makes you want to chase after it. I don't know how people can live at the beginning of the continent instead of here at the end. That's like going to the movies and only watching the first reel."

"When have you ever seen the sun come up over the water?" I asked.

"When we were in New York," Molly said. "There's a clothing-optional beach at Sandy Hook I wanted to go to and Daddy took us."

"Us?" I said.

"Yeah, Echo went too," Molly said. "She wasn't as uptight about it as you. She got into it. It was fun."

"Wait a minute," I said. "I don't remember this at all."

"You were asleep," Molly said. "Like I said, we went to see the sunrise. We got back at noon and you were still sleeping. Which doesn't sound like such a bad idea right about now . . ."

Apparently it wasn't a bad idea at all: when we pulled up into the driveway an hour later I had to shake her awake. "We're home," I said.

"Okay," she yawned. "What time is it? Wait—on second thought, I don't care. I'm going to bed."

"How can you be tired?" I asked. "At least the first time you could say you got worn out chasing the seagulls all day. This time you didn't do anything but lie around."

"And that can take a lot out of you if you do it right," she said. She yawned again and headed inside.

I went upstairs to find Echo still in her prom dress, still lying in bed staring at the wall three inches from her face. It'd been close to a day. "Uh, hi there," I said.

No answer. I watched her breathe for a minute just to make sure she hadn't stopped. "Um, any time you want to answer is fine by me," I said. Several minutes passed. "Well, this is just fabulous," I said.

Nothing had changed when I woke up for school the following morning. I went over and tapped Echo on the shoulder. "Wakey wakey," I said. "Schooltime for schoolgirls. Echo? C'mon, this is getting silly."

Echo blinked at the wall. "Very well," I said. "You vin zis round, Amerikanski. If you feel like waking up before school's out, let me know and I'll clear your absence."

But the school day went by and Echo still didn't show up, not even for the last period of the day. Benito was less than thrilled about this, making one of her rare forays into the *Iliad* room to complain about it. "Where is Echo?" she asked. "We have vital business to attend to."

"She's absent," I said. "Maybe for a few days. Gonna flunk her too?"

Benito stomped out of the room. "Hmm," Hayley said.

"What?" I said.

"Well, this would seem to add credence to the word going around," Hayley said. "I'd been skeptical, but—"

"Word?" I said.

"Yes," Hank said. "The word in question being 'marmoset.'"

"Actually, Carver's been moping around all day, and when someone finally asked why, he said he was bummed out because Echo had said she wanted it kind of rough, but then started crying after it was over and that made him feel bad," Hayley said.

"Oh, you've got to be—" I hadn't expected even Fringie to sink this low. "I suppose it'd be too much to expect people to doubt his story?"

"Well, it didn't sound all that likely to me," Hayley said. "But staying home strikes me as more consistent with something traumatic having happened than with an uneventful evening . . ."

"Well, yeah, true enough," I said. "Does getting felt up against your will count? Because that's what actually happened."

Hayley shrugged. "Maybe if you're really sheltered," she said. "I don't know. I have to admit, Carver's account made a lot of sense. Every time I try to imagine Echo in a sexual situation I get torn between two scenarios. On the one hand, she's so tightly wound that she's practically the poster girl for the whole idea of trapdoor release—the people who're extremely repressed and deliberate most of the time are the ones you can count on to snap and turn out to be really ferocious and animalistic lovers, with the growling and the scratching and the biting . . . but then on the other hand there's a real self-hating streak there and I could easily see her being totally submissive and asking her lover to hurt her, you know, like the basket cases who hook up with Kevin Love. Carver's account reconciled the two scenarios nicely."

"But that's ridiculous," I said. "This was a *first date*. This was Echo's very first date ever. Come on, she's only sixteen. We're talking kiss-on-the-cheek territory here. Trying to identify which stripe of sadomasochism suits her best is like trying to figure out which brand of chardonnay to put in a toddler's baby bottle."

"I don't see any reason to make a virtue out of immaturity," Hayley said. "She's more than old enough to have had a few flings by now. When I was sixteen—"

"When you were sixteen is totally irrelevant," I said. "People are different. Echo wasn't getting it on with boys when she was twelve. You weren't doing calculus. If you can get on Echo's case for being 'immature' then she can get on yours for being stupid. Echo wasn't club-hopping when she was thirteen. You weren't dealing with the deaths of both your parents. If you can get on Echo's case for being 'sheltered' from your oh-so-sophisticated lifestyle then she can get on yours for being sheltered from any kind of real hardship. That doesn't make either of you better and it doesn't make either of you worse. So let's can the condescension, okay?"

"It's all just talk anyway," Holdn said.

"What's that supposed to mean?" Hayley said.

"It means you're the last person to talk about having 'flings,'" Holdn said. "You talk like you're a chapter in *Cap'n Groovy's Voices of the Sexual Revolution* but you don't have 'flings'—you don't even let people within five hundred yards. It's overcompensation is what it is. Jethro's got you acting like a fifties housewife so you talk like you're turning your bedposts into doilies. Kinda pathetic if you ask me."

"I didn't," Hayley said. "And being in a relationship doesn't mean I couldn't have flings if I wanted to. Jefferson and I are mature enough to know the difference between sex and commitment. Three months from now we'll be living together. No reason we shouldn't have some fun in the meantime. I just haven't found anyone in Orange County I have the slightest interest in spending a night with."

I didn't really have much more interest in listening to this conversation. I went next door to Benito's room and listened to some of the vague people talk about scrunchies.

When I got home I found Echo still in bed, still staring blankly at the wall; I saw no evidence that she had moved an inch the entire time I'd been at school.

I knocked on Molly's door. "Who is it?" she asked.

"Me," I said. The door lock clicked open and I went in. "So, uh, have you given any thought to this Echo thing?"

"Some," she said. "I've been meaning to talk to her but the door's been closed and she hasn't answered when I've knocked."

"That's because she's been catatonic for the last forty hours," I said.

Molly blinked. "What?" she said.

J'accuz

"Echo?" Molly said. "Echo? Can you hear me?" She stroked Echo's cheek. Echo just blinked at the wall. Molly bit her lip. "What happened?" she asked. "Why is she like this?"

"I don't know," I said. "I'm betting it has to do with Fringie." I briefly recapped the story for her. "So I drove her home, and at first she seemed okay—she talked to me and everything—but then she didn't get up the next morning. Or the morning after that."

Molly nodded. She stepped out into the hall and beckoned me to follow. "Okay, I have a plan," she said. "First, we need to set up a place for her that isn't depressing."

"Sunny Acapulco?" I suggested.

"I was thinking about my room," Molly said. "I'll dress it up a little."

"You're not exactly the first person I'd pick to dress anything," I said. "But sure, go for it."

It didn't take long. I hadn't even finished my homework before Molly sauntered back in. "Okay, take a look and see what you think," she said.

I went next door. It didn't look much different from the way her room usually looked. I suppose it was a bit tidier. Also, the curtains and windows were open, but despite the light streaming into the room, every single one of Molly's 1,369 halogen lamps was pumped up to maximum intensity. With the high-gloss walls, it was like standing inside a lightbulb. "Step one to fighting depression," Molly explained. "Turn the room into a sunlamp. So much of mood is a matter of light intake. Every little bit helps."

I saw that she'd affixed some sort of gauzy material along the top of the window screens. "Are those . . . fabric softener sheets?" I asked.

"The box says they're 'outdoor fresh,'" Molly said. "Which is good because the actual outdoors is more like smog and asphalt fresh."

It was then that I noticed the music. "Heh," I said. "I'd've thought you'd be the last person to go for ocean sounds."

"Oh, I'm just having my computer run though some ambient background sounds," Molly said. "I thought it'd be more pleasant than silence."

I nodded. "Okay, so you've turned your room into a big Skinner box," I said. "Now what?"

"Is Bobbo home?" Molly asked.

"Not yet," I said. "Why?"

"Because that means we can use the bathtub in the master bedroom," Molly said. "If Echo really did go from dancing to climbing rainy hillsides and then straight to bed for two days, it's safe to assume she's probably fairly rank by this point. Which isn't good for anyone. You can't help feeling miserable if you're not clean. And if she isn't cleaned up before we move her into my room then I'll be the one who's miserable."

"Okay, but why Bobbo's tub?" I asked. "What's wrong with ours?"

"Ours is right up against the wall," Molly said. "Makes it awkward to get at her left side. Besides, it'd be a whole lot easier for me to just get in with her, and Bobbo's is the only one that's big enough. Maybe I can even figure out how to turn on the Jacuzzi part. Anyway, I need your help getting her down the hall. Let's get this done before Bobbo gets back."

"Fair enough," I said. We went back into my room where Echo lay staring at the wall. "Hey, kid," I said. "Bath time. I don't suppose you feel like waking up, hmm?" I waited. "Okay, that's what I figured," I said. I turned to Molly. "Er, how do we do this?" I asked.

"I was just trying to figure that out," Molly said. "I guess we just drape her arms over our shoulders and walk her over—"

"Like she's taken a couple bottles of sleeping pills and has to keep moving till the paramedics arrive?" I said. "Okay, I can dig that." I grabbed her right arm and wrapped it around my neck; Molly did the same with her left arm and we lifted Echo to her feet. "Urgh," I said. "What did they serve at that prom dinner? Do hunks of steel count as a food group?"

"Iron helps us play," Molly said. "Come on, she's not *that* heavy."

With some difficulty we managed to half-walk, half-drag Echo to Bobbo's room; the adjoining master bathroom was dominated by the home spa that Bobbo had had installed shortly after he'd moved in. It even had a little ledge for people to sit on. I started to maneuver Echo inside but Molly stopped me. "Wait," she said. "Forgetting something? It's kind of hard to bathe her with her dress on."

"Right," I said. "Okay, have fun. Let me know when you're done and—"

"Wait," Molly said. "If she doesn't cooperate, I won't be able to get this dress off her unless I cut her out of it."

"I'll get some scissors," I said.

"Don't be silly," Molly said. "How are you going to help me bathe her if you can't even help me undress her?"

"Say what?" I said. "When did I sign up for that? I'm not going to *bathe* her."

"Why not?" Molly said. "I seem to recall that you used to bathe *together*."

"Not since we were six," I said.

"I really don't see why you're so hung up about this," Molly said. "You've never seemed to freak out about *me*."

"That's different," I said. "I'm used to you. And, I mean, look at her and then look at you. Echo's a chick now. You're still basically a kid."

Molly rolled her eyes. "Okay, let's put that to the test," she said. She set Echo down on Bobbo's bed and went over to his dresser.

"What are you doing?" I asked.

"Giving you every advantage I can," she said. She pulled a T-shirt and a pair of shorts out of Bobbo's dresser and pulled them on; then she walked out the door and reappeared a moment later with her hair tucked up under one of Echo's old baseball caps. "Okay," she said. "Now not only am I dressed, I'm wearing boy clothes. So look at me. Don't just glance at me and say, 'Oh, that's Molly, I know what Molly looks like' and see what you expect to see. Actually look at me. Is there anyone in the world who wouldn't be able to tell I'm female? Ain't I a chick?"

I had a good look at Molly. And, of course, she was right. Echo and Jerem and I had always had fairly unisex features, at least as kids, but just as Krieg had looked like a boy—or at least some sort of male beast—from day one, Molly had always looked like a girl. She never would've been able to pass for a boy the way Echo had, and though I'd filtered out the evidence for months, she now had the figure to go along with the face. "Okay, I give," I said.

"So there you go," she said. "It's more than a little insulting for you to treat me like some kind of mythical sexless creature just to be able to deal with me as a person, like the fact that I have a gig disqualifies me from the human race or something. And the same goes for Echo. So the fact that she's female is more pronounced than it was when she was six. So what? What does that have to do with anything? You're acting like that makes her radioactive or something. You're twins. You should be more comfortable around her than anyone. Now be mature and help me take her dress off."

The phone rang. "Um, I'll get that," I said. I picked up the phone on Bobbo's night table. "Hello?" I said. I looked up at Molly. "It's for me," I said. "You should probably get started." I fled downstairs. Only once I reached the bottom of the staircase did I register that the person on the other end of the phone hadn't stopped talking: "—attendance office. Our records indicate that Madeleine Eve Mockery missed one or more periods of class today. Unexcused absences can lead to disciplinary action. Beep!"

"Ah, yes, 'beep,'" I said. "How true that is." The attendance computer replied to my rapier wit by hanging up.

I flipped through the TV channels a few times and then heated up a couple frozen tamales. I was halfway through wolfing down the second one when the phone rang again. "Hello?" I said.

"Is Molly there?" asked the voice on the other end.

"Molly?" I said. I couldn't recall having ever received a call for Molly before. "Sure, I guess," I said. "Who's calling?"

"This is Rachel," said the voice.

"Rachel Monihan?" I said. "Hunh. Okay, hang on."

I went upstairs and stood at the threshold of Bobbo's room. "Molly, phone," I said. "It's Rachel. Should I have her call back, or—"

"No, I need to take this," Molly said.

"So take it," I said.

"Can you come in?" Molly said. I took a couple steps into the room. Molly hopped out of the tub and dried herself off. "Look, you don't have to get in, or even help," she said. "Just make sure she doesn't drown while I'm on the phone. If you want to wash her hair that's what I was about to do next. The shower head's already hooked up to the faucet."

Molly headed off to her room to take the call and I went into the master bathroom to watch over Echo. If she was bothered by me seeing her naked she didn't show it; she just sat in the bathtub staring at nothing. "Uh, hi there," I said. "How's it going?"

Echo blinked. "Glad to hear it," I said. I waited for Molly to come back. Minutes passed. I dipped my fingers in the water. It was tepid at best. "Hrm," I said. "Okay, I suppose we'd better get this finished before it starts getting chilly. Close your eyes if you don't want to get shampoo in them."

To my surprise, Echo shut her eyes. "Hey!" I said. "If you can—" I stopped. "Okay, no pressure," I said. "If you want to, you know, talk or something, feel free." She didn't say anything. I set to washing her hair.

I'd just finished rinsing the conditioner out of her hair when Molly returned. "Good," she said approvingly. She hopped back in the tub. "Yipes, it's getting cold," she said. She turned the hot water back on and I went to go finish my homework. "Don't go too far away," Molly said. "We still have to take her back to my room."

So twenty minutes later I returned to find the tub empty and Molly drying Echo off. "Want me to get her a bathrobe or something?" I asked.

"Why?" Molly asked. "There's nothing wrong with the way she is now. Well, her hair could stand to be combed. We can take care of that once she's in my room."

"So I take it your plan is to treat her like she's you?" I said. "I think the general idea should be to treat Echo to what would make *her* comfortable, not what would make *you* comfortable."

"That sounds reasonable," Molly said. "The problem is that you're suggesting that we return Echo to her usual routine, which made her not comfortable but miserable. Trust me, I know what I'm doing. Let's get her settled."

So a couple minutes later Echo was back in bed, only this time it was Molly's bed and instead of staring at the wall she was staring at the ceiling. And of course she was no longer wearing her prom dress. For the first time I really looked at her. I had to admit that Molly had had a point: Echo and I *had* bathed together until we were six, and though adolescence had wrought its predictable changes, to a great extent the six-year-old Echo, the one whose body I knew almost as well as my own, was still present in the sixteen-year-old version. And the reverse was also true: as Molly fluffed up her pillows for Echo, I looked at the age-progression portrait of Molly at thirty tacked to the wall and had to admit that I saw hints of her future self in Molly at thirteen. I'd always sort of thought of the five of us as just a passel of kids, but suddenly I couldn't help envisioning us as the women and men we would eventually become. Jerem, long-haired, bespectacled and pale, locked up in the basement of a university computer lab, completely unaware that it was two-thirty in the morning; Krieg lifting weights in prison; Molly, bandana around her head, naked body spattered with paint, glancing over from her canvas to her daughter in her crib—I couldn't decide whether it was a studio apartment, or a room in a house she shared with a dozen of her friends from college, but always she had a baby, always a daughter, and always hers alone, even in the scenario with eight men in the house. And Echo . . . Echo, thirty, and somehow broken, still virtually catatonic, still living with me for lack of anywhere else to go. I shuddered.

"What?" Molly said.

"Nothing," I said. "Just saw a ghost."

A matter of convenient spacing

Afternoon turned to evening turned to dusk turned to night. I checked in on Echo to find Molly gently stroking her left side. "Hey, what's all this?" I asked.

"The centerpiece of the plan," Molly said.

"Which is?" I asked.

"Touch therapy," Molly said. "Have you ever seen an infant on life support?"

"Not personally," I said.

"Well, they used to stick premature and sick babies into incubators and wait for them to get better," Molly said. "Some did. A lot didn't. Until finally someone pointed out that for babies to thrive, they need to be touched. Nothing stunts the will to live more than the lack of physical contact. Once hospitals started programs of stroking and massaging infants on life support, survival rates skyrocketed. And that goes for healthy babies too. And toddlers. And kids. And everyone. People need to be touched or they get sick. It's as simple as that."

"But Echo always demanded *not* to be touched," I said.

"So she was self-destructive," Molly said. "That's not exactly news. But that's going to change. Until she wakes up, not a moment is going to pass that Echo isn't touched. She is going to be touched, constantly and all over. Until she's up and about again."

"All over?" I said.

"That's right," Molly said. "Every last square inch. Being so alienated from her own body is probably a big part of the reason she seems to have fled it. But this is Echo right here on this bed and every single bit of her is deserving of love."

"And the way to show her we love her is to molest her?" I asked.

"It's not molestation!" Molly said. "Molestation is about exploitation. It's about touching someone for your own pleasure and not caring about its effect on the other person. Touch therapy is the opposite. It's all about its effect on the other person. People are just so paranoid about touch these days that everyone just assumes it's automatically destructive when it's actually one of the greatest forces for healing that we have."

"Hrm," I said. "All right, I'm going to bed."

"Okay, cool," Molly said. "Hop in."

"Er, what?" I said.

"Part three of the plan," Molly said. "We all sleep together. My bed's big enough for all five of us."

"You can't be serious," I said.

"Why not?" Molly said. "It's only been in the last hundred years or so that people have got it into their heads to lock their babies away in cribs and exile their children to empty beds in a dark room far away from everyone. The psychological damage is enormous. It's *unnatural* to sleep alone."

"Have you been eating crystals again?" I asked.

"Come on, I need you to take over so I can ask Krieg and Jerem," Molly said.

"Take over?" I said.

"Constant contact, remember?" Molly said. "You don't have to actually massage her if you don't want to, but you do have to touch her. Even just holding her hand is fine. But she is not to be left untouched for a second." She took Echo's hand, placed it between both of mine, and headed across the hall.

"So," I said to Echo. "Are you having fun yet?"

Echo blinked at me. "That's nice," I said. "You know, if all you wanted was for us to start taking care of you, the traditional method is to turn into a beetle." I was sitting at the edge of the bed; it occurred to me that since there was no question I was going to cave in to Molly's plan eventually, I might as well save myself some time and cave now, so I climbed in between Echo and the far wall. Molly returned a moment later with Jerem in tow. "What, no Krieg?" I asked. "And here I thought he'd jump at the chance to try smothering you to death again."

"He said he wasn't interested," Molly shrugged.

"Actually, he said, 'Suck my cock, you cocksucking bitch,'" Jerem said.

"Hmm," I said. "Would that count as 'touch therapy'?"

"I doubt I could get him to agree to the bath first," Molly said. She hopped into bed and snuggled up next to Echo. Jerem set to work ripping Molly's computer out of the wall and hooking his own up in its place. He turned it on, started downloading something, undressed, and climbed into bed.

"What, you too?" I said.

"It's hot in here," Jerem said.

"Eighty-four degrees," Molly said. She reached over Jerem, took the remote control off the night table, and clicked off the light.

The next morning I was woken up by the sound of my alarm going off. I reached over to turn it off but ended up smacking Echo in the shoulder instead. "Uh, sorry," I said. I rubbed my eyes and realized the alarm was in the next room—my room. I climbed over my sleeping siblings, stumbled into my room—which, compared to Molly's, might as well have been a meat locker—and shut off the alarm. It felt very lonely getting ready for school without Echo downstairs reading the newspaper. A minute before I left I poked my head into Molly's room. Molly had migrated over to my spot so Echo was between her and Jerem instead of her and the wall. "Are you staying home from school?" I asked.

"Of course," Molly said sleepily. "This is way more important. I'm weeks ahead in all my classes anyway."

"Okay," I said. "Have a good day. I'll be back after peer counseling."

"'Bye," Molly murmured.

At school I couldn't help but wonder whether I should've stayed behind myself. I was pretty sure that Echo was *aware* of external stimuli; she just wasn't responding to it. Meaning that she knew I'd bailed out on her in favor of inconsequential things like advanced placement tests and *Iliad* layout. Once September and I had finished off our last case of the day I hurried home to find Molly's room much as I had left it: Jerem and Molly and Echo all still in bed, Jerem typing away on his computer, Molly sitting up feeding Echo some tomato soup. "How's our little naturist community this fine afternoon?" I asked. "Hey, how'd you get her to start eating?"

"Just a little trick from home ec class," Molly said. "Rubbing stubborn babies behind the earlobe can get them to swallow. I figured it was worth a shot."

"Great!" I said. "But, uh . . . if she's eating now, then—"

"I'm taking care of it," Molly said. "So are you just going to stand there or are you going to cuddle?"

"Well, I can do the cuddling thing for a bit," I said. I put down my backpack and got under the covers. "But I have an AP test tomorrow that I really should study for at some point."

"Too bad there's no AP Cuddling," Molly said. "You could do both at once."

"I think that kind of remark has been proven to cause cancer in laboratory animals," I said.

"Tell him about the dress," Jerem said to his computer screen.

"Oh, right," Molly said. "I asked Jerem to go hang up Echo's prom dress. I assumed he knew I meant to put it in with the dry cleaning, but he just stuck it in the closet instead."

"Wow, that *is* a good story," I said. "You should send that to 'Life in These United States.'"

"It wasn't meant to be a comedic masterpiece," Molly said. "Have you looked in your closet lately?"

"Sure," I said. "I don't really use it, though. Echo's got some of her old jerseys in there."

"Maybe you should have another look," Molly said.

"Okay," I said. I went back to my room and pushed back the sliding door. There were a bunch of clothes draped over plastic hangers. At the front was Echo's old Angels jersey, with her Kings jersey behind it. Behind that were just a bunch of black sweatshirts. I checked in with Molly. "I still don't see anything all that remarkable," I said.

"Keep looking," Molly said.

I shrugged and headed back for another look. After a couple more black sweatshirts, I finally reached the prom dress, wrinkled and stained from the trials it'd been through. Then I slid it out of the way. Behind it was another dress.

This one was white. It wasn't quite as daring as the black one: this one had a back, and sleeves (short ones, granted), and the hemline was just a smidgen above knee length; it was also looser, more summery than the one she'd chosen to wear to prom. I had no idea where she'd gotten it. I'd certainly never seen her wear it.

Behind that dress was another black dress, this one with long sleeves and an ankle-length skirt.

Behind that was a blue one.

Then another white one.

From there I didn't bother looking at them. I let my fingers do the walking to the back of the closet. There were a dozen more.

I went back to Molly's room. "Why does Echo have seventeen dresses?" I asked.

"We were wondering the same thing," Molly said.

I pondered this as I lay in bed that night. My first thought was that they'd probably been Mom's. But I thought back on every outfit I'd ever seen her wear, and I couldn't remember seeing her in a single one of the dresses in Echo's closet.

And me—I was wearing a T-shirt and boxer shorts. It was what I'd worn to bed from the time I was a little kid. And for my room, it was a perfectly sensible ensemble. But Echo and I didn't keep our room at eighty-four degrees and then climb under a thick comforter with a bunch of other people. Echo, Molly, Jerem . . . they were all sleeping au naturel. And they were, in fact, sleeping. Even Echo had her eyes closed.

I figured it was worth a shot.

And in the end I had to admit that once again, Molly was on to something. It didn't solve the heat problem right away—if anything, it felt even hotter—but it was still something like a hundred and fifty thousand times more comfortable her way. I could roll over in my sleep without my shirt giving me friction burns or attempting to strangle me.

The windows were still open, and though it was night, Echo's face was outlined by the blue light of the stars and streetlamps. At that moment my sister's profile seemed like the most beautiful apparition I'd ever seen. I was so overcome with love for her that I felt like I needed to jam my fist through my own rib cage and wring out my heart to keep it from rupturing. I wanted her life to be perfect, nothing but joy from that moment on. Molly had her arm draped across Echo's chest, her hand up against my shoulder; I mirrored her, held Echo close, tried to channel the warmth I was feeling into her, vanquish whatever it was that had chilled her till she froze. And it didn't feel sexual at all, and it didn't feel odd or uncomfortable or wrong. Quite the opposite. It felt familiar. Like I'd told Siren: Echo and I had shared quarters a lot closer than these for nine months. This may not have meant anything practically speaking, but it was fun to say. And while I certainly couldn't attest to any prenatal memories, neither could I swear they weren't bobbing there just below the surface of my consciousness.

So I switched my consciousness off and went to sleep.

Hooray for Mollyworld

When I was seven I opened my sock drawer one morning to discover that, to my horror, the laundry hadn't been done and I was left with one pair of underpants. It had been my favorite pair when I was five. How could it not have been? It had little rocket ships all over it.

Of course, at age seven, I would never have been able to live it down if anyone had discovered what I had on under my shorts that day. The potential for humiliation was staggering. The entire time I was at school I felt like I was carrying some deep, intense secret around with me. It lent the entire day a sort of surreal focus. Everything was brighter, crisper— too bright, too crisp, like wearing a pair of glasses with too strong a prescription. And now, nine years later, I felt that same intensity once again. Over the course of that week, school morphed before my eyes into something impossibly absurd. Conjugating *ser* and *estar*, mocking Zab's periodontal care, signing red tickets for girls with "bare skin on torso area" . . . it was hard to believe it was even real, let alone important— not with the secret of this parallel universe I was carrying around inside me, this bubble of null-time where we spent hours—or seconds, it was hard to tell—with one concern alone: slathering Echo with affection. A bright, shining, warm, sweet-smelling bubble with the sound of the ocean quietly churning and crashing in the background, where bare skin on every area was the order of the day and pretty much anything we had to say could be communicated by touch. This had been my problem at the start. I hadn't realized that in Molly's room, the laws of physics were different.

I got home from school, went to the kitchen, had a glass of apple juice, set my books down in the TV room, watched a few minutes of the local news, switched off the TV, went upstairs, and stepped through Molly's door into a different dimension.

"Allen!" Molly said.

"Hi!" I said. Echo's hair was glistening and wet. "Aw, you gave her her bath and I wasn't invited?"

"We didn't know when you'd be home," Molly said. She giggled. "If you want, we can do it again."

"Oh, that's okay, I guess," I said. I climbed over the three of them into my usual place in bed, shielding Echo from the wall. I tapped her on the shoulder. "Hey, you," I said. She blinked. I took her in both arms and held her tight for a couple minutes, stroking her back, stroking her hair, whispering baby talk into her ear. Molly fluffed up her pillows again. I propped Echo up among them and kissed her on the cheek, put my head against her chest and listened to her heart beat. "Hey to you too," I said to Molly.

"Hey," she said. "Do I get a kiss?"

"You bet," I said. She leaned over Echo and I gave her a peck on the cheek. Then she looked at me for a long moment and there was a little jump in time like an old record player skipping and before I had a chance to really register what was happening we were kissing for real. Not erotically, not passionately, but a kiss. It lasted a few seconds, and not for a moment was I tempted to break away. It seemed like exactly what we should be doing. She was Molly. I loved Molly. When you love people, you kiss them. The logic in this was perfect, exquisite, and absolute.

Molly sighed and we went back to cradling Echo between us. "We have a perfect family," Molly murmured.

Jerem was still typing away on his computer, his feet tangled up with the rest of ours but his mind on other things. "What're you up to?" I asked.

"Just a project I've been working on," he said.

There was a knock at the garage door. We listened to the echoes die down as they bounced around the house. "Someone should get that," I said.

"Maybe they'll go away," Molly said.

"Or just come in and steal all our stuff," Jerem said. "The door is unlocked, you know."

Another knock. "Right," I said. "I'll go get it." I got out of bed and dressed again and went downstairs into the cold.

I opened the garage door. It was Hayley. "Oh!" I said. "Uh, hi."

"Hi," she said. "Is Echo home? I know she's been sick, but I thought I'd at least drop by and say hi."

"That's sweet," I said. "I don't know if she's ready for visitors yet, though. Wait here, I'll check. Can I get you anything? Apple juice?"

"That's okay," Hayley said.

"I'll be right back," I said.

"Are you okay?" Hayley asked. "You're giving off kind of a weird vibe. You're not on squeak, are you?"

"What?" I said. "Of course not. Deeg city here. I'll be back in a second."

I went upstairs. "*¿Quien es?*" Molly asked.

"It's Hayley Kerensky," I said. "Hey, Eck, want to see Hayley?"

Echo blinked. "Is that a 'yes' blink or an 'I don't want my corneas to get scarred' blink?" I asked. Echo didn't answer. "What do you think?" I asked Molly. "She doesn't know about Echo's . . . condition. She just thinks she's sick."

"Well, how do you think she'd react?" Molly asked. "Not just to the sickness, but the treatment. I'm not about to mock up a traditional sickbed on a moment's notice."

"No idea," I said. "For all I know, she could be into it. I mean really into it—wanting to sleep over, even. Though probably not with me here."

"Well, you know her better than I do," Molly said. She kissed Echo on the neck. "It's your call."

I went back downstairs. "Sorry," I said. "I don't think it'd be a good idea. But Echo does know you visited, and it means a lot."

"Uh-huh," Hayley said. "What's she got, anyway? Is it contagious?"

"Contagious?" I said. "You might say that. Something around here certainly is."

Deus ex shoebox

That was Wednesday. On Thursday I came home and went to Molly's room to find her quietly dozing, curled up like a cat, her head in Echo's lap. She blinked sleepily as I came in. "Hi," she said.

"Hi," I said. I kissed her but her kiss back was perfunctory at best. "What's up?" I asked.

"What really happened?" Molly asked.

"Hmm?" I said.

"To make Echo like this," she said. "You left out part."

"I did?" I said. "I told you everything I know. Echo told Hayley that she was interested in that Fringie guy who used to live across the street. He asked her to prom for no discernible reason, and we argued about whether she should go. She said Fringie was one of the shining lights of Western civilization; I pointed out that he'd tried to rape Peggy Kaylin a matter of weeks earlier. So when after the dance he took her to some convenient scenic overlook and started pawing at her, Echo knew what was coming next and so bit his tongue when he stuck it in her mouth. She got out of the car, found a phone, called me, and I picked her up. Having invested herself in defending Fringie only to have him turn on her in dramatic fashion, she got all depressed. What am I leaving out?"

"How did you find out what happened?" Molly asked.

"She told me," I said.

"On the car ride home?" Molly asked.

"No, she was pretty quiet," I said. "It was later that night. She asked if she could sl—oh. Oops."

"What?" Molly asked.

"Well, she asked if she could sleep in my bed, like when we were kids and she had terrible nightmares all the time," I said. "And she told me what'd happened, and I went to sleep, and then I got woken up by her kissing me a little, and I, uh, kicked her out of bed."

"So the person who turned on her last wasn't Carver Fringie," Molly said. "It was you."

"Well, I didn't know!" I said, my face turning hot. "*Now* I know it was perfectly innocent. But at the time it seemed kind of creepy. I mean, for all I knew, she wanted to get it on."

"What if she did?" Molly asked. "What's wrong with that? Isn't that a perfectly reasonable thing for a healthy sixteen-year-old to want?"

"But I'm her brother," I said.

"So much the better," Molly said. "You'd rather she get asked out by someone she's seen at school a couple times and then after *maybe* a conversation or two start making out with *him*? That's better than someone she loves and trusts and knows inside and out and grew up with? Of course, the best thing would be for kids to be raised communally—that way we'd all have a pool of people we were intimate with from birth . . . but since we're stuck with families, that leaves us with siblings. Not to marry or have kids with, obviously, but to practice with? Why not?"

"But that's—I mean, that's perverse," I said.

"Why?" Molly said. "See, the fact that that reaction is so automatic is a sign that you shouldn't trust it. That it's not coming from any kind of considered or reasoned position but that you're just parroting back something you've uncritically *absorbed*. If you'd said that you and

Echo aren't very close, or that it'd be exploitative, or that in the long term it'd ruin your relationship, or something like that, and you had something to back it up with, then sure, tell her it's a bad idea. But to just flip out and kick her out of bed for daring to be so bold as to kiss you after you rescued her? That's just cruel. And the fact that you *didn't* think about it, that it tripped a little switch in your head and you responded like a robot, just makes it worse. And you're so *lucky!* You and Echo—you're well matched. Your strengths, your weaknesses, your experiences—they're not identical, but they complement each other. Sure, maybe it's a bit late. Maybe you each should've hit this stage when you were ten and moved on to other people by now. But I guess that's to be expected in a culture like this, one that stunts your growth. You and Echo together . . . I think it'd be great if you were to try it out just once or twice. I think it'd be beautiful. In fact, a lot of the time that's what I think about when I mastur—"

"Whoa!" I said. "Okay, see, that's just way too much information. Yeesh. That's more information than the Library of Congress."

"Well, you could use some information," Molly said. "In fact, I know some information you could use right now. Jerem, go get the box."

Jerem slipped out of bed and ambled out of the room. "The box?" I said. "That sounds suitably ominous."

"Jerem was up in the attic earlier today and he found this shoebox hidden under one of the air-conditioning ducts," Molly said.

"What was he doing up in the attic?" I asked. "You're not planning on pulling a Jane Eyre on Echo, are you?"

"On himself," Molly said. "He's thinking of moving up there. He said he couldn't go back to living with Krieg."

Jerem returned with the shoebox. "So what's in the box?" I asked.

"All kinds of stuff," Molly said. She opened it. Inside was the detritus of a bright kid's life: her Student of the Month awards, one every month for virtually her entire time at Ilium; good citizenship certificates from first grade, the long-expired Burger Despot coupons still attached; a little gold hockey player with missing feet.

"We shouldn't be looking at this," I said.

"Normally, I'd agree," Molly said. "But if we're going to help her get better we need as much information as we can get. And we don't need to read any of her letters or any kind of . . . private expression, nothing like that. Just mundane artifacts'll do the trick. Like these go club passes. Or these things." She poked around at the bottom of the box and came up with a dozen little scraps of paper.

"Movie tickets?" I said. "So?"

"Look at the times," Jerem said. "They're all late shows—"

"Makes sense," I said. "That's when she's up and alone. Better to go catch a movie than to spend all night in the garage pumping iron like she's doing ten to twenty for armed robbery."

"—and they're all children's admissions," Jerem finished.

"Oh," I said.

"Who keeps movie tickets, anyway?" Molly asked. "Sure, you might keep the ticket for a film that changed your life. Or for the one you saw on a really good first date . . ."

"So what's the point?" I said. "C'mon, I can do without the theatrics."

"Okay," Molly said. "Recognize this?"

She held out a Scam-A-Lot miniature golf scorecard. Along the top were the letters DAEKMJ. "Dad, Allen, Echo, Krieg, Molly, Jerem," I said. "Sure, I remember this game. Echo won, Krieg threw his putter at the group ahead of us . . . you know, the usual. So?"

"Now look at this one," Molly said.

The second card had scores just for A and M. "Hunh," I said. "I don't remember just the two of us ever going to play mini-golf," I said.

"Neither did I," she said. "I thought it was possible I might've been really little and just forgotten, but if you don't remember, I think that's pretty definitive. And besides, the answer's right here in front of us." She dug to the bottom of the box, produced a thin eight-by-ten photo album, and handed it to me. I flipped through it. It contained maybe half a dozen pictures of Echo. The first was from when she was about eight, the last from when she was maybe eleven. In all of them she was serious—not grim, but not smiling, just placid. "Look at the last one," Molly said.

I did. "What about it?" I said. "It's Echo sitting under a tree."

"Guess where it's from?" Molly said.

"Given the dress and the non-tropical nature of the tree, I'd guess it's from when we were in Pennsylvania," I said. "And *you* always said my extensive botanical training would go to waste."

"Flip it over and see if you're right," she said.

I pulled the photo out from behind the plastic of the album and turned it over. There was writing on the back. Though it indicated the time and place the photo was taken, the first word was all I needed to see. "Oh, duh," I said. "'Madeleine.' 'M.' Okay, I get it." I paused. "Wait, no I don't," I said. "I never went mini-golfing with just Echo either." I started to put the picture back in the album when I noticed that the pocket I'd taken it from wasn't empty. "What's this?" I asked. "A duplicate?"

"Not exactly," Molly said.

I took another look at it. The tree was the same, the pose was the same, but the person sitting under it was different. I knew who it was but I flipped the picture over anyway: the note on the back read "Susan." "Okay, this is slightly creepy," I said.

"Recognize the dress?" Molly said.

"You mean it's the *same dress*?" I said. I compared the two pictures. "Wait, no it isn't. They're both white but they're different styles. Which would tend to make sense considering that Mom's dresses wouldn't have fit Echo when she was eleven."

"But they fit now," Molly said. "Which is why even though she's not wearing this exact dress in the picture, it's hanging in her closet. Along with sixteen other dresses that Mom collected over the years but which we didn't know were hers because she didn't usually hang around the house in elegant eveningwear."

"So why did Echo take the dresses?" I asked.

"They were given to her," Molly said. "By the same person who took the pictures."

"Bugs Meany?" I said.

"Andrew Mockery," Molly said. "If you think about it, a whole bunch of stuff falls into place. Why did Echo have such an extreme reaction to Daddy's death compared to the rest of us? Because—"

"Because he was molesting her, right?" I said. "Father-daughter incest. Oh, our dark family secret finally revealed. We'll be right back with our movie of the week after these messages."

"What?" Molly said. "I mean, I suppose that's possible, but I really doubt it. I just figure that after Mom's death, Daddy sort of cathected onto Echo a bit overmuch. Increasingly so as she got older and started to look more like his Susan. They started going places, just the two of them . . . maybe he had her dress up and took her to departmental functions and stuff. And I'm sure Echo liked being the favorite kid. Who wouldn't? Except in Echo's case it was magnified because . . ."

Her voice trailed off. "Yes?" I said.

"Because, well, how to put this," Molly said. "Okay. We know Echo's an intellectual prodigy."

"Right," I said.

"And an athletic prodigy," she said.

"Correct," I said.

"And, as of late, an aesthetic prodigy," she said.

"Don't rub it in," I said.

"So why shouldn't she be an emotional prodigy as well?" Molly asked. "Except in this case it's more of a handicap than an asset. Haven't you noticed the way that if you show her the slightest bit of kindness she gets so overcome with gratitude that she can hardly speak? That if someone does her an injustice she gets so overcome with rage that she becomes more violent than Krieg? And sorrow . . . I mean, it took *me* months to get over Daddy getting killed. And I was maybe a tenth as close to him as Echo seems to have been. I'm not surprised she's spent the last four years crying every night."

"And when her date turns out to be a slimeball she just shuts down?" I said.

Molly shook her head. "I thought we covered this," she said. "You're blaming the wrong person. Let's look at a brief recap of Echo's life to date. When she's six years old, her mommy dies. She compensates by investing a lot of herself in her friends; they turn on her. She grows quite intimate with Daddy; he's killed. She puts herself on the line betting you that Carver Fringie is actually well-intentioned; she loses the bet. At this point, pretty much every single person she's ever risked getting close to has abandoned her in some way. Except you. And then when she's at her most vulnerable about exactly this, you kick her out of bed."

"Look, *I didn't know!*" I protested.

"Oh, I'm not blaming you," Molly said. "I think that in a way that's exactly the reaction she was trying to provoke. Think about it. In the last couple years, how has she acted toward you? Lots of arguments? Ultimatums? 'Do what I say or I'll never speak to you again'?"

"Lucky guess," I said.

"Not really," Molly said. "I live in the next room and the walls are thin. How about when she finally does goad you into lashing out at her? Does she act hurt? Or . . . satisfied? Even pleased?"

"She smirks a lot," I said.

"I think Echo's been hurting for a long time," Molly said. "Enough to tempt her into suicide. But she can't do that as long as the two of you are on anything close to friendly terms. Because that'd mean she'd be abandoning you just as she was abandoned by her parents and her friends. So she figures that if she poisons your relationship, you'll be glad to see her go. But there's the catch. When she finally does lose you, it hurts even more. Hurts too much to speak or move or do anything. Which is why when she does pull out of this state, *that's* going to be the most dangerous period. She's no threat to herself like this. It's when she's up and about and has the energy to do something drastic that we have to really watch out for her."

"This is really depressing," I said.

"Why?" Molly said. "This is the way it's been for years now. The difference is that now we know the score. Or at least the sport. And we've already done a lot to remedy the situation. We've tripled the number of people she needs to alienate before she can feel free to go. And you and Jerem and I aren't going anywhere."

That night as I was drifting off to sleep I heard my name. "Hmm?" I said. "Molly . . . ?"

"Shh," Echo said. I opened my eyes. Echo was staring at me intently, her cheeks wet with tears. "Don't wake her up," she whispered.

"What?" I said. "How long have you—how—"

"I need your help," she whispered.

"Help?" I said.

"I have a plan," she said.

"Seems to run in the family," I said.

Fringie gets the chair

None of us went to school the next day. The idyllic atmosphere of the previous few days kind of evaporated with Echo no longer comatose, however. Before, she'd exuded a sort of calm and serenity, like a sleeping pet; now, as she nervously paced around the house in her old black sweats, she seemed to broadcast her anxiety to anyone who came near, and the entire house teetered on the brink of panic. "You know, we don't have to follow through with this," I said.

"Yes we do," Echo said. "Jerem's already put the note in his locker. Molly'll be back any minute with the package from Rachel."

"So?" I said. "You can still back out."

"But I don't want to," Echo said. "This is something I need to do. I'll never be able to put this mess behind me if I don't." Her face softened. "Look, I realize we're both in for some fairly extreme disciplinary action here. If *you'd* prefer to back out and save your peer-counseling job, I understand." From downstairs came the sound of the garage door slamming shut. "That's Molly," Echo said. She checked her watch. "It's almost four," she said. "I'd better get going. Are you coming?"

"I guess," I sighed.

The *Iliad* room was empty when we arrived; it being Friday afternoon, we didn't have to worry about encountering any stragglers. Echo's breathing slowed as the minutes ticked by. "So what was it like?" I asked.

"What?" Echo said.

"This week," I said. "You know, the, uh, the way you were."

"I don't really want to dwell on it," she said. "I just woke up Sunday morning, and it was dark, and still, and there was this static in my head drowning everything out, and I thought about getting out of bed, but the thought just got drowned out in the static . . . and you came and asked me questions, and I tried to answer, but I just couldn't fight through the static, I couldn't summon up the energy, I couldn't . . ."

"Hold that thought," I said. "Here he comes."

I'd had my doubts about whether Echo's plan to settle accounts with Carver Fringie was a good idea, but after she made it clear that she wasn't out to do him any lasting damage but just wanted a conversation on her terms—"sort of an ad hoc peer counseling session"—I decided that the ends justified the admittedly questionable means. Of course, this was Carver Fringie we were talking about. I could've found a way to rationalize dropping him down an elevator shaft.

The first step had been to slip a note into his locker reading, "I've been doing a lot of thinking about Saturday night. I reacted badly. In fact, I've changed my mind about the whole thing. Can you come to the *Iliad* room at four? Maybe we can work things out and pick up where we left off. Echo."

I'd been skeptical. "I dunno," I said. "Seems pretty obvious that this is bait. You can practically see the fishhook."

"That's because you don't have Carver Fringie's ego," Echo said. "If this had been one of the other water polo players, I'd expect a certain amount of suspicion. When Sluggo gropes someone, for instance, even he knows it's a fairly safe bet that she's not thrilled about it. That thought would never occur to Carver Fringie."

Fringie did seem somewhat guarded when he came in, though. I'd ducked down underneath Hank's favorite table but he seemed to sense my presence, or at least sense that he wasn't alone. He waved the note at Echo. "So is this for real?" he asked.

"Absolutely," Echo said. "Every sentence is true. I *have* been thinking about Saturday night, all week—I've hardly thought about anything else. I did react badly, as my brothers and sister can attest. And I have changed my mind about the whole thing. So can we pick up where we left off?"

Fringie's eyes narrowed. "Eventually," he said. "At some point. At present I have a full schedule."

"That's okay," Echo said. "I only need a few minutes. See, if I'd had a chance, the next thing I would've done would be this."

And with that she tagged Fringie with a faceful of pepper spray. Getting a canister of the stuff on such short notice had been the trickiest part of the plan, but I'd suggested Rachel Monihan as a potential nearby source and sure enough, she had cases of the stuff. Fringie clutched his face and reared around wildly. Echo grabbed him by the collar and yanked him down sharply into a waiting chair. It was at this point that I emerged with a roll of duct tape to secure Fringie's feet to the chair's legs. After that Echo was able to pull his hands behind the back of the chair and use the tape to improvise a pair of handcuffs fairly easily.

"You fucking bitch," Fringie whimpered.

"Oh, quiet," Echo said. "Your glasses protected you from most of it. It could've been a lot worse." Echo's own glasses glinted in the flickering light of the *Iliad* room. She hadn't worn them while she was convalescing and they suddenly looked very odd to me. "So," she said. "Maybe now you have a bit more of a sense of what it's like to be helpless."

"Oh, you can't be serious," Fringie said, face crimson and eyes blinking violently. "Let me guess—you and our old friend Pathetic Loser Guy have put together a little play for my benefit? I sit here and watch while you make like a parochial school assembly and reenact my crimes until I burst into tears at what I've wrought. Right?"

"What?" Echo said. "Don't be ridiculous. I just want to talk to you. On my terms."

"Fuck you and fuck your terms," Fringie said.

"We'll be here all night if you keep up that kind of attitude," Echo said. "The custodian's not due to arrive until five. If you cooperate, you'll be free to go by then. If not, we can stash you somewhere until he's gone. I certainly don't have any other plans for the rest of the evening."

Fringie glanced over at me, his eyes stained a deep red. "I knew this deeg thing was just an act," he said. "Scratch the surface and you're just cheap thugs with cheap threats."

"No threats," Echo said. "No one's going to get hurt. You're perfectly safe whether you talk or not. It's just a matter of how much time out of your day you plan to lose."

"Let's drop the meta shit and get on with it," Fringie said.

"Fine," Echo said. She paced around the room for a minute. "Why did you ask me to prom?" she finally asked.

Fringie yawned.

"Why?" she demanded. "What happened to you? You were sweet to me once. I put my faith in you. Why did you have to break that trust?"

"Because you wanted me to," he said. "You're female. Therefore you are a masochist."

"What?" Echo said.

"Protest all you like," Fringie said. "It's a fact. All females are masochists."

He looked back at me again. "See, people often ask me, 'Hey, Carver, how is it that you get so many chicks?' And the answer is really quite simple. Getting chicks is not difficult. Once they sense that you can hurt them, they will flock around you despite themselves. Is it genetic? Is it cultural? I really can't say. But it's a simple fact: all straight women are mentally ill. You can tell by the fact that they're attracted to the masculine. What could possibly be the appeal of masculinity? It's intrinsically repulsive. It's no accident that Eve had to be forcibly torn away from her own reflection, from the delicacy and loveliness and exquisite balance that is the female, and compelled to submit to the crude kludge that is the male. There is no beauty in masculinity. No, the masculine attracts not through allure, but through the power to hurt. The feminine knows itself to be inherently superior to the masculine, but as long as the masculine can overpower it, cause it pain, make it hurt, the feminine will submit. It's the way of the world. The feminine has the merit; the masculine has the power.

"But power alone is not sufficient, of course," Fringie continued. "Those who have the power to hurt but will do none will never prosper so long as those who would be hurt know they will do none. Females are masochists. If they don't feel they're in danger, they get bored and find someone who'll hurt them. And the best way to establish a constant state of danger is to be unknowable. To suddenly employ a vocabulary beyond their comprehension, a register with foreign cadences; to slip an unexpected cruelty into a conversation; to refuse to divulge any information of consequence about your background; that's all it takes to make yourself mysterious, unpredictable, dangerous—and hence irresistible. Of course, the threat must only register on a subconscious level, for that is where the innate masochism of the female lies. On a conscious level, she will deny—or even be unaware of—the extent to which she secretly wants to be hurt. On a conscious level, you want to encourage the delusion that she somehow knows you."

Fringie looked at Echo and me appraisingly. "This, of course," he went on, "is why you don't see siblings hooking up. It's not genetics, or you'd see adopted sibs going at it all the time. But it doesn't work that way. Studies have shown that even in nonfamilial situations—communes, kibbutzes, you name it—kids who grow up together are disgusted by the idea of sexualizing their relationships with each other. Because when you spend that amount of time together, you get to know each other too well. You see her wet the bed, catch him tossing off to some magazine . . . every humiliation you spend your life hiding is an open book. Of *course* familiarity is going to breed contempt."

"Only if you're misanthropic," I interrupted. "For some people the better you get to know them the more wonderful things you discover."

Fringie snorted. "You'd like to think that, wouldn't you?" he said. "Of course, it didn't work out in practice. See, Peggy told me about your priceless advice. You know, that she should get together with a guy she knew? Sort of self-serving on your part, hmm? Except you weren't even a factor. You weren't on her list any more than her brother was. Because you're not a guy to her. You're a clown. Because you didn't keep anything from her. Because she knows you. On the other hand, you don't know her. That's how she got you to keep after her like a puppy for all those years. By not letting you get close. You've never even seen her room, have you?"

"You don't know anything about it," I said. "We *are* close. You're the one who doesn't know her. You don't know her at all. You don't know which teeth she had to have pulled before she got her braces on. You don't know what she named the goldfish she had when she was eight. You don't know—"

"Nor do I care about such inconsequential shit," Fringie said. "I know what I care to know. I know what the inside of her mouth tastes like. I know the nipple placement on those legendary breasts. And I know what kinds of sounds she makes when she comes."

"That's a lie," I said.

"Oh, true, she put up her little show at first," Fringie said. "Happens a lot. Never lasts long. And sure enough, in a matter of days—*days*—she came crawling back. She *begged* for it. Invited me up to her secret room and lay on her bed with her legs spread wide and *begged* me to jam my gig up into hers. Probably on some unconscious level she wanted to put herself in a position where she *had* to beg for it. I'm telling you, Al—females are masochists. She more than most. Even physiologically. She bled most magnificently."

"That's a lie," I repeated lamely.

"Ah, but you see, there's no way to test that assertion," Fringie said. "Can't repeat the result. Because once that cherry's gone you can't get it back. But wait!" he said. "I know what you're thinking. You're thinking, sure, there's never any such thing as *exact* repetition. If the experiment kills the rat you've got to try a different rat the next time around 'cause the first one's a corpse. But I can tell you from personal experience that it doesn't work that way. After all, you're not going to find a closer genetic match than Kelly, but she could hardly be more different. Kelly's had 'B-E aggressive' pounded into her since well before she learned the cheer: she bites and scratches and claws. Peggy just bites her lip and tries not to cry. Kelly's a screamer. Peggy's a moaner. They're as different as Snow White and Rose Red." He nodded thoughtfully. "And as similar, too. For all their differences, they *are* sisters. And at the moment of solvency they gasp just the same."

A smirk played across Fringie's face. "Is that rage I see?" he asked me. "Moral outrage? I didn't think so. It's jealousy, of course. Because, after all, it could've been you. I didn't have any advantages over you when I started. If anything, I was a few steps behind. At least *you* were healthy to start with. And *you* had the Proud African Warrior archetype to play with—that's a level of foreignness I could never hope to achieve. But you blew it. You didn't cultivate your masculinity—hell, you went out of your way to make it clear that you were absolutely harmless. As if a female is ever going to be attracted to a benign little elflike creature. You blew it, Al. And I knew you were going to blow it. I sat on my porch and I watched the two of you playing on her front lawn, always the two of you, never inviting me—and I knew I was going to get to her first. Because I *decided* to." He looked over at Echo. "Oh, and you were there too," he said. "You wouldn't play with me either. But when I got back from Chino I noticed that you didn't exactly have guys lining up around the block to get at you. So I figured I could take my time and work on more pressing cases. Then when Hayley passed me the word that you were interested, I figured I might as well get you out of the way. And this is how prom dates come to be. Of course, after everyone got a look at you in that dress, I had to rethink my calculations, make a move before I'd had a chance to lay the groundwork. So now we have our little show, just like with Peggy. And just like with Peggy, it won't be long before you're crawling back for real. That's why you brought him along, hmm?" Fringie jerked his head in my direction. "Because him being here is the only thing that keeps you from begging me to take you right here."

Echo jumped at him and for a second I honestly thought she was going to kill him—one hand at his throat, the other poised to rip his face from his skull. "I ought to pluck out your eyes," she hissed. And for the first time, Fringie showed a twinge of fear. For Echo's nails were glistening—she'd had her fists balled up so tight during his monologue that she'd drawn blood from her own palms. But then she took a step back and shook her head. "Come on, let's go," she said.

"Shouldn't we untie him?" I asked.

"This is farcical enough already," Echo said. "Let the janitors do it."

We went home.

Nine

I wasn't sure who the phone call would come from. I figured that after Fringie complained to the administration about the little stunt Echo and I had pulled, I'd be facing the end of my career as a peer counselor and a hefty suspension besides; it was just a question of who broke the news. If they wanted to let me down easy, they'd have September call me and pass the message along. Or if they wanted to get tougher, Doctor Todd might call to order me into his office on Monday. For all I knew they might even have the police look into the situation—Ilium had already had problems with one Mockery, so for all Echo and I knew they'd been waiting for the two of us to snap for months. So Saturday afternoon when the phone rang I knew it was going to be for me. It was September. "Hey, cool," I said. "Looks like I get the golden parachute, huh?"

"What?" she said.

"Nothing," I said. "So what's up?"

"Well, you weren't here yesterday, so I just wanted to remind you that you're signed up to work that party tonight," she said. "At Greg Garner's. Remember?"

"Hmm?" I said. I thought back. "Oh, right. That's tonight?"

"Sort of," she said. "Technically, tomorrow morning. Starts at midnight."

"Terrific," I said. "Hey, I don't suppose you've heard from Doctor Todd in the past day or so?"

"Nope," she said. "Why? Should I have?"

"Just wondering," I said.

We didn't order a pizza

When I went downstairs I found muddy tracks across the foyer—it looked like someone had gone wading in butterscotch pudding and then pranced into the kitchen without washing their shoes. This didn't bother me so much as the fact that I was pretty sure I was the last person to come downstairs and yet no one else had cleaned the damn floor. I got out the mop and a few minutes later the tracks were gone, but I was pissed.

Since it was the weekend, I'd slept in, but still, when midnight rolled around, I felt much more like turning in than heading out for the evening. There had been a time, not too long before, that I still got excited about doing key patrol at parties; there was the warm and toasty feeling of knowing I was doing my bit to make the streets safer, and the prospect of maybe hitting it off with some cute designated driver . . . but now I couldn't help but feel I was kidding myself, just going through the motions of being a deeg. The main reason I kept it up wasn't because I felt I was doing anything valuable, wasn't even to keep from disappointing September: it was because every time I went to one of these things, some generous soul would insist that one beer wouldn't kill me and that the conversation they were having about the best way to get into an over-21 club was really quite fascinating and that the part where they all tried to remember who they'd slept with the previous weekend promised to be even more enthralling. If I were to give up key patrol, no one would conclude that it was because I no longer cared whether they lived or died. They'd think I'd been tempted by the allure of their little urine specimen cups. And I didn't want them to think for a second that I'd become one of them.

The music that greeted me at Greg Garner's doorstep was more than a little disconcerting: bleeps, bloops, and blorps like those I'd heard coming from Jerem's computer, overlaid with samples of what seemed to be porn stars being brought to the throes of fake ecstasy by the sound of trucks downshifting on the highway. Ringing the bell had no effect and the door was open so I stepped inside. I didn't see Greg Garner anywhere, nor anyone with a salad bowl full of keys; what I did see was that the front chamber, which I'd remembered being sunken, was now raised slightly above the hardwood of the foyer, with some people standing, others half-drunkenly lolling around on the floor. I took a step onto the raised area and felt the floor give under my feet. Because it wasn't really the floor. The room had been packed solid with mattresses.

I retreated back to the corner and watched people come in— always couples, though they didn't necessarily stick together. In fact, a quick survey of the room indicated quite the opposite: clutches of guys here and there, groups of girls other places, and more than once I saw a guy and a girl come in and head in opposite directions the moment they cleared the threshold. Which made sense, given how mismatched the couples usually were: scruffy college-age guys accompanied by girls fresh from having their eighth-grade class picture taken. Unfortunately, it was the former who gravitated toward my corner of the room and whose conversation I had to hear.

"Seen Garner?"

"No, why?"

"Need to get that ID from him—"

"Don't give it to her *now*, dumbass—she'll just leave—"

"I'm not going to *give* it to her, I just need to *show* it to her so she'll know it's for real and stay—"

"Promising her an ID's fucked up anyway—you don't get her an ID, you get her some *beer*. That way when she needs more she has to come back again. What's that saying? 'Teach someone to fish and you feed them for a lifetime, give someone a fish and they have to give you a hummer every time they want another fish'?"

I tried to maneuver away from that particular pocket of conversation but the crush of people suddenly became more intense and I found myself pinned against the wall as a dozen couples came in at once. It was the water polo players and their dates. Most of these dates were Carver Fringie's castoffs—Linda Garcia, Erika Christensen . . . I didn't know whether they'd ended up with members of Fringie's supporting cast because they simply hung out in the same circles, or if the lesser water polo players actually bid formally or informally for the rights to

Fringie's exes like hockey draft picks. It occurred to me that maybe I'd been mistaken in thinking that the water polo team was popular. Maybe they just seemed popular because Fringie's various conquests couldn't escape the gravity well.

"Where's Fringie?" someone behind me asked. No one from the team even noticed, and I don't suppose he'd been asking them anyway.

"Dunno," someone else said. "Doesn't look like he's with them. Guess he's coming later. Or maybe he's late 'cause he's coming now, huh-huh, huh-huh."

"Hey, who's the blonde?"

"Which? With Kevin Love?"

"Yeah."

"Lemme look. Oh, that's Peggy Kaylin."

I came very close to choking on my own esophagus at that one. I craned my neck to make her out in the crowd but couldn't see her through the sea of bodies. I saw Kevin Love—he was a full head taller than everyone else—but who he had with him I couldn't tell.

"Peggy Kaylin? The squeak queen?" said one of the guys behind me. "Heh. Wouldn't have recognized her with—"

"—with the peroxide? Yeah, she's been like that for a couple weeks."

"I was gonna say without come dripping down her chin."

"Oh. Huh-huh. Well, just wait till she needs more pills."

I followed Kevin Love's head into the living room, and at that point the crowd thinned out enough for me to see that he was with someone with unevenly bleached hair wearing a thick black leather jacket. I couldn't see her face, but I didn't have any reason to doubt it was Peggy. Still, I had to see. When I did catch a glimpse of her face, a twinge of pain flashed across her features and she bobbled unsteadily on her feet: not because she was curtsying to me—I doubted she'd even seen me—but because Kevin had twisted her wrist or something. I was about to go up and say something to him when I felt a hand on my shoulder. It was Greg Garner. "Excuse me, but who're you with?" he asked.

"Ilium High School peer counseling," I said. "But—"

"I mean which person," Greg Garner said. "This gathering is, shall we say, couples-only. And I certainly didn't call for any—"

Kevin Love came up behind him and whispered something in his ear. Greg smirked. "I see," he said. "Heh. It seems there's been something of a miscommunication and we won't be requiring your services this evening after all. So run along now. I assume you can show yourself out."

I tried to catch Peggy's eye before I left, but Kevin gave her wrist a jerk and dragged her into the next room. At that point all I could do was hope that the stories I'd heard about him weren't true.

There's always a catch

When I got home that night I found my room cold and empty, as was becoming usual. Echo had taken to spending her nights in Molly's room, not just for the three hours that she actually slept, but pretty much from dusk to dawn. I slept in our room by myself. I did miss our little parallel universe, but still, when it comes right down to it, when you're asleep you don't know who is or isn't in bed with you. Of course, this didn't stop me from trying the door to Molly's room when I got home from the party. It was locked.

But when I got up the next morning—okay, afternoon—Molly's door was cracked open, a rare enough event that I took it as an invitation. And sure enough, when I tentatively pushed the door open a bit more, Molly looked over at me and beckoned me inside. She was sitting at her easel drawing something—I couldn't tell what until I went inside.

It was then that I saw the subject of Molly's sketch: Echo, naked as the week before, cradling a pair of apples in her left arm and contemplating a third apple in her right hand. "She's supposed to be Atalanta," Molly explained.

"Atalanta?" I said. "Isn't that the one who got chained to a rock for being beautiful or something?"

"That's Andromeda," Molly said. "Atalanta was the one who vowed not to wed until she met a man who could beat her in a race—losers were put to death. So this guy petitions Aphrodite for help to win her, and she gives him three golden apples which he uses to distract Atalanta when he races her. Not that she was averse to being distracted, wink wink. So they get married, but they're so overcome with desire for each other that they take each other right there in the temple instead of offering thanks to Aphrodite, so she punishes them by turning them into lions. Though I never really understood how that's a punishment. Who wouldn't want to be a lion?"

"Tigers are cooler," Jerem said. He was perched on Molly's bed typing away on his computer (as if that didn't go without saying).

"That's debatable," Molly said. "Anyway, I'm not saying it's *better* to be a lion than a tiger, or a lion than a girl, just that if you do get turned into a lion there's no reason to wish you were anything else. Lions are glorious. Of course, girls are glorious too." She gestured at Echo with her piece of charcoal.

I looked at Echo. "Hey, how long have you been holding that pose?" I asked.

"About an hour," Molly said.

"Really?" I said. "Don't you think she's spent enough time frozen in place as it is?"

"I've got a camera in my room," Jerem offered. "You could snap pictures and draw them off the screen. Save time."

"It's not the same," Molly said. "I guess I could use them for preliminary sketches, though . . ."

Jerem fetched his camera from the other room and Molly hooked it up to her computer and snapped off a dozen pictures of Echo from a variety of angles. "Okay, now you," she told me.

"Say what?" I said. "Not a chance."

"Don't tell me you're embarrassed," she said. "Not after last week."

"Not exactly," I said. "But I can't follow Echo! It'd be like going from the ceiling of the Sistine Chapel to 'Dogs Playing Poker.' Maybe some other time." I went back to my room.

Eventually Echo joined me. "So how'd you get roped into mannequin duty?" I asked.

"She asked me," Echo said. "After last week I owe Molly a lot more than modeling time." She rummaged through the stack of books on our desk, selected one, hopped onto her bed, and started reading it.

"So, um, were you planning on getting dressed at some point?" I asked.

"Yesterday I went for groceries and when I got back I had no reason to get undressed," Echo said. "Today I modeled for Molly and I have no reason to get dressed. I don't have an agenda, I'm just being efficient."

She grabbed a notebook off the desk and started scribbling stuff in it. I noticed it was the one she usually kept her English notes in. "So you're going back to school tomorrow?" I asked.

"I guess," she sighed.

"You don't sound thrilled," I said. "If you want, I could probably work out a deal for you to take your finals and stuff at home—"

"No, I want to go back," she said. "I want to see Hayley, at least . . ."

Muchas smooches

I had a different reason to be eager to get back to school: I had me a theory what needed confirmin'. The first thing I did when I got to school on Monday was go to the office and have another look at the key patrol sign-up sheet. The party at Greg Garner's was right on the first page; the name in the adjoining column: "Carver Fringie." I made a note to have September's thumbs broken for not including this little tidbit of information when she'd asked me to take the assignment.

On the other hand, I felt a weight lift from my shoulders as I put the sign-up sheet away. Okay, that may be overstated. But at the very least I felt as if someone had taken the weight on my shoulders and tied a bunch of helium balloons to it. For I realized that I no longer had to worry about Fringie reporting me—that having me summoned to the sex party and orchestrating the water polo players' arrival to make sure that I caught a glimpse of Peggy there had been his revenge for the incident with the chair. We were even. Of course, five seconds later I remembered that he'd signed up weeks earlier and thus thanks to the laws of cause and effect the chair bit couldn't have had anything to do with it. The balloons popped.

When I got to the *Iliad* room I found that Echo and Hayley had already been reunited—they were talking when I walked in. "Hey, it's great to have you back," Hayley was saying. "I missed you."

"That's nice of you to say," Echo said, staring at the floor.

"Sure," Hayley said. "I mean, it's been a while—I haven't seen you since . . . since before prom, now that I think about it. From what I hear your prom dress was quite a stunner, too. Wish I'd seen it." Sluggo sniggered. "What?" Hayley asked.

"Nothing," he simpered.

"So what happened?" Hayley asked. "Allen said you got sick. Was it the dinner? I hear the prom dinner's always a regular E. coli festival."

"No . . . it wasn't the dinner . . . ," Echo said. She turned to stare at the chalkboard. "I just . . . didn't feel well . . . but thank you for visiting . . ."

"Hmm?" Hayley said.

"Allen said you visited," Echo said. "Sorry I couldn't see you . . . it means a lot . . ."

"Well, sure," Hayley said. "You sound surprised. If I were sick you'd visit me, right?"

Echo smiled, but it was the kind of smile that comes unbidden after you crack your shin on the coffee table. "You'll never get sick," she murmured.

Hayley gave Echo a curious look. "Echo, did I do something wrong?" she asked.

"What?" Echo asked.

"Well, I couldn't help noticing that you haven't looked at me the entire time we've been talking," Hayley said. "You're all twisted up in knots. Did I do something to upset you?"

"No," Echo said.

"Well, I'm having a hard time believing that," Hayley said.

Echo blinked at Hayley. She seemed to freeze for the tiniest moment—and then she grabbed her by the shoulders and kissed her. A second passed, then five; Echo didn't seem inclined to pull away.

"Whoa!" Sluggo said.

That shattered the moment. Echo drew back; horror flashed across her face, almost too quick to register; and then she was gone, the door slamming loudly behind her. I started after her, more out of habit than anything else, but by the time I stuck my head out the door to see where she'd gone, the hall was deserted. Not even Echo was that fast: she'd either evaporated into the ether or locked herself in the faculty bathroom a couple doors down. I decided it'd be kinder to leave her alone for the time being.

"That was, um, unexpected," Hayley said.

"Whoa!" Sluggo repeated.

"I would say that qualifies as not upset," Cat said.

"Hmm," Hayley said. "There's apparently been some kind of mis-understanding here. I'll talk to her." She smiled faintly. "On the other hand . . . if Jefferson could kiss like that," she said, "I never would've left Seattle."

You know where you stand

"I ruined everything," Echo said.

Echo sat disconsolate on the edge of her bed. "You didn't," I said. "Hayley'll understand."

"'Understand'?" Echo said. "'*Understand*'? You act like that's a *good* thing. That she *understands*. What she *understands* is something she was never, *ever* supposed to find out about. And now not only does she know, but she found out in the worst way *possible*. How am I supposed to go back there now?"

"Well, Min-Hsun Lee somehow managed to recover from wetting himself during the sixth-grade school play," I said.

"This is completely different," Echo said. "It'd be one thing if I'd just embarrassed myself. This is worse. Hayley was just trying to be . . . sisterly . . . and I—she's not—she'd never—"

"Running away from home?" I asked. Through the door frame I'd caught a glimpse of Jerem as he emerged from his room with a heavy backpack. I didn't let go of Echo's hand, though.

"Actually, yes," he said. "Though I'm not running. I'm taking a limo."

"What?" Molly cried. Her door flew open and she ran out into the little alcove. "You're going somewhere?"

"I'm moving out," Jerem said.

"Moving out?" I said. "I thought you were just moving to the attic."

"That was last week," he said. "Remember that project I was

working on? I was designing some new Bloodgnarl levels. And while I was at it I optimized the game engine a bit. Anyway, I sent them a copy of my work and they offered me a job."

"What?" I said.

"I guess they'd rather have me working on the sequel than taking what I learned from reverse-engineering their program and applying it to a competing product," Jerem said. "So now I can finally afford to move out of this hellhole. They've already got an apartment waiting for me in Mountain View. I probably could've just stolen the money but this is nice and legal and I don't have to worry about looking over my shoulder all the time."

"But that's—I mean, that's ridiculous," I said. "They can't give you a job. You're nine years old."

"And they're all nineteen," Jerem said. "Hacking is one area where competence is all that matters, not anything as stupid and inconsequential as age. Besides, they have no idea how old I am. They might've been a little suspicious about the fact that I wouldn't meet them in person or talk to them on the phone. But that's not really all that rare in the hacker community. And in any case, I was able to . . . compensate them for overlooking that."

"You bribed them?" I said. "With what, your inheritance money? *Our* inheritance money? Or did you just plunder some bank with an 'insecure server'?"

"Actually, I just copied those pictures of Echo off Molly's computer," Jerem said. "Once they got a look at a couple of those they would've given me a yacht."

"*What?*" I said.

Molly threw her arms around Jerem and started to cry. "How—how can you just pick up and leave?" she asked. "Why didn't you tell me?"

"Please, let's not turn this into cheap melodrama," Jerem said, wriggling loose. "My ride'll be here any minute. If for some reason you need to get in touch with me you can reach me on my cell phone. Though I don't see any reason you'd need to."

"Don't leave, Jerem," Molly said. "I love you. I l—"

"That verb doesn't mean anything," Jerem said. He looked over my shoulder through the window to see the limo pulling onto our street. "Hmm," he said. "White? I ordered black. Someone's not getting a tip." He went downstairs. Molly dashed back to her room. I heard Jerem's phone go off as he walked down the driveway.

Echo sighed. "Can I sleep with you tonight?" she asked. "I think Molly may be busy."

"Absolutely," I said.

It's a crash, crash, crash

That night I was awakened by a soft feathery sound. It was a sound far more familiar than I would've liked. I wondered who Echo was crying about tonight. Jerem? Hayley? Fringie? Dad? The length of the list of candidates was itself worth crying over. I was about to draw her close and try to comfort her when I suddenly registered what I was really hearing. I don't know what tipped me off—a slight difference in the catch in her breath, maybe—but all at once I knew that Echo wasn't crying. She was up to something far different. Apparently at least one element in Molly's case for sticking around had been convincing. To tell you the truth, it was quite cheering: for once, Echo's sighs signaled something good. They meant she was embracing life even in the face of all these crises. I couldn't help but wonder who she was dreaming of as her fingertips worked their magic. It occurred to me that the list of candidates hadn't changed much with the difference in the question.

Naturally, when I got up the next morning I didn't tell Echo what I'd heard. I did ask if she was planning on going to school and she just shrugged. I decided to see what Molly had to say about the matter—as far as I knew, she hadn't even heard about the kiss—but when I went next door to her room, I found her with her eyes all red and her face somehow puffy and drawn all at once. "Are you okay?" I asked. "You look awful."

"I was on the phone with Jerem all night," she said. "Or I tried to be—he kept hanging up." She shook her head. "How could he just leave?"

"He's an ass," I said. "I think he proved that fairly definitively yesterday. Forget about it."

"But I love him," she said.

"Why?" I asked. "He doesn't love us. Yesterday you told him you loved him and he treated you like something he was scraping off his shoe. The whole time you and I were trying to help Echo get better he was trying to figure out the best way to translate her into Internet porn."

"But he's my brother," she said. "There's only one person in the entire world that I'm a big sister to, and it's him. That's all that counts." She sighed. "What happened?" she asked. "I mean, it may never have been paradise around here but at least things were stable. Now it's all collapsing. And I don't even remember what started it . . ."

I kissed her on the forehead. "I'm betting on the Big Bang," I said. "Okay, school awaits. See you later."

It was a blisteringly bright morning: for some reason the summer sun is always fifty times harsher at seven in the morning than it is at seven at night, even though the light is coming at more or less the same angle. Echo winced the moment we stepped out the door. "Looks like when you decided to come to school after all you hadn't factored the weather into the equation," I said as we strolled into the wheel. "Let's see. Con: charred retinas. Pro: at least it's not raining."

"Whatever," she said.

Suddenly I bumped into Echo—she'd stopped in her tracks and was staring at her locker. I looked up. Emblazoned across it in bright red spray paint was the word "DYKE."

"Okay, I think it's safe to count this as a 'con,'" I said.

I thought Echo would be upset. Instead, she calmly walked up to her locker, carefully dialed her combination, and opened it up.

Then she ripped the door off its hinges and bent the flimsy metal in half between her hands.

"Eep," I said.

Echo tossed the remains of the door over her shoulder. Then she started grabbing the books in the cubbyhole that had once been her locker and stuffing them into her backpack. She got about two-thirds of the way through before giving up and sinking to the ground.

"I can't deal with this anymore," she said. She held her head in her hands. "I can't—I don't—I can't cope with this." She sighed. "I can't . . ."

"Okay," I said. "Here's what we're going to do. First, you're going home. But don't just sit around all day. Go to the beach or something. Or pick up Molly after school and go with her. I'll talk to Doctor Todd or someone and get you on an independent study program. You can take all your finals and you'll be done with school for the year."

"You mean home schooling?" Echo asked. "Daddy asked about that after the hockey playoffs. The school psychologist said I needed to stay in school for the social skills or I'd never learn how to relate to people in the real world . . ."

"Okay, one, they're idiots," I said. "First of all, school is nothing like the real world. It's the most maladaptive environment you could come up with. And two, you're not ten anymore, you're sixteen. You're better off just getting on with your life anyway. Get your equivalency this summer and spend a year or two doing something. I'm sure Professor Katie or Professor Danny would take you on as a research assistant or something if you wanted to do that, or you could volunteer for the city, or look for something outdoorsy—I mean, there are a million things you could do that'd be better for you at this point than school. I don't know why I didn't think of this till just now. How does that sound?"

"The going home part sounds good," Echo said.

We got back home just as Molly was heading into the bathroom to wash up for school. "You're back!" she said. "What's going on?"

Echo climbed back into bed and pulled the covers over her head. I hopped up onto the bathroom counter and told Molly all about the kiss and its aftermath while she showered. "It had to be Sluggo," I said. "Maybe he wasn't responsible for the spray paint, but he told whoever was. Maybe it was the water polo players, but I'm actually betting on Echo's old hockey teammates. I'm just trying to figure out what came over her."

"It was bound to happen," Molly said. "I've heard her talk about Hayley—she's probably wanted to do that for weeks now. The only thing that stopped her was her protective ice coating, and once some of that got melted away, she didn't have any other means of dealing with that feeling. She just has to learn how to channel her impulses in a productive way instead of acting on them without thinking or quashing them altogether." There was a squeaking sound as she turned off the water. "Maybe I should stay home again," she said.

"Though I did get a note about all the school I missed last week . . ."

"I think she'll be okay," I said. "I just hope she does something fun instead of lying around here feeling depressed." I went back into our room. "Hey, sis," I said. "I think I'm going to be heading back now. I'll come back for lunch, okay?"

"Okay," Echo said from under the blanket.

"And . . . I mean, you know it doesn't make any difference to me, right?" I said. "Whether you are or not."

Echo pulled the covers down around her neck. "Whether I'm what or not?" she demanded.

"You know," I said. "If you're, you know, gay. I mean, are you?"

Echo glared at me. "That doesn't mean anything," she said. "That's just a label. Life is more fluid than that. How can you tell who you're going to be attracted to before you are?"

"Okay," I said. "Anyway, it's all cool by me. I just wanted to make sure you knew that."

As I headed downstairs for class I couldn't help but muse about this. When I gave it some thought, I could easily see Echo at age thirty happily married to some woman. The picture just seemed right to me. I smiled. I wondered if at some point I could convince her to trade in our car for a convertible and we could go cruising for chicks together.

"What are you smiling at?" Peggy asked.

Decayde

Peggy had been waiting for me in the garage. "Yipe!" I said. I looked at my watch. I was already a couple minutes late for class, but at this point that was no longer a consideration. "Wow," I said. "Uh, hi. Isn't it kind of early? It isn't even seven-thirty yet."

"Early to you, maybe," she said. "I was just getting ready to go to sleep."

I looked at her: flat, greasy blonde hair with black streaks showing through the bleach, black leather jacket now adorned with mysterious discolored patches, lips red and swollen, eyes a faded gray. She looked like she hadn't slept in three days or changed her clothes in thirty. How my brain managed to process this information and register it as beauty I have no idea. But she couldn't have looked more beautiful to me had she shown up freshly scrubbed and shining in her Catholic-school uniform.

"So?" she said. "Aren't you going to ask me why I'm here?"

"You're here," I said. "I don't see any reason to spoil that by questioning it."

Peggy blinked. I couldn't help noticing that she was blinking about five times faster than normal—I would've attributed it to the bright sunlight but in the garage it was actually quite dim. "Well I'll tell you what it's not," she said. "It's not because you saw me at that party and I came to give you some explanation. I don't have an explanation. I was there for the same reason as everyone else. What do you think of that, huh?"

Peggy was seething, yet somehow her fury could hardly have been less contagious. I felt a remarkable serenity descend over me. Or maybe it was just exhaustion—suddenly I felt like *I'd* been the one up all night. "It was good to see you again," I said.

"But that's *not* why I'm here," she emphasized. "I'm *not* here to tell you that you didn't see what you think you saw and that it's not as bad as you think. That's *not* what I'm here to tell you. It's *worse.* It's *much* worse. I've done things—things—"

"Yeah, I heard a little about that," I said.

"But you don't *know,*" she said, pacing around the garage. "The thing is, you don't *know.* You think, you think that the things you don't know about are pretty much the same as the things you do, but you're *wrong.* I did things—Kevin—just tonight, just last night, we—he—see, you don't *know* is what it is. But I'll tell you. I'll t—"

"Why?" I asked.

"What?" she said.

"I mean, if you came to tick off a list of drugs you've taken and demeaning sex acts you've performed, I'd prefer that you didn't," I said. "I don't know how to run a confessional and it's not anything I'm particularly interested in hearing."

"*See?*" Peggy hissed. "You don't know. You just want to cling to some illusion about who I am and—"

"I don't think it's necessarily that," I said. "It's just that I really don't see the point. If you want me to 'take you more seriously' or something, that's not the way. If you want me to forgive you, then I forgive you already. If this is a test to see if I'll be shocked and repulsed and kick you out of the garage, then you're going to be waiting for a while because that's not going to happen. But on the other hand, I don't really see this turning into any kind of meaningful conversation, because you don't seem like you're in the state for it and I kinda doubt that we have enough in common to have anything to talk about anymore. So—so what can I do? Is there some kind of help I can get you?"

"Help?" Peggy said. "Help? You mean send me away, right? Like Kelly got sent away. Well, it didn't work. Because my parents ran out of money and so now today they have to go pick up Kelly before she's better. Of course, she's still better than *me.* I'm—"

"*Oh,* now I get it," I said. "This is your way of redeeming Kelly, right? You're trying to make her look like the good sister by acting like the bad sister. Except it's a paradox, since that's a generous impulse Kelly would never have and just goes to show who's really the good one."

"Shut up!" Peggy said. "*You* don't know what I'm thinking. *You* don't know what's in my head. You don't—"

"But after ten years I have a pretty good idea," I said. "It's a little voice telling you that you're vile and disgusting and dirty and stupid and worthless, and since I'm the only kid you know without an underlife, you want me to tell you that you're a vile and disgusting and dirty and stupid and worthless person so that you can consider your mission accomplished. But that's not what I think. I think you're still sweet and kind and good and that's why I l—" I paused. "No, wait. That's totally untrue."

"I *knew* it!" Peggy said triumphantly. "I *knew*—"

"I was going to say I love you for being sweet and kind and good, but you know what?" I said. "That doesn't even enter into it. I really don't care about those things. I love you for—for—*nothing,* really. I just love you. No matter how you look, no matter what you've done, no matter what state you're in. There's absolutely nothing you can do to make me love you any less. I guess that's how you're supposed to feel about your kids, or your brothers and sisters, but for some reason I've got it for you. And I have no idea why and I really don't care. I love you, Peggy. You're my best friend in the world."

Peggy stamped the floor in frustration. "Don't *say* that!" she demanded. "Don't *ever* say that! I can't be your *friend*! I'm the worst friend a person could *have*! I'm the worst—"

"Yeah, maybe," I said. "I mean, you have a point there. Sometimes you really *aren't* very good at being a friend. I don't care about that either. You're never going to convince me that you're anything less than the crowning glory of the universe. Apparently you can't see it or else you wouldn't be trying to peel the skin off your face or starving yourself into the hospital or setting dates to have your breasts chopped off, but that's what you are."

Peggy squinted at me. "What're you on?" she asked.

I shrugged. "I mean, just look at yourself," I said. "How did you get here? Even in the last few seconds before you were conceived, there were hundreds of millions of cells competing, hundred of millions of possible combinations. The most minute difference—a hundredth of a degree difference in temperature—and some other cell would've won. And in place of Peggy Kaylin would be one of your brothers and sisters who never came to be. And that's just the last few seconds. A hundredth of a degree difference a generation ago, and your parents would've been their own siblings, had completely different lives with different people, and no one remotely resembling you would ever have existed. And that's the space of one generation out of eighteen billion years. If *anything* in the history of the universe had gone differently—if a supernova five hundred million light-years away had happened a tenth of a second later—you wouldn't be here. How many things could be different in any given second? How many chaotic subatomic blips could blip some other way? And then how many seconds are there in eighteen billion years? Not even Echo could multiply all those numbers by each other. And yet they all worked out to produce you, *you*, Peggy Kaylin. I think this is as close to the definition of a miracle as you can get."

"Not just me," Peggy said. "It's—"

"You're right, it's not just you," I said. "You could make the exact same argument for anyone. And I don't know, maybe that's where I picked up this impulse to try to help people. Even though I suck at it. Because I spend a couple minutes with someone and they start to seem less like a miracle and more like an unfortunate accident. But not with you. You're the one person where I always see the miracle. I have no idea why. And I don't care. I love you."

Without warning, Peggy burst into a hysterical crying fit. I wish I could say it was because she'd been so touched by what I'd said, but these weren't the kind of tears that come from being moved. This was what in ancient texts is invariably described as "the lamentation of the women." I drew her close to me and held her tight—mostly because, you know, I had a *soul,* but also partly because the neighbors were less likely to call the police if her wails were muffled against my shoulder.

"Shhh," I said. "You do realize it was totally hopeless from the start, right? You could spend the next ten thousand years throwing kittens off of cliffs and you still wouldn't come close to balancing everything out the last ten. Every good memory I have revolves around you, kid. You are my happy childhood."

Peggy kept on crying for a few minutes but she burned out pretty quickly. Soon she was quiet save for the occasional hiccup. "Okay," I said. "You need to get some sleep. Let me walk you back to your house." She nodded and I escorted her back to her front porch where I gave her a last hug. "I love you," I whispered.

She whispered something back, but I couldn't quite make it out. I thought that it'd spoil the moment to say "What?" so I just held on to her a moment longer and then let her go. There was a soft click as she closed the door behind her. As I walked to school I wondered what she'd said.

And I still do.

I didn't hear the first vehicle to arrive at the Kaylins' house that afternoon—the Kaylins' van was remarkably quiet for a vehicle that size. I did hear the second one, because an ambulance with its siren going tends to be pretty loud. Molly came into my room looking rather alarmed. "Wow, what happened?" she asked.

I didn't know how to answer. I felt like someone was scraping at my heart with an ice shaver. "Some kind of emergency," I said stupidly.

Molly looked at me expectantly. "What?" I said.

"Aren't you going to find out?" she asked.

"I'm sure I will eventually," I said.

Molly seemed quite stunned by my callousness. "What?" I said. "I mean, of *course* I want to know what's happening. Of *course* I want to run over there and help. But there's nothing I can do. I'm no paramedic. I'd just be getting in the way. I mean, it seems like the admirable thing would be to rush to the Kaylins' and ask what's wrong and how to help, but if you think about it, if Kelly *has* overdosed or Mr. K. *has* had a heart attack or something then the last thing they need is me asking a lot of questions."

Molly looked at me sadly. She must have known that in picking those examples I was desperately flailing around for an alternate scenario to latch on to. But still, I didn't know. I'd always been kind of proud that in moments of crisis I was able to switch off my emotions, keep my head, but really it was more a matter of keeping my head *about* my emotions: as I sat in bed, working on my homework, I was able to avoid getting upset not because I was numb to everything, but because it wasn't *rational* to be upset yet, because it made no *sense* to start tearing myself up inside when I didn't know who was hurt or how seriously. On the other hand, it was entirely rational to be scared to death. My hands were shaking so badly as I worked on my algebra problems that I might as well have been writing the answers in Chinese. And when the phone rang at long last I was hyperventilating so heavily that I could barely choke out a "hello."

"Beep! This is a recorded message from the Ilium High School attendance office. Our records indicate that Madeleine Eve Mockery missed one or more periods of class today. Unexcused absences can lead to disciplinary action. Beep!"

That was the only call that came before sundown. I tried to force myself to sleep, but my heart was beating about four times too fast for that. I was going to have to find out. I dressed again and walked two doors over to the Kaylins' house. All the lights were on. I prayed I was doing the right thing. I knocked timidly on the door, which swung open.

The first two people I saw were Dooj and his wife, and for a moment I thought I had the wrong house. But then I saw Mrs. Kaylin, and she saw me. I would not have been the slightest bit surprised if she'd screamed at me to get out. But she didn't. She beckoned me inside, and when she spoke, the words were muffled as if there weren't enough air in the room to carry the sound. "She was already gone when we got home," she said.

Peggy had killed herself.

The girl who never was

The three-ring binder September and I had received for peer counseling had a checklist of signs that someone is suicidal. One was talk of suicide; I hadn't heard a word. One was giving away possessions; I hadn't received a thing. But this had been no snap decision. Or if it had been, Peggy had done a lifetime of thinking in the space of a snap.

I obviously have no idea what the exact sequence of events was. But for some reason I'm inclined to believe that she started with the photo album. It was open on the coffee table in the living room when I came in. I don't know whether Peggy had left it there, or if the family had discovered it after seeing what had happened to the pictures on the wall. But Peggy had cut herself out of every picture in the house.

You could tell which she'd started with. Some of the pictures had been cut very precisely; even with Peggy herself missing, the photos bore the mark of her characteristic neatness. But then time constraints or simple despair had taken their toll, and she'd gone from leaving a perfect outline to erasing herself with two or three quick strokes of the scissors to simply ripping the photos into pieces.

"Do you . . . have any pictures of her?" Mrs. K. asked.

"No," I said. "I have some index cards she gave me . . . with license plate numbers on them . . . but no, no pictures." I swallowed. "Are there . . . were these the only . . . ?"

"My mother has one," Mrs. K. said. "One . . ."

Dooj scowled at me as Mrs. K. buried her face in her hands. The kids showed me the rest.

I'd never been to Peggy's room before. And I still can't say I ever have. For after finishing with the pictures, Peggy had taken every book off her shelves, packed them away in boxes, and stacked the boxes in her closet. She'd boxed up her clothes and disassembled the dresser: taken out the drawers, wedged the mirror behind the shell that remained. She'd stripped the bed, taken down the canopy, left the bare mattress. It hadn't taken long. The room was tiny. And when she was done erasing every sign that this room had ever belonged to a living breathing dreaming girl, she'd gone to the garage, found some of the blue-gray paint Mr. K. had used to touch up the window frames, and splashed it all over the walls to hide the delicate pink underneath. Peggy's room no longer was. This barren chamber was just an empty box.

I didn't get the significance of the shattered pile of wood next to the bed at first glance: I'd taken it to be a night table, but Grant set me straight. "She broke her dollhouse," he said quietly.

"Dollhouse?" I said.

"Yeah," Cheese said. "This was the second one. The first one was just a house. She and Dad made it when she was little. From a kit. And then she decided to make one all by herself. A copy of our house. She wanted to get all the rooms exactly the same. She didn't work on it much. Just every so often. If you ever saw her in the garage sawing wood, or staining wood, or something? She was working on this."

And now it was firewood.

I can only guess that wrecking the dollhouse had been the last step: after that there was nothing left in the world to bear the mark that Peggy had ever lived except for her body. And she couldn't even find it in her heart to treat herself to the kindness of going to sleep for the last time in a warm, familiar place. Apparently she hadn't planned on being found at all. She hadn't left a note. She was found at the top of the stairs, as if she'd been felled as she was about to head out the door. Maybe she had been. Squeak is a fairly mild tranquilizer, mild enough to be legal in most countries, and people who use it recreationally generally tend to take a handful of the stuff without passing out. Peggy had taken several handfuls, but even that probably would've left her enough time to lock the door behind her and go . . . where? To curl up under a tree in the park? How far ahead had she thought? But then she'd taken a sudden detour into the bathroom. Had that been part of the plan? Or had emptying out the medicine cabinet been a spur-of-the-moment stratagem? A few handfuls of pills would've given her time to get away from the house and hide. But with a bottle of aspirin and two bottles of cough syrup to keep them company—not to mention half a bottle of mouthwash and a month's supply of Kelly's birth control pills—she hadn't even made it to the end of the hallway.

And so that's where she was found when the rest of the family got home from picking Kelly up at rehab. They'd called the ambulance before they'd even had time to close the door behind them on the way in. But the only good it had done had been to attract the neighbors' attention.

Peggy was gone.

And as I sat in the hallway where she'd been found, as I listened to the murmurs of her shell-shocked siblings, I felt blessed. Peggy and I could have had a fight that morning. We could have had some inane conversation about guest stars on TV reruns. But by blind, ridiculous luck, the last thing I'd told her was how much I loved her, how much I'd always loved her. I'd been saving it up for ten years and I hadn't been too late. It still hurt like a punch in the gut—like a punch *through* the gut—and I knew it was going to hurt for the rest of my life. But when I looked back on these days I'd be able to live with how things had played out.

So I thought, anyway.

I heard the Kaylins' station wagon pull up: Mr. K. had had some business to take care of at the hospital, I'd gathered. Or the police station. I looked at my watch. I'd been up since six and needed sleep desperately. "I should go," I said. Cheese and Kelly and Grant didn't say anything. I went downstairs. Mr. K. was still standing in the little foyer. "I'm so sorry," I told him.

He nodded. The little red light was blinking on their answering machine. He pushed the button.

"Beep! This is a recorded message from the Ilium High School attendance office. Our records indicate that Margaret Hannah Kaylin missed one or more—"

He stabbed the button again. We stared at each other for a long moment.

I had dealt with the death of my mother, and the death of my father. I was prepared to deal with the death of Peggy.

I could not deal with the death of Margaret Hannah Kaylin,

daughter of Robert and Josephine Kaylin of 151 Hyacinth Avenue, Fullerton, California.

I took off running.

There's a bear in the woods

Molly found me in Acacia Park. I don't really know how long I'd been out there, sobbing. To me it felt like hours but it may have been only a few minutes. She didn't say anything, just put her arms around me and sat with me till I was cried out. "You know," I finally said, "you're very sweet. But your oracular powers could use some, some *fine-tuning*, you know?"

"Still making with the funny?" Molly said. "Even now?"

"It's either that or go off the deep end," I said. "And I don't think there's any water in there. C'mon, I need some sleep."

Echo was waiting up for me when we got back up to my room. "Hey, you," I said.

"Allen, I'm sorry," she said. "About what I said . . ."

"What did you say?" I asked.

"When I said that Peggy Kaylin was nothing special," she said. "It was just the heat of the moment. I didn't know this was coming . . ."

"Tsokay," I said. "Don't beat yourself up. I know how you can make it up to her, though."

"How?" Echo asked.

"Don't copy her," I said.

When I woke up the next morning the sun was streaming in the window. Even this close to summer solstice, it usually hadn't made it over the Monihans' house when I woke up. I looked at my watch. It was past ten. Molly was nowhere to be found. "She went to school," Echo said. "She had a test she couldn't miss."

I went over to the window and looked at the sun. It was the first morning Peggy had missed since the day she was born. "That thing," I said, "is the cruelest ball of hydrogen in the universe. Would it have been too much to ask for it stay down for a few days? Show some fucking *respect*?" I looked down at the street. I'd thought I might head over to the Kaylins' to see if there might be any help I could offer, but the driveway was clogged with cop cars. "What do you suppose that's all about?" I asked. "I know you're supposed to notify the police whenever there's an unnatural death but I thought they already took care of all that."

"Strange," Echo agreed.

I washed up and got dressed and lay in bed and stared at the ceiling for a while and eventually went downstairs to find Echo transfixed by the television. I looked to see what she was watching and she immediately changed the channel; for a moment I thought it was to cover up what she'd been watching, but I quickly discovered that it was just to take advantage of the fact that the local newscasts weren't in perfect sync.

"—Buena Park woman as a dead body is discovered in a shallow grave in her backyard," said the TV. "Police were called to investigate after thirty-four-year-old Thelma Warner returned home from visiting her parents to find a freshly dug area behind her house. The gunshot-riddled body they retrieved has been identified as belonging to seventeen-year-old Carver Fringie of—"

"Oh, *shit,*" I said.

"There's more," Echo said.

I turned my attention back to the TV. "—complicated when it was discovered that Fringie's longtime girlfriend had taken her own life the day before the body was—"

"Turn it off," I said. "Turn it off." She did. "Oh, god," I said. "Oh, I am such an *idiot.*"

"Why?" Echo asked.

"*Things!*" I said. "Yesterday morning Peggy came here distraught because the night before, she and Kevin had done *things*—I thought she meant *sex* things, like he coerced her into something humiliating—but I think she *saw* it. I guess Fringie and Kevin Love had a falling out and—I mean, that guy is *demented.* Everyone says—and she saw him do it, and she couldn't deal with it, and—oh, Echo, what am I going to do?" I collapsed onto the sofa. "And the Kaylins!" I said. "They must be going through hell. Their daughter dies and they immediately get peppered with questions from the police—"

"We have to tell them about last Friday," Echo said quietly.

"What?" I said.

"We have to go to the police and tell them about what we did," Echo said. "We left Carver helpless. Do you know of anyone who saw him between then and now?"

"Oh, *god,*" I said. "Oh—oh—" I tried to take this in. Two days ago I'd been worried about being suspended. Now we were accessories to murder. I wondered if the prison system would be amenable to letting us share a cell. "You're right," I said hopelessly. "We might as well go now."

"You're not going anywhere," Krieg said. "Sit the fuck down."

I'd been too overwhelmed by the news to have heard him come in. "Sit the fuck down," he said, "and shut the fuck up. You are not going to fucking tell anybody a fucking thing. Because if they latch on to you that brings them closer to me and that's not going to fucking happen."

I'd barely even heard the name the first time, since I hadn't been paying close attention until Fringie was mentioned, but suddenly I remembered who they said had lived in the house where his body was found: Thelma Warner. Daisy's mother. And instantly an alternate scenario snapped into place. The tracks on our floor, where the body had been found . . .

"If you say a single fucking word," Krieg said, "and I mean a *single fucking word,* I am going to kill Molly. And don't fucking think about pulling any fucking tricks. Even if you get me before I get her, I'll have friends on the outside who'll get her. 'Cept they'll have some fun with her first. Do you hear what I'm fucking saying? One word, and she is fucking *meat.*"

Echo leaped at Krieg but I was able to grab her before she cleared the sofa. She struggled like a bobcat and I wouldn't have been able to hold her for very long but Krieg didn't need much time to stop her. "Yeah, just fucking *try* it," he said. "You just try it, you fucking cunt. Warder's got the car running. If I'm not out there in a minute or two, he's going over to her fucking school to plug her right now. So don't fuck with me. Carver Fringie fucked with me and now look at him. I *told* him I was gonna fuck him up. And I don't say shit unless I fucking mean it."

For a moment I couldn't figure out what he was referring to, but then suddenly the phrase connected. "Wait," I said. "You—*killed*—Carver Fringie . . . because HE BUMPED INTO YOU at a *PARTY*?"

"He hit me with the fucking *door*," Krieg said. "And if you hit me with a fucking door, that's what you get. So you just fucking *imagine* what Molly's gonna get if you breathe one fucking word of this. One fucking word." He sneered and headed out to the driveway.

Echo and I sat on the couch and tried to get a grip on the situation. You might as well have asked us to get a grip on an electric fence.

"What are we going to do?" Echo asked.

"I was going to ask you that," I said.

"Daddy would know what to do," Echo said.

"We could ask Bobbo," I said.

"Get serious," Echo said.

"Well—we have to tell *somebody*," I said. "Don't we? Who knows how many people could get hurt between—"

"I don't care," Echo said. "You can run that number out as many digits as you want. Molly counts more than all of them. We're not going to do anything that compromises her safety."

"Does that mean we don't talk to the police?" I asked.

"I don't *know* what it means," Echo said.

By this point the news was over—the news about Fringie, anyway. I went upstairs and turned the radio to the news station. I listened to Fringie's dad explain that Fringie had always pretty much looked after himself and often didn't come home for a few days and so he hadn't thought much about his son having been missing for so long. I heard Daisy's mom tell reporters that she'd been in Arizona trying to convince her parents to loan her a couple thousand dollars to pay some bills and she had no idea how a dead body had ended up in her backyard. But no one on the radio could explain why if Peggy hadn't even known about Fringie being murdered, if it hadn't been that trauma that had sent her over the edge, then why wasn't she still here, why couldn't I go two doors down and ask my best friend what I should do?

When Molly came home from school that afternoon her shirt was covered with a hideous red stain. "It's the strangest thing," she said, peeling it off. "I was just walking home minding my own business when this gangly guy all dressed in black came and splashed spaghetti sauce all over—"

"You walked home by *yourself*?" Echo cried. She shot me a frantic look. "How could we have forgotten to walk her home? How could—"

"Walk me home?" Molly said. We filled her in. Her eyes went wide. "We should go to the police," she said.

"We can't risk it," Echo said. "Maybe they can protect you from him, but not from everyone he knows. We've got to hide you somewhere." Her eyes lit up. "We could go to Hayley's!" she said. "Hayley'll know what to do, and we could hide there, and . . . and I need to talk to her anyway . . . about things . . ."

The phone rang. "This is probably the president calling to let us know the nukes are on their way," I said. I picked it up. My bets were on either Krieg or the police or the Ilium attendance computer. Instead, it was September.

"Are you okay?" she asked. "You've been missing school a lot lately. Are you sick?"

"Only at heart," I said. "Are they canceling school by any chance?"

"Because of Carver?" September asked. "It didn't happen on school grounds, so no. But they're having an assembly on Friday to talk about it. They're bringing in professional counselors and everything. But—well, Mrs. Handey's here, and she wants to talk to you."

"Yes?" I said.

"Hello, Allen?" Mrs. Handey said. "It looks like we're going to need you to work extra hours for a while. We've got a lot of kids who're torn up about all this and—"

"Yeah, and I'm one of them," I said. "Mrs. Handey, I'm really in no shape to do peer counseling right now. I just lost the best friend I've ever had and—"

"I didn't know you and Carver Fringie were that close," Mrs. Handey said.

"Carver—" I came very close to slamming down the receiver. "I'm talking about Peggy Kaylin," I said. "Look, I—I'll be right down." I hung up. Maybe September would have some ideas. "I have to go to school for a bit," I told Echo. "Why don't you go to Hayley's and I'll meet you there."

So I headed back to Ilium. The crowd was far larger than the usual crowd of people waiting for buses to arrive; I quickly discovered that most of the little groups weren't people waiting for buses at all but rather were clutches of Fringie's various conquests over the previous few years commiserating about their loss. I felt sick. I couldn't help these people; I didn't even want to help these people. I just wanted them to go away. I wanted it all to go away.

I went into the conference room. "You look exhausted," September said.

"Really?" I said. "I can't imagine why. Okay, send in the clowns."

I was surprised by how few of the people September and I talked to over the course of the next few hours actually knew Fringie on any kind of personal level, or were distraught that he'd no longer be in their lives; most of the comments were more along the lines of, "If *Carver Fringie* can be found in a shallow grave in Buena Park, what chance have *I* got? They're gonna find pieces of me in someone's freezer before I'm twenty." There were enough people waiting to talk to us that it eventually became clear that we wouldn't be done before dinner, so we ordered some pizzas; this turned out to be a bad idea, since once the pizzas arrived people started making up problems as an excuse to snag a couple of slices. Finally the place started to clear out, but it seemed like every kid who left was ambushed by reporters doing live reports for the local news at four, at four-thirty, at five, at five-thirty, at six. I figured I could wait them out. There was a bed in the nurse's office, so after September left, I headed over there and figured I'd take a quick nap till the eleven o'clock news was over and then go home. I couldn't find a light switch, though—all the lights in the office seemed to be on a timer—so I wheeled the bed into an acceptably dark storage room and closed the door. I was incredibly tired.

Molotov cocktails

My sleep was plagued by an insistent buzzing sound; every time it stopped, it seemed to return a moment later. At first I dreamed of bees and wasps, but eventually reconciled myself to the fact that my alarm clock was trying to wake me up. I opened my eyes and found my alarm clock nowhere in sight. I was still in the storage room. The buzzing had been the muffled sound of the bell at the start and end of each class. I slipped back into the nurse's office and found a clock. I could hardly believe my eyes—the bell that had finally succeeded in waking me up had been the one that signaled the beginning of lunch.

Once I got my bearings, I found myself thinking a lot more clearly than I had in quite a while. I decided that going to the police had to be the best option. Krieg was probably lying about being able to effortlessly orchestrate a murder from a prison cell, and more to the point, there was no reason to expect that he wouldn't hurt Molly anyway even if we didn't turn him in. And if it meant that Echo and I would end up doing time right along with him, well, maybe Molly could bring us a cake with a file in it or something.

So now it was just a matter of finding out whether Echo and Molly were still at Hayley's house or if they'd returned home. I found Hayley in the *Iliad* room so I figured I'd just ask her. "Hey, any idea where Echo is?" I asked.

"How the fuck should I know?" Hayley snapped.

"Eep," I said.

"Sorry," she said. "Look, this isn't a good time. It's over between Jefferson and me."

"Really?" I said.

"He's been fucking some trollop for the past six months," she said.

"I thought you said you were okay with that," I said.

"Oh, piss off," Hayley said. She sighed. "Look, I'm sorry. I just need to be left the hell alone for a while. Tell Echo I'm sorry too."

"For what?" I asked.

"She didn't tell you?" Hayley asked.

"Tell me what?" I said.

"Well, she came over last night, and Jefferson and I had just finished breaking up, and I was kind of tipsy, and I kind of told her that she was the last person on earth I wanted to see, or something like that," Hayley said.

"What?" I said. "Oh, that's just gr—"

"And she still wouldn't leave—something about having been trying to find me all afternoon, or something—and I was still all worked up from arguing with Jefferson, and so I guess I sort of took it out on her," Hayley continued. "I may have said something to the effect that the only reason I ever talked to her was because it was fun to watch her moon after me just because I pretended to be interested in listening to her go on and on about her pathetic, miserable little life, or something like that . . ."

I blinked. "Did you just say what I th—"

"And I might possibly have left the impression that every afternoon after she was gone Holdn and Cat and I got together and laughed at how she was still falling for it," Hayley said. "There may have been something in there about a betting pool as to when she'd finally figure it out . . ."

"She—you—what the hell is *wrong* with you??" I asked. "Oh my *god,* Hayley. Do you realize what you've done? Do you have any *idea*?"

"Look, it's not my fault," Hayley said. "I'm not a cruel person, really. Most of that stuff wasn't even true. I'd just had a little too much to drink. I'm sorry."

"Fair enough," I said. "You're right. It's not your fault. The fault lies with the gang of thugs that held you down and poured the booze down your throat. I'll be sure to explain that to my sister's corpse."

I slammed the door and took off running for home. It was kind of hard to see where I was going through the tears in my eyes, and while I didn't bump into anyone, I also didn't quite clear the fence and ended up sprawled on the other side bleeding from the shins. It was then that I decided that unless Echo specifically asked me not to, I was going to have to dismember Hayley with my bare hands.

"Where've you been?" Echo asked.

I looked up. Echo was standing over me, hair matted, eyes running, mouth twitching, clutching a stack of papers to her chest—she looked like she hadn't slept for a month. Molly was standing behind her and didn't look much better—her "76" T-shirt seemed to have been dug out of the bottom of the hamper. "I fell asleep at school," I said, clambering to my feet. "So, um, are you okay? Did Hayley—I mean, aren't you—"

"I'm not going to talk about that," Echo said. She climbed over the fence and Molly and I followed her into the crosswalk. "I *told* you I ruined everything," she muttered.

"You didn't!" I said. "You didn't do anything wrong. It's her. I swear. This is just a long string of coincidences—"

"I'm sure," Echo said darkly.

"Where are you going?" I asked.

"I'm turning in these tests and then I'm done with this place," Echo said. She turned to Molly. "You know, you don't have to follow me around now that Allen's here. I just didn't like the idea of you being alone in the house."

"Don't be silly," Molly said. "I'm not leaving you."

So the three of us took a tour of Ilium's lovely teachers' lounges, dropping off Echo's finals in the appropriate cubbyholes. Our last stop was the English lounge, where I'd had my chat with Siren a few months before; Molly was about to pour herself a drink from the water cooler before I pointed out all the bugs floating at the surface. "Yecch," she said.

Echo found the stack of inboxes and slid her paper into the one marked with Benito's name. "Okay," she said, rubbing her temples. "That's it. Let's get out of here."

We walked down the hall and out to the wheel. I was the last one out. The door clicked shut behind me, and that's when the alarms went off.

Ten

When the alarms died down, over fifty people had been wounded. In twenty-five of those cases, the wounds had been fatal.

The victims did not represent a true cross section of the Ilium High School student body. For the bullets didn't come raining out of the sky. The gunfire came in bursts, leaving some cliques leveled entirely while others went completely unscathed with no one even grazed. The list of casualties I read in the next day's newspaper had been in alphabetical order. But as I read it, I knew which names belonged together.

The moment I saw Clement Campbell's name, for instance, I knew which other names were likely to appear on the list. Clement had been the one to score the winning goal in the youth league hockey championship game, and he and most of the rest of the roster had continued to hang out together. And sure enough, most of the names I expected to find were waiting for me further down the page. Vance Judden. Jay Kyeutter. Min-Hsun Lee. Neal Navarre. All of them were dead now. Some of their wounds had been from quite a distance; others were from point-blank range. Not one of them had lived even long enough to be loaded into an ambulance.

The water polo players had gotten off comparatively light. Many of them hadn't even been on campus at the time of the attack, but had been stuck in the drive-thru at Taco Junta or the Burger Despot. This, of course, came as no consolation to the loved ones of Arnold "Lemming" Armstrong, who'd been killed after taking a pair of bullets in the chest.

But the relatively minimal casualties among the actual water polo team didn't extend to its hangers-on. It didn't take long for me to pick out the names of Fringie's exes from the list of the dead. Erika Christensen. Amber Flores. Linda Garcia. Shelby Streicht. All of them had been involved with Fringie, and now all of them had been shot to death, mostly at point-blank range. It was almost like a modern form of suttee.

Shelby hadn't been standing with the other three, though. She had her own clique, and it too was well represented among the victims. Missy Schaeffer was dead. Brad Chasintek too. And Siren Delaney. That one hit hard. We'd had a scattering of moments together, which she'd most likely forgotten and I would never, ever forget. I'd even planned out our futures one afternoon. Now she had no future. This was the end. Siren Delaney belonged wholly and completely to the past. Of course, it was Sarah I'd cared for, and she had been consigned to the past quite some time before. Maybe now I'd be able to mourn her without Siren walking around to make me feel stupid about it.

Jessica Pound was dead, too. She'd been the defining influence in Siren's life, and as far as I knew, they'd never even met. I'd checked up on her a little after things fell apart with Siren. She was every bit as unpleasant as Siren had described. Being violently beaten and molested by one's father and uncle from the age of three tends to do that to a person. For Jessica, getting shot to death counted as a comparatively good day.

The names kept coming, names of people who hadn't had anything in common except for the fact that they'd been in the same wrong place at the same wrong time. There was a Jonah Barry and a Brandon Vane on the list: I had no idea who they were, and now they were dead. Other names were more familiar. Sharon Sharalayek. She'd been September's and my first peer counseling case. Now she was dead. Shot in the heart. Ingrid Escajeda. She'd been the first person I'd ever called a ride for. Now she was dead. Shot in the head and chest.

There were even a few names I recognized from the *Iliad*. Minh Tran. For a few days it had looked as though Benito's never-ending outbursts of passive cruelty were going to lead to Minh Tran's elevation to editor-in-chief; now he was dead. Marie Lasker, who'd taken over Siren's spot as the third writer on the page I worked on, and done a fine job of it: she was gone too. And Gayatri Tamar. She'd been Mrs. Wennikee's pick to be editor-in-chief in a few years. But now those were years she wouldn't get.

Krieg Mockery was dead, and Mark "Warder" Warner with him. Less than a week earlier, they had found Carver Fringie conveniently tied to a chair in the *Iliad* room, beaten him unconscious, freed him from the chair and thrown him in their trunk, driven him out to Buena Park, waited for him to reawaken, and tossed him, his hands and legs still bound, into a swimming pool. I had loathed Fringie. Still, not even the basest part of me got any joy out of imagining this scene. I thought about the moment when his lungs started screaming for oxygen, when he suddenly realized that this wasn't a joke, that they weren't going to fish him out, that when he finally did black out he wouldn't be waking up again, and the sheer chemical terror of it made me sick. Even though it was Fringie. When I pictured him at the bottom of the pool, I didn't see him as the predator who'd been the author of so much of Peggy's and Echo's misery; I saw him as the poor sick kid across the street who wasn't strong enough to play with the others. And when they did at long last fish him out, how long did it take for his swagger to return? How long before the pre-human core of his brain ceded control back to its superficial overlay, before the howls of an animal faced with death quieted down and allowed his sneering voice to return? How long before he once again saw no reason to doubt that he still had at least sixty more years coming to him to do with as he wished? And when Krieg and Warder went out to their car and came back with their guns, when he realized they'd just been toying with him, when the bullets ripped through his body, what had his last thought been? Who had he been thinking of at the moment of his death? I tried not to dwell on it, but my thoughts kept returning to that scene against my will. I didn't even know whether that was the way it had happened: it was just the way I'd reconstructed events. Which just made things worse. It meant that every time I flashed back to the scene, I had to pay attention to it to see which details had changed since the last time through.

I never wondered what Krieg and Warder had been thinking about when they'd been shot to death in turn. I strongly doubted that either one of them had ever had a thought worth noting.

I didn't get around to reading the list of names until the newspaper was already a few days old. It looked a lot older than that: I found it in tatters out on the driveway as I was packing my stuff into the car, and couldn't help but pick it up and glance through it. Nothing I read surprised me. I went back to packing.

I'd already told Bobbo where I was going; I also tried to pay the Kaylins a visit to say my good-byes, but no one was home. I slipped a note under their door and went back home to take a last look around and see if there was anything I'd forgotten. I was just about to head out to the car when the phone rang. Half an hour later I found myself at the Lord of the Pies Family Restaurant and Bakery on Imperial and Lemon. It was the sister chain of the juice shop chain Peggy had worked for. Even that distant a connection made me wince.

September Young and I had worked together just about every afternoon for the past two years. Now she was the last entry on a list I knew by heart. But her family and I hadn't exactly been on the best of terms, and since there was nothing I could do for September herself, it was my relationship with the Youngs who had survived that counted now. I'd figured I'd send them a card. But August had had other ideas, and so I found him and April sitting at a booth, April with a cup of coffee, August starting into a slice of apple pie with melted yellow cheese, his shoulder heavily bandaged. They were both wearing white. "Glad you could make it," August said. "Have a seat."

I sat down. "I realize you're on a tight schedule, so I'll get right to it," August said. "September obviously didn't leave a will, so I've taken it upon myself to distribute some of her personal effects." He handed me a little bound book with a swirly sky-blue cover. "I thought the most appropriate person to give this to would be you, seeing as you're the one it's mainly about."

"What?" I said.

"Go ahead, have a look," he said. "See, pretty much every night she made a special note of whether you seemed to have 'noticed' her that day. If you said something about what she was wearing, or made an inside joke that only the two of you were inside, or things like that." He gestured at the book with a forkful of pie. "Go ahead, read it," he said. "She would've wanted you to know. Now that it doesn't matter anymore."

I felt my throat get raw and tight like I'd swallowed a plateful of thumbtacks. "Please don't," I said.

"Please don't what?" August said.

I couldn't even choke out an answer. At least with Peggy's death there was the minuscule consolation of knowing that it was something she'd sought for herself. But September had been bright, cheery, optimistic, heartbreakingly earnest . . . I looked down at the little book full of her bright and cheery thoughts and optimistic hopes and heartbreakingly earnest dreams and it all seemed just so fucking unfair. Peggy's death had hurt on a personal level but September's struck me as just plain objectively cruel.

"There's also this," August said. He handed me a book titled *Ameliorate Your Vocabulary in a Fortnight*. "You probably don't need it, but she bought it specifically to impress you. When you read the diary be sure to note how she kept waiting for you to compliment her on her newfound word power, which you never did."

"I'm sorry," I said. "I'm sorry. There were times . . . there were times that I really wished I could've fallen for her, you know? It would've made things a lot easier . . . for both of us, it looks like. I did . . . love her . . . in a way . . . I wish I'd actually told her so . . . she's the one I didn't get to tell . . ."

"I'm getting a cigarette," April said. As she stood up to leave I noticed that her midriff was bare, revealing a new tattoo: the symbol for the planet Mercury in purple around her navel.

"She thought it was a female symbol with devil horns," August explained once April was out of earshot. "She was fairly bright at one point . . ."

"And you weren't," I said.

"Is that supposed to be an insult?" August said calmly.

"No," I said. "I just mean that . . . you've changed. Since the last time I talked to you. A *lot*."

"And I owe it all to *Ameliorate Your Vocabulary in a Fortnight,*" he said. He had another bite of pie and chewed thoughtfully. "What can I say? This is the kind of thing that makes you completely reevaluate what kind of life you've been living. I've never been *stupid*—I just haven't been applying myself. But I kind of think I owe it to my sister to lead a life that honors her memory. I'm the one responsible for what happened, after all."

"What do you mean?" I asked.

"Well, the three of us happened to be standing together on the wheel when the alarms went off," August said. "Arguing, as usual. After a couple seconds people started screaming, and September and April both kind of froze, not realizing what was going on. And the gunfire started getting louder, and they were standing on opposite sides of me, so I had to make a choice. And I chose. I screamed to September to get down, and threw myself on April. I took a bullet in the shoulder. Well, let's not get carried away here—it grazed me. And September . . . didn't get down in time."

"Was she—I mean, she was killed instantly?" I said. "You're sure she was killed by a shot from the tower?"

"Yes," August said. "I . . . checked. Before April and I made our break for it. She was gone. And that was my choice. If I'd jumped the other way, September would be the one sitting here, helping me hand out April's stuff. And you want to know what I was thinking, what the basis was on which I decided who lives and who dies? It wasn't anything I had time to mull over or anything—my brain wasn't in control, just my brain stem. And even though my brain knows it's a crock, my brain stem has been programmed from day one to believe that good kids go to heaven, and bad ones—don't. I saved April because I figured that on the off chance that turns out to be true, I know where September's going."

He polished off his pie. "So," he said, "it seemed to me that if I'm going to be the kind of person who goes around making life-or-death decisions, that didn't seem to be compatible with me being a cretin. So I decided to finally grow up some. Let's just hope April does the same. She's been taking it pretty hard. A couple days ago we found her sleeping on the floor. This morning it was the front lawn. Sleepwalking. Poor kid."

August dabbed at his mouth with his napkin and threw a few dollars on the table. "Well," he said, "I've got to get going, and so apparently do you. Enjoy the book. You know, when I first decided to give it to you, it was supposed to be a punishment—my kid sister was a very special person, and you never quite seemed to twig that fact. But I suppose you did try to be a friend to her, so you also get a reward. And the punishment and the reward are the same thing. See, all that's left of September now are the things she touched. You're holding an important chunk of a special girl's life right there in your hands, buddy. And you better be feeling pretty damn honored."

And I did. And I do. Every day I take out September's book and look at it.

But I still haven't opened it.

Lemming Armstrong. Jonah Barry. Clement Campbell. Brad Chasintek. Erika Christensen. Siren Delaney. Ingrid Escajeda. Amber Flores. Linda Garcia. Vance Judden. Jay Kyeutter. Marie Lasker. Min-Hsun Lee. Krieg Mockery. Neal Navarre. Jessica Pound. Missy Schaeffer. Sharon Sharalayek. Shelby Streicht. Gayatri Tamar. Minh Tran. Brandon Vane. Mark Warner. September Young.

Twenty-five dead.

And if you've been counting, you know that doesn't add up.

Eleven

When the fire alarm was pulled, every door in the entire school automatically switched into the locked position. The doors locked from the outside, meaning that people were free to exit the buildings, but not to enter them. This had been Doctor Todd's idea. The theory was that it was a good safety measure to keep people from running back into a fiery building to retrieve their belongings (or to dodge a fire drill). This was all well and good when the danger was coming from inside. This time it wasn't.

It was quite a few seconds before I figured out what was happening. I heard the alarms go off, and just as I was about to make some oh-so-pithy comment about Doctor Todd's timing, I heard a chorus of screams over the wail of the alarm bells and I realized this wasn't a fire drill. But I had no idea what it was.

I heard a sort of unfocused popping above both the screams and the alarms, but before I could identify it, a wave of people came hurtling toward the door directly behind me and I was shoved to the ground. The door was locked. No one was on the other side to open it. I was knocked over as I tried to get back up and banged the side of my head against someone's locker. I lost track of where I was, where Echo was, where Molly was. "Run!" I yelled stupidly. The world was spinning and that was when I finally caught a glimpse of what was happening.

Warder was running around the wheel shooting people.

I knew exactly what I had to do: get the hell out of there. But I was still dizzy and couldn't find either of my sisters. *"Molly! Echo!"* I shouted. "Where are you?"

The second half of my question was answered a second later, as I saw Echo take off running—*toward* Warder, *toward* the danger. *"Echo!"* I cried. "Echo, don't—"

She couldn't hear me. And this turned out to be a very good thing. For if she had been able to hear me over the screams and the fire alarm, then that meant Warder could've heard me as well, and he might've turned around. Instead, he saw two of Echo's old hockey teammates charging at him, gleefully shot them both in the chest, and was taken totally by surprise when Echo hit him from behind with a flying elbow-first tackle that sent him sprawling to the ground and his gun skittering across the wheel. He tried to get up, but she threw an arm around his neck and choked him out in a matter of seconds.

And the shots kept coming.

I'd been so focused on Warder that I hadn't even seen that people on the other side of the wheel were also being felled as they ran. It probably didn't help that I couldn't see the shooter. I saw people getting gunned down as they fled for cover, but had no idea where the shots were coming from until I heard the taunts. Krieg always was a coward.

"READY, OKAY!" he warbled from his perch on top of the clock tower. *"BE AGGRESSIVE! B-E AGGRESSIVE! IS THIS AGGRESSIVE ENOUGH FOR YOU?"* He fired into a group of people struggling to yank one of the doors open. *"IS THIS FUCKING AGGRESSIVE ENOUGH?"*

And for a moment I felt a rush of hope. There was no way Krieg was getting out of this one alive—Warder was unconscious, so the cops would have to just arrest him and throw him in jail, but unless Krieg surrendered, there was no way they were going to be able to get him down from on top of the tower without using lethal force. And then Molly would be safe, and Fringie's killers would both be in custody, and everything would be fine.

Except I couldn't find Molly. For all I knew she'd been trampled, or shot already, or—

"Craig!"

I heard Molly's voice ring out across the wheel. She was standing near the base of the tower, calling up to him.

"Craig!" she cried. "Stop! I know what's wrong! I can help—"

She was trying to talk him down. She was trying to *talk him down*. "*MOLLY!*" I screamed. "*You can't—*"

Krieg casually glanced in Molly's direction, pointed his gun at her, and fired. A salvo of bullets punched through her chest. She crumpled to the ground.

The air was pierced by a wild, inhuman scream as I ran to her. Krieg saw me make my move and fired in my direction. Or tried to. This time the gun jammed. "Fucking Soviet piece of shit!" he shouted. He grabbed for another one. I didn't much care. If Molly wasn't okay—and I couldn't see how she could be—then I could not possibly care less about what happened to me. At this point survival was a meaningless consideration compared to touching Molly one last time before we were dead.

As I ran toward the tower, Krieg pointed a different gun at me. But before he could fire it, the gun flew out of his hand. Or at least that's what it looked like. What had actually happened was that his hand had flown off his wrist. Echo had picked Warder's gun off the ground and shot Krieg's hand off. Then she fired at his head. The impact almost knocked him backward off the tower, but then his knees buckled and he slumped forward. The police ended up needing to call in a crane to pull the body off the top of the tower.

Echo and I were the only ones left on the wheel still moving. I reached Molly—she was still breathing. It was shallow, but it was breath. "Hang on, Molly," I said. I sat down beside her and cradled her in my arms. "Please, please, just hang on."

I heard still more shots. Molly swallowed heavily. "What's that?" she asked, her voice a harsh whisper. I looked up.

Now Echo was shooting people.

She started with Warder, unconscious on the ground—put the gun to his head, and fired. Warder had been lying right next to the hockey players he'd killed the second before Echo tackled him. And as she stepped over his body, she fired into both their corpses as well. That was strange, but meaningless—they were already dead. But Warder hadn't been.

Echo had just committed murder. I looked at her face.

There was nothing human there.

And she kept shooting. There were plenty of bodies left to go between her and us.

"It's nothing," I said to Molly. I stroked her face. I didn't have much time. "Molly," I said. "Molly. I love you, Molly. I love you, kid. I love you forever." I looked back up at Echo, still shooting people. Most of the people she was shooting were already dead. Some of them probably weren't. That wasn't what upset me. What upset me was that she was taking so long. That if she didn't hurry up, she wouldn't get to us in time to say good-bye.

Molly shivered. I prayed that she'd heard me. "Please," I whispered. "Say something."

"I'm dead," she whispered.

"You're not," I said.

"I'm going to die," she said. Her voice was shaking violently. "In a minute or two I'm not going to be here, there won't be a me, and there'll never be a me ever ever again. Never—oh—oh god—" She sobbed, great gulping violent sobs, gasping for breath, tears streaming down the sides of her face. "I'm never going to grow up—I'm never going to go to college, or—or have a baby, or—or—or anything, or anything, it's not fair, I was trying to help, I could have helped, I was trying to help, it's not fair, it's not fair, it's not fair! It's not fair! *It's not fair!*" She pounded the ground with her fist, but all that did was make her bleed faster. My clothes were already soaked through with her hot sugarsweet blood.

There was a clack as Echo set the gun down against the volcanic rock and sat down across from me. "You killed those people," I said quietly.

"I was putting them out of their misery," she said, the wildness in her eyes subsiding as she took Molly in her arms. "They were already dead."

"Not all of them," I said. "Some of them—some of them might've gotten better—"

"No," Echo said. "This much I've learned. None of them would ever have been any better."

I heard sirens in the distance. "Molly?" I said. "Molly? Molly, listen—ambulances—you'll be okay, you will, you will—"

She swallowed. "i'm thirsty . . ." she said. Her voice was nothing more than a breath now. It was entirely possible that I'd imagined it.

"Get her some water," Echo said, her voice ragged.

"But—"

"You heard her," Echo said. "Get her some water."

"You're not going to—" I looked at the gun on the ground.

"Of course not," Echo snapped.

"Not on her?" I said. "And not on yourself?"

"Of course not," she repeated. She paused. "The clip's empty."

I got up and dashed to the nearest water fountain, on the other side of the wheel. My hands and forearms were dripping with Molly's blood, and for a moment I hesitated—it seemed very pure and holy to me and I didn't want to defile that by touching this contraption full of chewing gum and half-dried phlegm. But I didn't have any time to waste. I grabbed the handle and gave it a twist—and the handle snapped in my hand and dangled loosely from the fountain. And then suddenly I heard shouts behind me.

The police entered the wheel first, fanning out to make sure the paramedic crews wouldn't be in any danger. Echo saw them too. And she picked Warder's gun off the ground and pointed it at the first cop she saw.

"*NO!*" I screamed. "IT'S EMPTY! IT'S *EMPTY!*"

The cops, who had come in with their weapons drawn, instinctively pointed them at me: I was the one shouting. But I was also clearly unarmed. The second it took for them to identify where the real threat was coming from—or what seemed like the real threat—was all I needed. I threw myself between Echo and the police, in front of the empty gun.

And they didn't open fire.

In an instant four of them had Echo pinned to the ground, a fifth had grabbed the gun, and two others were frantically radioing for the paramedics to come on in. "Molly," I said, "I'm sorry, I'm sorry, the fountain was broken, I couldn't get you any water—"

"that's okay," she murmured. "it's raining . . ."

I looked up. There wasn't a cloud in the sky.

Twelve

Molly Abigail Mockery died in the ambulance on the way to the hospital. She was the twenty-fifth and final casualty.

The police and paramedics were somewhat puzzled to find that, other than Molly, every single victim left in the wheel was dead—all the survivors had managed to escape under their own power. There were scores of injured people to treat, of course; some had been shot in the shoulders or arms, for instance, or had bones broken in the mad dash to find an open door or gate. But Molly was the only one they'd found in critical condition. Everyone else either had no life-threatening injuries, or was dead at the scene.

They also found it odd that some wounds seemed to be from a gun fired from dozens of yards away while others had apparently been inflicted at a distance of mere inches. But that was consistent with the story the survivors told. Warder and Krieg (or, as the news called them, Mark Warner and Craig Robert Mockery—they always used all three names) had killed Carver Fringie a few days earlier. They'd dumped his body in Warder's mother's backyard, but had immediately sensed police closing in on them, knew their lives were effectively over. So fueled by cocaine and the desire to take as many people with them as they could, Warder had pulled the fire alarm and then run out to the wheel and started shooting people from point-blank range, while Krieg fired away from the top of the clock tower. A number of news outlets reported that the shootings had taken place not long after school had started, since the clock they saw in the footage they received clearly read 9:07.

Every tragedy needs a hero, and Echo got some perfunctory plaudits for having knocked out Warder—as the last few people to get away had seen with their own eyes—and then having used his gun to shoot Krieg, as I told the police later when they questioned me about it. But then the news coverage would immediately focus on the juicier aspect of Echo's story: that, distraught over the mortal wounding of her sister by her brother, she had tried to bait the police into shooting her in turn. Which meant that Echo's name became synonymous not with "hero," but with "nutcase." Or, at least, that's what it became synonymous with for the two or three days that Ilium was in the headlines. Then Fullerton got tacked onto the list of cities to be trotted out the next time something like this happened, and Echo's name, like the rest of the specifics of what happened that day, was only remembered by those of us involved. Which is a small mercy, at least.

I too had my moment on the news. I'd been allowed to ride with Molly in the ambulance, and then after she was pronounced dead on arrival, I was taken to the police station for what I can only call interrogation. After a couple hours I was released. At first I waited around for them to finish up with Echo, but it turned out that she wasn't going anywhere—they were keeping her in custody for psychological evaluation. So I was driven in a squad car back to my house, where I found troops of reporters camped out on my driveway. As I got out of the car they started peppering me with questions. Or rather, with *a* question, asked over and over again by twenty different people:

"Why? What caused your brother to do such a thing?"

I didn't see any reason to dignify that with a reply. I weaved my way through the crowd, but as I reached the garage door, I heard someone shout, "Come on—you *owe* us an answer!"

I turned around. "You think there *is* an answer?" I said. "This isn't a *mystery*. You can't count up a handful of clues and come up with a neat little Reason for why people are the way they are. Molly thought she could, and—and—I mean, do you *really* expect that you can sum all this up in a sound bite? Find out that he had some defective gene, or that he was toilet-trained wrong, and there's your answer? You can't understand Krieg until you understand our parents, and you can't understand them until you understand their parents; you can't understand Krieg until you understand Echo and Molly, and Jerem and me; you can't understand me until you understand September and Sarah, and Peggy, or her until you understand Kelly, and Fringie . . . and you can't understand any of us until you understand biology and psychology, and sociology, and *economics,* and *astronomy*—are you listening? Do you hear a word I'm saying? To even come close to understanding a single human life you've got to understand the entire *universe.* Let me know when you get close."

I went inside.

Naturally, they only used part of that clip. I saw myself on the news, asking, "You think there is an answer?" Then the commentator came on. "Yes! There is an answer!" he declared. "And that answer is this generation's *moral depravity*! The liberals'll blame it on the guns, but the guns didn't fire themselves—if these young sickos hadn't been able to get hold of some guns, they would've found some other way! Run around stabbing people, or sat on the top of that tower and thrown rocks! But you don't hear anyone trying to outlaw rocks, do you? It's—"

I turned off the television and went upstairs.

I went into Molly's room. It was still warm. Eighty-four degrees. Everything was just as she'd left it, waiting patiently for her to return.

And she never would.

It was then that I realized that Peggy had been exceptionally kind in erasing the reminders that she had ever been. Because when I walked into Molly's room with the bed where we all had slept, the easel with a still life half-drawn, her scent still clinging to the air, I fell into a trap, found myself thinking how we'd really messed up this time, really just done everything completely wrong, and how the next time I saw her, when she got home from school or wherever she was, we were really going to have to sit down and come up with a better strategy for the next time we found ourselves in this situation.

But there was no retest in two weeks. Molly wasn't coming home. The woman whose portrait hung on the wall was someone I would never meet.

There had been a time when I'd expected that one day Peggy and I would be married. When I was a little kid, I just sort of assumed it. But that had changed in the intervening years. On the surface I pretended I thought of her as "just a friend." Deeper down, I was hopelessly in love with her. But deeper still, I knew that the surface was closer to the truth than my supposed "hidden feelings." That those feelings were a function of needing to be in love with someone, anyone, and she was just the most convenient candidate. That really we had next to nothing in common and that soon we would drift even farther apart than we had already, the visits turning to phone calls, the calls to cards at the holidays, and then one year even the cards would stop coming. On some level, even though it hurt, even though it hurt worse than anything, I knew I would lose her.

But Molly was my sister. She was never, ever supposed to leave. When I finally kicked off at age one hundred and six, Molly was supposed to be there at my bedside, hale and hearty at a hundred and three. We were supposed to have a century together. We were supposed to have a *life*. *She* was supposed to have a life.

Now, when I died at age one hundred and six, Molly would have been dead for ninety years.

I curled up on her bed and waited. I was willing to wait as long as it took.

It didn't work, of course. I was trying to hold on to Molly as firmly as I could, but she slipped from my grasp. I don't know how many nights passed—more than one, I know it was more than one—but there came a point where her room stopped smelling like her and started smelling like me. It was just a room. And there was no more point in staying in that room than in any other.

I needed to talk to someone. Desperately.

But the person I needed to talk to was Molly.

The night that Peggy had killed herself, I was able to get through it because Molly had been there to comfort me. She was the one I could always turn to. For anything. Except this.

So I had to find someone else. I needed to talk to Peggy.

But she was dead too.

That meant September.

But she was dead too.

I needed to talk to someone who wasn't dead.

And I honestly believe that the only reason I'm still here to write this is that there was still one person who fit that description.

Someone who had the power to decide such things declared that Echo needed further time under observation. Not because of what she'd done before the police arrived—Echo claimed, and claims to this day, that the next thing she remembered after she saw Molly get shot was waking up the next morning, and I certainly didn't volunteer any information about why Warder had suffered point-blank wounds even though Krieg was supposedly the one who had taken him down. Nevertheless, waving an automatic firearm at uniformed officers was deemed sufficiently questionable behavior to keep her from being released, at least right away. She was sent up the coast to some sort of psychological treatment center. When I found out, I followed her, of course. I didn't have anywhere else to go.

Naturally, they wouldn't let me stay in the hospital with her. Their budget was already stretched to fairly ridiculous extremes: they couldn't afford to replace their old light-blue uniforms, so every time I go to see Echo, she's wearing an orange jumpsuit designed for prisoners. They were cheaper. At least she was deemed sufficiently well that they let her wear cloth instead of paper.

I'm only permitted to see her on Sunday afternoons. We meet in a little room that smells of stale tobacco. The room has a pair of fraying couches and a water cooler and a big boxy radio out of which a little black-and-white television screen pops up with the push of a button. We are not permitted to be alone, but the nurse keeps her distance and watches the television while we talk. We are permitted to hug when we first see each other and then again when we part, and we do. We are permitted to hold hands while we talk, and we do. Any other contact draws the attention of the nurse and might prolong Echo's stay. So covering the back of her hand with my palm as we talk somehow has to function as shorthand for the fact that she is the only remaining connection to the life I had before. If she were to leave me, I would have absolutely no reason to move or eat or do anything but lie in bed, blinking at nothing. I think she's pleased that I finally understand.

. . .

Like I said, I wasn't allowed to move in with Echo when she was remanded for further observation and treatment. I had to get a motel room down the street. That was the beginning of summer; now summer's almost over. And I've spent more or less every moment in this little room, writing. The day after I moved in, I booted up my computer and typed, "The day I turned sixteen years old I had no idea that in four months nearly everyone I cared about would be dead. Unburdened by this foreknowledge, it was with a free and unclouded spirit that I went down to the DMV and failed my driving test." Nearly three months and hundreds of pages of virtually nonstop writing later, I'm almost done. It was important to me that I get it all down on paper. Not because I was afraid that I'd forget. Quite the opposite.

You see, Echo isn't the only one with a gift. I can't multiply hundred-digit numbers in my head, or pick up foreign languages in a week, or stop a hockey puck. But I have a talent Echo doesn't have. I remember everything that's ever happened to me.

When Echo and I were little, Bobbo used to make us do tricks for the women he brought over. First he'd have Echo do some long division, with a square root or two thrown in for fun. Then he'd ask me things like "What was I wearing forty-seven days ago?" and I'd say "The same thing you're wearing now" and his dates would be less than impressed. Eventually he figured out that a better trick was to pick up a random book or magazine or something, have me read it, and then instantly quote it back to them. Of course, this doesn't mean that I necessarily had any comprehension of what I'd read. I just flashed back to when I was reading it and the words once again appeared before my eyes.

When I first started this project, it was because I *wanted* to forget. I knew that someday, someone close to me would ask me about my past, and why I never talked about it, and I'd be able to just hand over this stack of paper and not have to think about it ever again. But as I got deeper into it, I found that far from being a chore to get over and done, it was a wonderful escape. Instead of living in a cramped motel room with stains on the carpet and fuzzy TV reception, I could spend my time in a world where Molly and Peggy and even September and Sarah were still alive, could talk with them once again, even if only to recite the same lines, even if only to make the same mistakes. If I'd let Peggy get a word in edgewise the last time I saw her, would she still be working on perfecting her dollhouse even as I type these words? If I'd demanded that we go to the police the moment Krieg left the room, would Molly still be here to visit him in prison or place flowers on his grave? I'll never know. I can only speak the words I hear myself say when I remember what happened the first time through. And yes, that's good enough. I've never exactly been reticent in conversation, but now more than ever, I feel the need to keep talking. As long as I keep talking, I can conjure the people I've loved back into being. As long as I keep talking, I can once again live the life I had before. As long as I keep talking.

As long as I don't shut up.